Whispers in the Darkness

Lemuel Lomeda

Ukiyoto Publishing

I dedicate this to my late father, who sparked my love for reading and consequently, writing.

Contents

Volume I: The House of the Night

Chapter 1 Snow-White Skin

When Pandora was about to be born, her grandmother, *Lola* Sabrina, had a strange feeling that something bad would happen.

It was a foreboding feeling that only her type of person with her particular experience could recognize. She didn't know when, how, or who was it happening to. She unmistakably knew this to be real, like understanding the natural law of gravity.

It originated from a voice in her head, and she would only heed it when something bad was imminent. She verbalized this concern right after Pandora popped out of the womb, which, in hindsight, nobody understood or even paid a great deal of attention to. She was, after all, an old woman approaching senility, and the people who saw her in the hospital thought she was simply a patient with a mental disorder.

She was standing outside the delivery room, trying to get a clear view of her granddaughter's birth through the glass window. As Baby Pandora came out of the birth canal, she yelled: "The baby is black! Beware the darkness, as it will arrive soon!"

Pandora's mother, Angelica, the assisting nurse, and the obstetrician became silent and stared at the newborn infant. She was covered from head to foot with gooey vaginal discharge. Yet the color of the skin can be seen clearly due to the bright fluorescent fixture: NOT black but preternaturally white, luminescent even.

A shade too white, which shocked Angelica. She wouldn't feel this way if the baby came out dark-skinned since the supposed father was also a dark brown Filipino man. The baby's pale skin might make everyone think the dad was a white guy or something.

The doctor proceeded to cut the umbilical cord, wrapped Baby Pandora with a blanket, and gently handed her over to Angelica's waiting arms. Despite her pallid skin color, she was a beautiful and bouncing baby girl. Angelica knew she would love this tiny human being no matter what happened.

Angelica asked the doctor why her daughter's skin was this white and was told not to worry and that it was normal for babies to come out this pale from the mother's womb. "Her skin will change and be rosy-colored later, once both of you are stable," the doctor said authoritatively.

After the commotion of childbirth was over, Angelica and Baby Pandora were wheeled over to the maternity ward, where there was an awaiting bed in a private room. Lola Sabrina followed closely behind and waited patiently for the nurses to leave.

Once the nurses left and only they remained, she approached and stood by the bedside. "Mama, meet your new granddaughter, Pandora," said Angelica. Lola Sabrina looked on silently. "What did you say earlier?

The baby is black? Can't you see that she's as white as snow?"

"Did I say something earlier, dear? I don't remember doing that."

"Never mind, but the doctor is wrong. I think Pandora might be an albino or something. We have to talk to another doctor, maybe a skin specialist."

"You should rest first, dear. We can talk to a doctor later. Do you want me to get you something?"

"Mama, can you get me something to drink? I'm a little thirsty. I think we packed some bottled water in the bag."

~O~

It was nighttime, and Angelica was sleeping soundly on the hospital bed. Baby Pandora was beside her, also asleep, wrapped in a clean blanket. Lola Sabrina was resting on a couch in the corner of the room, about to doze off. The room was almost soundless except for the slow and steady buzzing sound of an ancient A/C that the hospital staff didn't bother to fix or clean.

At first, the A/C noise was irritating, but as time passed, it became the soothing sound of white noise. It soon became an integral and familiar part of the hospital, like its antiseptic smell.

As Lola Sabrina was about to fall asleep, she began to hear a steady whispering voice coming from an unseen source. It was a familiar voice she had heard before, but she often didn't understand what it was saying, and she only knew it meant there was something bad that was going to happen. She'd always yell out what it said to make sense of it, but it was confusing and nonsensical nonetheless.

All the same, she couldn't comprehend what it meant and was too sleepy to shout. However, the whisper, along with the buzzing sound of the A/C and the general state of comfortableness inside the hospital room, made her nod off immediately.

She began to dream.

She had this recurring dream of flying. She had read somewhere that when it happens to you, it's an out-of-body experience like undergoing astral projection. Your spirit or astral form then leaves the body and flies to whatever place it went.

Whenever this happened to her, she only remembered the flying part but never the specifics, and she always felt like a million bucks in the morning after she woke up. She had wished she had a better memory, like in her younger years so she could remember them.

However, this wasn't a dream about flying but something else entirely. It wasn't a dream but a nightmare about death and destruction.

The dream was too much for Lola Sabrina. There was too much killing, too much blood, and too much death. It was senseless, without any rhyme or reason. However, she felt there was something familiar about it, someone she knew, even though everything was a bloody blur. Amidst the devastation and gore, there was a pale figure standing calmly, raising her hand as if motioning to stop the violence.

The chaos stopped, and there was a momentary peace, but then, she woke up. She knew there was something important about this dream and tried to force herself to remember it, but alas, she couldn't. Her faulty old brain prevented her from retaining it.

All she could recall was the hand of a pale figure motioning to stop, but to what kind of force it was trying to forestall, she couldn't remember.

Chapter 2 Growing Up Rapunzel

Angelica was right: Baby Pandora was an albino. She determined this diagnosis after consulting with a dermatologist, which meant that Pandora has a genetic condition where her body produces little or no melanin, which determines hair, skin, and eye color. She will have vision problems later in life and hypersensitivity to sunlight. Otherwise, she'd be healthy growing up.

Another aftereffect of her condition was the color of her eyes, which was pale blue. The only part of her body seemingly unaffected by albinism was her hair, which was jet-black in color. All the same, these features gave her an ethereal and otherworldly quality, which left her mother, grandmother, and many who saw her in complete awe. People in her immediate circle soon treated her like extra-special cargo that could easily be broken if careless.

Angelica refurbished her house to be acceptable to the standards of an ultrasensitive infant with many perceived shortcomings. Sunlight and other bright lights were going to be an issue, so she had to find some dark-colored curtains to block any outdoor brightness and install dimmer switches to dim her household fluorescent tubes. She also had to make her home safer for a growing child by baby-proofing it further, which she had learned from her mother. She only wanted her to be free of danger, and if it meant locking her up in a tower like Rapunzel to protect her, she wouldn't hesitate to do it.

In time, she grew older. Her Lola Sabrina was always by her side, watching over her like a hawk. Even though she was long in the tooth and foggy-brained, she was still strong and nimble-footed. She would run after her and scoop her up whenever she was about to slip and fall.

When Pandora was three years old, something happened, making her mother Angelica more worried, thus forbidding her to go out alone. This, in turn, trapped her further inside the proverbial tower with a lock and key.

~O~

It was Sunday, the usual time for Lola Sabrina to attend Mass. She had given up on her daughter Angelica to go with her since she had decided to be an atheist after she became pregnant.

Since it was too late for her daughter, she wanted to introduce Catholicism to her granddaughter. She had hoped to have her baptized, but Angelica didn't want to. She had no choice but to acquiesce since she was the true decision-maker in her daughter's life.

Pandora was hyperactive at this age, always running around the house with Lola Sabrina in tow. They bought her a child leash so she would be within their reach whenever she'd try to commit some toddler-like catastrophes in their home.

The plan was simple. Lola Sabrina will have to walk to church (which was thankfully not that far) with little Pandora leading the way, like a dog leading its master. Lola knew how weird it would look to others, but she'd reached this stage in her life where she didn't give a damn anymore what other people thought. She also accepted it'd be doubly odd due to her granddaughter's otherworldly appearance but didn't care nonetheless.

Angelica, on the other hand, did care and was worried that something bad would happen. However, she had been tired for a few days already from taking care of a hyperactive child and her fatigue won over.

She watched as they went outside the house, a strange-looking pair, merely walking on the sidewalk, going to church. She looked skyward and was thankful the cloudy weather cooperated with their trip. She had dressed up Pandora with a new colorful dress she'd bought, with ribbons on the neckline and waistband.

She still watched as they reached an intersection, crossed the road, and disappeared. She closed the door and went straight to bed.

People did stare, but only in amusement. Her perceived paleness wasn't always an issue to others since people were used to seeing foreigners as white as her everywhere in the Philippine archipelago.

And they were a funny pair indeed, with Pandora always trying to run but prevented by the harness and leash held by Lola Sabrina. Also, Pandora was barking like a dog, which surprised Lola and made her think about where she copied it. *Maybe from Paw Patrol, her favorite show?* She thought and smiled.

They arrived at the church. As they climbed the steps and proceeded to enter the somber establishment, Pandora stopped right outside the entryway, seemingly afraid to enter. Then Lola Sabrina began to hear the same familiar whispering voice, saying something opaque. It was saying: "Do not enter! Darkness will come outside! Fire! Fire! Fire inside!" All these, she reiterated in a screaming fashion.

As if on cue, Pandora screamed and cried bloody murder. People looked behind and were startled by the commotion, especially from the word "fire!" They proceeded to stand up and ran towards the exits, almost trampling over both of them. Pandemonium ensued.

Amidst the commotion, Lola grabbed the screaming Pandora and ran downwards, away from the church, bound for home. She could hear the siren of an approaching fire truck, which she paid no attention to. She was focused on sprinting and carrying this precious cargo, hoping she wouldn't drop her on the ground and everything would be alright.

Unfortunately, it wouldn't. The commotion at the church was witnessed by some people who had known Lola Sabrina and reported her to the authorities. They charged her with falsely reporting a fire, which was a serious offense. However, due to her age and status in the community, it was dropped to a misdemeanor and made her pay a fine instead.

After this happened, Angelica vowed never to let Pandora go outside and out of her sight. She'd remain indoors and hopefully be an innocent child forever, locked inside a metaphorical tower.

Chapter 3 Cinderella's Ashes

Being indoors all the time didn't seem to bother young Pandora. The house they were living in was a large mansion with many nooks and crannies and a wide and enclosed backyard where she could play all day. Their family came from old money, and their ancestors were notorious land barons who owned most of the land in town.

However, the men in their family seem to always die young, either due to bad health, accidents, or fortuitous events. The women always remained to live out their lives in riches until seniority.

Pandora's father, who was Angelica's groom-to-be, suffered the same fate and also died young during her third trimester of pregnancy under mysterious circumstances from a business trip outside the country. His corpse was cremated, put inside an urn, shipped through Priority Mail Express International Services, and addressed to Angelica. She'd supposed to receive it after a month or so, well after her due date.

It was a package she dreaded receiving from USPS, and once she knew she'd get it on the day, she arranged a little funeral ceremony with her mother and house helpers present, who functioned as mourners and dressed up in all black.

She had set up a special place to put his ashes on a shelf atop the fireplace. While the embers were roaring, she delivered a prepared speech to commemorate the short life of her so-called husband-to-be, her Prince Charming.

~O~

What can I say about Henry? Was he a prince? Well, not really. He was a bit of an asshole, and Mama can attest to that. He was also a degenerate gambler who always lost the money he earned as the proprietor of his family's business. He had many faults and may not be made of suitable husband material, but I still loved him nonetheless.

We met during a low point in both our lives. It was during my rebellious phase when I went out all night, drinking and partying.

Henry, on the other hand, loved playing mahjong at that time and would play with some of the most affluent people in town. They'd hang out in a house that our families were close to and played mahjong all night.

This house was like a palace. It was owned by the Pabuaya family, who were neck-deep in local politics. There were many rooms inside that functioned as various entertainment venues. There was a big room with more than ten tables set for playing mahjong and another as a karaoke bar. There were still other rooms for purposes I wasn't aware of and didn't care to find out.

On weekends, we'd go to the karaoke room to drink, sing, and be a rowdy bunch of spoiled brats.

On the day we met, I was supposed to be grounded. I had snuck out earlier that night but had to go home by twelve since Mama always checked on me at that time.

My friends and I went straight to the karaoke room. We were there early, and no other people were present yet, except for one person sitting alone by the bar. It was him, of course, looking like an unkempt prince carrying the world's problems on his shoulders.

My friends had sat at their usual table and were busy choosing the songs they wanted to sing on a songbook while I walked directly to the bar to order drinks.

He noticed me while I motioned to the bartender. Our eyes met. His eyes looked tired and red due to lack of sleep, but I also noticed something that made my heart flutter. I didn't know how to describe it; maybe it was love at first sight. I am not sure, but yet I knew I wasn't the only one feeling this way. He also did.

He awkwardly introduced himself to me, and I to him. He readily admitted that he came here to play mahjong and always lost loads of his family's money. I appreciated his honesty and became all the more attracted to him.

He also said he had seen me a few times before but was too embarrassed to approach her since he knew about my family's stature and wealth in town. We talked, drank, and sang for the rest of the night. We lost track of time.

When I saw the clock again, it was almost midnight, and I panicked. I ran immediately outside without informing Henry or my friends and hailed a public tricycle to bring me home.

When I got home unnoticed and went to my room, I discovered I had forgotten my shoes and was barefoot. I laughed at my carelessness and was thankful nonetheless I was able to get in without Mama noticing, or else it was my ass on a sling.

I replayed everything in my mind: the happenings earlier in the evening, the singing, about Henry and our conversation. We had clicked and hoped to see him again soon. However, reality came crashing down. I knew that Mama didn't like him and wouldn't accept him as part of the family due to his unsavory reputation as a gambling addict. I decided then that family was more important and tried to forget the events earlier.

But I didn't know then that Henry was a relentless son of a bitch. He had a gambler's attitude of persistence, after all, to never give up even if the odds were stacked against him.

Early the next day, he came by our house. He was holding the shoes I had left behind. He wore the same clothes he did last night and was doubly unkempt, but his eyes, even though appearing red and tired, were shining happily. It demonstrated the promise of love, which I had longed for.

We soon became lovers and promised to marry each other when the time was right.

Three years into our relationship, there were still no marriage plans or even an engagement ring on my finger. We went through many ups and downs. Mostly down because of him.

And then I became pregnant. He was aloof and withdrawn during those months and disappeared for many weeks. I was worried for him and suspected he was spending all that time gambling.

Then, one day, he was completely gone, and his parents said he left for a business trip to the US. I didn't want him to go since I was already in my third trimester and for him to be present for our daughter's birth. I pleaded with his family to tell him to return for his child's sake, and they said they'd pass on the message.

I never heard from him again. He had cut contact entirely until someone called from the US to tell me he died.

~O~

Angelica took out a silk handkerchief, wiped the tears from her eyes, and blew the mucus from her nose. She continued:

"Henry, even though you had many faults, I loved you. We have a daughter now, and her name is Pandora, which you had insisted on naming. I need help in raising her since she has special needs, and you're not here. Thankfully, Mama is here to help me. You're dead now, and I hope you can find some peace at last.

"So, rest easy my dear prince and goodbye. We'll see each other again soon."

Chapter 4 Little Red Riding Hoodlum

The speech took a lot out of Angelica. She thought she'd feel some semblance of relief after, but instead gave the opposite effect. It was like she was now carrying Henry's weight, including all of his perceived issues and hang-ups on her shoulders.

It was this kind of weight that had burdened Henry and drove him ultimately to an early grave. It was a type of affliction like a contagious disease that degenerate gamblers, hard drinkers, and drug addicts had and passed on to people close to them.

And to relieve herself from this heavy burden, Angelica took up drinking, which made things worse. She always drank alone in her room after Pandora was asleep. She'd drink until she passed out and do the same thing the next day and every day since.

~O~

Time went on excruciatingly slow for Angelica but moved quickly for Pandora. She was innocent and happy for a short time but slowly became aware of her situation.

She was almost seven years old. By this time, she was old enough to notice that she never went outside their home, and when she asked why, no one gave a straight answer. It was always "when you're older Pandora," or "you're still a baby, Pandora," or "you're not old enough yet."

But now, she *was* old enough to go to grade school. She wanted to meet and be friends with kids her age. She didn't want to play with Lola Sabrina, Matteo, the family gardener, or *Tiya Domeng*, the cook, anymore. She wanted to go out and about doing stuff normal kids her age did.

One day, she decided to sneak out of their house and see the whole world. She put on a bright red hooded cloak that Lola Sabrina had sewn to protect her from the hurtful rays of the sun. For her, it was a disguise, but her young brain couldn't comprehend that her overall appearance could bring more unwanted attention instead.

There was a small hole in the corner fence in the backyard, just enough to fit her or a tiny animal, which led to a forest and then to town. She brought a small basket filled with her favorite snacks in case she got hungry.

It was her first time in the forest. She'd always see it from the second-floor balcony and wondered what lay ahead. She imagined it inhabited by fantastical creatures: *Duwendes, Engkantos, Tikbalangs*, and other mythical creatures her lola Sabrina often told her about. She was an imaginative child, always playing make-believe games alone if she couldn't find anyone else to play with her in the house.

She had waited for the right time to sneak out when everyone took their early afternoon *siesta*. And fortunately, it was also gloomy out. In such a manner, she could stroll along the forest without worrying about the sunlight hurting her.

Outside the hole, she saw a small pathway leading inward to the forest, which she took.

She glanced upward. There were various kinds of trees, mostly coconut and bamboo, some tall Narra trees, and a few sturdy Molave trees. Their branches seem to interconnect like they were deliberately forming a natural canopy to ward off encroaching sunlight.

She heard the natural sounds of the forest: birds singing, a gentle breeze blowing, and crickets chirping. So far, nothing was out of the ordinary. She walked on.

Then, she heard something unusual, something not part of the natural surroundings. It was the sound of a whispering voice.

It was unintelligible as if it was speaking in a language Pandora couldn't understand. It was slow and steady at first but rose in crescendo and urgency that changed into a growl of a ferocious animal. It frightened her so much that she ran.

She ran and ran. She glanced behind, but no one was there, yet the growl was still within earshot and seemed to follow her. She continued running and reached a clearing.

She stood in the middle, looking left and right, front and back, to see if someone or something was approaching. She heard leaves rustling on her left, and a shrub began to move. *What's coming out?* She thought frighteningly.

Out came a small animal that looked like a cross between a kangaroo and a goat, covered in black fur, and had sharp teeth. She recognized it as a *Sigbin,* another mythical creature mentioned by her Lola Sabrina. However, its demeanor didn't seem violent but curious. It approached her and sniffed her shoes. She reached inside her basket and broke off a piece of ham sandwich, which she handed over to the animal. It grabbed the piece with both claws and devoured it.

Pandora began to think. *Was this the one running after me?* It didn't seem to be since the kind of animal she'd heard before was angry, and this one appeared friendly. It also looked like it was fond of her and yelped happily as she gave it the rest of the sandwich.

She was about to walk away and return to the original pathway, but the Sigbin appeared to be motioning her to follow deeper into the forest. She hesitated, yet her curiosity got the best of her and went after it.

By and by, the surroundings seemed to become darker and murkier. They were approaching the lowland portion of the forest, which was a swampland. The ground became muddier, the atmosphere wetter, and the forest sounds creepier. The Sigbin was hopping along, thus leading her further and deeper into the forest.

It was leading her toward what appeared to be a giant termite mound, but upon closer inspection, it was a house made of mud. She knew this to be true because there was a wooden door in front and had a brass doorknob to open it. She went towards it, reached out, and twisted it open.

A fiery bright light emanated from inside and hit her open face. She cried in pain and covered her sensitive eyes. She retreated and fell backward. She rubbed her eyes with both hands as if trying to scrape the pain away. Through her fingers, she could see the Sigbin walking towards the doorway and entering.

She stood up, dusted the dirt off her red cloak, and followed suit. The door closed behind her. She didn't bring the basket of snacks with her since she had accidentally dropped it outside when she fell earlier.

Chapter 5 Under the Juniper Tree

By the time they discovered Pandora was missing, it was already too late.

Angelica and Lola Sabrina thought she was playing in her favorite spot in the house, under the juniper tree, in a secluded area in the backyard. It was her special hidden nook, away from prying eyes, where she could play and imagine fantastic scenarios with her toys.

They would often hear shrieks of laughter as she conversed with imaginary friends at fancy tea parties and fought invisible monsters in fantastical realms. She was Princess Pandora, after all, the soon-to-be Queen in the Kingdom of Make-Believe.

They'd be comforted by her childish noise, which meant everything was alright with the world. As she grew older and put away childish things, she still went to her special nook to elude the people in the house and be alone. She'd play games and watch videos on her tablet and be momentarily content.

However, the juniper space didn't emit any sound whatsoever: no screams of laughter or electronic sounds. It was completely silent. Angelica called out her name, but there was no response. She called again and again and again and ran towards it.

She wasn't there. She yelled out her name again and again, and panic began to seep in.

Lola Sabrina and the household helpers came out of the house to see what the commotion was about. They saw Angelica in complete panic mode, weeping and wailing Pandora's name. When they realized what had happened, they split up and began searching the wide expanse of the household.

Minutes became an hour. They heard a shout from Matteo, the gardener, and everyone ran towards him.

Matteo had discovered the small hole in the fence, which they correctly surmised Pandora went through. Angelica told Matteo to get any gardening tool from the shed that could be made into a weapon and follow her outside to the forest.

Matteo brought a pitchfork and an electric lamp since it was almost dusk. They saw the same pathway Pandora had taken earlier and sprinted towards it.

They ran and ran deeper into the forest. Matteo was familiar with the surroundings and told Angelica that Pandora might have gone to the swamplands, so they made a sharp turn and ran as fast as their feet could carry.

Deeper and deeper they went, and darkness began to fall. They stopped running, and Matteo switched the lamp on. They saw something ahead, which looked like a large boulder. They crept towards it, not knowing what to expect.

It was the largest termite mound they had ever seen, which was significant unto itself, but what was more substantial was a familiar-looking basket beside it with Pandora's favorite food inside. Angela gasped, picked the basket up, and looked within. There was still uneaten food, which meant Pandora might be close by.

She yelled out her name but was hushed by Matteo. He said: "You shouldn't shout, Ma'am, we are in an enchanted part of the forest where elemental spirits live. They might curse us or something. Do you see that in front of you? It is a dwelling place of a *Nuno*. Some people also say it is an entryway to an enchanted realm."

"I don't care if it's where the devil himself lives, Pandora might be somewhere, maybe hurt or unconscious. We have to find her! Search the area on the left, and I'll go to the right."

"Yes Ma'am."

They searched and searched everywhere, but Pandora was nowhere to be found. Suddenly, they heard something coming from the giant mound, like the creaking sound of an opening door. They ran towards the sound and saw a blackened form standing there.

It wasn't something, but *someone*. It was Pandora.

Her whole body was covered with black mud, and she seemed dazed and confused. When she saw the shocked face of her mother, she fainted and fell to the ground.

"Carry her Matteo, and give me the lamp and pitchfork. We have to go home now."

"Yes Ma'am. We should come back here tomorrow and offer a gift to the spirits and thank them that your daughter is safe and sound."

"Fuck that Matteo, I don't believe in that shit. We are going home right now!"

"But Ma'am…"

"RIGHT NOW!"

"Yes Ma'am," Matteo said and made the sign of the cross.

Chapter 6 The King of the Golden Mountain

The town of *Gintongbayan* held many secrets.

In the past, way before Lola Sabrina was born, it was a town that exclusively mined for gold and made many of its citizens rich.

Gold was discovered in the streams and basins close to the fabled Golden Mountain, which the original settlers said was the source of this precious metal. People were in a feeding frenzy, trying to get their grubby hands on any land they could find close to it, including Lola Sabrina's grandfather, Don Marcus Ponce de Leon.

Don Marcus was one of the most ruthless of the lot. By sheer will and intimidation, he acquired most of the land in the nearby region of Golden Mountain, including some farther away (now most of the town), and locked out many of his competitors. He hired locals to become miners and then monopolized this venture. He became incredibly wealthy, which gave him power and influence in Gintongbayan.

However, he became too greedy. He wanted more gold, more money, and more power. Since the Golden Mountain was a mostly unexplored and unmapped territory, he needed to know if gold was there to be mined and thus, owned.

He had heard of the many tall tales told by the settlers about the legend of the Golden Mountain, which was supposed to be the dwelling place of mythological creatures and elemental spirits. The locals were scared of going there, and those brave enough came back different, and some say, cursed. Some had lost their humanity and became like animals, and some were so traumatized and shell-shocked by the experience that they died young in mysterious circumstances. Yet some were strong enough to go through with it and returned relatively unscathed and continued living their lives until they grew old. However, most didn't return and were never heard of again.

Don Marcus wanted to know who these people were who survived the ordeal, gather all pertinent information, and possibly recruit them to be explorers once again. He found one such person, Henry Teves the 1st, the first of his line and great-great-great grandfather to Henry.

Henry was a huge man, built like an ox, with ferocity, to boot. He was strong-willed and unrelenting and didn't suffer fools. He survived his journey to the Golden Mountain before, apparently, due to his force of character and general foolhardiness. While others have likewise befallen on hard times and soon died, one way or another.

Don Marcus got hold of his whereabouts in a neighboring town near Gintongbayan and paid him a social call. He wanted to know what made him tick and determine why he wasn't affected and why the others did.

He discovered they were quite similar men with strong and unrelenting character traits. He found a kinship with him, which, in turn, loosened his tongue and soon spoke openly.

However, Henry told a story that was so unbelievable and horrifying thus changing everything for Don Marcus. He was never the same ever again.

~O~

I recognize a bullshitter when I see one, and you, my friend, are not one of them. You see this here on my right bicep? It's a tattoo of *Dwende*, a dwarf who lives in the deep caverns of the Golden Mountain. This one, in particular, is the king whom I met and made a deal with. I'm getting ahead of the story.

Dwarves love gold, you know. They love it so much that they even sleep with it in their beds. There are scores of these little bastards there, along with many other creatures and monsters.

The trick is not to be scared of them. They smell fear, and if you reek of it, then you're dead. They're going to make a feast out of you, literally.

Back then, I was a young man attracted to the possibility of getting rich with gold. The mining location was still virgin terrain and up for the taking.

I came to your town penniless but driven to succeed. I befriended a few local panners who brought me to the nearby streams where they panned for gold.

As you know, the panning process is slow. We use a pan to separate the heavy gold particles from lighter particles with water. It is a hit-and-miss, a slow and tedious process, which sometimes takes weeks before hitting pay dirt.

I got impatient and wanted to get a lot of gold as soon as possible. The only way to do that is to go directly to the source: the Golden Mountain.

The locals told me about the elemental spirits and fantastic creatures living there, deep in the caves and caverns under the mountain, which they said is the location of large quantities of gold. The small nuggets found on the streams and lakes were supposedly just discarded gold particles, thrown away and unusable by the dwarves' standards.

Back then, I didn't believe it, like I didn't believe in ghosts, vampires, and werewolves. For me, they're all nonsense and superstitious bullshit.

Since nothing else held me back, I decided to go straight to the source. I packed a small knapsack with a few essentials and brought my American long rifle, which is good for long-distance shooting. I picked this gun especially because it is big and scary, and it also packs a loud punch and will likely scare away any pesky creatures within earshot.

I started my trek to the Golden Mountain early the next day. To get to the caverns supposedly where the gold is located, you have to go through a thick forest, and some portions of it are wetlands.

I walked and walked. I passed the dry forestland with many plants and animals we'd seen before and were all familiar with. Soon after, I noticed the natural scenery slowly change and became wetter, darker, and stranger.

The plants became more twisted in nature and vine-like. These things littered the forest floor like large snakes trying to grab my legs. The sounds became creepier and unnatural. To me, it was a clear indication that I was entering another place, not part of planet Earth but in another realm entirely. It's like when Dorothy said in The Wizard of Oz: "We're not in Kansas anymore Toto."

I wasn't in Gintongbayan anymore. I was in the land of the *Dwendes, Engkantos, Diwatas,* and many more creatures you've only read in books about myths and legends: I was in the magical realm of *Batala.*

I had imagined a doorway going to this fabled domain, but there wasn't. It was a gradual transformation into this place. Maybe it was purposefully done to discourage people like me, like a warning that something creepy was heading my way, so I had to turn around.

But I didn't and soldiered on, trampling over those crawling vines and going through the muddy vegetation.

Soon, I came upon the base of the mountain that had a cave entrance. This was it, I'd arrived, and the gold was waiting for me inside. I unsheathed my rifle, pointed it to the darkness ahead, and cocked the trigger.

I was ready to shoot any creature coming my way if it proved to be dangerous. I slowly walked in, and what I saw...

~O~

Henry paused and took out a cask of homemade *tuba from* a cupboard, which was fermented coconut liquor. He poured two glasses full, took a large swig of the bubbly liquid, and handed the second to Don Marcus. He took a small sip and made a face.

"You don't like it? You've been drinking too much of the expensive stuff, your taste buds won't take any of the local shit anymore. This is what we poor folks get to drink nowadays."

"This I don't understand," said Don Marcus, changing the subject. "Why aren't you a wealthy man? You went to the Golden Mountain and came back. You didn't find any gold there?"

"Yes, I did, I found so much gold that could make me rich hundred times over."

"You didn't fill your bag or even take one nugget? Why?"

"Well, I'm going to tell you. The story isn't finished yet. I think you should drink the tuba, and you're going to need it."

Don Marcus did, and Henry smiled.

~O~

I saw a bright light at the end of the tunnel, which I cautiously approached. The light was yellow-orange, the color of fire. As I drew closer, the light became bigger and brighter, but I didn't feel any heat emanating from it. I remember feeling warm and cozy as I walked closer and closer.

I reached the entrance to another inner cavern, which was enormous. The bright light came from a humongous tree whose branches were inflamed. When I looked much closer, it was a magical fire that didn't burn out or even die down. It was a ceaseless and comforting flame, which also provided illumination to the place.

I saw many fantastic-looking beings within the vicinity. At that time, I didn't know about the different types of fabulous creatures in Philippine mythology, which I learned later. Aside from the creatures I've previously mentioned, there were the gigantic *Kapres*, the ape-like *Amomongos*, the *Lakivots* (huge talking civets), and many more.

I also discovered later that there was some conflict going on, between the white and black creatures, and unwittingly became involved.

From what I've gathered, the white beings wanted to share their precious commodity—the gold—with us humans since they have more than enough already. In addition, they want to engage in commerce with us, thus fostering peace and prosperity with both parties.

While the black creatures, led by a black dwarf, didn't want to engage in any dealings with us since they knew about our greedy nature.

We both know they're right. Humans always want more of something we crave, be it money, gold, or power. We want more and more of it and never get satisfied.

The creatures then saw me as I was marveling at the burning tree. It was as if they were waiting for me all along. A black dwarf approached and introduced himself.

Now, this dwarf was an impressive-looking creature, as you've seen from my tattoo. He was less than four feet tall, had long white hair and beard, and wore a golden tunic. He also had dark skin like an African. He was holding a staff, which I learned later was magical.

He said: "I am Axe-Grinder, King of the Golden Mountain. I may be the king, but I don't have a palace, royal court, or any kingly accouterments like a normal king has. Well, maybe this gold tunic only.

The magical beings in the domain of Batala designated me as their king because I have a talent for organization. I have created three different castes to help us function as a society. There is the higher caste, which includes me and the ruling class, the middle caste for the workers and soldiers, and the lower caste for creatures who don't have rational minds and are more barbaric.

Nevertheless, it appears that the organizational caste system I've created is failing. The creatures have formed factions instead based on their skin color and pitted one against the other. I didn't plan for this and wasn't aware of their propensity to look at the color of their skin as a reason for division. They seem to have lost their faith in me.

The latest issue is about the humans who have taken up residence down by rivers and streams. Humans like you, who have come here to get some of our gold to get rich."

I felt danger was afoot and slowly unholstered my rifle. I held it in both hands, ready to fire if something happened.

Axe-Grinder tapped the staff on the ground, and the rifle suddenly and magically crumbled into dust. I didn't have any weapon anymore to defend myself in case the shit hit the fan.

He said: "I need your help, human. You can help me win back their faith in me by dealing with this human situation. In return, I'm going to give all the gold you can carry and leave here unharmed."

I was overjoyed by this news and was eager to listen to what I was supposed to do. Axe-Grinder took me to his domicile, away from the others, to speak in private.

His homestead also looked like a giant termite mound but hollowed out inside for the placement of the pieces of furniture. There was a table, chairs, a bed, and a makeshift kitchen, but all in his diminutive size. There were also heaps of gold littered everywhere.

I had to crouch down to enter the doorway and sit on his tiny chair.

He gave me something to drink, some sweet drink I hadn't tasted before. I drank the whole glassful and licked my lips.

Soon afterward, I became sleepy. Then I realized that Axe-Grinder had put something in my drink. I began to panic and tried to run towards the door, but I fell flat on my face. I tried to get up and saw Axe-Grinder smile, which made me deathly afraid for the first time.

Then I fell asleep.

~O~

"Then what happened? Were you able to escape?" Said Don Marcus.

"Yes and no. I was able to come here and live with other humans but Henry didn't. He remained there and became a prisoner of the black dwarf, my Lord, and King Axe-Grinder," said Henry, but it wasn't him after all.

The thing that wasn't Henry stood up and transformed. His skin began to split open, his head became bigger, and his mouth suddenly grew sharp fangs. Out came a terrible-looking and dark-skinned creature, which was an *Aswang*.

It stood up, attacked Don Marcus, and bit him on the neck. It began sucking his blood until it was satiated. He dropped the blood-soaked body on the floor, unconscious but still alive.

The creature transformed back into the human form of Henry and wiped the blood off his face. It didn't want to kill him but merely to infect and ultimately make him a servant to his Dark Lord Axe-Grinder. He had fulfilled, once again and many times before, his goal of living with the humans: recruiting them one by one to become part of his Dark Lord's army.

Chapter 7 Matteo, the Wise Servant

asa de la Noche was the name of the ancestral home of Don Marcus Ponce de Leon and his descendants. There was even a metal sign mentioning it above the wrought iron gate for everyone to see. He named it as such because it evoked fear among the townsfolk and hindered them from visiting or even approaching the gate. He only wished to be left alone. He also loved the night and slept during the day.

It was built in 1888, just ten years before the end of Spanish colonization in the Philippines. Don Marcus was part of the educated upper class of Filipinos at that time called the *Illustrados*, who held power and influence over the lower class. One prominent member was Jose Rizal, who later became a national hero.

At the height of his wealth and power, Don Marcus acquired one hectare of land five kilometers northward from Golden Mountain. He immediately had the mansion built in the style of Spanish Colonial architecture. He hired an architect from Spain who specialized in this architectural type and paid him handsomely.

Casa de la Noche had all the trademark features: clay tile roofs, soft arches, white stucco walls, and carved wooden doors. He had many rooms built for his family, which he assumed would become numerous one day, including a few underground rooms for his clandestine activities. These rooms served a special purpose that he didn't want the rest of the world to know about.

He hired local people to be his servants and whose direct line of descendants remained working for his family.

The majordomo was the chief butler in the mansion but strangely didn't follow the tradition of hiring direct descendants as household help. There was a new one every ten years or so, and nobody from the family knew where this new person came from. He'd appear one day as a replacement for the old butler and would automatically become the new one for the family. It was one of the pre-arranged stipulations left by Don Marcus for his family. He particularly instructed them to never inquire about it.

Matteo, the family gardener, came from a long line of servants working for the Ponce de Leon family. His great-great-great grandfather was a servant hired by Don Marcus himself to be a groundskeeper, and his mother was a former maidservant to Lola Sabrina herself.

Matteo was a good servant; he always did what he was told and kept his head down. He was a simple man with simple joys in life, and one such joy was seeing his young ward Pandora grow up.

He always saw her from afar, playing with her toys under the juniper tree. She'd sometimes call on him and ask him to play with her, and he'd readily do what she told him. One day, he was supposed to be a grumpy old king who scolded her naughty dolls, and another day, a terrible dragon play-fighting with the warrior-princess Pandora.

The day Pandora ran away was an awful day for everyone in the household. All the servants were shocked and dismayed by the news, but the butler was the only one who didn't seem affected and merely frowned after hearing it. He went about doing his work as if nothing had happened.

After Pandora was found in the woods and carried home by Matteo, the servants were overjoyed. He gently put her down on her bed while the other servants prepared a basin of lukewarm water and a washcloth to wash the black mud from her body.

Angelica was still beside herself and went to the room to take a secret swig of vodka to calm down her nerves while Lola Sabrina bathed Pandora herself. Matteo left them and went downstairs to the servant's quarters to his room.

He tried to wash the black mud off his clothes and body. It was a sticky and greasy type of mud that couldn't be washed off easily, as he discovered. It was some black dye that could hardly be removed by ordinary soap and water. He needed to find a strong chemical detergent to take it out.

He went outside and walked towards the family washerwoman's room to get some of the strong stuff. On his way, he noticed the majordomo walking towards the basement stairs, which were supposed to be off-limits to everyone, including the servants.

Matteo thought there was something strange about the butler, which he couldn't fathom what it was. He was relatively new and arrived at Casa de la Noche only a year ago.

He was a stern taskmaster who often scolded the other servants if they made mistakes. He was in his mid-fifties, shifty-eyed, rotund, and balding, which made him all the more unlikeable and unappealing. Every one of the servants hated him, but Angelica and Lola Sabrina seemed to like his dour nature and often commended him on a job well done.

Matteo knew little about those underground hidden rooms that Don Marcus had built. He was never curious to find out since it was simply against the rules to even ask about them. He prided himself on being a conscientious worker who always did the right thing.

However, if something untoward was about to happen, he would intervene for the benefit of the offended party and would find a way to make things right again.

He felt the butler was about to do something inauspicious and had to find out what it was. He might be a thief looking for something to steal since everyone else was upstairs attending to Pandora's needs. He waited for a few minutes and quietly followed him.

The basement stairs were leading his way, way down below ground level. There was a fluorescent bulb on the wall every tenth step to illuminate the way, and by his count, stopped at the hundredth step. There was a steel door at the end of the stairs, which was partially open. He peeked inside…

But there was nothing, only a dark and empty room with cobwebs on the walls. He had thought it was a wine cellar containing expensive wine or hidden family heirlooms. There was nothing there except emptiness.

Nevertheless, the majordomo had disappeared out of thin air.

Where did he go? Matteo thought. He was perplexed and climbed back up the stairs.

He waited for thirty minutes for the butler to come but never did. He soon gave up and went to the washer woman's room to get some strong detergent.

The next morning, he asked Pandora's nursemaid about her condition. She was happy to learn she had woken up and was in relatively good spirits. He was also surprised to see the butler had reappeared, doing his usual rounds. He glanced a wary eye at him as if he knew what had transpired the night before, which made Matteo self-conscious.

He regrettably knew he was now in the major domo's sights, and sooner or later, he'd find something to blame him for. He wanted to care, but Pandora was more on his mind, instead of any petty retaliation the butler would likely throw at him.

He decided to get back to the forest. He needed to find out what had happened to Pandora, get some clues, and give some appeasement in the form of offerings to the elemental spirits for any seeming transgressions committed yesterday.

Chapter 8 Snow White and Rose Red: Best Friends

Pandora could hardly remember what had happened in the forest. The occurrence felt so alien to her, like she was recalling a hazy memory that occurred to a different person. Thinking about it exhausted her mentally and emotionally, so she resolved to sweep everything under the rug and continued living her life as she grew to teenhood.

Nevertheless, her mother, Angelica, was freaked out by the whole situation, which drove her further into alcoholism and depression.

With her mother sidelined from parenting duties, it was her Lola Sabrina who picked up the responsibilities of being a mother to Pandora. She wasn't strict and gave her some semblance of freedom to be her adolescent self, with all her natural inclinations.

She was allowed to go outside and attend school, not because she was now trustworthy enough to do things on her own, but because of another person who was responsible enough for both: a girl named Ruby Rose.

Ruby Rose was Matteo's daughter. She used to live with her mother elsewhere but soon lived with him in Casa de la Noche when she was old enough to be a maid-in-training.

They became fast friends.

They were total opposites. Pandora was outgoing and free-spirited, while Ruby Rose was studious and introverted. Pandora was like Pinocchio, always getting into trouble, and Ruby Rose was her Jiminy Cricket, the protector and conscience of the pair.

Lola Sabrina had tasked Ruby Rose to always be at her side and never leave her wherever she went. It was up to her to get her prepared for school and be on time. Soon, her duties also included doing her schoolwork and making her assignments. She never complained for one bit because she loved it since, in return, she had a best friend who was also like a sister.

~O~

They were now teenagers in high school.

Pandora grew up to be a beautiful yet frail-looking girl. Her paleness now had a rosy-colored tint due to the Philippine heat, and she often brought an umbrella everywhere to cover her sensitive skin. She also hadn't lost her elfin features, which still left people in awe after seeing her.

Ruby Rose was also beautiful in a traditional sense. She looked like the typical pretty provincial lass that parents wanted their sons to marry. She always had good grades and was often on the honor roll. However, she was sometimes bullied by some of her wealthy classmates due to their presumption that she was a social climber because of her closeness to Pandora.

She'd often just turned a blind eye and avoided them whenever the taunting started.

They were the most popular girls in their high school but for different reasons: Pandora for her looks and wealth and Ruby Rose for being smart and nice. Pandora thought it was the most important thing in the world, while Ruby Rose was indifferent about the whole thing, thought it silly, and was more concerned about schoolwork.

To remain popular, she thought she needed to get a boyfriend. She told Ruby Rose about her plan one day when they were both in her room one evening doing homework (which meant Ruby Rose was writing hers).

"I should get a boyfriend. What do think?"

"Are you serious? Your mom would throw a fit and go crazy. Your Lola will be fine with it I guess."

"Who cares what my mom thinks? She'll be too drunk to be aware of it anyway. She won't find out."

"But Lola Sabrina might."

"Lola can't even remember what she ate for breakfast, more so recalling me having a boyfriend. But she'll be ok with it, as long as you'll go along with me on our dates."

"You're assuming you will easily find a good boyfriend material in our little town of Gintongbayan. Have you even seen the boys in our school? Most of them are sons of rural folk."

"I don't care about that. As long as he'll look cute holding my hand."

"He will have rough and callused hands. He'll also stink of doing manual farm work. Are you ready for that?"

"Stop it, Ruby. I'm being serious."

"I'm also serious. Eighty percent of the boys in our school are like that."

"And what about the remaining thirty percent?"

"You mean twenty percent."

"Sure. Twenty."

"The remaining boys are like you, children of rich landowners."

"Well, do you know of any cute boys like that?"

"I don't know, we'll have to look into it."

"You'll have to do it alone Ruby. I can hardly go out you know, because of my sensitive skin. You have good tastes anyway and I trust you."

Ruby Rose groaned. She hated Pandora when she was like this, always involving her in her numerous hair-brained schemes. When things go bad, she'll end up being blamed and has no choice but to put up with it.

"You want me to interview boyfriends for you?? What am I, a pimp?!"

"Haha. Very funny, Ruby. You mean you won't do it? For all the things my family gave you and you do this to me? Wow, it really hurts," said Pandora, and mock cried.

"Oh, stop it. You look silly. You know I'm still going to do it anyway like I've always done in the past. But you have to promise me this: don't sleep with him, alright? You're still sixteen years old, too young for that stuff. Both of us *are* still too young. Do you understand?"

"Yeah, yeah, yeah. Are you finished with my homework?"

"Almost," said Ruby Rose. She was miffed for always being the sucker for the stupid situations Pandora always got herself involved in. She finished up both of their homework and walked out without saying anything.

~O~

Matteo noticed her daughter coming inside their room in the servants' quarters in a huff. He wanted to ask why but decided not to since he intimated what had transpired beforehand: Pandora. It was always about Pandora, how irresponsible she was, and why she had to do whatever she asked, even though it was constantly stupid.

He'd always tell her to remember her place since they were just employees in the household. No matter what they asked, you always have to say "Yes Ma'am," and never "No Ma'am." They have to be right all the time even though, in your mind, they're dead wrong.

However, if the situation was so bad and going along with it would make it worse, then you have to do something about it, without them even knowing, he had told her. It's still your responsibility to fix whatever needs fixing in the household because you wouldn't want it to come back and bite you in the butt.

The same thing had happened to him before, and he had to do something about it. He remembered the occasion he had to deal with a particular situation concerning the new majordomo, which made him cringe in disgust.

Chapter 9 The White Snake

The majordomo's name was Pluto, which Matteo thought was weird for a butler. The previous butlers had normal names like John or Jacob, monickers so mild that nobody would remember after hearing them. But "Pluto," was a strong and unusual one that elicited conversation and more questions like: "Who gave you that name?" Or "Did your parents name you after the cartoon dog?"

It always looked like Pluto didn't know how to respond to these questions and showed a constipated smile that looked more like a painful grimace.

But for Matteo, it was one more thing added to a list of things very unusual about Pluto.

Another strange thing about him was he never seemed to sleep or even take naps.

Similar to all servants in Casa de la Noche, they had one room each in the servants' quarters. Ruby Rose had one reserved for her, and she'd get it once she reached eighteen years old. She slept in his room in the meantime.

Since Pluto was the chief butler in the household, he was provided with a bigger room with better amenities. However, Matteo had never seen him coming in or out of his room. He'd only see him as he did his usual rounds within the household. He tried to follow him, but he'd magically disappear whenever he wasn't looking, even for a second.

Another strange thing happened the day after Pandora was lost in the forest, which didn't particularly occur to Pluto but prompted Matteo into action nonetheless.

~O~

The morning after Pandora was found, he went back to the same spot in the forest, by the giant termite mound. He had brought a young goat, which he tied up and carried on his shoulders.

Once he arrived, he unburdened the kid off his shoulders and tied it to a shrub close by. It was bleating noisily like all younglings do when taken from their brood.

The young goat served as an offering to the elemental beings of the forest, as thanks for bringing back Pandora safe. He made a sign of the cross, turned around, and was about to take the first step homeward…

Then he heard a hissing sound. When he turned around, he saw a gigantic white snake slithering towards him, coming from behind the termite mound and heading towards the goat. Matteo stepped back and was about to run but suddenly decided not to.

He watched in morbid fascination as the snake opened its mouth and swallowed the goat whole. He could still hear the goat bleat as it slowly passed through the snake's stomach. The bleating soon stopped.

Once it was full, it turned around and slithered back from whence it came.

As he was walking back, he replayed in his mind the scene of the snake swallowing the goat repeatedly. Then he had an epiphany, something that would fix his little problem with Pluto and keep everyone he cared for in the household safe from potential harm.

~O~

Matteo knew of a local witch or a *Mangkukulam*. She was reportedly a half-crazy old woman that people go to for herbal medications. For additional money, she supposedly could cook up magical potions that gave any desired effect to its drinkers, and he needed one such concoction with powerful life-altering properties. Yet he was not sure if he could afford it, but needed to check its viability and effectiveness nonetheless.

The Mangkukulam lived in the poorest part of town. Most of the people living there were squatters, too poor to own land but tolerated by the landowners because of their balloting potential. They were block voters told to vote for whoever the preferred politicians were and would always guarantee landslide wins for them. In return, they could live in the land for free and do whatever they pleased.

The squatters' village was aptly named: "Land of Broken Dreams." Its inhabitants were too many, and the area was too small to accommodate all of them.

The settlement was ten hectares of land supposed to be utilized for farming purposes but instead used as living quarters for the poorest of the poor of Gintongbayan. It was a makeshift shantytown of broken dreams and broken promises populated by broken people.

The witch was one of the less pathetic but seemingly learned people in the village and thus was designated as one of the village leaders. She was also one of the few that outsiders visit for her particular tradecraft of witchery.

Matteo already knew about the squatters' camp and the Mangkukulam and was aware of the rules. He had to pay a toll to enter, keep his head down, and avoid eye contact at all times.

When he arrived at the witch's hut, she was already standing by the doorway as if she knew he was coming. She beckoned him silently to follow inside.

He imagined a witch's lair as a place full of vials on shelves, a black cat on the table, and a bubbling cauldron in the middle of the room. However, it was like any other home of poor people with scant furniture and a wood-burning stove. The witch looked like an ordinary old woman but whose eyes were crossed. Matteo correctly guessed that she wasn't crazy at all; it was her eyes that made people think she was.

Matteo told her what he wanted her to concoct. She thought for a minute and nodded. She then said how much it would cost and told him to return in two weeks to get the finished product.

~O~

The week prior, he had worked on a plan for Pluto to ingest the potion. He watched him more closely than usual and memorized his daily habits. He liked to eat *budbud* or glutinous rice rolls and *tsokolate* or hot chocolate as an afternoon snack, so he had to, in some way, secretly put the potion in any of those.

The day came when it was time to fetch the concoction from the *Mangkukulam*. She was waiting in the doorway like before, as if she knew he was coming, and handed a vial to him. He looked questioningly at her, and she just nodded and winked. He was slightly creeped out at seeing one of her crossed eyes close and immediately left after paying.

The plan went into motion. The right time to secretly pour the contents of the vial into the snacks was in the afternoon inside the kitchen when Tiya Domeng, the cook, wasn't looking. He quickly poured a few drops into the steaming cup of tsokolate meant for Pluto and watched what would transpire.

He knew what was supposed to happen if the potion was done right. He watched as Pluto gingerly sipped the tsokolate and bit one mouthful of budbud.

He watched and waited, which seemed like forever…

Chapter 10 Donkey Cabbages

Pluto loved to eat all the human food it could find but had to do it secretly because he didn't want anyone in Casa de la Noche to be suspicious since he wasn't like them.

He wasn't even human. He was a *Pugot*, a shape-changing being whose true form was a large, black, and headless creature. Aside from his shapeshifting ability, he could also move at great speeds that humans couldn't perceive through their five senses. Only creatures of his ilk could keep track of him.

He came from a long line of Pugots Don Marcus made a secret bargain with. Their abilities could only function for roughly ten years aboveground, and the strain of more than that would cause untimely demise, so they had to return to their home realm of Batala when the time came. Therefore, they must replace one another every decade or so.

Eating became his favorite pastime. Human food was more delicious than the sloppy mush he used to eat in Batala, so whenever the opportunity arose to overeat, he'd do it without hesitation.

He especially loved the delicious rice rolls Tiya Domeng made from scratch every afternoon. He devoured them two at a time and can finish ten in one sitting. He liked to chase them down with a hot pot of *tsokolate*, which hit the spot.

He had been trying to get away from Matteo and be alone for once, but everywhere he turned, he saw his face peeking, which massively irritated him. He could hardly enjoy his favorite pastime after seeing his annoying face everywhere. *One of these days, I'm going to have to eat him if he keeps up with this,* he thought.

He decided to forget about Matteo in the meantime and go ahead with his gluttonous pursuits and reprimand him later. He demolished one plateful of budbud and drank one large mug of tsokolate.

He burped loudly. He was so happy and satisfied with his full belly. However, something strange was happening: his stomach started to grumble loudly like a storm was brewing inside his body. Then, he began to transform into something else but not of his own volition. Something, or someone else was forcing him to change into another creature he didn't know.

He found himself on all fours and galloping. *Am I a horse?* He thought. *Anyway, being a horse is not so bad.* He trotted towards a mirror hung close to the doorway to see his face: it was the face of a miniature donkey.

He hee-hawed in surprise. He also saw in the mirror that Matteo was behind him, holding a piece of rope and an empty sack.

Then, it was lights out.

~O~

He awoke in a darkened room. He tried to move, but he was still tied up. He could see the room even though the light fixture was switched off. He saw that he was in one of the secret underground rooms he frequently visited for nefarious purposes.

He had extreme night vision, which was one of the endowments of being part of Lord Axe-Grinder's black army. All of them had various abilities, which they used to infiltrate the human population of Gintongbayan.

His duty, like all the others like him, was to live among the humans and remain with them until their time was up. He was a lookout man and kept a close watch on one of the most important families in town.

Pandora's disappearance caused quite a stir among his ilk. They were close to being discovered, and additionally, it seemed that Matteo was trying to undermine everything they had built and planned for decades.

He saw someone enter the room, which was his abductor, Matteo, of course. He brought along a plastic bag filled with cabbages, which smelled so good to him. His donkey mouth began to water.

Matteo began to strip a leaf off one cabbage and dropped it close to Pluto, which he immediately gobbled. He did the same thing to all the heads of cabbages he brought.

Pluto never knew before that cabbages tasted this good. His donkey taste buds went into overdrive as he ate them with gusto. He was in a state of complete bliss and almost forgot the situation he was in and his protracted hatred of Matteo.

At this juncture, Matteo said: "I want you to listen. I know you can still understand me, even though you can't reply, so here's what I have to say: whatever you're planning, stop it. I've been observing you since you first showed up in this house, and you're doing some suspicious things I don't understand. If you keep on doing this, then I have to do something about it."

Pluto looked inquiringly at him. Matteo understood the look and said: "I'm going to feed you to a giant snake in the forest. You're just a small donkey the size of a goat and the snake can easily swallow you whole. Do you understand?"

Matteo's donkey head nodded in fear. He knew about the giant white snake in the forest, which was one of the most feared and terrible foes of the black army.

"So, we are in agreement. You'll remain as our butler and do nothing that will cause harm to anyone in the household. If I find out you're doing something shady, I still have the power to change you into a donkey then feed you to the giant snake. Do you understand?"

Pluto nodded.

"You're going to change back into your old self in a few hours, so you'll go back upstairs and act like nothing has happened. I'll be watching you always."

Pluto hee-hawed in somber understanding.

Chapter 11 The Willful Child

Pandora's plan of finding a boyfriend didn't go as smoothly as intended. Most of the boys in her school were intimidated by her and the wealth and stature of her family. Yet Ruby Rose was able to scrounge up a few likely candidates, which included a couple of rich and poor boys.

She whittled the list down to two potential boys: one poor, smart boy and one rich, handsome boy.

The rich boy had mestizo good looks and was also popular in school. He was the mayor's son, whose family got rich by mining gold in the past. He was also an athlete and captain of the local basketball team. He was the perfect boy for Pandora.

Meanwhile, the poor boy was the most diametrically opposite person to Pandora in every way possible. They were like oil and water together. On paper, it shouldn't work. However, being intelligent was the ace up his sleeve since Pandora loved talking to smart people. It leveled the playing field in a big way.

Ruby Rose arranged dates for both of them. It was difficult to plan one for the rich boy since he showed little enthusiasm in this undertaking in the first place. Yet he still agreed to do it since Pandora was a great catch and a girl the whole male population in school had a crush on.

She went on a date with the rich boy first. Ruby Rose predicted this would not go well, and she was right on the money. It was like two alpha dogs meeting for the first time and immediately at each other's throats. The date was a disaster of epic proportions.

Ruby Rose scratched the rich boy's name off the list.

The poor boy was the last candidate, and Ruby Rose had an inkling that they would hit it off. He was her classmate, after all, and was included on the same honor roll. He was more similar to her, and since Pandora loved her as a sister, it was a reasonable assumption that she would also have great affection for him.

The date went well, as expected. Ruby Rose thought the idiom "opposites attract" was all hogwash but now believed it to be true. It seemed people who have nothing in common would seemingly make ideal partners.

Then another idiom, "too much of a good thing," suddenly popped into her mind, which was something Pandora always tended to personify. If she liked to do something, she would excessively do it until the wheels fell off. Then, it would be her job to fix it like she did many times before.

Hence, she hoped and prayed this undertaking wasn't foolish and provided value to everyone involved, especially herself.

~O~

At first, Pandora was filled with enthusiasm for having a suitor. It was a novel experience for her, having someone who supposedly wanted to gain her affections to be her boyfriend, so she had to play it cool and not appear overexcited.

Andreas was known by everyone as a nice boy, which in essence, he was. However, he was aware of the situation he was in and how it was a favorable opportunity for himself and his family. Being in a relationship with one of the wealthy Ponce de Leons was like finding a goose that laid golden eggs. He wasn't going to ruin his golden chance by any means necessary.

Soon enough, they became boyfriend and girlfriend for real. Ruby Rose was always by their side, a ubiquitous third wheel who acted more like a parent to the young and immature couple.

~O~

It was almost prom. it was an important event for Pandora, thus causing everyone in the household to be on edge. The helpers were in a constant state of agitation, forever at the whims of Pandora's hissy fits. Her Lola Sabrina couldn't assuage her since she was the reason for spoiling her rotten, which, in turn, lost Pandora's respect for her. It was her mother, Angelica, who could mollify and reprimand her in one of the few times she sobered up. She told her the hard truths about being a growing woman, the sort of intimate womanly knowledge passed on from mothers to daughters.

The day of the high school promenade came. Angelica bought the girls expensive dresses from top Filipino fashion designer Michael Cinco. Ruby Rose's dress was more conservative by design, which was her preference, while Pandora's was sexier and more revealing, which was what she wanted.

They had a black Toyota Lexus in the garage reserved for special occasions, which they used and driven by a uniformed chauffeur. They were ready and excited. They were like two princesses, all geared up for the ball, made up, and dressed to the nines.

They picked up Andreas along the way. He dressed modestly in a Barong Tagalog, which Pandora had chosen for him to wear. She didn't want him to look too flashy and wanted everyone staring at her. His role was no more than an unfabulous window dressing to the flashier main attraction—Pandora.

They arrived at the high school gymnasium, which was the venue for the prom. Pandora led the way as they strolled inside. She expected to get everyone's attention, and she did. Some students stood, with their mouths agape as if seeing a popular celebrity for the first time. Mission accomplished.

At the same time, Ruby Rose, who looked equally as beautiful, wasn't used to getting all the attention and didn't have Pandora's confidence. She aimlessly walked with her head down, trying to find a hole she could crawl into. She saw a classmate who, like her, didn't have a date and rushed towards her side.

It was now Pandora and Andreas as the main center of attraction. Everyone was thinking the same thing, and from the looks of it, they had a good chance of becoming Prom King and Queen. The music played a love song, and they started dancing.

It was the happiest day of Pandora's life. She danced and laughed and enjoyed herself. She feverishly wished the night would never end.

Nevertheless, something sinister was permeating in the shadows, and they had no idea it was heading their way.

Chapter 12 The Raven

A lone blackbird had flown far from its nest atop the Golden Mountain. It was looking for carrion to feed its hatchlings, and its journey had brought it to the high school gymnasium. It had a keen sense of smell and could detect the slightest scent of deathly odors and even smell a living organism close to expiry. It had perched atop the gym because it sensed soon-to-be dead meat it could feed on and bring to its baby birds.

It knew it would happen anytime soon, and it did not need to wait long.

~O~

As anticipated, Pandora and Andreas won the titles of Prom Queen and King. She was overjoyed as a golden crown was placed atop her head, and a sash labeled "Prom Queen" was pinned on her dress. She glanced at Andreas by her side, who was equally glad and smiling from ear to ear. She saw Ruby Rose among the crowd, smiling and clapping her hands.

Amidst the cacophony of noises in the gym, she suddenly heard a hushed whisper from a woman who eerily sounded like her Lola Sabrina. The whispering voice was saying something unintelligible, and the only phrase she could understand was: "darkness is coming!"

She heard loud caws from a mob of crows perched atop the rafters. They were agitated, and some were flying to and fro from the wide ceiling space. She sensed something horrible was approaching, which would ruin her moment in the sun.

It angered her. Whatever was coming, it was going to have a taste of her terrible wrath. She felt a surge of energy forming in her core, emanating and trying to go out.

Then, seven little people barged in from the gym entrance. They were *Dwendes*, black dwarves dressed in golden tunics led by Lord Axe-Grinder. They were holding scary-looking battleaxes as big as themselves.

The students thought they were part of the show and applauded them. The dwarves were heading to the stage towards Pandora. As the first dwarf approached, Andreas knew something was wrong and stepped forward in front of her, attempting to shield her. The dwarf cut him down like a scythe to a rice stalk, and his upper torso fell backward with a sick thud. There was blood everywhere: on the floor, on the walls, and Pandora's expensive dress. She screamed bloody murder, and the whole gymnasium erupted in chaos.

In her wrath, the energy forming in her core transposed to her limbs and suddenly issued forth in her hands in the appearance of pure light. She pointed her lighted right hand to the first dwarf and obliterated him into nothingness.

The flying crows swooped down and shapeshifted into numerous dark and terrible monsters from Batala: vampiric *Mandurugos*, horse/human hybrid *Tikbalangs*, and boar-like *Kiwigs*. They began attacking the students. Pandora saw this taking place and started blasting at them, scorching their dark body coverings and destroying them. They had thought no one would fight back, and most had retreated after witnessing Pandora's emergence of power.

Lord Axe-Grinder's original plan was to take her by force and bring her to Batala. He wanted to recruit her as an ally of the black army as he had originally intended when she was still younger and lost in the forest. But he saw now that they couldn't. She was too powerful and wrathful, and anyone who came close was blotted out from existence. Nonetheless, he planned to try again in the future, when the time was right. They might have lost this battle, but the war between the black and white forces was still ongoing.

He motioned his remaining minions to fall back and retreat, which they gratefully did. They transformed back into flying crows and flew out of the gymnasium.

The gym was empty of living people since the remaining students and teachers had fled, all except Pandora and Ruby Rose. They ran towards each other and embraced and cried. Then they heard a wail of police sirens from afar and were comforted by the notion that the horror was now over and grownups with authority had arrived.

They glanced at the horrifying image of Andreas cut in half at the stage. They sobbed, wailed, and hugged each other tighter. Ruby Rose comforted her and told her that everything was going to be alright. She nodded. They sat down and waited as the sirens became louder and came closer.

~O~

The raven surveyed the scene. It flew downwards to get a better look. There were numerous dead bodies scattered on the cement floor: some were humans, and some were monsters. Then it saw a ghostly form of a boy on the stage, swooped down and alighted on his shoulder.

The boy had a shocked expression on his face like he couldn't believe what had happened to him. He looked at the bird and was surprised by its friendly disposition. The bird cawed like it was telling him that his time in the physical world was over and to follow him to the realm of the spirits.

However, he disagreed. There was still yet unfinished business, and he wanted to remain and help the girls since he loved one of them.

The bird cawed in agreement. It would also stick around to help achieve the ghost boy's goals, and once it was over, it would bring him to paradise.

Chapter 13 The Ungrateful Son

Lola Sabrina had a sudden clarity of thought she hadn't felt for a while. It was like a dark cloud had parted in her mind, and the sun emerged to bring light to the world.

She had these abrupt lucid moments a few times each month, wherein she could remember everything distinctly: the past, present, and future events. These moments would last for a few minutes only, and after they passed, she would go back to her previous state of constant forgetfulness.

It occurred a few minutes before the black dwarves attacked the high school gymnasium. She saw these events happen in her mind's eye and sent a telepathic message to her granddaughter Pandora, which she knew later had worked and was crucial in her defense against the dark monsters.

She was thankful both girls were alright but was aghast after learning about the gruesome death of the boy. It reminded her of what had happened to her father, who likewise perished under the fiery hands of fate.

~O~

Romeo was bleeding again. He had been out in the forest with his friends, looking for adventure and engaging in boyish shenanigans.

His friends were like him in demeanor, a bunch of reckless teenagers out for fun of the destructive kind. They were previously warned of the haunted nature of the forest, but they didn't care, and their wanton aggression took over.

Their group included one girl named Dolores, Romeo's high school sweetheart. She was young, innocent, and stupid and followed him around like a puppy, reveling in everything he did.

Whenever he was on one of these foolhardy excursions, he would leave destruction in his wake, often resulting in bruising and bleeding of his entire body. His mother Dona Corazon, tended to his wounds and reprimanded him for his behavior, but he never listened. He wasn't afraid of her and often disrespected her. The only person in the house he was scared of was his father, Don Marcus, who would severely whip him with a belt when he badly behaved.

His father often admonished him to tread lightly, literally and figuratively, whenever he went to the forest since elemental beings lived there and didn't want to be disturbed. He warned him of their vengeful nature and to respect their elemental laws.

Romeo didn't believe any of it and thought it was all bullshit, so he, along with his unruly friends, proceeded to demolish everything they could get their hands on in the forest when any opportunity presented itself. He was immune to his father's whippings and didn't care anymore.

Nothing ever happened to them, which made them arrogantly self-righteous, and went on with this kind of conduct. Soon, they grew to young adulthood, and Romeo married Dolores when their ages permitted and immediately birthed an offspring—a daughter named Sabrina.

There wasn't any consequence to their actions because he didn't know of Don Marcus' previous agreement with the elemental beings, a pact forged by blood.

~O~

Everyone noticed that Don Marcus was a different man after his visit from Henry Teves 1st. He was less of a tyrant and more patient with people now. He also became more furtive and would disappear for days at a time. No one knew where he would go, which made Dona Corazon worried.

She knew about the secret underground rooms she wasn't privy to that her husband had built for some arcane reason. She would see him go downstairs to those rooms but disappeared after she tried following him, and suddenly reappeared a few hours later.

What were in those rooms? She often wondered but didn't pry and never even attempted to ask. She was a simple barrio lass before marriage and was forever thankful that Don Marcus courted and married her. He had rescued her from poverty and obscurity and transformed her into a respectable high-society maven.

Any personal quirks or frequent marital abuses were ignored and forgotten instantly. She didn't even complain whenever he whipped their only son and always made excuses for both their behaviors.

Now, a drastic change has happened to her husband, but thankfully, not for the worse. It was a type of change she could live with and tolerate.

Therefore, life went on for her family in Casa de la Noche. Dolores lived with them after marrying Romeo, and Baby Sabrina was born.

~O~

However, Romeo became worse. Dona Corazon had thought his teenage shenanigans would disappear after growing to adulthood, but it exacerbated. He started to drink heavily and became abusive to Dolores and Sabrina. She tried to reprimand him but couldn't. He hadn't respected her as his younger self and wouldn't change now.

She asked Don Marcus to step in and be a father for once to Romeo, but he didn't seem to care. He wasn't like his usual self most of the time and was forever lost in his thoughts.

One day, in a drunken stupor, he ventured out to the forest alone. He remembered his younger years of destructive excursions in the forest and tried to replicate it. He had bought along a flame thrower that

Don Marcus had acquired after the Philippine-American War, which he had stolen.

He burned anything he could see: plants, bushes, trees, and small animals. He yelled expletives in insane glee, screaming that he didn't believe in elemental spirits and they should all go fuck themselves.

Then he heard a loud hissing sound, and coming out of the flames appeared a gigantic white snake.

He switched off the flame thrower and stared at the marvelous apparition, disbelieving it was real. It slithered straight to him, stopped, and stood up like a periscope.

Then, it transformed into a woman clad in flowing white light. She said in a whispery voice: "My name is *Bakunawa* and you have transgressed in my forest. What is your name?"

Romeo was so drunk that he could barely stand up but could still understand her. He said: "Romeo is my name baby, don't wear it out. Why do you want to know?"

"Romeo. I now remember. You are the son of Marcus, who had bestowed a powerful protection spell on you. We will not harm you, even though you have always disrespected my forest. However, we will give you a warning, which I hope you will heed."

"Warning, shwarning. Fuck you, you're not real. You're just a figment of my drunkenness. Suck my dick white lady."

"My warning to you is: if you still continue with this wanton destruction of nature, we will take one of your ancestors down the line and she will become one of us and you will never see her again."

"*She*? You mean my daughter Sabrina? If you touch one hair from my daughter, I'm going to…"

"You're not going to do anything, and we will destroy you if you will," Bakunawa said and transformed back into a white python. She slithered back into the now extinguished fire and disappeared.

He went home in a daze and went straight to bed. When he awoke, he tried to remember what had happened the day before, but it was so incredible he thought he might just be dreaming. He shrugged, stood up, went straight to the liquor cabinet, and opened a bottle of whiskey. He took a long swig and burped.

He continued his drinking spree until nighttime and became blind drunk. Yet he still had a few brain cells remaining and rambled towards the same spot in the forest where he encountered the white snake. He had brought a half-full bottle of whiskey, poured its contents on a nearby shrub, and lit it with a matchstick. The whole plant was instantly aflame and soon spread towards the nearby grassland.

Romeo cackled in laughter. He yelled: "Fuck you, white lady! Suck my dick!" He danced like a madman.

Unbeknownst to him, the flames slowly crawled towards him like an orange caterpillar. It started to grow bigger and bigger and became man-sized. It grew arms and legs, and the face of a woman began to form. It was Bakunawa.

The Serpent-Goddess Bakunawa, whose dress was made of fire, walked towards Romeo, the dancing buffoon. He didn't notice her until it was too late: she hugged the living daylights out of him.

He had nothing to eat all day and drank whiskey the whole time thus pure alcohol was coursing through his entire body. He was instantly lit ablaze, yet he continued to dance like a cha-cha dancer from hell until he couldn't anymore.

He dropped dead on the forest floor, burned to a crisp.

~O~

Lola Sabrina remembered seeing the charred remains of his father's body as it was brought back home. She was shocked beyond belief, and her young mind hadn't known how to process this unfolding tragedy properly.

Her mother and grandmother cried and cried and were stricken with grief. Yet her grandfather, Don Marcus, didn't seem affected and looked on indifferently.

She had thought the worst was over after her father died, but something much worse was yet to come, which had involved her.

Chapter 14 The Godfather

In the aftermath of the attack at the high school gymnasium, thirteen humans were recorded as having "traumatic death by wild animals" by the coroner's office, including one victim that made everyone in town truly concerned: the mayor's son. He was the boy who nearly became Pandora's boyfriend but intentionally took himself out of the picture.

When Mayor Edilberto Pabuaya (or Mayor Eddie to his constituents) found out his son was one of the victims, it hit him hard like a punch in the gut. It felt so unreal that he stubbornly didn't believe it at first. He thought he had gained so much power and controlling influence in Gintongbayan that no one dared to undermine or seek to harm him and his family.

After seeing his son's ravaged body in his own two eyes on the autopsy table at the coroner's office, he felt weak in the knees and then broke down sobbing. His wife was with him, who also wailed in grief. The boy was their only offspring after all, and no one was going to carry on the family name.

The coroner's office was located in the same building as the office of the police chief, which he went to after seeing the grisly remains of his dead son. He was let in by the Chief, who was sitting behind his desk.

"Please come in, Mr. Mayor, and have a seat. My heartfelt condolences to the loss of your son sir, I truly am very sorry," the Chief said somberly.

"Chief, I want a complete report of what happened," said Mayor Eddie. He tried to remain calm and collected in his usual functionary affectation as the town leader. However, his severe melancholia stripped away his façade of coolness, and his true feelings broke through. He seethed: "Fuck this. Who the fuck did this Chief? I'm going to kill this motherfucker, if it's the last thing I do."

"Whoa Mr. Mayor. Don't say anything you might regret later. We are still gathering all pieces of information and I'll be able to give you a complete report by tomorrow."

"Don't give me this bullshit Chief. You've seen the crime scene and the bodies, and you have an intimation of what had happened. What is your expert opinion?"

"Well, a pack of wild dogs did it."

"What about the stab markings? Did the dogs also do that?"

"No, there were people. They were the ones who had brought the dogs inside and commanded them to attack."

"So, you're saying a group of people came into the gymnasium, stabbed the kids then told their dogs to also attack them?"

"Yes, all evidence points to that direction."

"Any witnesses?"

"We're compiling their statements as we speak."

"Who did it? And why?"

"We don't know the 'who' and 'why' yet. I'm giving this to my top investigator to look into. Rest assured Mr. Mayor he will personally provide you with daily progress reports."

"I'll be looking forward to it," Mayor Eddie said and calmed down a bit. He left and went back to the coroner's office, where his wife was still weeping. He hugged her, took one last look at the dead body of his son, and went home.

~O~

Most of the younger people in town addressed Mayor Eddie as "Godfather Eddie," since he was forever being called upon to sponsor their baptisms. He was happy to be involved with these events because it made him more popular, and increased popularity translated to additional votes in the next election.

His ancestor Carlito Pabuaya was one of the founders of the town, who, like Don Marcus Ponce de Leon, also struck gold and became wealthy. But unbeknownst to him, he had likewise made a secret pact with the elemental beings.

He wasn't a believer of supernaturalism and regarded himself more of a pragmatist, so any news coming to his desk that can be considered "supernatural," would automatically be disposed to the garbage bin.

He believed in facts, truth, and justice. He regarded himself as an honest-to-goodness public servant and a true believer in these concepts, which he held in high regard.

Yet all these didn't seem important to him now after learning about the gruesome death of his son. Revenge was on his mind, and he would make certain to get it by any means necessary.

~O~

The next day came and brought nothing but sadness to Mayor Eddie's home. His wife couldn't be consoled and locked herself in their bedroom. He dressed up and went downstairs, and found out that a smartly uniformed police officer was waiting for him in the dining room.

He walked gloomily towards him and shook his hands.

"Mayor Eddie, I'm from the Criminal Investigation and Detection Group, Police Officer Michael Collins."

"*Collins?* You're not a Filipino? But you look like one."

"I am sir. My father is a Filipino-American who married my mom, a pure Filipina. You can call me Mike, if you want."

"Okay Mike, tell me. Who killed my son and why?"

"Well, Mr. Mayor, my colleagues and I talked to the witnesses, mostly students and a few teachers who were present during the attack. They said that a bunch of midgets—or to be politically-correct—*little people* barged inside the gym and started killing people with axes closest to them. Then a few wild animals appeared and started attacking. And then, the next part isn't clear yet..."

"What happened?"

"The ones who were still alive and saw what happened next said that a girl by the name Pandora was able to kill some of the attackers and drove the remaining away."

"A girl? All alone? With what?"

"Some said she was holding a gun, some said a torch. But fire appeared to come out of her hands and incinerated the attackers."

"Maybe she was holding a weapon of some kind?"

"That's what we're trying to find out."

"Did you talk to this girl, Pan..."

"*Pandora.*"

"Pandora. Were you able to talk to her?"

"Well, we found out she's from the Ponce de Leon family, who lives in Casa de la Noche."

"Oh Christ. It's one of those assholes. I was friends with his father Henry in high school, who was also an asshole, but now dead."

"We tried talking to her, but her mother and grandmother prevented us from doing our job. They said we couldn't due to her sensitive nature and unless there's a warrant of arrest. We explained to them we're not charging her with anything yet and we only need to listen to her side of things."

"Then *what?*"

"They still wouldn't. You're right, they *are* a bunch of assholes. However, we still need to talk to the daughter, so this is where you come into the picture, Mr. Mayor."

"Yes, I'll talk to them. Both our families have a long history together as family friends, since the origin of this town. So much tragedy happened to that family, and now with mine…"

"I'm truly sorry for what happened to your son, Mayor Eddie, and we're going to catch the culprits to this heinous assault on the school. The girl might hold information we need, so please talk to them."

"Yes, I'm going to, but later. For now, I have to comfort my wife and arrange for my boy's funeral. After I talk to them, I'll call you immediately."

"Here's my calling card. Call me anytime Mayor Eddie."

"Yeah, talk to you soon…"

Chapter 15 The Spirit in the Glass Bottle

Andreas had a difficult time getting used to being a ghost. He didn't feel any different; he could still do pretty much everything a living person could, but two things he immediately discovered were different: he could walk through walls, and people couldn't see him anymore like he was unreal.

In essence, he was, since he wasn't alive anymore in the conventional sense. From what little knowledge he gleaned about spirits, he knew he was an entity moving between two different planes of existence, which made his sojourn only temporary and volatile. Time was his enemy, so he needed to do the thing he had to do as soon as possible.

But what am I supposed to do? He thought. Helping Pandora was already a given, but what kind of help should he contribute? From what he saw, Pandora could defend herself from those horrible things that attacked them. She incinerated them using only her hands. *Maybe I could protect her if those creatures tried to find her again.*

But he knew he couldn't. He wasn't able to defend her when he was still alive and couldn't when he was now dead. There wasn't much use for an invisible ghost boy who could move through objects. He had to know how to help her as soon as possible so he could leave and finally cross over from the physical world.

He went to Casa de la Noche to see what was happening with Pandora and Ruby Rose, his two most favorite people in the world.

~O~

Angelica was mad at everyone in the house. Her mother especially, because she was the one who helped her prepare for the prom. But deep down, she knew it was her fault since Pandora was her daughter in the first place and could have given her the help she needed and not left the responsibility to her mother.

She had been looking for a sign to stop drinking, and once she found it, she vowed to herself she would and what had happened to Pandora was a definite sign to stop. She went to the liquor cabinet to empty its contents of booze, but as she arrived, she discovered everything was gone. Every whiskey, gin, vodka, and rum bottle had disappeared.

She had the only key to the liquor cabinet since no one else in the house drank except her. *Did I throw them away while I was drunk last night?* She thought. *Maybe I did since I blacked out.*

She remembered the story of her ancestor Romeo Ponce de Leon, who had died by lighting himself on fire with a bottle of whiskey in the forest. Her mother, Sabrina told this story to her as a lesson about the danger of excessive alcohol consumption, and she had thought that if she started drinking, she wouldn't go that far. But now she knew that unless she stopped, she was on her way to killing herself with the devil's juice.

The sign she had been waiting for definitely told her to stop drinking and be a mother for real to Pandora. She closed the empty cabinet, threw away its key, and went to Pandora's bedroom.

~O~

Pandora was in her bedroom still crying, and Ruby Rose was consoling her. She had been sobbing nonstop the whole day, and Ruby Rose was getting tired and wanted to leave. She was looking for an excuse but couldn't think of anything Pandora would believe.

Then, there was a knock on the door.

"Who is it?" Said Ruby Rose.

"It's me. Please open the door Ruby," said Angelica.

"Hey Pandora, your mother is here, maybe she wants to talk to you alone."

"Huh? Okay. Come back when she leaves, alright?" Pandora said. Her eyes were bulging with tears.

"Sure," said Pandora and opened the door. "Hello Ma'am Angelica, I'll go so you can talk with her alone."

"Thanks Ruby."

Angelica walked to the dresser beside the bed, sat on the stool, and said: "Pandora, are you okay?"

"Are you okay?? *Are you okay?* That's all you can say to me?"

Don't start Pandora. I'm here as your mother, trying to talk to you. I know I haven't been much of anything since your father died, and I'm sorry."

"He died a long time ago Mama, and I don't even have any memory of him. All these years, you didn't seem to care about me and always lock yourself in your room."

"Yes, I know. I'm so sorry Pandora. I promise I'm going to be here and help you process what happened to you in the gym."

"I don't know what happened Mama," she said and began sobbing again.

"The police will try to talk to you again, but don't worry, you don't have to. Don't talk to anyone outside the house, alright? Just stay here for the meantime. I've called your school already and you're taking a few weeks off."

"What will happen to me? Will I go to jail?"

"You're not going anywhere Pandora. Your Lola and I will handle everything, I promise."

"But Lola Sabrina can't even remember what she ate for breakfast. How is she going to help?"

"Your Lola is more capable that you know. She might have a few memory lapses, but she still has the ability to do amazing things."

"What kind of amazing things?"

"Things you might think are unbelievable or even impossible."

"I don't understand."

"Your Lola has powers, alright?"

Pandora stopped crying, and her eyes widened. She had always felt something was peculiar about her family but didn't know what. Whenever something weird happened, she always dismissed it as everyone in the house seemed to do, and she just followed suit. Now she was about to find out there actually was a reason for those strange occurrences.

"What kind of powers?"

"She is a telepath and can see the future."

"Wow. Really? How did she get them?"

"It was something supernatural, which I don't really believe. I never paid attention to that bullshit whenever she told it to me. You can ask her about it later, if she's able to remember."

"Yes, I'll do that."

"Hey, where did you get that glass bottle of whisky? It's supposed to be in the liquor cabinet."

"I don't know how it got there, Mama. Maybe you brought it here a while ago."

"Have you been drinking it?"

"What? No Mom. Ewww, I hate it. Even the smell makes me sick. Can you bring it with you when you leave and throw it away?"

"Yes, I'll throw it away. It's a disgusting drink. It makes you forget things."

"Yes, it's disgusting."

"You feel better?"

"I do Mama, your visit made me feel better."

"We should talk more often."

"Yes, we should."

"Anyway, talk to your Lola Sabrina about her so-called powers. You're going to love it."

"Thanks Mama."

Angelica left the room and was glad she finally connected with her daughter.

~O~

A few minutes after Angelica left, Pandora went to Lola Sabrina's bedroom and knocked. "Lola, are you there? Can I come in?"

"Pandora, is that you?" Said Lola Sabrina.

"Yes, it is. Can I come in?"

"Sure. Come in."

Pandora opened the door and entered. Her Lola was sitting by her dresser, looking at her through the reflection in the mirror. She was smiling. She said: "You're here to ask some questions, right?"

"Yes Lola. How did you know? Well, I guess you do because you can see the future."

"Did your Mama tell you?"

"Yes Lola, she also said you have a telepathic ability. Is that true?"

"Yes, it's true."

"How did you get them?"

"It's a long story Pandora. Are you sure you want to hear it?"

"Sure, I do. I don't have anything else to do anyway. I'm not supposed to go out remember?"

"Yes, I remember."

"By the way, there's an unopened bottle of whisky on your dresser. I never knew you drank Lola."

"It's not mine, somebody put it there, and I know who."

"Maybe you forgot you took it Lola. Anyway, don't bother. Just tell me the story."

Okay. Have a seat, dear."

Pandora sat down on the bed and prepared to listen to the story.

~O~

Andreas, in his ghostly form, was in the room with Pandora and Lola Sabrina. He had been trying to lift various objects with his spectral hand but to no avail. The only objects he could inexplicably hold and lift were any glass bottles and he had been practicing all day with liquor bottles.

And strangely, Lola Sabrina was seemingly aware of his presence, which gladdened him. It *will make my job easier,* he thought.

He stood by the corner and waited to listen to Lola's story.

Chapter 16 The Good Bargain

Have I told you how my father died? I already did? Well, the lesson you must learn is this: never drink alcohol to excess, or else it will kill you. It's alright to drink a little occasionally and only in moderation.

How did I get my powers, you ask? It's a strange story, dear. I once told your mother the same story, and she didn't believe it. If you also don't, then it's fine. I hope you learn something from it that can help you when the time comes.

This story involves two brothers named Jacob and Wilhelm. They were so-called paranormal experts who had arrived in town to investigate the unusual circumstances surrounding my father's demise. I hadn't known his death was regarded as strange because he died under ordinary conditions by accidentally burning himself to death.

I remembered the brothers having a dull and creepy appearance like they were morticians. Maybe their grim look was part of the package. They had to appear in a particular way to lend credibility to their profession.

The brothers came to our house and spoke to my mother, grandparents, and me in that order. They told them the same story by accidentally burning himself to death when he was blitzed out of his mind. They explained there was nothing strange about it since he was an alcoholic after all and often went to the forest and vandalized it when he was younger.

However, the brothers said his death might be ordinary, but the place he died wasn't. Something strange was happening in the forest, and they wanted to find out what it was.

I knew then of the stories my grandmother used to tell me about elemental beings living in the forest, which they were already aware of. They said there were too many stories from dozens of people about strange goings-on in the forest that left them no choice but to investigate it.

Back then, technology wasn't the same as today. They only had books and notebooks to back up their findings. They were established authors who had published books previously about supernatural phenomena.

They wanted to visit the forest and see it for themselves and asked to hire someone from the household to accompany them as a guide. I immediately volunteered to go with them, but my mother said no and let two helpers keep them company instead.

At that time, I had never gone to the forest and was too scared because of the stories told by my grandmother. However, my fear was overtaken by curiosity, and I secretly followed them.

The brothers also brought one of those old photographic cameras the size of a small TV set and let the household helpers carry it. It looked heavy, and they had a hard time holding it, while I slowly followed, unseen, hiding behind every tree along the way.

Soon, they arrived at the exact spot where my father died. The surrounding area was scorched and blackened, and there was also a gigantic termite mound in front of them. I didn't know back then it was unusual and thought it was only an ordinary part of the forest. But now I know its large size was what made it strange.

They started setting up a large camera to take pictures. I sneaked closer and closer until I could hear them within earshot. The older brother Jacob told his younger brother Wilhelm to take photos of the surrounding area that had gotten burned, including the termite mound. If you've seen this kind of camera before, setting it up was complicated and tedious, and it would take about ten minutes to take one picture each.

After watching them briefly, I became restless and antsy and wanted to transfer to another area for a better vantage point. While I looked around, I noticed the giant termite mound began to tremble. The shaking became more pronounced and stronger, and a crack in the ground surface began to form in front of the mound. The brothers retreated, and the two helpers ran away, presumably back home.

At that point, I should have run away like the helpers and returned home, but I didn't. I just stood there transfixed and waited for what was supposed to happen next. I saw the brothers were also standing like statues, in complete awe of the occurrence.

The crack in the ground became bigger, and there was a white light emanating from it. Then, a grizzled hand appeared, grasping the edge of the crack. It looked like something, or someone was trying to climb out.

Out from the ground appeared a pale old man with a long beard and wearing a long white robe. It didn't look like a midget or a dwarf, but a human man who was just small in stature.

The brothers were also captivated by the sight, and Wilhelm began setting up the camera to take the old man's picture. The old man approached it, which, compared to him, looked huge. He looked at it in awe and tapped a part of it with his wooden staff.

Jacob started talking to him and addressed him as "*Nuno*." The old man didn't seem to understand and looked blankly at him. Jacob took out a book from his bag, opened it, and showed it to the Nuno but didn't seem to be affected by it.

The Nuno began to wiggle his nose like he had smelled something nasty and looked straight in my direction. I tried to hide but knew he had found out about me.

The brothers also saw me. Jacob motioned me to approach since I had already been discovered. I advanced in trepidation, a little scared but more curious than ever.

The Nuno had a dreadful face, full of creases, crinkles, and smeared of dirt. Upon closer inspection, his robe was more light brown than white. He began to tap the mound with his staff, and a wooden door appeared, complete with a brass knob. He opened it with his wrinkled hand and motioned for us to follow.

The brothers quickly packed the camera and approached to follow suit, and I also did. We were excited about the possibility of seeing a new world where elemental beings like the Nuno existed.

The Nuno closed the door behind him after we all entered.

~O~

"Lola, I remember something like that happen to me when I was younger and lost in the forest, but the memory felt so unbelievable I had doubts it's even real," said Pandora.

"It was. You might not want to believe it, but it really did happen to you. I saw it myself in my mind, before it happened."

"Why didn't you tell me? You could've saved me from the trouble I got myself into."

"As you know because of my age, I have memory lapses. On certain occasions, when I see something is happening in the future, I immediately forget it. I'm truly sorry for that, dear."

It's okay, Lola. Please continue with your story…"

~O~

It was dark once we entered, and I couldn't see anything. The tip of the old man's staff suddenly lit up like a flashlight. And yes, dear, it's a magic staff.

We saw that we were inside a tunnel going slowly downward, under the ground. The old man was quick to his feet for his age and dashed towards an unknown destination that I assumed was at the end of the tunnel. We quickly followed, half-walking and running, trying to catch up to him. The brothers looked awkward and funny since they lugged the heavy camera along.

We saw a tiny bright light at the end of the tunnel, which increasingly became bigger as we came closer and closer.

A few minutes into the tunnel, the light became man-sized, then soon as big as a house. As we finally reached the end, we saw the light come from a burning tree. It was a magic tree I suppose, since it didn't seem to burn out and give off any harmful heat. Different creatures didn't look human, which I learned later were elemental beings my mother told me about.

There were also dwelling huts of mud and grass that looked like the giant termite mound above the ground. The old man directed us to the largest and most elaborate-looking domicile, which we assumed was their leader.

This home looked even stranger compared to the other dwellings. There was no door but a large hole we couldn't fit, so we just stood outside and waited. The wizened old man was gone, which I guess he already did what he was supposed to do.

Out of the hole slithered a giant white snake. It looked magnificent in its size as it stood up like a periscope facing us. Then, it began to transform into the shape of a woman wearing a flowing white dress.

The woman looked beautiful in an otherworldly way, like she wasn't a normal human being, but someone more superior than us. She was, as I found out later, a goddess named Bakunawa.

The brothers had set up the camera and took many pictures of her and this magical realm we had traveled to. One brother, Jacob, started writing in his notebook, recording everything he saw.

Then Bakunawa spoke. She said she knew all about us: the brothers and their reason for coming there, and about me and what happened to my father. My father was punished because he had disrespected nature and her elemental brethren many times before and was warned to stop but didn't. I didn't know how to react after hearing it and just nodded numbly.

Meanwhile, Jacob was busy taking down notes, and Wilhelm was taking pictures. Bakunawa then told us a story, which explained everything.

~O~

"Lola, I don't understand. What do you mean by 'everything?' You mean why we were attacked in the gym?"

"Yes, and more. She told us what we wanted to know."

"Oh, okay. I'm sorry I interrupted Lola, please continue."

"It's fine, dear…"

~O~

She first asked us: did we notice how all her elemental brethren were similar? We glanced around and looked at various creatures in the underground realm: the ethereal *Engkantos*, the sprightly *Diwatas*, the centaur-like *Anggitays*, and many more. Jacob then said they were all fair and light-skinned.

Bakunawa nodded. She told us they were all from the same race of white elemental beings whose job was to protect nature at all costs, including the humans who respected them. There were other creatures like them living in a different domain, also underground, separated by distance and a magical force field. They were dark creatures who wanted to exploit and dominate the human race. They were in a forever war with these dark beings, and they were losing.

Bakunawa then proposed a bargain: the three of us remain with them indefinitely, and then train us in their ways. With us by their side, she said they might have a fighting chance in defeating them.

Jacob and Wilhelm were taken aback. They explained they didn't want to stay since they had a profession and personal lives to return to. They were only there to investigate and record all the happenings for their upcoming book.

Bakunawa was silent after she heard it. The brothers started to look scared and had probably regretted the whole journey. Then she looked directly at me, and I smiled and nodded.

~O~

"So, I stayed with them and the brothers left."

"Is that it? What happened to you and the brothers? Why have I never heard about them? They should have been famous by now if they've written a book about that magical realm."

"Well, that's another story for a different time."

"Won't you finish the story, Lola? I want to know what happened next."

"Sorry, dear, trying to remember all those events made my head hurt. I need to rest a bit."

"Ok Lola, I'll come back later after you've rested."

"Thanks, dear. Please close the door after you leave."

Chapter 17 The Blue Light

Pluto, the majordomo, was blatantly keeping a close eye on the goings-on in Casa de la Noche. He decided to do away with the pretense any longer and use his position to his advantage. He took note of Pandora leaving her grandmother's room looking somewhat joyful, and her crying fits seemed to be gone. He was sure Pandora had gleaned some important information from her grandmother that changed her mood for the better.

He was aware of the attack in the gym and was unhappy about the outcome, as many of his cohorts had perished. He knew Lord Axe-Grinder would be mad at him because he didn't give him any warning whatsoever about Pandora's burgeoning new power. He dreaded the incoming punishment, which surely would be inflicted on him.

He was becoming desperate to find crucial information that his lord needed, to appease him. He was already aware of each family member's backstory, which he had learned before arriving at the house for the first time. Any new information accumulated he'd record and gladly give to Lord Axe-Grinder for his perusal.

There was something important the grandmother had told Pandora, which he urgently wanted. This way, he wouldn't be punished and could stay in Casa de la Noche indefinitely.

The girl Pandora was the key to it all. Lord Axe-Grinder had wanted to abduct and recruit her to be part of his dark army, but his efforts had failed.

Then, a sudden revelation hit him: why not abduct her himself? He had the home court advantage and knew the house and its inhabitants, so he had to find a way to get her alone and take her. His lord would be so happy that he'd spare him from punishment or maybe give him a higher position in the army.

He would wait for the right time to strike...

~O~

Ruby Rose arrived in her room at the servant's quarters and was physically and emotionally tired. She didn't get any sleep for days and had been spending all her time by Pandora's side tending to her needs. She had reached her breaking point with Pandora's bratty temperament and almost decided to bang her head on the wall. Pandora was a difficult pill to swallow, and it took an especially patient person to deal with her. Ruby Rose was one of the few who could.

Thankfully, her mother had unknowingly rescued her, and now she can finally sleep. She lay down on her bed and closed her eyes, but quickly opened them after hearing a loud bang of a closing door. She saw her father Matteo arrive, looking agitated.

She arose and said: "Dad, what's up? Why are you angry?"

"Hmm? Oh. Nothing Ruby, go back to sleep."

She saw the vein on his head throbbing, and she knew something was going on. "Dad, is it about Mom?"

"No Ruby, it's nothing to do with your mother. It's about something else, I mean *someone*."

"*Who*? Maybe I can help."

"Don't worry about it. It might get a little dangerous if you will."

"Does it have to do with Pandora? What did she do now?"

"Yes, it is, but she didn't do anything. It's about someone else who might do something bad to her."

"Here in the house? Who would want to harm her?"

"It's that son of a bitch Pluto, the butler. He's been snooping around, listening on the outside bedroom doors of the three madams, and butting in on other people's business. He's done the same thing before and he's doing it right now. I have to put a stop to it."

"Maybe he's just doing his job Dad. I think he's harmless."

"Is being a creep part of his job description? Because it's not."

"Let me ask him what he's doing, and maybe he'll tell me."

"You don't know him, Ruby. He can be dangerous."

"I'm sure we could work it out. Have you no faith in your smart and beautiful daughter?"

"Beautiful yes but smart, maybe not. Foolhardy might be the right word to describe you."

"I'm probably the most careful and thoughtful person around here Dad. What would he do to me anyway? The worse thing he could do is to scold and tell me to mind my own business."

"I'm not so sure about that Ruby. After the attack at the high school gym happened, all of us from the household staff were shocked and dismayed, but not Pluto. It looked like the news brought gladness to his face and it was only after seeing Pandora safe and sound that his face changed to shock. I think he knew the attack was supposed to happen and was surprised after seeing Pandora safe at home."

"Really? You saw all that happen? Maybe you're misreading his facial expressions, since he's a weirdo after all."

"I know what I saw Ruby, and I'm always right. I knew about your mom screwing around before anyone else, right? I have an especially good sense predicting things before occurring, and I'm not making a mistake right now. He's up to something."

"Alright Dad, you win. Just don't do anything stupid that can cause harm to anyone, okay? I'm going back to sleep."

"Go to sleep Ruby, and gather your strength. Pandora will need you later."

Ruby went back to bed and immediately slept like a log.

~O~

Andreas discovered another ability his ghostly form possessed: he could observe many occurrences in the house simultaneously. It seemed that time and space were vastly different concepts from what a living person experienced. He could be in two places instantaneously and see what was happening in both. He was able to stay and listen to Lola Sabrina's story and also follow Ruby Rose to her room.

He heard about the potential danger Pluto might inflict on Pandora, and his spirit body suddenly branched out to a third spectral form and floated away to find the majordomo's whereabouts.

He saw Pluto outside Pandora's door, trying to listen in. He walked through Pluto's body and the doorway and saw Pandora sitting on the edge of her bed. She was flipping pages of a photo album and stopped at a picture of a man, and upon closer inspection was her long-deceased father.

She had never talked about her dad when he was still a full-fledged living boy. From what little knowledge he gathered, he had died abroad before she was born and didn't even know him. *Why the sudden interest?* He thought. *Maybe it had to do with the attack and the reason behind it.*

Or perhaps there was no reason at all, and she was just looking for something to do to kill time since she was grounded. But then he saw a single tear appear, fall, and drop on one of the photos. It looked like she was still sad and needed cheering up. However, there was a potentially dangerous person outside her door who might do some harm to her.

He had to snap her out of it and alert her of the possible peril outside. He looked for a glass bottle to displace, but nothing made of glass was on her dresser. He got more perplexed, and then his ghostly form changed in color and turned to a bluish light instead.

He then saw Pandora looking directly at him like she could see him for what he now was, as a blue specter. There was no fear showing in her eyes but recognition. She knew him.

She said: "Andreas, is that you?"

He tried to talk, but no sound came out of his mouth. The only thing he could do was to nod, which he fervently did. He realized that spirits like him couldn't talk, so he needed to find a way to convey to her that Pluto was outside posing a threat.

He pointed at the door and then to his right ear, mouthing that someone was listening outside. She was confused for a second but immediately understood. She tiptoed to the door and quickly opened it, but Pluto had disappeared. She looked at him bewilderingly, but her expression turned to surprise as she saw that he was beginning to fade away.

Andreas saw that his bluish light was slowly extinguishing. He was returning to his once ghostly form that no one could see.

However, now he knew that Pluto was dangerous and was a person he had to watch out for. He also needed to find a way to reactivate his blue light and make himself a useful entity for the family.

Chapter 18 The Young Giant

"Lola, are you asleep?" Pandora said and lightly knocked on her bedroom door. "I saw something strange, and maybe we could talk about it."

No response. She turned the doorknob to come in and saw her Lola on the bed, sleeping. She quietly closed the door behind her, tiptoed towards the bedside, and sat down. She saw her eyes rapidly shifting in REM sleep. She was moaning something incomprehensible like she was talking in a different language. She then stirred to awakeness, opened her eyes, and saw Pandora's face staring directly at her.

"You were talking in your sleep Lola. Were you dreaming?"

"You're there, dear. Sorry I didn't answer the door," she said and rose from her bed. "You have the most beautiful pale blue eyes. Have I told you that before?"

"You always say that to me Lola, but my eyes are always hurt by bright lights."

"I know, dear."

"What were you dreaming about Lola?"

"My dream? Oh. About flying. I'm always flying in my dreams, going to places I've been before when I was younger, soaring through the air like a bird."

"You mean the same place in your story, in the enchanted kingdom of magical creatures?"

"Sometimes, but I can only remember small parts of it when I wake up. It's called astral projection, dear, I've read about it somewhere. Whenever you dream about flying, your spirit leaves your body and flies in any place whatsoever."

"It never happened to me Lola. Is it one of the powers you got from them?"

"I don't think so, dear. Normal people can do it too, and you don't need to know magic to fly in your dreams."

"Have you previously dreamt about it?"

"I don't remember dreaming about it before, only recently. Maybe these dreams are trying to tell me something."

"Perhaps you're seeing the future Lola."

"It's possible, dear, and haven't figured it out yet. It's my faltering memory, sometimes playing tricks on me."

"It's because you're old, Lola. But don't worry, you're still my grandmother after all, and I'll always love you."

"You're sweet, dear, and I love you too."

"Lola, I saw something earlier, only for a few minutes, and then it disappeared."

"What did you see?"

"I saw Andreas as a ghost. He was trying to tell me something but didn't finish."

"Is he the boy who was killed? He's a ghost?"

"Yes Lola, a ghost. Are ghosts real?"

"After all the strange things that happened to you, and after the matter about astral projection, you're still having doubts about the existence of spirits?"

"I've never seen one before Lola."

"What about the dark creatures you saw in the gym, have you seen them before?"

"Only in books and movies, and yes they *are* real since I saw them with my own two eyes."

"If you saw Andreas in spirit form, it means ghosts are real, dear."

"If you say so, Lola."

"He'll come back, I'm sure of it. He has unfinished business in this plane of existence and can only cross over once it's done."

"You mean heaven? So, he has to do what he needs to do here and go to heaven?"

"It's not a simple as that, dear. There are various realms or levels of existence, and what you call 'heaven' is just another level, and our reality is some other one. Ghosts are in a different realm, trying to enter our own. Those dark beings that attacked you in the gym also live in another one in what you refer to as an enchanted kingdom."

"Wow, I didn't know that. Why are there many realms, Lola and for what purpose?"

"I don't know, dear. It's one of those eternal questions no one knows the answer to, like 'what is the meaning of life'. We just have to accept that life is full of mysteries, and all we need to do is respect it and everything it entails. And be kind. We must be kind to others."

"But some are bad. What will we do about them?"

"We have to destroy them."

Pandora was taken aback by Lola Sabrina's response. She looked into her eyes to check if she was serious, and she was. *Dead* serious.

What will happen next?"

"You'll need to learn about all the important things, dear, so you will be prepared if something bad happens again."

"So, tell me Lola."

~O~

Where did we stop? Oh yes. The grim brothers Jacob and Wilhelm had left the enchanted realm while I stayed. However, it's not the end for them, and will reappear later in the story.

Do you know what a '*Kapre*' is? It's a type of giant that lives on a tree. They are hairy creatures that like to smoke tobacco. I befriended one of them, a young giant named Jabber. He was also a BFG, which means a big, friendly giant.

He was quite young for a Kapre. He was about one hundred fifty years old, exceedingly tall, thin, and gangly, almost like a basketball player. He was also my first love.

We met a few days into my training and went with me during off days. We grew close and became more than friends.

On the first day of my so-called magical training, Bakunawa the Serpent-Goddess performed an attunement spell on my person to make me receptive to all forms of witchcraft. I had no history or anything that could be regarded as supernatural that happened in my whole life at that point, so something had to change inside me. Once I became attuned, the real training began the next day.

I also need to mention, dear, that the passage of time in the enchanted realm differs from what we're accustomed to. One year there is equivalent to one day here, so essentially, I was only missing one day in the real world.

I spent a year there. It was enough time to learn their ways.

Among all the various magical abilities taught to me, telepathy and divination were my strong suits, so I focused on mastering them. I often used Jabber as my test dummy and performed numerous magical spells on him. He was none too happy but assented nonetheless. He did care for me, after all.

In the last week of my training, the brothers returned, which took us by surprise. They said they changed their mind and returned many hours later, but for us, almost a year had passed. However, something was different with them. I felt their intentions were somewhat devious now since I still had an unpolished empath ability, which sometimes came in handy.

Indeed, something was *off* about them, and Jabber noticed it too. He had an acute olfactory perception, and he didn't like what the brothers smelled like. He said they didn't smell human but something else entirely. They reeked like their mortal enemies, the dark beings from the darker side of the enchanted realm.

If it was true, the real brothers were dead or held hostage, and these alleged "brothers" were dark beasts masquerading as them. Jabber went to find Bakunwa to tell her about this difficult problem.

I was left with these creatures posing as the brothers. I looked at them but didn't see any difference. They still appeared like ordinary, albeit weird-looking people. But then I remembered there was a way to see their true intentions by using a magical incantation: a truth spell.

I knew its exact words from the Book of Shadows, which I chanted to them:

For those who want the truth revealed,
Opened hearts and secrets unsealed,
From now until it's now again,
After which the memory ends,

So   magic   secrets   remain   secure,
I seek the truth for reasons pure.

One brother looked straight into my eyes as if he was hypnotized. He then asked me what I needed to know, and he would answer truthfully. I asked him why they were there, and he replied to take me and force me to join their side instead and kill as many enemies they could find along the way.

I was becoming a pawn in two warring factions, and I never wanted what was happening to me. I needed to look out for myself and wanted to escape.

The truth spell would last for ten minutes and leave the brothers in suspended animation. I didn't want to leave without saying goodbye to Jabber, but I had to since the time was almost up.

And so, I ran towards the tunnel passageway leading outside the enchanted kingdom. Then I heard growling behind me like a pack of angry dogs running after me. I glanced back and saw two dark shapes looking like misshapen monsters quickly gaining ground.

I ran faster and faster, but deep down, I knew I wasn't fast enough to escape them. I prepared for the worst as they came closer and closer.

One claw struck my leg, and I fell and smashed my forehead on a large boulder by the passageway. I screamed in pain. As I turned back and waited for what I assumed was the killing blow, someone else was behind and began striking them with a giant club. It was Jabber trying to save me.

Jabber delivered blow after blow and knocked them out unconscious. I was dizzy, and my legs were bleeding. I couldn't walk. He rushed over and carried me, not back to the enchanted realm but to the exit leading to the forest.

The blow had hit a vein in my leg, and I was quickly losing blood. Before I lost consciousness, I told Jabber to take me home to Casa de la Noche.

He ran and ran. I hugged his neck, trying not to fall. As I was about to lose the last thread of awareness, I chanted to him a communication spell, which enabled us to talk to each other at great distances via whispers, like having walkie-talkies inside our heads. Then, I drifted off into unconsciousness.

I awoke the next day in the hospital with my family around me. Both my mother and grandmother were weeping but were glad I was alright. I was only gone for one day in the real world but spent one year in the enchanted realm. They never questioned my whereabouts since they assumed I was only a rebellious kid doing stupid things.

I continued living in solitude, rarely going out of the house and seldom using my powers, only when necessary. Then I met your grandfather. It is another story for a different time.

~O~

"Wow Lola. That was an exciting story. What happened to Jabber?"

"I never saw him again. We were two beings from vastly different realms: he was a young Kapre and I was a young girl. It wouldn't work. However, the communication spell did, and we were able to often talk to each other in whispers and only for a few minutes each time, since the spell made me exhausted."

"Does he still talk to you?"

"Sometimes. On certain occasions, I forget it's him and I get confused, since it sounds like nonsense most of the time."

"What will happen now?"

"We go downstairs for a snack. I'm a little hungry. Maybe there's some *budbud* and *tsokolate* still left on the table."

"Okay."

"We're going to do things one step at time, dear. No more crying or childish tantrums, alright? You need to be brave and strong, and everything will be fine. Let's go."

Chapter 19 Godfather Death

Mayor Eddie thought his initial feeling of vengefulness would dissipate after time passed, but he was wrong. It rose in resonance and timbre and felt like a ringing in his ears, making him constantly see red. He yearned for retribution with all the fiber of his being and wanted it served on a bloody plate.

It was all he felt during the days after his son's death. The more he comforted his crying wife, the angrier he got. He put on the mask of a grieving father as he arranged for his son's funeral and talked to well-wishers and consolers.

But deep down, he wanted revenge, and he would get it sooner rather than later, and when he found out the person or persons responsible, he would have them killed.

Mayor Eddie told his secretary to clear his mayoral schedule the next day to spend the entire time with the Ponce de Leons in Casa de la Noche. He wanted to talk to the girl and ask about the part she played, which may lead to the culprits.

~O~

Pluto the majordomo didn't get any suitable information from the three madams, which was valuable enough to give to his Lord Axe-Grinder. All his snooping around was for naught.

He needed to crank it up a notch and be more forceful in his probing, which entailed talking to them. Generally, part of his job as a butler meant keeping his mouth shut for long periods and only supervising silently from a distance, but now he had to converse with them on purpose for a few minutes. He hated doing it since he thought of himself as superior to them.

There was one obstacle to his plans, which was Matteo, the thorn in his side. He had to deal with him first before speaking to them.

Then, there was a knock on the door, which he opened. It was the mayor. He said: "Good morning. Can I talk to the head of the household?"

"Please come in sir and sit down at the reception room. I'll call Madam Angelica."

Pluto was dismayed as he went up the stairs to Angelica's room to get her. The last thing he needed was the mayor poking around the house. But then he thought about it. The mayor would ask the hard questions that needed asking, which he could never do, so he had to find a way to listen to their conversations.

But how would I do it? He thought. They would go to the dining room, where they could talk privately. He would have to find a place to hide there and listen.

He decided he would shape-shift into a rat and hide in an area where he could observe, unnoticed. He waited for both to settle in the dining room, closed the door, and hurriedly went to his room in the servant's quarters. But he forgot to close the door behind him…

~O~

Matteo noticed Pluto rushing excitedly to his room from his room window. *He's up to something,* he thought. *I should put a stop to it, whatever it is.*

He went outside and tiptoed to Pluto's room, which was ajar. He peeked inside and saw something that boggled his mind but didn't change his resolve to take him down. It made him more worried instead because he wasn't dealing with someone human anymore, but something else entirely, which posed a significant threat to everyone in the house.

He saw Pluto transform into a disgusting rat. He hated rats and regarded them as a bane of his existence. If rodents were seen roaming the household, it was his job to eradicate them. He made a special tool for this lethal chore, which was a barbed wire-wrapped baseball bat. It constantly made a mess after whacking them, but he always brought a bucket of water, detergent, and brush with him, so that he could immediately clean after.

He knew there was something strange about Pluto, but this was too much. He only assumed he was either a thief or a pedophile and would never have guessed in a million years that he was a shape-shifting fiend.

However, he was a stupid rat he could handle, and he relished the thought of smashing him to smithereens.

He hid as he saw the rat scurry along the pathway towards the upstairs dining room, where he had learned earlier that Madam Angelica and the mayor were talking in private. He took his rat-killing tool with him and quietly followed…

~O~

"Hello, Miss Angelica. I want to talk to you first, then perhaps your daughter later," said Mayor Eddie. He had the grim and tired look of a man who had lost all hope.

"Mayor please sit down. I'm really sorry for what happened to your son. I do understand what you're going through since I have endured so much death in my family. You will get past it, believe me but it will take time."

"Thank you. I knew your late husband in school. He was quite a rambunctious fellow, and his death shocked all of us."

"Yes, I know. He sometimes talked about you and spoke fondly about your friendship."

"Really, he said that? I never thought of him as someone who tends to reminisce about past events. I knew him as a move-forward type of guy who always looked to the future instead of the past. Maybe he changed after he married you."

"He did, but for the worse. You know his gambling habits, and it became so bad that he began stealing some of our things to sell or pawn. However, there were calm moments where he was sweet to me, and that's what I missed most of all."

"Do you know how he died?"

"I don't know, he went to the U.S. for business, supposedly and knowing him I bet it was gambling-related. He was cremated and his ashes were sent over via USPS. Do you see the urn above the fireplace? That's him," said Angelica and pointed to the shiny urn on a shelf.

"And your father and grandfather too, all had died young. Maybe your family is cursed."

"You should talk to my mother; she believes in that kind of stuff, but I don't."

"Me too, and we're alike this way. There's only a few of us left. Most of the citizens in Gintongbayan believes in the supernatural: about dwarves, fairies and monsters. Even those people left alive from the attack in the gym talk about unbelievable creatures only found in stories and movies. As their mayor, what am I supposed to do with this information?"

"It's your duty to investigate it. You have to separate the truth from make-believe, and then find the one responsible."

"Yes, which means I have to talk to you daughter. Everyone pointed to her as the one who killed the creatures. And the first question everyone wants to know is: how did she do it?"

"Mr. Mayor, I wish I could, but I really can't. She had a delicate congenital condition that precludes her from any of this. Have you talked to the other victims?"

"The police did. She's the last one that haven't given her statement yet. I'm here in their behalf since she won't talk to them. We all want to know the truth, even you, and she can shed some light on this unfortunate situation and maybe lead to the ones involved."

"I'm worried about her safety. Will she be safe?"

"She won't need to go anywhere. I will be the one talking to her and no one else."

"She won't need to leave the house?"

"She'll stay here and I'll even send some police over to guard your house, but only after I talk to her."

"Yes, we may need them if there are really people out there intending to harm her. I'll talk to my daughter first," said Angelica and left the room.

~O~

Matteo was hidden behind the doorway of the private dining room when Angelica exited. He muttered a sigh of relief for not being seen since he didn't know how to respond if being asked about the reason for his attempted concealment.

He had been on his hands and knees trying to look for mouseholes on the walls and perhaps find Pluto in one of them. He saw only one behind a cabinet right beside the door, which surely Pluto went through. It was big enough to fit Pluto's rat size that led to a couch in the other room where he could have easily hidden.

He checked his rat-killing tool, which he discovered was filthy from all the rodents it had whacked many times previously. He had forgotten to clean it and made a mental note to do it after he had finished whacking Pluto, the rat.

He was still hidden when Angelica returned, now along with Pandora. He waited for both to enter the dining room and resumed his rat-smashing stance…

~O~

"Pandora, you know Mayor Eddie, right? He's your godfather after all," said Angelica and pointed to a seat where Pandora would sit.

"*Mano po*, Godfather Eddie," said Pandora took his hand and pressed it to her forehead.

"Thank you. I'm surprise you still do the traditional honoring gesture. Most of my other godchildren don't do it anymore."

"She's a good girl Mayor, we've raised her to respect her elders."

"Godfather, Mom said you wanted to talk to me about the attack in the gym. And I'm also sorry of what happened to your son."

"It's all very unfortunate. We're trying to find the people responsible for this and you might be able to help. Can you?"

"Yes, but I don't know what else I can tell you that everyone at the gym already seen…"

"They said you were able to defeat them by some sort of weapon in your hands, which had blasted them away. What did you use? A gun?"

"I don't know sir. It was all a blur. I had a strange feeling that some bad people were coming into the gymnasium to do harmful things, which made me mad. After one went up the stage and stabbed my boyfriend Andreas with an axe, something came out of my hands like fire and blasted him away. But it was too late, Andreas was dead.

I saw other creatures that looked like black monsters on the basketball court, along with students trying to run away. They were killing the students. I ran towards them and blasted those monsters one by one. The remaining fled after seeing they were defeated. That's all I did, and I'm sorry it sounds unbelievable, but it's true."

Mayor Eddie was incredulous as he heard the whole story. His mouth was open the entire time. It grew wider and soon hit the floor. He prided himself as a man who upheld facts and reason, but it always bowled him over that some people often engaged in flights of fancy and replaced them from the truth. He glanced at

Angelica and saw the same look of disbelief. He said: "Can you describe these bad people, these creatures?"

"They're all ugly and horrible-looking. A few were dwarves, who wore golden garments and held axes. Some were giants, some looked like vampires, some were man/horse hybrids, and some were indescribable."

"No one looked like actual people?"

"No, all monsters."

"Why do you think were they there in the first place?"

"I think they wanted to abduct me. The other people there were unfortunately just collateral damage, including your son. I'm so sorry Sir."

"Why are you so special to them?"

"Mayor Eddie, may I interrupt," said Angelica. "It's because of our money, specifically, our gold. Our ancestor Don Marcus Ponce de Leon amassed lots of it, which made us rich beyond our wildest dreams, which meant we never needed to work ever again. People had been targeting us because they want to get their hands on it."

"I had an inkling that was the reason. Where did you deposit your gold? In a bank?"

"No, Mayor Eddie, it's here in our house, in a secret place. You're one of the few people who now know, so please keep it a secret."

"You don't need to worry about me. Your ancestor and mine were among the first people who prospected gold in the Golden Mountain. We took our share and put it in a bank. Maybe you should do the same with yours since its safer there."

"Perhaps, maybe another time. We have something more serious to deal with. Do you have any more questions for my daughter?"

"Yes. Everyone else spoke about a leader among the dwarves, who directed the attack. Did you see and maybe can describe him?"

"Yes, it's the oldest among them that went up the stage. He had long white hair and beard and held a staff instead of an axe."

"Have you seen him before?"

"No, of course not. He's a dwarf, remember? Before the attack happened, I only saw their kind in books and movies."

"Dwarves are people like us, Pandora. They suffer from a medical condition called dwarfism," said Angelica.

"We don't have dwarves as citizens here in town, I can attest to that. Maybe they came from the neighboring towns, or more likely from a travelling circus or carnival? It would explain a lot about their appearance."

"Perhaps you're on to something Mayor Eddie. Maybe a group of circus folk found out about the gold in our house and attempted but failed to kidnap Pandora and take her hostage?"

"Yes, it makes sense now. The only thing that doesn't is the so-called "fire" coming out of your daughter's hands."

"We can make sense about it later Mayor Eddie. You now have possible suspects for the attack, which you can now give to the police."

"I have to talk to them. But what will I tell them about the fire in her hands?"

"Tell them she was holding a can of hairspray and lighter with her and used them to light the bad guys on fire."

"That could be a believable statement for the police. Thank you and goodbye. I have to go," said Mayor Eddie and immediately left.

~O~

Pluto the rat was excited. Now he had some important information he could give his Lord Axe-Grinder. He scampered along his hiding spot and went through the mousehole in the wall and…

SPLAT!!

He didn't see Matteo waiting for him on the other side of the hole, thus smashing his small rodent body with a bat. The last conscious image he saw was of Matteo picking him up and dropping him in a bucket of water, drowning him.

Chapter 20 The Master Thief

Mayor Eddie was in high spirits as he arrived in his office after visiting Casa de la Noche. The whole situation wasn't hopeless anymore since Pandora could provide probable suspects to the cops and be able to satiate his craving for vengeance.

He told his secretary, Michelle, to call the police station and have Police Officer Michael Collins come over the next morning for a scheduled meeting. After the call, he took his journal from his desk drawer and wrote down everything that transpired at Casa de la Noche: the conversation with Angelica and Pandora and every small thing he noticed.

He started journaling once he became mayor. It was an essential tool for his job that enabled him not to forget all the information he deemed significant. Inside were important dates, events, people, phone numbers, and many more. Once done, he put it back inside the drawer and told Michelle he needed to go home to check on his grieving wife.

He left the mayor's office, leaving only Michelle alone.

~O~

Michelle was hired as a secretary the previous year after the former secretary quit due to interchanging political alliances. She applied for the job and was hired due to her impressive résumé and proper references. She was also pleasing to the eyes and level-headed, which made everyone like her immediately.

However, everything she wrote in her CV was made up since she wasn't what she said she was, and even her name was false.

Her real name was Esmeralda *Tagapulot*: cat burglar. She was notorious in big cities and was on every law enforcement agency's most wanted list, which made her larcenous activities difficult to accomplish. She resolved to escape and looked for a smaller place where no one knew her. Her research brought her to *Gintongbayan*, a place brimming with gold to steal and especially ignorant and superstitious people to grift.

She infiltrated the Gintongbayan local government and was hired as a secretary to the municipal mayor.

She had been waiting and bided her time for the right opportunity to hit the jackpot. She had been secretly reading the mayor's journal to get clues on who had the biggest gold stash, and so far, nothing big enough yet that was worth her time.

After Mayor Eddie left, she opened his desk and read the latest journal entry, which piqued her interest. It referred to a house called Casa de la Noche that had large deposits of gold hidden in it. It belonged to the Ponce de Leons, which she needed to learn about. She also had to acquire the house blueprints and find out about its inhabitants.

It may be the jackpot she had been waiting for. Once she'd got it, she would get away to a non-extradition country in one of the Latin American countries where she'd lived her life in relative peace and wealth.

~O~

The next morning, Mayor Eddie met with Police Officer Michael Collins in his office. Every staff member noticed that he was relatively chipper as he greeted them and sat behind his desk.

He shook the officer's hand vigorously and said: "Please take a seat, Sir. I've talked to the Ponce de Leon girl and I have some good news to share with you. She was the main target for the attack. They tried to kidnap her for extortion purposes but failed. Look for circus or carnival folk as the chief suspects. I've heard there's a carnival temporarily stationed at the next town and you can look there first."

"Sir, but how did she defeat them? Witnesses said she had some kind of weapon that killed some of those attackers."

"She lit them up with a hairspray and a lighter. She brought them along inside her handbag. It was smart of her to do it, or else, many more could have perished."

"It seems unlikely that a flame coming from a lit hairspray could have killed many of the attackers."

"It's true and don't ever question my findings ever again. I'm the mayor of this town and my word holds meaning and importance. I bet there are some criminals hired as staff in the carnival at the next town. Go there now and come back once you find the perpetrators."

"Sorry Mr. Mayor. I'll go now and I'll be keeping you updated," said Officer Collins and left the office immediately.

"Michelle, do I have any more activities or events later?"

"Yes, Mayor Eddie. At eleven a.m. you have a lunch meeting with the School Board of Directors. The main topic for discussion is school safety measures so that the attack won't happen again. At three p.m. you will attend a funeral for a teacher that was also killed in the attack. That's it, Sir."

"Thank you," said Mayor Eddie. He took out his journal to write in.

~O~

Michelle, aka Esmeralda, took note of everything they said. She did it as part of her job and for her nefarious purposes. She knew the mayor was out the whole day, so she could go out and do some errands related to her plans.

She had no problem getting the blueprints of the house in the assessor's office due to her government credentials. They never asked her questions and readily gave them to her.

The next item on the list would take time, which was to scout and research Casa de la Noche. She drove over to the house for the first time to see what she was up against.

Casa de la Noche was in an ideal location not too far from town and still allowed for a semblance of seclusion and privacy. The area at the back was the fabled forest she had heard about from superstitious townsfolk, supposedly populated with supernatural creatures. The house had a haunted nature, which she thought she only imagined and immediately shook off.

Next on the list was to get information about its inhabitants, which might get tricky. She needed to befriend one of them to gain some inside knowledge, and she might have found the sucker to do it: their gardener by the name of Matteo.

Chapter 21 Cat and Mouse in Partnership

Matteo carried the bucket of water, along with the filthy remains of the banged-up Pluto in rat disguise, outside towards the forest. He was going to take him to the spot at the giant termite mound where he saw the gigantic white snake swallow a goat whole many years ago. He wanted to present him as an offering to the snake and, in return, perhaps get some blessings.

The snake wasn't there at the giant termite mound. He waited thirty minutes, but no other creature came crawling out to confront him. He emptied the bucket of water and left it behind, along with the dead rat formerly known as Pluto, the majordomo, and walked back home.

When he reached the front gate, she saw someone waiting outside, trying to peek through the iron railings. He was taken aback by her lovely and demure appearance and became immediately attracted. He said: "Can I help you, Miss..."

"Oh, I'm sorry. My name is Michelle. I work as a secretary to Mayor Eddie and I'm here on his behalf to ask follow-up questions."

"Do you want to speak to the madams?"

"Umm no. I understand the mayor already spoke to them so, no need. I want to talk to anyone from the household staff, to give an impression of what had transpired."

"You mean about the attack in the gym? Sorry, I wasn't there, but my daughter was. I was here all night."

"That's okay. I'm in a hurry to get back to work anyway. We can talk about some other time, in a restaurant perhaps?"

"You mean like a dinner date?" Said Matteo unbelievingly.

"Yes, a date. Would it be alright?"

"A date for real? With me?"

"Sure. Maybe about seven p.m. later? I'll give you my calling card so you can call me," she said and handed it to him.

He was struck dumb and couldn't speak. He just nodded as she left.

He couldn't believe what had just happened and thanked his lucky stars for this blessing he had received from the elemental spirits and given a new lease on his love life.

~O~

Matteo was anxious about his forthcoming date with Michelle. He hadn't been in one in a long time, and the last time he remembered was with Ruby's mother when they were still together.

From the beginning, he knew their relationship was doomed after their first fight, which became aggressive immediately. She was the main inflictor of the violence while he ducked and shielded himself from it. Yet he didn't break up with her because there was no other woman who took an interest in someone like him, who did lowly menial gardening work for a rich family.

They married soon after and had Ruby Rose. Nevertheless, they did separate once he found out about the affair, which was the straw that broke the camel's back. He took their young daughter to Casa de la Noche to live with him in the servant's quarters and never looked back.

Since then, he became cautious and distrustful of new people, and his instincts were correct most of the time. He was proven right by his suspicion of Pluto and his nefarious activities, which gave him newfound confidence. But this new girl was something else, and he couldn't tell if she was bad or good.

He wanted to know if the date was still on for later, so he texted her. She replied yes and to meet her in a restaurant named *La Cocina Secreto* in *Barangay Poblacion.*

The restaurant was one of the oldest establishments in Gintongbayan and opened about the same time the town was first established. Its décor was modern Spanish which was a mix of new and old colonial aesthetics. It served Spanish food, and its delicious *paella* was known throughout the province.

Matteo arrived at La Cocina Secreto thirty minutes before the agreed-upon time. He dressed up in Sunday's best and even had a new haircut. He chose a seat at the rear of the restaurant, with a direct line of sight to the entrance where he could see her come in.

She blew in like a fresh and fragrant wind exactly on time. She was a sight to behold and wore a feminine grey pantsuit and overcoat, which adhered to the current fashion trend called "quiet luxury." She took his breath away.

Matteo stood up and waved at her. She smiled once she saw him sauntered towards their table and sat down. She said: Hello. We haven't been properly introduced. My name is Michelle, and you are?"

"Oh, you mentioned you name earlier at the house. I'm Matteo. I work for the Ponce de Leons."

Have you been waiting long?"

"Not really, but it's fine. I came in early to check on the place first."

"Why? You don't like it here?"

"No. I've never been here before and only watched it from afar. This place is only for rich folk you know, not for people like me."

"It's one of the things I don't like about this town. The rich and poor don't seem to mingle. There's nothing like this bullshit in the big city. We do everything together, even fuck each other."

Matteo suddenly became uneasy and swallowed a mouthful of his saliva. He wanted to change the subject, or else he would faint if they continued on this topic. He said: "Oh, you're from the city, huh? What made you come here to this small town? I imagine the pay for government work is comparatively smaller."

"Yes, I know. Big city life is a rat race and the longer you stay in it, the more punishing it inflicts on your wellbeing. I longed for the simpler life in the province, where there's fresh air, less stress and very handsome people. Who, knows, maybe I'll find a man here that can finally sexually satisfy me."

(Gulp)

"Oh, right. Is it getting hot in here? I seem to be perspiring," said Matteo. He took a handkerchief from his back pants pocket and wiped his brow.

"Are you alright Matteo? You look pale. I think we should order some food. What's good here?"

"*Paella*. The paella is great here and famous throughout the province."

"We can order that and one more dish and a bottle of wine. I have a feeling this will be a wonderful night with a happy ending with both of us in my apartment. Do you agree?" She said and winked.

(Gulp)

~O~

They had finished the entire bottle of wine and got intoxicated, which loosened Matteo's inhibitions. He became braver and braver after every glass of wine and countered with witty banter from her straightforward seduction. She was surprised by his newfound courage, which appealed to her.

After dinner, he motioned to pay for their check, but she declined and said she had a budget given to her by her boss, the mayor, for discretionary purposes. It made him a little uncomfortable that taxpayers' money was used as payment for their dinner. He was about to give her a piece of his mind but suddenly glanced at her plunging neckline that now had a few buttons unfastened. Her ample breasts were almost showing, and he immediately forgot his train of thought. He was mesmerized and aroused.

As promised, she took him to her place, which was a one-bedroom house in a government-owned subdivision. They stripped naked once they entered and went straight to the bedroom. He had been chaste since the separation and was excited that he was about to have sex again after many years. He was surprised by her wanton sexual hunger and was more than happy to yield.

It took only thirty seconds of rhythmic thrusting for him to orgasm, which made him feel guilty. He knew she wasn't satisfied yet, so he performed cunnilingus on her for the first time. He was scared but quickly found out it was enjoyable for the both of them, and her vagina tasted surprisingly salty-sweet, like salt water taffy. She moaned with delight and climaxed after ten minutes.

They lay on the bed panting, satiated, and happy. She was earnestly surprised she enjoyed the entire undertaking and didn't feel like part of a long con. She suddenly thought that maybe there was a good life to be made in this town with this man. They might live modestly, but she'd be happy with him by her side. Nonetheless, she snapped out of it and quietly laughed at herself. There was lots of gold to take, and she overcame one hurdle to attain it. Now that Matteo was under her sexual spell, he would do anything she asked, even to go as far as committing murder.

Chapter 22 Rumpelstiltskin the Trickster

Lord Axe-Grinder and his surviving minions returned to the enchanted realm of Batala after failing to abduct Pandora. Most of his seven dwarves, whom he regarded as his inner circle, had perished, and all but one remained, whose name was Rumpelstiltskin.

He was regarded as the feeblest warrior of the seven and had spent the entirety of the attack outside the high school gymnasium as the lookout man. However, what he lacked in a warrior's skill and courage, he had one pernicious talent as a replacement: trickery.

Lord Axe-Grinder often used him for reconnaissance purposes in the human world since he could pass off as a tremendously dark-skinned Filipino man. He was their tallest dwarf with a height of four feet and eleven inches and a face that can be regarded as homely-looking. He didn't have his brother dwarves' penchant for long beards and hairs, while his preference was a close-cropped hairdo and a van dyke goatee. Their inborn pointed ears he could conceal by wearing a hat. People wouldn't give him a second glance after seeing him and left him to his own devices.

He could stroll the busy marketplace of Gintongbayan, talk to the merchants, and buy their foodstuff without anyone questioning his motives. He could even go to the local government offices and ask about the attack in the gym without anyone feeling suspicious, which he had done. To them, he was just an ordinary and concerned citizen who wanted to learn any new updates.

He found out that the police had primary suspects, which were carnival folk located in the next town. Police guards were sent over to the Ponce de Leon house to guard the young girl, who they said was the main target for the attack. Thankfully, no one suspected any supernatural involvement, which brought him momentary relief.

He reported all these to his Lord Axe-Grinder, who accepted the news coolly, which mystified him. It, in turn, made him reminisce about the glory days, when they were still on top of the food chain, and Ax-Grinder was regarded as a big deal in Batala.

Axe-Grinder was the oldest being in either the dark or light domains of Batala and had gone through all sorts of events known to man and elemental creatures alike. He was even older than his arch nemesis Bakunawa, the Serpent-Goddess, and prided himself on his near impregnability to any cataclysm. Nothing doesn't seem to bother him; he was always calm and level-headed, even if things went awry.

Since almost all of his cadre was dead, he had no one else to provide him counsel but Rumpelstiltskin alone, so he asked him what would be the next step to take. He said since most of their soldier were killed, they couldn't launch back-to-back attacks anymore as they lacked warriors to carry them out. What they need to do is send one creature—himself—to engage in deception and skullduggery with the enemy.

Lord Axe-Grinder thought for a minute and nodded. He told him to find Pluto first, his spy in the Ponce de Leon house, and find out what had happened to him. He then gave him five years (or five days in the human life cycle) to fulfill his plans, and he will be waiting for his return with hopefully glad tidings.

~O~

Police Officer Michael Collins dressed in civilian garb as he journeyed to the neighboring town of *Tamtam*, where the traveling carnival was temporarily stationed. He wanted to travel incognito and rode his motorcycle so as not to draw attention to himself in case the culprits were there, and might escape once they saw law enforcement looking for them.

Tamtam was less progressive and poorer, compared to the more affluent Gintongbayan, where many of its citizens were gold-rich. In contrast, it was an agriculture-based municipality whose main product was sugarcane, ironically called "white gold" by its citizens, as if to mock their unfortunate status in the district.

There was only one sugarcane plantation that occupied almost all of the agricultural land in town, owned by one family. While they became rich, the rest of the citizens were poor and thus employed as workers with meager salaries. As a way for the municipality to compensate, they let all sorts of unscrupulous businesses operate there, with little or no supervision. Soon, it became a haven for the illegal drug trade and many more prohibited and dangerous operations.

P.O. Collins knew this and came adequately prepared. He brought his personal sidearm, which he hid underneath his jacket in case the situation got hairy.

The carnival was situated on the outskirts of town, far away from any semblance of normalcy. It was a wild country filled with decrepit carnival rides, unclean surroundings, and odd-looking carnies. Some were dwarves, who looked scary by normal people's standards and were usually avoided by carnival goers.

P.O. Collins arrived at the carnival parking lot and parked his motorcycle. He checked his gun, cocked it, and put it back in the holster. He walked towards the entrance to pay the entrance fee…

~O~

Rumpelstiltskin arrived in Gintongbayan, determined to fulfill his mission. He wanted to give a victory to his Lord Axe-Grinder from the many defeats they had in the past. He first needed to check on his associate Pluto, the shape-shifting *Pugot,* who was missing in action.

How will he do it? He thought. His line of communication with Pluto had been mysteriously cut and no way of knowing about the goings-on in the house. He also knew that police guards were on standby there so he couldn't go through the front door.

He had to find a Casa de la Noche house dweller and extract useful information he needed, and fast. He only had five days to accomplish his mission. He must find a way inside the house or draw someone outside and manipulate him or her to answer his questions. If all options failed, his only way in as a last resort was through one of Don Marcus Ponce de Leon's secret rooms. It would be hard, but he figured out how to do it.

~O~

Don Marcus had a few secret rooms built for various reasons. Most were for storage for large quantities of gold, which he amassed during his lifetime, and one room for something else.

After he had spoken to the person posing as Henry Teves the 1st, who unwittingly infected and thus recruited him to be part of the dark army of Lord Axe-Grinder, his mind was lost for a time. It was like he was hypnotized and readily obeyed everything said to him.

He was told to build a few secret underground rooms to store their gold for safekeeping and one, as a means to travel from their realm to his. It was a passageway for the elemental beings to travel undetected into the heart of town. He obeyed their bidding without question and had them constructed.

Many years later, after the death of his son Romeo in the forest (who supposedly died from accidental burning), he had a sudden clarity of thought. He wanted no part in the war between the dark and light armies and needed to save his family from his misdeeds. He had the doorway of the underground tunnel permanently shut and cast a door-searing spell to prohibit any magical or elemental beings from entering.

He then became a hermit and never went out of the house for the remainder of his life. His family and descendants benefited from the gold and never needed to work again. However, he didn't know the enchanted doorway of the secret room that occupied the underground tunnel had one fatal flaw: it was vulnerable to ghosts.

~O~

P.O. Collins had successfully collared two suspects—dwarf carnies—while the others ran. He handcuffed them together and made them sit beside each other in one of the suspended seats of the Ferris wheel. They looked comical as they argued and fought while he called the local Tamtam police station for assistance and backup.

He hadn't wanted to make an unlawful arrest since he was outside his jurisdiction, so he had to provoke them to anger, and once they struck first, he brought the hammer down. The Tamtam cops found no issue in his collar and were glad to dispose of the perps. He called the police headquarters in Gintongbayan to have the culprits brought over to their local jail.

Mayor Eddie was waiting for him as he returned, which made him have a wide smile on his face. He commended him for a job well done. He wanted to be present in the interrogation and discover who masterminded the attack.

~O~

Rumpelstiltskin and his dwarf kind could see and talk to ghosts of the human variety. Since they dwelled in another level of existence, they weren't bound by the natural laws of the human world and could see, hear, and feel outside their cognition. He felt a spirit wandering in the household, which he could manipulate and exploit.

He performed a summoning spell to bring the spirit to his location, and once he arrived, he asked him to identify himself.

The ghost said: "My name is Andreas. Who are you and why did you bring me here?"

"I won't tell you my name since it isn't important but what I'm going to say to you now is. I have magical powers and I can give you whatever you desire, like making you human again, you just need to do one thing for me…"

"I don't believe you. And why won't you tell me your name? It's just name."

"My name isn't ordinary and holds power. No human, alive or dead, has ever said my name out loud, or else, something will happen…"

"Or else what?"

"Nothing you need to know right now. Trust me when I say, it can alter your life to be better."

"What if I find out your name, do I get a reward?"

"Yes, anything you wish."

"Or if I do what you ask, will you tell me your name?"

"Yes, and get your reward. Either way you win."

Rumpelstiltskin somberly watched Andreas, thinking his ghostly thoughts. He was smiling on the inside, happy that his power of manipulation was still in top form. He had everything he needed with the specter, and he could achieve his goals through him. Soon, he would get what he wanted and deliver a win to his Lord Axe-Grinder.

Before anything else, he had to know what happened to his cohort, Pluto. He said: "What happened to the butler by the name of Pluto? He's a friend of mine and I've been trying to contact him."

"The majordomo? He's dead. I saw him turn into a rat and was squished by one of the servants."

He was appalled by the news, but he tried not to show it. However, he knew if an elemental creature like Pluto died in this level of existence, he would be restored to life in another, so he'd see him again once he returned to Batala.

Chapter 23 The Moon

Lola Sabrina had a good night's sleep and felt refreshed the next morning. She was pleasantly surprised she was clear-headed and wanted to share some important details about her past as a white witch with Pandora before her mind became foggy again.

Once Pandora arrived in her room and sat by her bedside, she told her another story.

~O~

Do you know the moon holds magical power that can be harnessed by elemental beings, witches, and warlocks? People like us who are touched by supernatural forces can use the different phases of the moon to our advantage. The other phase you don't have to worry about. It is the full moon you need to watch out for.

You may have learned from school that the moon controls the ocean tides because of gravity, and more than sixty percent of the human body contains water. For this reason, whenever the moon is full and its gravitational pull is the strongest, any magic will be extremely potent for people like us.

After my stay in the enchanted kingdom, I learned to improve my two most powerful magical endowments:

divination and telepathy. I waited for the full moon to arrive each month either once or twice, and used them to their full potential.

I learned a trick when engaging in telepathy by whispering to the intended recipient, who was far away. It seemed to be more effective when done during the full moon and can reach someone located far off on another island in the Philippines. On ordinary days and nights, my telepathic reach could only be felt by someone within the town vicinity.

However, I had more control over my gift of prophecy. The full moon gave me extreme potency, and I was not only able to foretell the future of a particular person, but I could influence events to come true upon request. These are called self-fulfilling prophecies. If a person wants his or her preferred numbers picked in the lottery, I could make it occur. If someone wants someone else to die of natural causes, I could cause it to happen, but I never went that far. I'm only telling you that I could.

I became known in our wealthy circle of acquaintances as a *mangkukulam*. They came to me chiefly to ask their fortunes, and I told them what they wanted to hear, which I magicked to reality whenever the full moon arrived.

There were thirteen known witches in town (including me) who were all good. We got to know each other and soon formed a coven.

Then, one day, a man I knew casually around town approached me to ask who he would marry. When I looked into his future, I was surprised. I saw myself wearing a wedding dress and standing beside him in an aisle about to be married. He was your grandfather Galileo, my Starman.

We were both intrigued and began dating soon after. Before long, he asked for my hand in marriage, and I accepted.

The prophecy did come true, and we got married. Soon, I was pregnant with your mother and gave birth.

One day, I suddenly heard a telepathic whisper from Jabber the *Kapre*, who I became close to during my time in the enchanted kingdom of Batala. He had recently found out about my new family and was hurt. He wanted to come to the surface world and see me.

I became scared. Although I knew him to be tender and loving, I never saw him become angry, and I was afraid of what he might do to us. He said he would want to meet me at midnight during the full moon, in front of the giant termite mound in the forest.

I snuck out when everyone was asleep. I came prepared with a blasting curse in case he might become dangerous and hurt me.

What is it you ask? It's when flaming light emanates from your hands and disintegrates the target. Yes, I'm aware you inadvertently did it during the attack in the gym. It was unfocused and wild magic, which is dangerous. I'm going to teach you later to concentrate and rein it in.

Let's go back to the story.

We met during the wolf moon in January, which is a time when magical bearers and beings are the most powerful. It was a fortunate coincidence for me that on the off-chance Jabber would cause trouble.

But thankfully, he didn't. He was just sad and hurt. Even though he knew nothing could happen, he still cared for me and was distressed by our lack of communication. He only wanted to carry on with our friendship and to resume our telepathic means of communicating.

I agreed and promised to continue with it.

He told me that if it was all right, she could visit his realm for a day. I agreed, since their time was faster, spending one day there was equivalent to one hour here.

We went to the same pathway inside the giant termite mound through a tunnel. Have I told you before how beautiful it was in Batala?

Well, it was. The flaming tree that never burns out was still there, providing illumination and a warm and cozy temperature. Shiny gold nuggets were littered everywhere, which they paid no attention to and treated like ordinary stones and pebbles. When I glanced upwards, I thought I saw stars in the sky but was mistaken since we were underground in a massive cave. Those were millions of diamonds stuck on the rocky ceiling, looking like stars.

The various pale-skinned elemental creatures you already know were there: *Engkantos*, *Kapres*, *Diwatas*, and many more. They were all well-disposed and never disrespected me, compared to their dark counterparts, who were horrible and horrifying.

Jabber took me to a huge underground lake populated by mythical sea creatures like the half-men half-fish *Sirenas* and *Syokoys*, the great sea turtles, the *Bacobaco*, the *Gaki* or giant crabs, and many more. I watched everything and everyone with wonder and amazement.

Jabber then led me to the strange-looking dwelling hut of Bakunawa, the Serpent-Goddess. She slithered out and transformed into her human female form, whom I knew.

I was somewhat apprehensive from our last encounter when I was under her tutelage and suddenly left Batala without informing her. I thought maybe she held a grudge and might be mad at me.

Thankfully, she didn't and put all my worries to rest. I was welcomed with open arms by everyone like I was part of their tribe. She told Jabber to wait outside and took me inside her house.

I followed inside, where she directed me to sit on a bed. She explained she would give me a magical potion to make me sleep and dream. The dreaming part was important, and the potion would enable me to let my spirit leave my body and travel to different realms and levels of existence. In essence, it is like a drug that facilitates answering all my lingering questions about them and significantly about the origin of the eternal war between them and their dark counterparts.

There was no hesitation, and I drank it immediately. I lay down, slept, and dreamed about...

~O~

"Lola, this is great. You're telling me another story within the story. I hope I can still follow it and won't get confused."

"Don't worry, dear. I'll tell it clearly, and just try to follow and don't interrupt. I'm not sure how long my brain can handle this."

"Okay I'll shut up now."

Chapter 24 The Duration of Life

flying. I now remember. This was the first time I dreamt about flying. Astral projection. Remember when the spirit leaves the body?

Life is mysterious for us and even for their kind. Even though they live longer than us, they're not immortal and can still die. Yes, they are supernatural beings and have the magical means to defend themselves, and they can be killed. There are chinks in their armor, and it's one of the things I've learned in my dream state.

I flew in my dream. I felt a sense of freedom I had never felt before. I flew like I had wings on my back and soared to the night sky, trying to touch the moon. I discovered I couldn't even reach the stratosphere and learned then and there that the astral cord tied to my physical body has a limited length.

My astral form flew back here and saw everyone still sleeping. Your grandfather Leo was asleep on a spare mattress beside Angelica's crib. He had a bag with infant necessities beside him in case she'd wake up needing a diaper change or drink baby formula or something. He was a good father, and it was unfortunate he also died young. His death will come up later in the story, so hold your questions.

Then I flew again, away from Casa de la Noche, and hovered over the sleeping town of *Gintongbayan*. I had never seen it from this vantage point, and I realized there was a disparity between the rich and poor. We rich folk are located uphill, approaching the enchanted forest and the Golden Mountain, while the poor citizens are downhill to the sea. We were close to where gold was first discovered, and those who didn't join the gold rush lived far away.

I could project my astral form to the past and see how gold was first found and prospected by the first town settlers. Some greedier ones went to the caverns of the Golden Mountain to find more gold and were confronted by dark-skinned elemental creatures led by a dwarf with long white hair and beard. They offered them all the gold they could carry in exchange for dominion over them. Those who agreed were infected and recruited by blood-sucking *Aswangs*, and those who declined were rendered insane by a madness curse.

However, the pale beings from the light domain took issue since they regarded the human race in reverence. They fought with their dark counterparts whenever they saw them engaging in their blood-sucking recruitment methods and were able to spare many humans. They won many of those fights, yet they couldn't save everybody, and some continued to ally with the dark creatures.

I flew away from the past into the dark realm of Batala. It had many similarities with the light side and even had the same type of tree that burned an unceasing flame.

Yet the resemblance ended there. The whole cavern was dingy and muddy, and its inhabitants scary-looking. They had more gold there, which they made into numerous accouterments, effigies, contrivances, and articles of furniture. They demonstrated their adoration for gold and its importance, much unlike their lighter counterparts who valued human life more.

Have you discovered their weakness already? It's there in the story. If you've listened attentively, you'd know already. No?

Gold. Their love of gold is their weakness. Even though they use it as bargaining chips and a means to corrupt humankind, they still want it back. It's theirs first and foremost, and they expect to take it back once we humans outlived their usefulness.

Thankfully, our pale-skinned friends have fought and will continue to fight for us. Nevertheless, the war still rages on.

~O~

"Sorry Lola, I have to interrupt. If gold is their weakness, how can we use it to defeat them?" Said Pandora.

"It will take time to plan, and it's still too early. We need many people by our side as well as our pale-colored friends."

"How, Lola. *How?*"

"We will set a trap using their love for gold. I don't know how to do it yet, but it is the key in defeating them."

"Okay."

"Alright, dear. Back to the story."

~O~

My astral form flew away from Batala and crossed over to the astral plane of existence. It is a realm of spirits, angels, and other immaterial beings. It's similar to purgatory, where the souls of the dead go after dying. Some may think of this place as heaven or paradise, but not quite, but I understand why.

The place looked and felt like heaven. It made me feel so happy that I didn't want to leave. I saw other astral beings like me floating in technicolor light and gossamer clouds. It looked like it continued on and on with no end in sight.

It was explained to me later that I was floating in the celestial universe. It was a thousand times bigger than the material universe, with many astral planets and abundant with their beings.

I could stay there forever, but I knew I had a family expecting me at home and had to leave.

I awoke and stood up. Bakunawa wasn't there anymore. I went outside her dwelling and saw Jabber still waiting for me. I asked him where Bakunawa was, and he just shrugged.

I told him what I saw in my dream, and he told me what he knew about the places I went to. We continued to chat for a while and to catch up on his status. He told me he took in a mate and had a little Kapre baby along the way. I was happy for him and also felt relieved.

I suddenly realized the time and told him I had to return home. He said he would take me as far as the entrance to the giant termite mound. I opened the doorway, went out, and glanced at my watch. It was one a.m., and the full moon was still up. I walked the pathway going home, full of energy and high spirits from what I had experienced earlier.

I saw something ahead, which looked like a sack of rice in the middle of the road. Upon closer inspection, I was taken aback: it was a man lying on his stomach. I turned him over and was shocked beyond belief: it was your grandfather Leo, dead.

I then saw bite marks on his neck. It was a telltale sign of an Aswang bite. I screamed and ran towards home to see if Angelica was alright. I was relieved to see her sleeping soundly as if nothing was wrong. I ran back to where I saw Leo, and he was gone. I realized he wasn't dead but forcibly recruited by the dark creatures, which meant he was as good as dead.

I had to report him as missing to the police and left out the Aswang bite mark on his neck. I knew I would never see him again, and he was in a place I could never physically go to.

However, I tried to look for him through astral means whenever I slept, but never did. He was wiped off the face of the earth.

I blamed myself. I should have been honest in the first place and told him of my journey to Batala, instead I snuck out like a thief in the night. He must have tried to look for me when he woke up and was attacked by the dark monster.

His duration of life was cut short just because of my foolhardiness. You see, Pandora, this will be a lesson to you: you should always be aware of your surroundings whenever you go outside since malicious creatures are out there trying to harm you. You need training to use your powers properly, which I will teach you very soon…

Chapter 25 The Tale of the Two Brothers

Police Officer Collins knew the two dwarves he arrested were innocent of the crime. He did it anyway because he was overambitious and overeager to rise to the top of the police hierarchy. He was willing to sacrifice them to achieve his goals. To him, they were inconsequential and mere driftwood in his overflowing river of ambition.

The dwarves were ideal patsies since they could hardly speak normally and defend themselves properly. When asked anything about themselves, they responded by mumbling incoherently. The most the police found out was that they were brothers. They couldn't even tell who was older from all the overgrown hair on their bodies. They looked like balls of hair with eyes. They couldn't write their names since they were illiterate and had no IDs. They were written as "Juan de la Cruz 1 and Juan de la Cruz 2" on the police blotter for identification purposes.

They were brought to the interrogation room one at a time for questioning. Mayor Eddie was keenly looking at each of them on the two-way mirror in the observation room. He was elated by what was transpiring, even though P.O. Collins was coercing them to admit to the crime. It didn't take long, and they soon unknowingly signed their confessions.

After both dwarves were formally charged for the attack in the high school gymnasium, Mayor Eddie rushed to P.O. Collins, grasped his hand, and fervently shook it. He said joyously: "Officer, I'm so glad you caught the killers! Now my wife and I can breathe a sigh of relief. I'm going to recommend to your bosses that you be promoted immediately!"

P.O. Collins smiled. All his dreams were seemingly materializing. Yet he knew his achievement wasn't his alone but also for his secret benefactor and Lord Axe-Grinder, who had put him in his law enforcement position as a spy.

His recruitment was different compared to the other humans. While the others had undergone the usual bloody route of being bitten and infected by *aswangs*, he was spared because the dark creatures recognized a fierce ambition within him. He was taken instead to the dark domain in Batala and brought to Lord Axe-Grinder himself.

The dark lord saw a similarity in him, which was a ferocious desire to achieve his goals by any possible means. He told him they could help each other get what they wanted, and he would be spared from the bloodshed. He agreed since his life was on the line, and had no other choice.

Hence, he slowly but surely climbed the ladder of the police power structure, and any supernatural situation reported he'd underhandedly find a way to quash. In return, he and his immediate family were promised safety from possible incursions from the dark army.

~O~

The two brothers weren't as stupid as the police thought. They could comprehend what was happening to them but couldn't express themselves intelligibly because they had their made-up language to speak to each other.

They grew up in the circus by illiterate deaf-mute parents, who mostly signed as a means of communication. They never went outside their family circle to converse with other people. The two dwarf children grew up only knowing sign language but haven't learned to speak vocally. To compensate, they made up a language only they understood with a series of different grunts and whistles.

They became expert carnies, and everyone came to rely on them for their willingness to do the most disgusting tasks with the measliest of wages. Who will clean the elephant dung? Let the brothers scoop them up!

What they lacked in height, they grew in muscular strength. Even though they were incredibly short, they were unbelievably powerful, so much so that they could bend metal with their hands.

That night, after everyone was asleep in the local jail, they escaped their prison cell by bending the iron bars with their hands and wriggling themselves free. Then they sneaked outside without anyone seeing them.

They had the last laugh and were home free, away from the tall bad men who wanted to fuck with them.

The next morning, the jail guard noticed that the two brothers were missing in their cells. He immediately called the Chief of Police to inform him of the bad news and prepared for his incoming dismissal.

The Chief blew his top and immediately called P.O. Collins. He dressed him down, even though he knew he had nothing to do with the escape and wasn't at fault. P.O. Collins told him he'd go back to the circus in the neighboring town the next day to find them and bring them back.

He knew he would never see them again. However, he had another plan, something that would make Mayor Eddie and the Chief contented and not ask him any longer to find the true criminals who attacked the high school gymnasium.

~O~

The brothers knew they couldn't return to the carnival since it would be the first place the police would look for them, and they had to look for another area to lay low for a while.

Before long, they decided to hide in the forest, which they had previously heard to be a place where supernatural beings resided. It was the perfect place to hide out since locals would assume they were elemental creatures themselves and leave them alone.

Once they arrived, they built a makeshift hut from available resources in the forest and made tools for hunting and scavenging. They were used to this wretched existence and didn't think it a problem.

They eagerly welcomed their new life and remained there indefinitely. The two brothers finally found some semblance of tranquility that had eluded them all their lives, away from the cruel intentions of men.

Chapter 26 The Wolf and the Fox

Rumpelstiltskin missed his friends. They called themselves the "wolf pack," with Lord Axe-Grinder as their alpha, of course. The seven of them fought various battles and skirmishes for eons, from the time there was no division between the black and white elemental beings. Back then, they all lived in harmony as brothers and sisters of the elements.

The wolf pack was often sent out for dangerous missions and always came prepared for every eventuality. He was typically utilized as a scout and lookout man due to his viperous talent, while the others for their fighting skill and courage.

He had thought they came adequately prepared for the girl's abduction, but by the worst of luck, they sorely weren't because Pluto screwed up and didn't warn them about her supposed powers of witchery. He paid dearly for his incompetence and, as the ghost boy told him, was killed by a gardener named Matteo.

The gardener. Something was off about him. He seemed always happy and whistled whenever he did yard work. Nobody could be that joyful when doing back-breaking manual labor.

He needed to know who the gardener was and began following him around whenever he went out to town. He found out he was dating a foxy lady working in the local governing body, which intrigued him further…

~O~

Esmeralda, a.k.a. Michelle, had asked for all pertinent information she could think of from Matteo about Casa de la Noche and its inhabitants. She casually inquired so he wouldn't get suspicious. One crucial question she asked him immediately after having vigorous sex while he was in complete bliss after ejaculation: "Matteo darling, where is the gold located in the house?"

"Ohhh…. That was great! The gold? It's in one of the underground rooms."

"Have you gone inside in any of them?"

"I've only been inside one room, which was empty. I don't know exactly which room it's in. Only the two Madams have gone there. They have keys."

"Keys, huh? They have keys each?"

"No, there's only one set of keys for all the rooms, and Ma'am Angelica has them always in her person."

"Why her?"

"Because Ma'am Sabrina is old, and always forgets things."

"Have you seen the gold with your own two eyes?"

"No. Somebody from the bank visits the house once in three months who brings money, gets a couple of gold nuggets and puts them inside an attaché case."

"Who is this person and which bank?"

"Hey, your questions are getting intrusive. I'm not supposed to tell you any of this."

"Oh, I'm sorry darling, I'm just making conversation. Are you ready for the second round?"

"Am I? Of course! Start your engines!!!"

~O~

Rumpelstiltskin had rented a small bachelor's flat in the heart of town that he made as a temporary home base. He made Andreas the ghost his errand boy and spy, which was a happy chance since nobody could see him and could walk through walls.

Andreas returned after tailing Matteo, who had checked in a seedy motel. He told him: "Matteo is currently having sex with a woman, the mayor's secretary, in a motel. He's making stupid car sounds, which is funny. She's asking him about the gold and he's telling her everything."

I knew it, Rumpelstiltskin thought. *She's also after the gold. I have to do something about it.*

"Good work, ghost. I'm curious. Did you feel anything after seeing them having sex?"

"No and it's weird. I should feel titillated or horny but nothing. Why?"

"Because you're dead and don't have human desires or urges anymore. We're similar in a way, since we're travelers from different realms and don't have the same feelings as humans do."

"I don't understand."

"We're beings not of this realm. I'm a dwarf from another plane of existence and you're a spirit on your way to the astral plane but got stuck here due to unfinished business."

"Oh okay, I get it now. I need to finish my business here so I can go to heaven."

"Yes, if you want. Or I can make you human again, just as long as you help me."

"Help you? Why?"

"Because you have to. Do you want to be a ghost forever?"

"No. I want to be able to feel again and be with Pandora. Will you help me?"

"Yes, or course. Once you do, you'll get your wish. Now go back to the motel to follow the girl wherever she goes and report back to me."

"Yes sir. You haven't told me your name yet."

"My name is inconsequential and you don't have to know it."

"But how will I address you?"

"Call me lone wolf. Follow the girl. She's a fox and not to be trusted."

"Yes Mr. Lone Wolf, sir," said Andreas and disappeared.

Whew, that was close, Rumpelstiltskin thought. *If he only knew that my name has power, and if someone ever uttered it aloud, something terrible would happen.*

~O~

Esmeralda returned to the office after the quickie with Matteo in a motel. She regretted doing it. While she did like having sex with him, it was beginning to feel like a distraction from her ultimate goal, which was to get as much gold as she could in the Ponce de Leon house.

She switched on her desktop computer, clicked on a locked file marked "₱," and typed the password. It was an Excel sheet of all the information she had collected about her plan to steal gold. She typed the new information she got from Matteo and made a reminder to research known banks in the area that transacted with the family.

Once done, she waited for everyone to leave the office, opened the mayor's drawer, and took out his diary. She read the latest entry, which had no information she wanted. There was something about dwarves being taken into custody but escaped. She returned the diary, locked the main office door, and went home.

Chapter 27 The Shoes that were Danced to Pieces

Angelica heard something through the grapevine that the culprits from the attack in the gym were caught by the police. She felt relieved after learning it and wanted to take a swig of Absolut vodka but forgot she had disposed of every bottle from the liquor cabinet. She realized she made a promise to herself earlier not to drink anymore but still wanted to blow off steam.

Instead, she wanted to dance. She had been a dancer in her youth and often joined dance contests in town with her rich group of friends called: "Golden Girls," which she had belatedly realized was too on the nose. They were a decent dance group that had often placed in the contests but never won first. Their specialty was modern dance, and their favorite singer to dance to was Britney Spears.

She remembered she still had her old dance shoes in her shoe rack and an old Britney Spears compact disc on the CD stand in her room. She took them, including an old CD player, to the ballroom.

The ballroom door was closed. She took out an immense set of house keys, chose the right one, and opened the door. The room was dirty and dusty and hadn't been utilized for many years.

Angelica recalled the last time the ballroom was used, which was her engagement party to Henry, and never materialized in marriage. It was the last time she remembered both of them entirely happy, even Henry who was a perennial pessimist. He forgot his gambling addiction for once and enjoyed the merriment. Then, it was all downhill after that.

She remembered dancing for four hours straight, either with Henry or someone else, wearing her trusty dancing shoes. By the end of the night, both were danced to pieces. Afterward, she had them repaired to be usable again.

She placed the CD player on a dusty table, inserted the Britney Spears CD, and played her favorite song, "Oops, I Did It Again." She remembered the song being scandalous since Britney Spears was still a teenager singing a hypersexualized song while wearing a sexy school uniform in the music video. At that time, all the adults were shocked, but kids like her loved it.

She put on the dance shoes and began dancing. She was rusty and weightier than her former lithe teenage body, but she still had the moves. She moonwalked towards the center of the ballroom, hit something on the floor, yelled: "oops!" and fell. She did it again.

She remembered what the thing on the floor was that hit her foot. It was a protruding knob from a secret trapdoor. She thought it shouldn't be jutting out this way and should be leveled and concealed on the flooring. She took the set of keys, chose the right one, and opened it.

She saw a roomful of glittering gold nuggets, big and small, still there and closed it back. She saw a spare hammer lying on the floor, picked it up, and hammered the protruding knob back.

She resumed dancing and reminiscing about the good old days.

~O~

Pandora had also heard that some of the gym attackers were apprehended by the police. She wondered how they caught them since they were only human and the purported arrestees were creatures with magical abilities. She became suspicious of the news and decided to look for better information.

She took out her smartphone, clicked the Facebook app, and logged in to her profile. She scrolled and scrolled to look for any news about the arrest. He saw one from a local blogger who wrote about the two brothers' arrest and subsequent escape the next day. She stared at a photo of the supposed dwarves, which distinctly were not the ones who tried to abduct her.

They had caught real human dwarves, not the magical kind garbed in gold. She was glad they had escaped since they were innocent. She scrolled down for other news and saw a post about Andreas' funeral the next day, which she'd attend. She clicked "like" and logged out of her account.

She went upstairs to check if Lola Sabrina had awakened from her nap.

~O~

Angelica danced continuously for two hours without resting. By the time she stopped, she was covered with sweat from head to foot. She grabbed all her belongings, exited the ballroom, and locked the door behind her.

She saw Pandora on her way to her mother's bedroom. She thought she was responsible and old enough to learn about the location of the hidden gold in the ballroom. She called out to her to follow her downstairs, and she wanted to show her something.

After showing her the gold, she said: "Now you know the source of our wealth. This is our legacy from our ancestor Don Marcus Ponce de Leon. I'm trusting you this knowledge because soon, when you grow older, you will be the one who will convert some of it for our use and guard the rest of it. Make sure no one sees you coming in here, even the helpers. They know the existence of the gold but never where we hid it."

"I already knew about the gold, but not where it was. Is it true it's cursed and the reason why all the male members of the family died young?"

"Don't believe in that horseshit. They all died naturally."

"What about my dad and my lolo? They died mysteriously."

"Yes, there might still be unanswered questions about their deaths, but they died by natural means."

"You really think so?"

"Yes, dear. I was told the same supernatural stories by your Lola, but I never believed any of them."

"But why?"

"I'll tell you the reason some other time. For now, I have to take a bath."

"Were you dancing?"

"How did you know?"

"You're carrying dancing shoes, and it looked like it's danced to pieces."

"I should buy new ones. Do you want to go for a shopping spree downtown? I'll buy you anything you want for being a good girl."

"Am I supposed to be grounded?"

"Not anymore. Have you heard? They arrested the attackers. We can go out now. We have police guards anyway to follow us."

"Let's also bring Ruby Rose. She's also been cooped here like me. She'd want to go out."

"Sure dear, anything you want."

"Thanks Mama."

Chapter 28 The Poor Boy in the Grave

Andreas was present at his funeral and was surprised many people attended. He recognized some of them as family members, relatives, and friends from school. Most he didn't know and assumed were townspeople paying their respects.

He had almost forgotten about the crow, whom he met in the gym right after he was killed, and could seemingly understand him. He saw it perched atop one of the gravestones, cawing incessantly like a pet mourning the death of its master.

Then he saw his lady love and the cause of his demise: Pandora. She still looked as ethereal as the first time he laid eyes on her: pale blue eyes, jet black hair, and pale complexion that made him sigh with regret.

He thought she was alone, but when he glanced back, two uniformed police officers were situated at the rear of the crowd of mourners, watching over her. They wore earpieces and were talking to each other.

He saw her crying, which broke his spectral heart. He had thought he was immune to human feelings anymore since he wasn't technically human, but he still felt a profound sense of sadness. He also felt love for her, which reinvigorated him.

He saw himself turning blue, like what had happened before when he was excited. He knew if it persisted, people would see him, so he went to the back of the crowd among the tombstones and mausoleums where no one could. But it was too late. Pandora could see his blue-colored luminescence as he hid behind a man-sized headstone.

As the funeral winded down and his corpse was buried in the family lot, people started leaving. Soon, only Pandora remained, along with her two police guards waiting for her in their patrol car. The blue light still illuminated outward his ghostly body but had dimmed a bit. He saw Pandora approaching him and waited for her arrival.

When she arrived and was face-to-face with him, she said: "You're here Andreas. I saw you before in the house, but you suddenly disappeared. Why?"

He opened his mouth to talk, but no sound came out. He felt weird since he could converse with the magic dwarf but not with her. As a response, he pointed to his mouth and shook his head.

"You can't talk? Why?"

He shrugged.

"Maybe because you're a ghost?"

He nodded.

"Alright. From now on, I'll ask close-ended questions."

He nodded.

"How come I could see you?"

He shrugged.

"Oh sorry, I forgot. Only close-ended questions."

He nodded.

"Are you okay being a ghost?"

He shrugged.

"Are you stuck here?"

He nodded.

"Do you want to stay?"

He shrugged.

"Or leave?"

He shrugged.

"You mean you can't decide?"

He nodded. He knew that becoming human again was a long shot, and he was only following the dwarf's orders on the off-chance he would be rewarded with humanity. If it wouldn't happen, going to heaven was still a wonderful alternative.

"I wish I'd know how to help you, if only you can talk. Maybe there's a way you could. Follow me back home."

He nodded.

Pandora left and rode the awaiting police car to return to Casa de la Noche.

Andreas reappeared in Rumpelstiltskin's rented place. He was sitting on a wooden chair that was too big for him, with his dangling feet not touching the floor. He was waiting for his return with news.

"You're back. What happened in your funeral? Did many people cry?" Rumpelstiltskin said.

"Yes. She was also there and was able to see me. She told me to follow her to her house."

"Well, you should do what she asked and maybe she'll tell you some information I want."

"What do you want from her? You never said what it was. You just told me to follow her and listen to their conversations."

"Nothing will happen to her, I promise. She just knows something I need. No more questions, go now."

Andreas smelled something fishy and began to regret allying himself with Rumpelstiltskin. He was going to find out what, even if it was going to kill him again.

~O~

Pandora returned home and went straight to her Lola Sabrina's room. She was sitting by the dresser and reading a big leather-bound book with a three-pronged star in front. She wanted to say something but instead waited for her to finish and sat on the bed. After a few minutes of silence, she said: "Lola, are you done? I saw Andreas again."

"Hello, dear. How was the funeral?" She said, closed the book, and set it aside.

"Sad. Many people attended and Andreas' parents cried. I wish we could do something for them."

"We could. We can give them money."

"Oh yeah! Good idea Lola."

"I know your mama told you already about the gold. Have some of those converted to cash and give it to them."

"I'll tell her about it Lola, thanks. And another thing, I wanted to ask you a question…"

"Go ahead, dear."

"Why can't I talk to ghosts?"

"Yes, you can, not audibly but through telepathic means. You haven't been taught yet how to do it. It's one of my most effective abilities, you know."

"Can you teach me? I saw Andreas as a ghost again and I think he wants to tell me something."

"I know you were going ask me that question. I was reviewing about it in this book."

"I haven't seen that book before Lola. What is it?"

"It's a spell book called the Book of Shadows. I borrowed it from Bakunawa, the Serpent-Goddess. I'll teach you the basics to develop your telepathic ability, which you can use for your ghostly friend.

First, you should learn to meditate. Close your eyes, still your mind, and center your energy. You must find the stillness within you and achieve the right state of awareness. Focus on your breathing, and you become less aware of your surroundings. When some mundane thought enters your mind, redirect it to your breathing so you won't get caught up. By combining relaxation and focus, your mind will quiet and become still.

Imagine the person you want to contact using telepathy. Focus your energy outward on this person. Doing this will create a psychic bond and make telepathy possible.

Then send a simple clear message to this person. Start with a short and simple message, keep repeating it, and visualize him receiving it. You can try my whispering method, which is effective.

Go back to meditating and ask him to respond. Be patient because it may take time for him to answer back."

Pandora left her room and went to hers. She locked the door, closed the windows, and turned off the light. She sat on the floor with her legs crossed and followed everything Lola Sabrina had told her to do.

Chapter 29 The Golden Key

There were many keys to lock and unlock all the doors in Casa de la Noche. It was attached to a keychain and was hefty. It held the keys for all the known doorways throughout the house and also for the ones unknown and hidden from sight. They were made from different types of metal: brass, nickel, silver, bronze, steel, and nickel-brass mixture. There was only one unique key made from real gold; the most important was the key to open the door to the hidden tunnel going to Batala.

It looked like an ordinary and dull-looking bronze key but, in truth had magical abilities of its own. It was also a master key that could fit and open any locked entryways made by man, and even doors magicked with a door-sealing spell. It was a type of key that could be dangerous if fallen into the wrong hands.

The golden key was never used even once, by anyone in the Casa de la Noche household. Only Lola Sabrina knew of its existence but hadn't felt the need to utilize it. It looked inconspicuous and merely included among dozens of ordinary-looking keys in a set hanging on a hook inside Angelica's bedroom.

~O~

After one hour of trying and failing to talk telepathically to Andreas, she gave up. She felt she was doing something wrong but was disinterested in asking her Lola for help. Instead, she went to her mama's room.

Pandora told her that she wanted to get a little of the gold to give to Andreas' parents because she was partly to blame for his death. She agreed and pointed to the keys hanging on the key hook. She told her to look for two similar-looking bronze keys to open the main ballroom door and trapdoor. And also to make sure no one would notice her going in.

She grabbed the bunch and walked furtively to the ballroom. She picked the first bronze key to open the main door, glanced back to check if anyone was looking, entered, and closed it behind her.

She had forgotten exactly where the hidden trapdoor was situated and spent ten minutes looking for it. Once she found it, she selected the second bronze key and opened it.

She saw a ladder going to the gold, which she used to climb downwards. She immediately felt creepy once she set foot on the cement floor amidst piles and piles of gold nuggets. She quickly grabbed a good handful, rushed back up, and locked the trapdoor.

She put the fistful of gold inside her shoulder bag and went out of the ballroom.

~O~

"Do you know the exact location of the keys in the house?" Esmeralda asked Matteo after the umpteenth time they had sex for the day. By this time, he was physically and emotionally drained of all bodily juices, and his inborn suspicious nature had seemingly stripped from his psyche. Her plan of turning him into an oversexed simpleton worked.

"It's in Ma'am Angelica's room, hanging on a wall," Matteo said robotically.

"Would you be a sweetheart and get it for me when you get back? I'll make it worth your time," she whispered close to his ear, then kissed it, which gave him immediate goosebumps.

"Yes of course, when I'll get back."

"It will be for short while only. Once I make copies of the ones I need, I'll give it right back. No harm, no foul."

"Yes."

"Thank you darling! Are you ready for more? I'm not tired yet."

"Yes."

~O~

Dwarves were known to be expert craftsmen and miners in Batala, and also for their great affection for gold. They love it so much that they become greedy for it, and every gold nugget given to humans as a means for extortion and domination, they intend on getting back.

Dwarves make gold into many accouterments, contrivances, and weapons for various reasons. With every creation, they imbue a sprinkling of dwarf magic, like making golden apparel impenetrable to human-made sharp tools or making golden keys to open all kinds of doors.

The golden key was made by a dwarf named Gunnar the Gold-Crafter who was the most skillful craftsman of the rest of them. He was among the seven who were killed in the gym, leaving no one in Batala to forge for them anymore, and training someone else to be as proficient as Gunner would take eons.

Gunnar then gave the key to his Lord Axe-Grinder, who then handed it over to Don Marcus Ponce de Leon, who was told of its use. He thought nothing of it since and secured it among the set of keys in the house.

The golden key was the last of its kind, and not even Lord Axe-Grinder or Rumpelstiltskin hadn't considered its significance to their cause and possible solutions to their problems.

Until Andreas told Rumpelstiltskin about it offhandedly.

~O~

Andreas had heard Pandora trying to communicate with him telepathically but didn't know how to respond to her. He wanted to tell her about the danger posed by Rumpelstiltskin but was hesitant because he participated in the scheme, which he now had misgivings. He was scared she'd hate him forever if she discovered his involvement.

Instead, he followed her around. He wanted to avoid anything that might excite him and activate the blue light in his spectral body, so he always made certain to be fairly far away from her.

He followed her as she took the keys inside her mother's room and went down to the ballroom where the hidden trapdoor was. He saw her get some gold and then returned the keys to her mom.

He was with her when she visited his parent's home after the funeral. She gave them a bagful of gold nuggets, which made them happy. He, too was also pleased that his parents were compensated for the trouble his death had caused them.

He left her when she returned home, then reappeared in Rumpelstiltskin's place. He was still unmoved and sitting on the same high chair with his feet dangling. He asked him what had transpired and mentioned everything. He told him about the set of keys, the gold under the ballroom, and her visit to his parents' home.

Then, a wide and evil smile began to form on his face, which frightened Andreas.

Chapter 30 The Old Man Made Young Again

Ruby Rose noticed a definite change happening to her father. He didn't engage in things people his age tended to do anymore, like eating early dinners, watching TV game shows, or playing cards with other household helpers, but trying to do stuff younger people did. He looked awkward and silly, dressing in young people's clothing like oversized shirts, hoodies, and wide-legged jeans, and even had his hair cut in a faux hawk style.

Another new thing she observed was going out at night, which he never did before. When he finished his household chores, he would take a long hot bath, drench himself with god-awful-smelling cologne, and dress in age-inappropriate clothes. She'd ask him where he'd go but gave the same short and nebulous answer without further explaining himself: "*Out.*" When she asked where, it was already too late, and he had left.

She also observed that he was becoming nosy all of a sudden, to the point of inducing discomfort with the other household staff. He was becoming like the old butler Pluto, who always stuck his nose in other people's business. He was turning into someone his old self would hate.

She deduced there had to be a reason for his complete one-eighty-degree change. It couldn't just be a midlife crisis; it had to be something deeper and ominous. She was appalled and resolved to take some action.

That night, she waited for him to leave and secretly followed him. She had previously hired a motorized tricycle to wait for her a short distance from the main gate so she could go after him.

He also hired a tricycle ride that drove him straight to a government-owned subdivision, then was waved through by the security guard stationed at the main gate. She correctly surmised he was a regular visitor and was already recognized by the guard.

However, her tricycle driver was motioned to stop and then asked to give his ID, which he complied promptly. They continued following them from a distance. When they stopped, she told her driver to do the same and then to wait for her for a few minutes. She climbed down.

She hid behind a tall shrub and saw her dad walk on a narrow cement pathway to a small one-bedroom house. He rang the doorbell, and the door was opened by an attractive woman wearing a see-through nightgown. She grabbed and hugged him, then smothered him with kisses. She took out her smartphone and snapped a couple of pictures.

He looked like he was overwhelmed by the woman's lustful embraces and struggled a bit in reeling her in, then closed the door behind him.

It was a woman that was driving her father to do stupid things. From the looks of it, she was alluring and sexy as hell. Her dad was hooked.

She checked on the pictures she took on her phone and was glad she got a clear image of her face. She went back to the awaiting trike and told the driver to take her back home.

~O~

"Darling, did you get what I wanted?" Said Esmeralda after the initial coition. She intended to do it all night until she was satiated, which usually happened after two more vigorous rounds.

"Yes, I got it."

"Where is it?"

"My left pants pocket," he said. He took it out of his pants, strewn on the floor, and handed it over to her. She looked at the set of keys for a few minutes and unfastened a couple from the key holder.

She rose from her bed, still naked, and pulled out a few expired credit cards and plastic gift cards, a roll of Scotch tape, a cigarette lighter, scissors, and pliers in her bedside drawer.

"What are you going to do with those?"

"I can quickly copy them using these simple objects. Watch me." She said.

She first took the pair of pliers and held the teeth on one side of a key over the open flame of the lighter until charring it. Once charred on one side, she placed it on the table to cool it.

She cut a wide strip of Scotch tape and stuck it on the blackened side to transfer the char.

After ten seconds, she peeled the tape slowly from the key, with the impression on it, and stuck it in one plastic card.

She took the pair of scissors and carefully cut the shape of the key. Then, she repeated the same process to the few keys she had selected.

In less than an hour, she had created a few plastic keys from the expired credit and gift cards. She wiped the real keys with rubbing alcohol, then refastened them into the key holder and gave the complete set to Matteo. She said: "Here, bring it back to her room before anyone notices it's gone."

"Thanks. I should go now. My daughter is beginning to get suspicious."

"Alright. But I'm not finished with you yet. Get ready for two more rounds then you can go."

"Yes ma'am."

~O~

Ruby Rose switched on her laptop and uploaded the picture of the mystery woman's face onto Google Images, a search engine that allowed its users to search the internet for particular images. Technology in this day and age can, fortunately, make ordinary people like her become proficient detectives.

The first link was for the Philippine National Police website, which she clicked. She immediately hit paydirt and saw the picture of the woman included in the Top Ten Most Wanted List in the Philippines. She saw a somber-looking image of the same woman named Esmeralda Tagapulot, with a reward of five hundred thousand pesos for the criminal offenses of grand theft of the first degree, extortion, and arson.

She saved the wanted poster on her flash drive and switched off the laptop.

~O~

Matteo arrived at midnight in Casa de la Noche. He crept slowly, trying not to make a sound towards his room in the servants' quarters. He saw Ruby Rose asleep on her bed, with her laptop beside her.

He tiptoed out towards Lola Sabrina's room and placed the set of keys outside her door. He put it there because he knew she was an ideal scapegoat due to her forgetful nature and might even have thought she accidentally left the keys there.

He quietly went back to his room and closed the door behind him.

Chapter 31 In the Pink

Mayor Eddie was in his office attending to town-related issues with his constituents when he received a text message from a girl named Pandora, wanting to talk to him in person. He was a godfather to many kids in town and couldn't recall all of them. Then it hit him: she was the girl at the center of the recent attack in the high school gymnasium. She said she had some new information and to please come to her home as soon as possible.

What new information? He thought. The case was already as good as solved, even though the culprits escaped, he was still content with the result. It meant the criminals were on the run and wouldn't set foot in Gintongbayan anymore. The citizens would be relatively safe from possible assaults from strange-looking carnival folk.

He asked Michelle, his secretary, if he had any upcoming events or meetings scheduled for the day, and he didn't. He told her he would be going to Casa de la Noche for a personal visit for a few hours and to call him immediately on his mobile phone if there were any mayor-related concerns. Otherwise, he'd return before the workday ended.

Mayor Eddie left.

~O~

Michelle, aka Esmeralda, didn't like coincidences and found it ill-timed and weird that Pandora wanted to talk to the mayor when she was so close to attaining her goals. *Had they found out about what Matteo had done? She thought.*

In her other profession as a world-class grifter, she had to assume the worst and make contingency plans. Someone from the household surely had discovered what Matteo had done and told the madams, so she had to move up her timetable and create a workable exit strategy.

This con game is getting a little bit complicated, and I need to leave anyway before it all turns to shit.

She didn't need to get anything from her desk since the persona of "Michelle the mayor's secretary" wasn't real and all the stuff had no use to her. She looked at her workplace for one last time and left.

~O~

Mayor Eddie promptly arrived at Casa de la Noche and rang the doorbell. He expected the butler to answer the door, but instead, it was a young girl who said: "Good afternoon, Godfather Eddie, I'm your goddaughter Ruby Rose. I'm friends with Pandora and also work here." Then she performed the honoring gesture to him.

"Where's the weird-looking butler that used to answer the door?"

"He quit without saying anything, but some new butler will arrive any day now to replace him."

"He didn't tell you why? He just disappeared?"

"No."

"And you didn't find it strange?"

"It was, but with him everything was strange, and him leaving without telling us was just another weird thing he did."

"Alright, if you say so. Where's my other goddaughter Pandora? She texted that she wanted to talk to me face-to-face. Are your other madams here?"

"Not yet. They'll be coming shortly. Please follow me to the dining room, where you can talk in private," said Ruby Rose and turned around.

Mayor Eddie followed her to the same room he went to on his last visit. Pandora was waiting for him, sitting on a chair. She stood up and also performed the honoring gesture. Ruby Rose closed the door behind her after coming inside.

"Good afternoon, Godfather. Please sit down."

"Thank you. You have some new information you wanted to share with me? The police caught some of the attackers, you know. They did escape but no matter, they won't come back because they're wanted men. Sooner or later, they're gonna get caught."

"No sir, it's about something else. Two separate and unrelated people after the same thing. Well, one you might know and another one you won't believe."

"Tell me everything. I have nothing else planned for the rest of the day and I've told my secretary Michelle to call me if they'd need me at the office."

"Oh, your secretary? Because coincidentally, it's about her."

"Huh? What did she do?"

"Well, Ruby Rose can tell you. Go ahead Ruby…"

~O~

Police Officer Micheal Collins had a voicemail waiting for him at his desk at the police station. He had been out of town chasing so-called leads, which was all a pretense since he knew the perpetrators of the attack weren't even human and not of this earth.

He was looking for other people with diminished mental capacities who could serve as ideal fall guys for the attack in the gym. The two dwarf escapees would have been perfect but had seemingly vanished.

He returned to the neighboring municipality of Tamtam, but the traveling carnival was gone, and had moved to another town to engage in commerce. He didn't go after them anymore since their new location was too far and he lacked funds.

He returned with no success and needed to do some police work to redeem himself in the eyes of the top brass.

He sat on his desk and pressed the # button on his landline phone to play the voicemail. It was from the mayor, who wanted to talk to him about the case and to meet him in the Ponce de Leon house as soon as he got the message. Mayor Eddie's voice sounded urgent, which made him worry.

He told the reception desk officer of his new assignment from the mayor and then left the station.

~O~

Andreas reappeared in Rumpelstiltskin's place and saw him still sitting on the same big chair, unmoved. He had a slight smirk on his face and looked creepier than he had ever been.

"I discovered some new information, something that you might want to know. A secret door to an underground tunnel, and another to the gold. Are those what you're looking for?"

"Yes. Yes! You've got both? How?"

"Ghosts have ways to find any sort of information, since no one could see us, we could go wherever we want and listen to secret conversations."

"Good work! Do you know where the keys are?"

"They're with this girl who is a thief. She's planning to steal the gold anytime soon."

"Do you know where the girl is right now?"

"She's at her home in a government-owned subdivision, preparing for tonight's burglary. You can go there right now and catch her red-handed."

"Tell me where this subdivision is located..."

Chapter 32 The Nail in the Coffin

It was the fifth year (or five days in human time) since Axe-Grinder sent out Rumpelstiltskin on his mission of skullduggery and deception with the enemy. Those were his specialties, and he was confident in his abilities.

He had waited patiently and remained on standby, and now it was the time to take action. He rounded up his minions—dark beings with no capacity to reason, feel fear, or love. These were monsters who only knew bloodlust and chaos: the vampiric *Aswangs*, the ape-like *Amomongos*, the cannibalistic *Busaws*, the human/horse hybrid *Tikbalangs*, and the giant headless *Pugots*.

He was going to engage in a full-frontal assault into the heart of town through an underground tunnel leading to the house owned by his former human ally turned traitor Don Marcus Ponce de Leon. It was time to take all the gold back from the humans since it was theirs, to begin with.

He was sure Rumpelstiltskin had secured the master key to open the enchanted door. He hobbled using his staff to the front of his dark battalion and screamed in Dwarvish tongue: "It is time to destroy the humans and their allies and take our gold back. Forward, my dark brothers!"

~O~

After Ruby Rose found out about the woman who had seemingly bewitched his father, he went to Pandora first and showed her the wanted poster saved on her flash drive. After seeing it, she needed to bring in her mom and Lola to provide advice on the best way to handle it.

Ruby Rose thought he might have been enchanted by magic since he couldn't believe his father had turned into this awful person with the capacity to steal and be in cahoots with a criminal. Lola Sabrina said she sensed no enchantments imposed on him but was captivated purely by her feminine wiles.

They decided that the best way to deal with him was by enchanting him for real with a forgetfulness charm. This way, his memory of the woman will be wiped clean from his brain. Once done, it would be like waking up from a bad dream and being his old self again.

The next issue was the woman herself, who wanted to steal the gold from them. Angelica told Pandora to contact the mayor and bring him to the house. He needed to know that a wanted criminal was working in his office.

Pandora said she had been seeing Andreas as a ghost, who had been trying to talk to her. She had followed all the steps Lola told her and tried conversing with him telepathically, but it didn't work.

Her Lola said she did everything correctly, and it was Andreas, who was afraid to talk to her. She used her power of divination and ascertained the reason for his fearfulness: an evil dwarf was manipulating him.

Then Angelica thought of a plan: why not have both interlopers eliminate each other? It would be like hitting two birds with one stone. They all agreed, and it was a brilliant idea. But how?

They needed to bring in Andreas and have a genuine conversation with him. They will tell him of the plan and his part in making it successful. He just needed to be firm for a short while, and they will take care of the rest.

~O~

Police Officer Michael Collins arrived at Casa de la Noche and knocked on the door, which was answered right away by Ruby Rose. He was led to the private dining room where the plan was about to be set into motion. He naively thought he was there for a new assignment but didn't know he was about to be thrown into the lion's den, which was only fitting due to his collusion with the enemy.

Once inside, the mayor explained to him that two criminals were planning to raid this house, and he had to use his law enforcement know-how to set up actual police surveillance, complete with listening devices, video cameras, flying drones, etc. And after getting the necessary evidence for a conviction, he would arrest them immediately. He had to do it alone since he was the only cop they could trust in the Gintongbayan Police Force.

P.O. Collins beamed and was overjoyed that the mayor and one of the wealthiest families in town trusted him. His overambitious nature began to rear its ugly head with drool spilling from its mouth.

~O~

Rumpelstiltskin was agile and stealthy by nature and could spy any place almost unseen. His lord-Axe Grinder valued those abilities and often sent him on intelligence-gathering missions. He was only effective at a distance, watching the supposed target from afar, but was ineffective in actual combat. Any physical confrontation he had in the past always ended in defeat. He knew of his weakness, so to compensate, he used all sorts of trickery to gain advantage.

He arrived at Esmeralda's one-room apartment, crept by the outside window, and peeked in. The place was bare except for a well-worn bed and a few kitchen appliances. He saw a curious-looking black backpack on top of a table. The supposed woman suddenly stepped out of the bathroom with a towel wrapped around her body.

He could ascertain she was an attractive member of the female gender but felt no attraction. For him, humans were lower lifeforms comparable to all the other substandard creatures populating this lower level of existence. He was a *Dwende* of the superior race of black dwarves who resided in the magical realm of Batala.

He immediately knew how to trick her, which would take every ounce of his willpower not to be disgusted.

He went to the door and knocked.

"Who is it?" Yelled Esmeralda. He heard a tinge of panic in her voice and a rustling of clothes being worn hurriedly and strewn about.

"It's me, the man of your dreams," he said, his voice suddenly changing into someone she knew.

"Oh. It's you Matteo. I thought you've been discovered by the three madams. I was about to…"

"No, they didn't. You've taught me how to be as sneaky as you, remember? You're really a great teacher with a fantastic body," said Rumpelstiltskin, who had suddenly morphed into the bodily representation of Matteo. Transmogrification and mimicry were among his special talents, which made him an effective warrior of the dark army without the physical act of fighting.

"You mean this body?" She said and unfasted the wrapped towel on her torso, showing a glistening and lithe naked body. She then grabbed him indoors and shut the door.

She hungrily kissed him on the lips and inserted her left hand in his pants, feeling her way to his penis. But to her utmost shock, his groin area was bare, missing a human male reproductive organ. Her eyes bulged, and she stopped groping. She took a step back and said: "Where's you dick? Who are you or *what* are you?"

The face of Matteo disappeared, and the sinister and dark-skinned image of Rumpelstiltskin returned, sneering at her. "We *Dwendes* have evolved to become higher lifeforms, not needing copulation anymore. You are like a bitch in heat needing to be put down," he said and hit her with a right hook on her lower chin, knocking her out.

~O~

When Esmeralda woke up, she saw she was tied to a chair. She struggled to get herself free, but the binds were strong. Rumpelstiltskin was sitting on the opposite side of the table, smiling his evil smile.

"Who are you and what do you want from me?" Said Esmeralda.

She was fearful for her life because of the unknown element in front of her, which she didn't know how to deal with. She had been in bad situations before, but she had always managed to escape due to her craftiness and mental fortitude. She knew how to control any situation and turned it to her advantage because she was attentive to all the moving parts and the means to overcome them. But now, she was dealing with a supernatural creature she thought existed only in books and movies. How was she going to handle an actual magical dwarf?

"We want the same thing: to get in the house and access their hidden doorways. I understand you have the keys?"

"What made you think I'm going to help you?"

"Because if not, I'm going to eat you. I've eaten human meat before and it's delicious. It's a bid bland, so we include lots of spices to make it taste delightful. If I cook you on a spit right now, you'll be yummy."

"Oh no you won't."

"Oh yes, I will. Where are the keys? I'm still going to find them, by telling me now will save time."

"I don't know."

"You don't or you won't?"

"Both."

Rumpelstiltskin slapped her on the cheek. Her nose bled immediately and was discombobulated. She then said: "Alright. Alright! Stop hitting me, please! The keys are in the black bag over there. You can't do it alone. You'll need the help of a professional thief, which is me."

"What can you do?"

"I have ways to enter the house undetected by any people or electronic device. They might be expecting us, so we have to create a diversion and distract them, then we could come in and get what we want."

"I'm listening."

"You will provide the distraction, with your ability to transform into any person. Then after leading them away from the house, I'm going in."

"Tell me how we're going to accomplish this…"

~O~

Andreas reappeared in Pandora's room after following Rumpelstiltskin. Only Pandora was there while the others were downstairs in the dining room with Mayor Eddie and P.O. Collins, helping to set up the surveillance equipment in hidden areas throughout the house.

Pandora had properly learned to communicate telepathically with Andreas, which almost felt like talking. Their whole conversation took place in their minds.

What happened? Are they doing what they're supposed to be doing?

Still on track. But the woman maybe won't last the day because he's beating her. But she's strong and can probably survive it.

Are you sure you weren't seen?

I've turned my blue light off. I can now do it by will, as your grandmother taught me. I can go anywhere like the wind without anyone seeing me, even with magical creatures. I saw the dwarf transform into the image of your father, which was how he was let inside the house.

Oh my. He's going to be tough to beat. Do you have any ideas about his name? Lola Sabrina said saying his name out loud is the best way to defeat him, which will neutralize him.

I don't know, and I haven't heard him say it yet. How could we trick a trickster?

I don't know yet, but if all else fails, I could still blast him to pieces like I did in the gym.

Are you able to control it?

I hope so. Lola taught me a little. When will they come here?

I could see them. My ghost body can be in two places at once. They haven't left the house yet. They're talking about creating a diversion to lead all of you away while the woman will enter alone and steal the gold then open a secret door.

We're prepared for that. Good work. Still, follow them, and don't let them see you. Everything will be fine. I hope.

Don't worry Pandora, it will be okay. I trust your Lola, and she knows what she's doing.

Yes, but she tends to be forgetful. I hope her memory won't slip through this entire ordeal.

She won't. I trust her.

I trust her too. Be careful.

Andreas disappeared.

~O~

Police Officer Collins was done setting up video cameras and listening devices throughout the house. He went to the dining room where Mayor Eddie and the others were congregating. He said: "I've finished installing the bugs in each room. When they will come here, we will see them. The monitoring devices are set up in the guest room where I'll be in for the duration."

"Good work, Officer. I'm finishing up with my conversation here and I'll be with you shortly," said Mayor Eddie.

P.O. Collins went to the guest room and switched on the monitors connected to the cameras and listening devices hidden throughout the house. Each camera was installed close to the ceiling and provided a bird's eye view of each room.

He didn't know what the thieves would steal in the house and didn't ask, although he had heard before of the rumors about a roomful of gold in a secret hideaway. But regardless, he would just catch them in the act and arrest them.

Simple, he thought. *I hope I don't screw this up.*

Three hours passed, and he was getting antsy. He glanced at his watch, and it was ten in the evening. In his experience, any incoming house burglary can occur when everybody is soundly sleeping, which should be after midnight.

So, he waited and tried to relax his nerves. He brought out a small thermos of hot chocolate that Sabrina, the matriarch, gave him and took a sip. It was refreshing, but he noticed a slight bitter taste he didn't recognize.

A few minutes later, he felt drowsy and sat on a sofa to lay his head. He felt tired and wanted to rest his eyes for a few seconds…

~O~

Ruby Rose entered the guest room and saw P.O. Collins snoring. She went back to the dining room and told them what she witnessed.

"It worked. I thought he was never going to drink it. While he's out cold, we can talk about the plan," said Lola Sabrina.

"Let me get this straight: you want me to believe that dwarves and other mythological creatures we saw in books and movies are in fact, real?" Said Angelica incredulously.

"I've told you that before, dear. You've never once believed it."

"Because it's all so unbelievable and ludicrous. A giant who smokes tobacco? A shapeshifting headless monster? Magical dwarves?"

"Yes, they're all real, Mama. Lola Sabrina is also a *mangkululam*: a witch. Even I exhibited some witchy powers and Lola is teaching me how to use them properly."

"I've always suspected there was something strange in our town. I only thought it originated from the townspeople's silly superstitious beliefs, and nothing more. Now you're saying it's all true? Even ghosts are real?" Said Mayor Eddie.

"Yes. Dark forces have been present since the time our town was established. They have killed, kidnapped, and enslaved many of us in secret. They have infiltrated our living and work spaces, and disguised themselves as humans. You can't trust anyone."

"What are we going to do about it?"

"We have a plan and the police officer sleeping in the next room is a part of it. He's one of the humans who allied themselves with the dark creatures, so we can't trust him."

"*Him*? But he's a cop. He took an oath to protect and serve."

"He's also overambitious and greedy. When this is all over and the plan worked, he will either be killed like the rest of them, put in prison or a mental asylum."

"I hope so. Tell me about the plan again?"

"Alright. The plan is a little bit strange and might be scary but should work…"

~O~

P.O. Collins woke up and glanced at his watch. He had dozed off for only ten minutes. He checked the monitors; everything was the same, and still no movement. Then he heard some noise from the main gate and checked the monitor. He saw a raven perched on the iron railing, cawing loudly. The wind also blew the small bell attached to the push button ringer as if some unseen person was ringing it. He stared again at the screen to be sure, but no one was there.

He felt a cold chill at the back of his neck, like a sudden blowing of cold air from an A/C. He checked if it was on, but it wasn't plugged in. He was a bit disturbed but shrugged it off.

Then he saw something move on the screen coming from the old ballroom. It was someone dressed in blue moving quickly, like this person knew where the camera was hidden, trying to escape its reach. He was crouching in the middle portion and then opened what looked like a secret trapdoor.

It was them. He unholstered his service pistol, cocked it, and rushed outside the guest room towards the ballroom. He stopped at the main door and peeked in. No one was there, but the trapdoor was still open. He entered, with his gun directed at the opening on the flooring, slowly walking towards it.

Once he arrived, he saw a flight of stairs going down, toward a darkened room under the floor. He thought of following but resolved to wait for this unknown person to return. This way, he would surprise the thief in the act of stealing and arrest him or her immediately.

A few minutes had passed, and nothing happened. He was still in a shooting position, with the gun aimed at the hole in the floor.

Then he saw someone slowly going up, but he was ready. The person turned around, not showing a human being at all, but the most terrifying-looking ghost anyone has ever seen, either on TV or in the movies. This thing that wasn't human had maggots going out its eyes, a decomposing face, with teeth falling out. It had greasy hair that looked like strands from a wet broom.

Other apparitions suddenly came out of the woodwork as if on cue and more terrible than the next. They begin swirling around P.O. Collins, then entering his different bodily orifices. They were consuming him from the inside, stripping away his soul and humanity. He screamed continuously until he couldn't anymore. He dropped on the floor, unconscious and still alive but barely.

~O~

Lola Sabrina had magicked P.O. Collins' spirit form and transported it to the astral plane, the realm of ghosts. It was a place that mirrored the real world but was murky and had no light.

There was a replica of Casa de la Noche in this other dimension but populated by horrible ghosts who couldn't leave due to the sins they committed on Earth. They were trapped there forever and where the spirit P.O. Collins would remain until the end of time.

His body was still in the real world but was now like a robot who could be coaxed into doing and saying anything. It was in this state that Lola Sabrina wanted him to be in, to become their fall guy in their plan.

They had given the helpers a day off with pay so they could have full use of the house undisturbed and be able to use whatever magic without getting them involved. Then they heard a knock on the main door, which Ruby Rose went to answer.

She returned and told Angelica: "Someone's looking for you."

Angelica was surprised. She had lost contact with all her former school friends after she became an alcoholic and shunned the public. *Who might it be?* She thought and went to the door.

It was Henry, her former fiancée and father to Pandora, whom she thought had died. She was shocked and speechless.

"Sweetheart, it's me. I've finally come home," Henry said.

Angelica couldn't believe her eyes and thought she was hallucinating due to alcohol. She hadn't been drinking since she made a promise to herself a while ago to stop for the benefit of being a good mother to Pandora.

"Henry, is that really you? I don't believe it. Where have you been all this time?"

"It's a long story, which I'll tell later. But now I'm back to finally be a husband to you and a father to our daughter."

"But you were cremated and your ashes sent to me. So, who's inside the urn on top of the fireplace?"

"Not me. My parents may have sent it to you, sorry. They were always embarrassed with me and might have concocted my death abroad."

"It figures. Anyway, come in! Come in. Everyone is at the dining room," said Angelica and hugged him tightly. "Follow me! You have to meet your daughter who's amazing."

"Really, oh my gosh. Who does she look like?"

"Well, no one because of her skin condition. You'll understand once you see her."

They entered the dining room, and Angelica said: "Mama, Look who's back! It's Henry, Pandora's dad whom we thought died abroad."

"Dad? You mean my real father?" Said Pandora.

"Yes, dear."

"Henry? Is that really you? You look the same, after all these years," said Mayor Eddie.

"Eddie? My old school classmate? What are you doing here?

"If you don't know yet, I'm the town mayor here to visit with my constituents. I'm just checking up on them. And how about you? Where have you been all this time?"

"Alright. I should tell all you what happened to me…"

Chapter 33 The Riddle of the Name

I never went abroad. I was close by, but not exactly near, and located in a different dimension. I was held captive in the underground realm of Batala.

One night, when I was walking home after playing mahjong, I was suddenly grabbed by a dark and awful creature and brought there as a captive.

Many Gintongbayan citizens were also there as prisoners like me. They were there for various reasons the supernatural beings had conceived of us committing. What they imagined were offenses were merely slights and doled out unjust punishments. I saw lots of familiar faces, some, who had been missing and many I thought had passed away. I saw someone who might have been one of your ancestors, Madam Sabrina, who had been there longer than me.

We humans were held in a separate encampment away from the supernatural creatures. We were given materials to make shelter, like bamboo and nipa palm, and food that looked and tasted like rice gruel twice a day.

We were there for many years. The passage of time in Batala was strange. Some days we thought were long were, in fact, short, and vice versa. Then we discovered that time passed differently for various people and never knew why. Some grew older quickly, and some remained young for a long time. I was fortunate to be among the ones who aged longer, so you see me now as hardly older than the last time you saw me.

What have we been doing all this time? We were surviving mostly and trying not to get eaten. You heard right. When a special occasion happens, they grab one of us for the slaughter. We tried to look as unappealing as possible, or else it would be one of our heads on a plate.

I think we were there for what felt like eons. Then, one day, some gigantic hairy tobacco-smoking creature suddenly grabbed me and took me aside. He whispered to me a strange and almost unpronounceable word: *Rumpelstiltskin*. He told me to remember the word and tell it to you, Madam Sabrina, because you were his old friend and you'll need it when the right time comes.

He then helped me escape by smuggling me in his clothes and taking me outside the giant termite mound. We said our goodbyes, and then I resolved to come here and knock on your door.

~O~

"Did the giant mention his name?" Said Lola Sabrina.

"Yes. His name was Jabber."

"Yes, he was a good friend of mine in my younger years in Batala. Rumpelstiltskin, you say? What a strange word. Maybe it's a magic word, said at the right time."

"We're currently in a crisis, Henry. Good thing you're here to help us. One of those creatures who abducted you is planning to raid this house. They'll be coming soon."

"What can I do to help?"

"You know these creatures and spent the longest time with them. What should we expect?"

"They're relentless, and will never stop to achieve their goals. If they get beaten, they will merely regroup and attack again."

"What do they want?"

"Their ultimate goal is you, my daughter and the gold is just secondary. It's because you have abilities that can rival their arch-enemy Bakunawa the Serpent-Goddess. With your powers, they have a chance to win the war between them and their lighter counterparts."

"But I won't join them, D-d-dad," she stuttered like she was unaccustomed to saying the word.

"We know, dear because you're a good girl. In the off-chance they kidnap you, they will siphon off your powers and transfer it to themselves, making them more powerful."

"What will happen now?"

"We wait. They don't realize we've become stronger with the inclusion of your father and the magic word that Jabber sent to us."

~O~

Rumpelstiltskin had decided to transform himself into a police officer since people would let cops enter their homes without asking questions. Once he gained their trust, he would bring them outdoors so his one-time partner in crime Esmeralda, would sneak in and open the hidden doors that needed to be opened.

He had resolved to do the deed early the next morning, which they wouldn't expect. He untied Esmeralda from the chair and tied her ankles and hands together so she could lie on the floor and sleep.

Early the next day, he arrived at the front door of Casa de la Noche and knocked. Ruby Rose answered the door and asked inquiringly what was the matter.

He said: "My name is Police Officer Dinklage. I have reason to believe you have my colleague Officer Collins held captive. Is that correct?"

"No sir, he's in the guest room still asleep. He's currently under assignment by the mayor to do surveillance work for us."

"I want to talk to the three madams right now! Especially the girl, who's still a witness in another crime."

"Sir please, you have to talk to Mayor Eddie. He went home and will be here shortly."

"What's all the commotion down there?" Said Angelica, coming down the stairs and followed by Lola Sabrina, and Pandora.

"Ma'am, can all of your come outside? I want to talk to you."

"Officer, what seems to be the problem?" Said Lola Sabrina.

"Let's talk in the veranda, where we can have some privacy," he said and turned around.

"Rumpelstiltskin. RUMPELSTILTSKIN!" Yelled Lola Sabrina.

"What did you sa…"

A small black hole began to form out of nowhere, becoming bigger and bigger. It was drawing the policeman in, who was Rumpelstiltskin in disguise. He tried to get hold of anything, but by pure misfortune, Pandora was closest to him. He grabbed her arm and pulled her along, into the dark hole of nothingness.

Both of them were sucked in. The hole became smaller and smaller, then disappeared. Everyone was shocked beyond belief, not because of witnessing the scientific impossibility of a black hole but of Pandora vanishing right in front of their eyes.

Volume II: Into the Realm of Batala

Chapter 34 The Griffin is No Family Guy

Batala is a place of beauty and wonder but also danger. It is an interdimensional world situated belowground in an immense cavernous chamber hollowed out of limestone. It is a realm where magical creatures and beings populate, congregate, and sometimes agitate one another.

It is a complete biosphere: with breathable air from natural exhaust vents on the cave ceiling leading above ground, heating and light sources from magically illuminating trees, lakes, and rivers providing water and residency for aquatic creatures. There are numerous vast floating plateaus in midair with livable surroundings. There are large plant farms cultivated for food and also for magical potion ingredients. There are also many human pens filled with abducted humans for slaughter.

Batala and its inhabitants were borne from the Filipinos' need to make sense of the unknown. The intense force of their superstitious beliefs brought forth this magical yet treacherous place where it is not even entirely safe for its inhabitants to dwell. It is the realm where magic is real, impossible acts are everyday occurrences, and the passage of time inexplicably deviates from one inhabitant to another.

Its first indwellers only knew love and peace and never once fought. In time, they visited the human world above ground and were influenced by their corrupt acts. Soon, everyone drank from the well poisoned by human corruption and became afflicted.

Before long, the division started among themselves that begot discord. A set of rules was soon imposed by its oldest living inhabitant: the egomaniacal *Dwende* known as Axe-Grinder. Many opposed those rules, which formed an opposition led by the often apathetic *Diwata* named Bakunawa, the Serpent Goddess.

Thus, a force field was magicked into existence by the two opposing leaders to separate their tribes from potential conflicts. Yet it never seemed to work, and problems always happened. The dark creatures were a troublesome and greedy lot who managed to find ways to inflict their special brand of torment on humans and supernatural beings alike.

And the forever war between the light and dark beings began.

~O~

Pandora woke up and found herself riding on top of a winged monster with the head of an eagle and the body of a lion. They were flying in some humongous cave, which she assumed was Batala, from all the stories told to her by her Lola Sabrina. The eagle-headed flying lion screeched in protracted fragmentary bursts like it was communicating with someone.

Where is it taking me? She thought aloud.

You will know when we arrive there, someone whispered to her, which she guessed was the flying creature responding to her telepathically.

Who are you, and where am I?

I am Peter, and you already know where.

Wait a minute. So, your name is Peter, Peter Griffin? Really? Hah!

Yes. Why is it funny? I am named after one of your greatest saints, St. Peter.

Don't bother. I guess you don't have Fox Channel down here. Where are we going?

You will soon see Pandora, granddaughter of the mighty Sabrina.

Do you know my Lola?

Yes. Everyone knows your grandmother. She was the best student of our goddess, Bakunawa, who taught her magical arts from the Book of Shadows.

Are we going to her?

No, someone else will meet us when we land.

Where?

Peter didn't respond anymore.

Pandora never thought how beautiful Batala was. When Lola told her stories about it, she only imagined a dark cave filled with terrible monsters. On the contrary, it was an awe-inspiring and beautiful place filled with magnificent creatures. There were many marvelous flying beasts in the air with them and equally splendid-looking creatures on the ground.

She also noticed something odd that pleasantly surprised her: various creatures with different skin pigmentations intermingled with each other and weren't fighting. She had only heard about the forever war between the dark and light beings, but by the looks of it, everyone was peacefully coexisting. *Wait. Is this place Batala?* She thought aloud.

Well, sort of. We are in a pocket universe where we all live in peace and harmony, far from conflict. There are fantastical creatures from other mythologies throughout your world, not exclusively from your own culture. You might even see the most extraordinary creature in any mythical setting: a dragon.

Oh. I'd love to see one.

They rarely venture out from their horde and like to keep to themselves, but sometimes, a dragon can be spotted alone.

I better not see Khaleesi riding in any of them or else I'll be jealous.

Khaleesi who? Please do not talk nonsense. If you continue this way, I will not respond.

I'm just trying to make a joke. And I see it's not landing. I guess you and your kind don't have a sense of humor.

We don't traffic in nonsense. One can easily get killed when conversing like that, so for your sake, do not attempt to be humorous to any inhabitant of this realm.

"The key to life is to lie to yourself about reality. Smile through everything. All the bad things, you just pile them away in a place that will come back one day in the form of rage."

What are you talking about?

I remember your namesake saying that in one episode.

You are an extraordinary but strange girl.

They flew silent for a few minutes. They soon approached a floating plateau, where a group of creatures gathered.

We are almost there. Look below.

Pandora looked down and saw several mythological creatures she recognized: a centaur, a unicorn, a manticore, a minotaur, and many more magnificent-looking beasts. She also noticed a creature her Lola particularly described in her stories as a *Kapre:* a hairy tree giant that smoked tobacco.

It was Jabber.

Is he the one I'm supposed to meet?

Yes. He is an old friend of your grandmother. He is the reason you are here.

You mean it's his fault that I'm taken away from my family?

We do not see it that way. We are about to land, so hold steady.

Peter Griffin landed amid the fantastical beings. She climbed down and was immediately approached by the Kapre. She said: "I know you. Are you Jabber?"

"Yes. I presume your grandmother told you about me?"

"Of course. She said you were good friends when she was younger. Why did you bring me here?"

"I would never bring you here if it wasn't important. Don't worry, we will return you to your family once you have helped us."

"I'm sure my parents and Lola are worried right now about what happened to me. A hole suddenly appeared out of nowhere and sucked me and a dwarf in. By the way, where is he?"

"He's back in his own realm, while you're here with us."

"But my family. Someone should tell them I'm okay and will be back home soon."

"I keep in frequent contact with your grandmother, through telepathy. I'll tell her later."

"Okay. What am I doing here?"

"You're the only one that can help us, and it's a matter of life and death."

"WHAT? Why me?"

Chapter 35 The Crystal Ball

Immediately after Pandora and Rumpelstiltskin, the dwarf disappeared, everyone was appalled, except for Lola Sabrina. She had seen this type of magic before, a teleportation spell activated by a magic word. The word itself was inconsequential, but if invoked close to a magical being of Rumpelstiltskin's magnitude, it can open a portal to another dimension.

Rumpelstiltskin was transported to the darkest corner of the enchanted kingdom of Batala: a prison institution where the worst elemental creatures were confined. There was no escape in this place, and he was trapped there forever.

Pandora was sent to the same magical dimension but a different place altogether: a world within a world populated by peace-loving elemental creatures throughout the mythologies of the world.

This pocket dimension was like a reward destination for beings who left a positive impact on humans. It was a Realm of Complete Happiness, a kind of heavenly afterlife for these creatures, where they could live out the remainder of their lives in complete bliss. However, the place was in a crisis of epic proportions due to the impending invasion of Lord Axe-Grinder and his dark army.

Axe-Grinder knew about this place but was certain he couldn't access it due to his many evil deeds. Yet he discovered a tiny loophole and could make it large enough for his army to enter. Instead of attacking the above-ground world of Gintongbayan, he pivoted completely and planned to invade this previously inaccessible place instead. He desperately wanted what it offered, which was utter contentment. There, he could finally rule in complete happiness, minus his unnatural lust for gold.

The creatures in the pocket universe knew how easily Pandora dispatched Axe-Grinder and his minions in the gymnasium and sent the rest running like cowards. They wanted her to do it again for their sake. Nevertheless, it wasn't a certainty since Pandora wasn't properly trained, which meant she had to go to Batala and be taught by Bakunawa, the Serpent-Goddess.

~O~

After Lola Sabrina explained to everyone what had happened to Pandora and assured them she was alright, they were still hesitant to believe it. They wanted proof, and to see her alive and well with their own eyes. Lola Sabrina remembered she had a magical item that could allow Angelica, Henry, and Ruby Rose to watch Pandora as if she were on TV: a crystal ball.

But she couldn't remember where exactly she put it. Her faulty old brain had struck again. It was either hidden in the house or left behind in Batala when she was younger. They needed someone with an extra-special talent to find lost things, and by pure chance, they saw Esmeralda on the surveillance monitor climbing the walls to the upstairs window on her way to steal the gold.

~O~

Esmeralda had woken up alone early in the morning and discovered her binds were untied. The dwarf had left presumably to Casa de la Noche to carry out his end of the deal. She breathed a sigh of relief. Any normal person in her situation would immediately leave Gintongbayan and go as far away as possible, but she was made of sterner stuff. She was still proceeding with the plan by any possible means.

She stood up, went to the faucet to wash the dried blood off her face, and put on her cat burglar attire. She picked up the small black knapsack filled with essential burglary tools and left her apartment.

She arrived at the Casa de la Noche gate. She peeked in and saw a small group walking towards the veranda, which was part of their initial plan for distraction. It was still minutes before the first light of dawn and still relatively dark out, which provided her with a favorable opportunity. She jimmied a hole in the welded mesh fence to let herself crawl in.

She pussyfooted towards the back area of the house and adeptly climbed a vertical metal downspout towards the upstairs window. She was about to open the windowsill and was face to face with Matteo, staring at her through the glass. He gazed at her blankly without any semblance of recognition, which confused and scared her tremendously.

He opened the window and grabbed her hand to pull her in. Once inside, he said: "I'm supposed to bring you to the dining room so they can talk to you."

"Matteo, what's going on?! Are we in trouble?"

"I-I-I don't know. Am I supposed to know you?"

"Of course! You mean you don't know me??"

"I think I've seen you before but don't remember. Have we met?"

"Yes. Yes! What's wrong with you?"

"I don't really know. When I woke up earlier, I couldn't remember what happened yesterday and the day before. When I thought about it, it seemed like I couldn't remember the last month of my life."

"It's about the same time we first met."

"We did?"

"We're talking in circles. I think we should go and see what your bosses want with me."

She followed Matteo as he walked downstairs to the dining room, where everyone—including Mayor Eddie, who had just arrived and was updated on the recent happenings—was waiting.

She could have easily escaped the house, but her curiosity was stronger. She wanted to know what the hell was going on and why Matteo, her pussy-whipped sex puppy, didn't recognize her.

They arrived, and Matteo exited, closing the door behind him. She looked at the people present, one by one: Lola Sabrina, Angelica, Ruby Rose, and Mayor Eddie. No one appeared to be especially angry at her, but the predominant expression on their faces was fear.

Afraid of what? She thought.

"Michelle, my supposed secretary. Your name isn't actually Michelle, right?" Said Mayor Eddie.

"No Mr. Mayor. It's Esmeralda."

"And you're a professional thief and scammer. Among all the places in the Philippines, why did you pick my town?"

"Because your town is particularly superstitious and still way behind the times compared to the other places with regards to technology. You didn't even do a background check on me and could've found out that I'm wanted by the police. By the way, are you going to turn me in?"

"No. Because we need your help."

"You need *my* help? What made you think I'm gonna say yes?"

"We're going to give you enough gold to make you rich then disappear to any place the police won't find you, perhaps in a non-extradition country."

"Tempting, but it will depend on what you're going to let me do."

"You're going to help us find a missing crystal ball."

Chapter 36 The Water Nix

"**N**ow you know why you should help us. Your previous tormentors the dark *Dwende* Axe-Grinder and his minions want to invade this peaceful place and rule over it. You've defeated them before and hopefully can do it again," said Jabber.

"What little information I know about dwarves is their lust for gold. Does this place have lots of it?" Said Pandora.

"No. The most precious commodity in this realm isn't any raw material, but its denizens, the various magnificent creatures inhabiting the myths and legends from the different cultures of your people. This place has a way of making its dwellers feel eternally joyful, and the dwarf yearns for it."

"I don't know if I can do it again."

"You can, you just need proper training."

"Who will train me?"

"The one that taught your Lola Sabrina: Serpent-Goddess Bakunawa. She's presently in Batala and Peter will take you to her."

"Do I have time for it? When will the dwarves make it here?"

"They will arrive in a week's time here. Yet time passes differently in every realm. You can train for a long time there while time goes on in a snail's pace here. Once you're done, only a few days has passed here. No more questions. Go now and may fortune be in your favor."

Peter Griffin approached, and Pandora rode on his wide backside. He flew away from the assemblage of majestic creatures towards the enchanted realm of Batala.

~O~

A tiny water nix was listening to the conversation between Pandora and Jabber, along with various creatures in the realm of complete happiness. She was unseen by the others due to her minuscule frame and could be almost invisible if she wanted to. She was the size of a hand and could easily fit herself on an adult human's palm.

She wasn't a dweller of the realm but merely an uninvited visitor originating from the underground lakes and rivers of Batala. She was there for one reason: to spy on Pandora.

After the conversation ended, she latched on to Peter's tail and held on tightly as they took flight. She was aware she chose a spot to attach herself near the anus, so she barely breathed, or else she might accidentally inhale poop-filled air particles.

They flew to grand heights that only winged beings could go. She saw majestic vistas and other marvelous flying creatures roaming in the air. She felt a reckless abandon she had never felt before, a kind of freedom she had longed for all her life. She almost forgot her spying chore, the main reason she was attached to the stinky tail of a griffin.

~O~

She was known as Nixie by her community of *Diwatas*, or water sprites, who resided in the various watercourses in Batala. Similar to many of the aquatic and semi-aquatic beings there, they were neutral to the conflict between the dark and light creatures. They preferred to keep to themselves and let the land-dwellers do the fighting.

But Nixie was different. She had an adventurous spirit and wanted to roam far and wide in all four corners of Batala, so one day, she decided to do it. She left the underground stream, which she had lived all her life, and began her adventurous trek.

Her lilliputian size was her advantage, and she could go anywhere and do anything without anyone noticing her. Her first foray into risky venture was into the dark side of Batala, where she had been told by her elders that was the one place she should never go. She was thirsty for adventure and disregarded all good judgments, thus entering the forbidden realm.

But her quest for adventure was immediately cut short: she was snatched up by someone with large and hairy arms. She formed into a ball while the creature held on to her with one dirty paw.

A few minutes later, she noticed the creature stopped walking. She unballed herself and stood up, facing the scourge of Batala, her Diwata elders had warned her about—the dark *Dwende* known as Axe-Grinder.

"What do you want with me?" Nixie frighteningly said.

"Do not be afraid little fairy, you are safe here."

"I'm no threat to you, I'm merely an adventurer wanting to explore your place."

"We aren't fond of visitors, especially creatures with your lighter-toned complexion. Didn't your elders warn you about us?"

"Yes, but I figured you wouldn't notice me because of my size."

"We see everything, even tiny sprites like you."

"Don't kill me, please. I'm not part of your forever war. Our Diwata community doesn't support either side of the conflict. I'll leave and never come back again."

"No, you can't, but I'm offering you something better, something I know you want. In return, you have to do something for us."

"What do I want?"

"Flight. You want to fly like your cousins the woodland fairies. Since you're a semi-aquatic water nix, you couldn't. Yet you wish for it so much that you're willing to go against the warnings of your elders. I could give that to you."

"I don't know. What will you want me to do?"

"Since you can access difficult to enter places and can seldom be seen, you can get in to this hidden realm where not one of my kind could enter. Once inside, then observe any the important occurrences there and report back on what you find. In other words, be a spy for us."

"Once I've done all of it, then you can make me fly?"

"Yes."

"How can I get into this secret realm?"

~O~

Are we almost there? Pandora whispered telepathically.

Not yet, but we're close, replied Peter Griffin. *Once you see a large enough portal located in a cave ceiling, then we're close. Then we're going to fly through it to enter Batala. This entryway is a secret, so don't tell anyone.*

Okay. Will you remain with me after we land?

Of course. I'll be with you for the duration of your training.

Tell me, Peter: do I have a reason to worry or be scared? I've never been on my own or even ventured this far from home.

Truthfully, there is danger everywhere. However, we would never leave you and always protect you, wherever you go.

Thank you, Peter, that's good to know. And one more thing...

What is it?

When you get home, please say hi to Stewie for me. He's my favorite character in Family Guy.

Here we go again...

Chapter 37 The Glass Coffin

Since Andreas was a ghost and merely a temporary visitor in the real world, his astral body fluctuated constantly between two different levels of existence. One minute, he was among humans, the next in a mirror dimension on the astral plane. He was often confused by it and would sometimes mistake one for the other.

He was still in Casa de la Noche, but he wasn't sure if it was the real house with actual people he had grown to care for or a creepy reproduction populated by ghosts like him. He soon found out it was the latter because of the appearance of a terrifying-looking ghost with maggots coming out of its eyes on a decomposing face. It was roaming in the house, along with other horrible spirits.

He also saw a raven perched on the ceiling rafter—the same one he could talk to that had promised to accompany him to the afterlife.

He asked the blackbird: "Are you finally taking me to paradise?"

"Not yet. You still have unfinished business," the bird responded.

"I've given as much aid I could muster to the people living in this house. What more can I do?"

"Your ghostly business is linked to the girl, who's now missing. She's asleep in a glass coffin, waiting for his Prince Charming to give her the kiss of life, which is you."

"She is? I am?"

"Yes, in a manner of speaking. You have to help her return back home safely to her family. And then, Prince Andreas, you can finally cross over."

"How am I able to help? I can't even stay in one plane for a long time."

"You have other ghostly powers, remember? Your spirit form can be in two places at once and you can communicate telepathically to people. You can also travel to different planes of existence, and the girl is in one of them."

"But how will I find her?"

"The grandmother. Offer her your help in locating the missing item and any more after that. Go back to the real world and find her."

"I don't know how."

"Concentrate and think about your ultimate purpose in finding girl. If you end up back here then refocus on the girl again."

"Okay, I'll try."

"I'll try to be with you and help you whenever I can. Good luck," said the raven, and flew towards an open window and vanished.

Andreas concentrated intently, and the mirror dimension changed to the real world. It was like the light of the whole world was suddenly switched on. The roaming spirits had vanished, replaced by actual household helpers in Casa de la Noche.

He had to find Lola Sabrina and offer his help.

~O~

After everything that had happened, Angelica had mixed emotions. On the one hand, she was glad that her long-lost husband-to-be Henry, was miraculously back home after years of thinking he was dead. On the other hand, she was bewildered that her daughter had disappeared in front of her to an unknown place, not part of the real world. The family curse had struck again.

And she noticed another emotion rearing its ugly head at the worst time possible: horniness. She hadn't had sex for many years and had lost interest in the act itself, but Henry's sudden appearance brought about long-gestating feelings of sexual arousal. She could feel blood rushing to her groin and making her feel light-headed.

She looked at Henry's wild-looking appearance after many years in captivity in Batala. Any other person might be repelled, but she was turned on instead. She felt a hunger that needed to be satiated immediately.

She went to him, took him by the hand, and led him to her bedroom. The others were too preoccupied to notice they were gone.

She had told Henry to take a bath earlier. He had worn clean clothes, but his hair and beard were still uncut and unshaven. She caressed his thick beard and gently pushed him towards the bed, where he landed on the soft cushion. She unzipped his pants and pulled it off his legs. Henry wasn't wearing underwear, and his member was already standing at attention as if anticipating incoming action.

Angelica stripped down naked and slowly and tentatively bent down on all fours, like a tigress ready to attack. She settled herself on his penis and gasped. She felt a slight tear within her vaginal wall but felt great instantly. She straddled him like she was riding on horseback, mimicking the slow, rhythmic trotting of a horse getting steadily faster. From what she remembered about Henry, it will only take a few minutes for the ride to be over.

And it was done in less than a minute. Both of them climaxed at the same time, and it felt like all pent-up emotions had formed into a cannonball being shot out of her. She screamed in pure orgasmic release.

"Thank you. I needed this," she said and lay down beside him.

"I was surprised earlier and didn't know what was going on when you brought me here. I missed this," said Henry.

"Me too. Do you know I became an alcoholic after you died? I was so depressed that I started drinking and did it every night until I was hammered."

"Oh. I'm sorry."

"Don't be. It's not your fault. Well, maybe to some extent. But it was the only way I thought I could cope."

"What made you stop?"

"You still don't know the whole story. Our daughter was attacked by your captors and almost kidnapped but she was able to fight them off. After that happened, I promised myself to change and be a good mother to her, so I stopped drinking."

"You made an effort to change. Good for you."

"Our daughter deserved it. She needs a normal mother and finally, a father that loves and cares for her."

"*Our daughter.* It still feels weird saying it. She needed a father and I wasn't here. Sorry."

"Stop apologizing. It wasn't your fault you were abducted. We can still find our missing princess, don't worry."

"I hope so. We need some catching up to do. Do you call her princess?"

"When she was little. She used to play make-believe and imagine herself as a fairytale princess, like Snow-White. Maybe she needs an actual Prince Charming to rescue her or to wake her from an enchanted sleep."

"Or maybe she just needs her family to find her."

"Yes. We should."

Chapter 38 The Two Brothers Return

The grim-looking brothers Jacob and Wilhelm were held in the same prison camp of abducted humans as Henry, within the darker side of Batala. However, they didn't interact due to its immense size, and the captives were inclined to keep to themselves.

The two brothers were only two years apart, and due to the unusual effects of Batala's inconsistent time duration on humans, Jacob didn't seem to age at all, while Wilhem aged tremendously. The younger brother now looked like the grandfather of the older brother.

However, Wilhelm was still spry for an older-looking man and wasn't helpless. On the contrary, his mind was still like a steel trap and often did the thinking and decision-making for both. He was also the more courageous of the two, and it was unfortunate that his body was aging rapidly compared to his brother.

There were many human encampments in the dark realm of Batala, but theirs were the largest, filled with all sorts of humans ranging from children to old people, men and women alike. They had makeshift huts made from bamboo and nipa, potable water, and gruel given to them twice a day. Terrible-looking creatures served as guards outside the fences, which kept constant watch.

There was no chance of escape, and those who did were smuggled out by the monsters themselves. Wilhelm witnessed something like this happen recently and wondered every day since how it was done: a *Kapre* or a tree giant had smuggled out a human by hiding him within the folds of his clothing.

Was the human friends with the creature? He thought. He couldn't imagine one of those monsters befriending either of them since they only thought of humans as meat for the slaughter. He also noticed the giant wasn't like the other dark-skinned creatures: his complexion was artificially blackened by mud that further confounded him.

He could only assume the mud-caked monster wasn't supposed to be there and had gone as a pretense to smuggle out the human because they were previous acquaintances. If it was the only way to escape, then they had to find a monster foolish enough to make friends with him.

He considered the creatures guarding them. There were two: one was stationed at the front gate, the other at the back gate. The front gate guard was a *Lobo* or a gigantic feral dog, and the one guarding the back was a *Lakivot* or a huge talking civet. The Lobo looked wild and menacing, while the Lakivot didn't. On the contrary, it looked like a large kitty cat malleable enough to be influenced. And by happy chance, it was able to hold a conversation with a human similar to him.

Wilhelm began saving some of his food, then giving it to the Lakivot when opportunities presented themselves. He was building rapport with it, which soon led to a casual friendship. He introduced Jacob to the talking cat but balked because he was too freaked out by it.

He also learned that some *Dwende* festival was approaching, and when this event occurred, many humans were butchered for food. And so, Wilhelm decided if they were to escape, it had to be in the immediate future, with the Lakivot abetting them.

Slowly but surely, he gained the Lakivot's trust. He found out he was part of a family of peaceful giant talking civets but was forced by Axe-Grinder and his minions to be part of their army. If they declined, they would be killed, so they had no choice but to join.

Due to their immense size and propensity for ferocity, each of their family members was dispatched to various flashpoints in Batala, where potential trouble might occur. It was assigned to their encampment, where it had remained for a while.

He found out it was lonely and missed its family. It was still a youngling and yearned for its mother. Wilhelm told it that since their situation was similar and held against their will, they had to help each other escape.

The Lakivot became silent and thought for a long time. Then it nodded its head in agreement, and Wilhelm secretly sighed with relief.

~O~

Bakunawa, the Serpent-Goddess, wasn't available when they landed in the light side of Batala. When Pandora inquired about her whereabouts, everyone didn't know. It was part of her mystique to be missing for long periods, and they were used to it.

Where is she, and what am I supposed to do? She thought. Since time was crucial, she had to do something.

She decided to go inside Bakunawa's strangely-shaped domicile. It had no conventional door, so she crawled inside a narrow hole, which she assumed could fit a python or a slim teenage girl like her. Once inside, she inspected the surroundings, looking for anything and nothing in particular.

One thing caught her attention: a large leatherbound book with an embossed three-pronged star in front. It was the fabled *Book of Shadows* that Lola Sabrina mentioned in one of her stories. It was the book in which Lola had learned all her magical powers if she remembered them on occasion.

She leafed through the book and noticed it was written in a language she couldn't understand. It also had many illustrations and drawings that she assumed referred to particular magical rituals and incantations. Then she browsed upon a drawing of two men riding a giant spotted cat, leading a herd of animals. She didn't know what it meant, but she felt it was important. She made a mental note of the page number and promised to get back to it later.

In the meantime, since Bakunawa wasn't there yet, she had to do something constructive, thus deciding to see the entire terrain of Batala for herself, along with its magnificent-looking inhabitants, and find out if all the stories Lola Sabrina told her were true.

Chapter 39 The Water of Life

Nixie, the water sprite, had followed Pandora everywhere, with nobody seeing her. She had a way of making herself almost unseen due to her minuscule size. Peter Griffin had a saddle on his back with a saddlebag attached, which made a viable hiding place for her.

She could peek out and view the many places they traveled to in the light side of Batala. Its vast underground caverns had many wondrous sights to behold: the flaming trees, floating plateaus, underground watercourses, and cultivated farmlands. But it was the magnificent-looking residents that impressed her the most. Seeing them in front of her eyes felt more exhilarating than swimming in the underground lake that she called home.

While the *Sirenas*, *Siyokoys*, and numerous merfolk looked splendid in their fins and scales, they couldn't compare to the land-based creatures—some of them human/animal hybrids—that imbued a different kind of gravitas that aquatic and semi-aquatic beings and like her didn't have. Maybe it had to do with walking on the ground using their hind legs that did the trick. Swimming didn't have the same effect and looked cumbersome at times.

And flight. Flying, for her, looked cooler than swimming and walking combined, which was one of the reasons she yearned for it so much. Exploring and going on adventures would be easier and less cumbersome. She could cover more distance and go to many places in a day, compared to hiking.

Her resident lake had the most diverse beings in the Batala, ruled by the *Bacobaco*, the great sea turtle who, legend has it, caused Mt. Pinatubo to erupt. Its most terrifying resident was the *Nanreben:* a sea serpent, who had shining eyes like torches, horns like a water buffalo, long tusks and teeth, and tough scales throughout its body.

Her home lake had one feature that the other underground waterways didn't have: the Fountain of Life. It was a natural outflow of water in the middle of the lake that, if consumed, gave the drinker eternal life and enlightenment. Most of the creatures living in the light side of Batala drank from the fountain at one point in their lives, thus affording them the necessary fortitude to combat Batala's peculiar time duration, which made them nearly ageless.

After the conflict between the light and dark beings began, no one from Lord Axe-Grinder's army had access to the life-giving fountain anymore, which further degraded them in mind, body, and spirit. Most regressed to become the dark and terrible monsters of Batala that the other peaceful beings feared.

Hence, the Fountain of Life was fiercely protected by the Nanreben, and only those who were given special permission by Bacobaco himself were the only way to consume it.

Before Nixie had left her home lake to go on an adventure, she stole a whole flask full of the Water of Life, which she had brought with her in a tiny backpack. She knew she'd need it later and use it at the most suitable time.

~O~

Andreas saw the whole Ponce de Leon family in distress. They were in a group huddle in the dining room, along with Mayor Eddie, Ruby Rose, and Esmeralda, which surprised and confounded him. She was talking to them like she was an integral part of the group, and everyone was intently listening to her. He didn't know what had transpired that changed their opinion of her.

He concentrated on altering his spectral aura to blue to let himself be seen. The nearest person to him was Ruby Rose, who yelled in surprise after seeing his light-blue ghostly form.

He tried to speak, but no words came out of his mouth. He had forgotten that the only way for an apparition like him to be understood was through telepathy and thought: *Can any of you hear me?*

Yes, I can.

Who among you is talking to me?

It's me, Lola Sabrina. I can hear you. Why do you want to speak to us?

I want to help in finding Pandora. I can go to places that no mortal man could.

Yes, of course. Our immediate concern is finding a missing object: a crystal ball. You will partner with Esmeralda, who has expertise in finding lost things.

Do you trust her? She was planning to steal from you, you know.

Things have changed, and she's with us now. I trust in her abilities to get the job done.

If you say so, but can she hear me?

No. You'll have to find another way to communicate with her. To Esmeralda: "Don't be scared of the ghost boy. He was friends with Pandora when he was still alive and he wants to help. You can use him in going to places you could never go."

"First things first. Is he dangerous?" Said Esmeralda.

"No, he's not. I admit, there are other malevolent spirits out here that can be a danger to people, but Andreas was a good boy when he was alive and still a good boy after he died. He has unfinished business in this mortal realm and he can only cross over once his business is fulfilled."

"What's his unfinished business?"

"Helping Pandora get back to us safe and sound."

Andreas nodded and made the shape of a heart with both hands.

Good work, Andreas. That's a great way to communicate with people. Simple sign language does the trick.

"Is the ghost saying he loves her?" Said Henry.

"Yes. At one point they were boyfriend and girlfriend. Then they broke up after he died." Said Angelica.

We never broke up.

"I don't think they broke up," said Ruby Rose.

"Sure they did. When a person dies in a relationship, the living one is forced to discontinue the relation. Am I right, Mr. Mayor?"

"I think we veered off topic."

"And Angelica, when you thought I died, you have every right to go into a relationship again. Why didn't you?"

"Mayor Eddie was right, we should get back to the issue of our lost daughter," Angelica replied.

"Be that as it may, it is still an important topic to discuss. Perhaps another time Henry."

"Okay," Henry said sullenly.

"Alright. About the crystal ball. The last thing I remembered seeing it was in one of the underground rooms in this house, but I forgot which one."

"Yes, I've been wondering about that Lola Sabrina. Why did Don Marcus had those rooms built? For what purpose?"

"Esmeralda might know. She even made copies of the keys."

Esmeralda took a set of keys from her pants pocket and dropped it on the table before everyone. She said: "Here they are. I wasn't able to use them since you found out about me."

"Wait. It gives me an idea. Ruby Rose, please get the original keys hanging on a hook in Angelica's bedroom," said Lola Sabrina. "And to answer the question: I don't know. My grandfather, Don Marcus was a secretive man. There are some underground rooms we use for storage purposes, but for the other rooms, I have no idea.

Among the set of keys, there is a skeleton key made of gold that can open all the underground doorways, and we will use it to find the crystal ball."

"Finally! Some progress," exclaimed Henry.

"When Ruby Rose returns, Esmeralda will use it to open each underground room and find the crystal ball. Well, except for the one under the ballroom."

"What's in the ballroom?" Asked Henry.

"Shhh! I'll tell you later," whispered Angelica.

"For the rest of us remaining, how can we help?" Said Mayor Eddie.

"For now, nothing. But for me, I have to rest. I need a clear head to locate my granddaughter. Wake me up when the crystal ball is found."

"Yes Lola," said everyone in unison.

And Andreas, since you can pass through solid objects, please go through every underground room to look for the crystal ball. Once you find it, tell Esmeralda.

Yes, Lola.

Andreas dimmed his blue light and vanished. However, he was still there but merely invisible to human eyes. He passed through the dining room wall and went to the cellar, where the first underground room was located.

Chapter 40 The Beam

Pandora felt a cold draft of air wafting over her as they flew to the highest point of Batala. She thought: *I'm freezing. Do you have a coat I can wear in your saddlebag?*

Yes. Grab it right by your knees. I think you will recognize it, replied Peter.

She rifled through the bag and pulled the first one that felt like clothing material. It was the bright red hooded cloak Lola Sabrina had sewn for her when she was younger. She put it on, and it still fit.

Do you remember when you were little and unknowingly ventured into this realm?

Just bits and pieces. It's like a bad memory that my brain wants to erase.

The dark creatures got hold of you and tried to paint you with their black mud in hopes of changing you to be like them. But someone rescued you and returned you safely to your mother.

Who did?

Jabber the Kapre. He's been looking out for your family since he met your grandmother. To some extent, you are indebted to him. Do you understand?

Yes. I have to help him. I mean all of you.

And that coat you left behind here. Jabber found it, cleaned and hid it for safekeeping in case you returned, which you did.

Where are we going?

We are going to the highest point in Batala, where the Yeti lives.

Do you mean Bigfoot?

Or the Abominable Snowman. He lives on a snowy plateau all alone. He used to live in the Realm of Complete Happiness but was cast out.

Why?

That place is supposed to make its inhabitants feel contented, but for some reason didn't work for him. It made him feel sad instead, so he was banished. They didn't want his sadness to infect the realm. We have to find out why he felt that way, and the realm did nothing to change it. Maybe we could use it in our fight against Axe-Grinder and his army, or rather, we can ask him to join us. He's a formidable creature that can be useful to us. I see a safe place to land. Hold on.

A light snow was falling on the plateau. They landed on a wide enough spot beside a frozen pond where they could see a cave entrance just a short distance away, with a faint light glowing inside.

In that small cave is the Yeti.

Is he dangerous?

No. He is the friendliest creature you will ever know. But he suffers from depression from time to time.

What's his story?

We'll ask him ourselves. Come on.

They moseyed towards the cave entrance. There was a makeshift door made of pine that fit the entire opening. Peter screeched loudly, and a steady thumping sound of someone with heavy footing approached them from the inside. The door opened.

Pandora saw a huge gorilla-like man with white fur all over his body. Peter screeched again, which sounded like an eagle's peal call to express greetings. The Abominable Snowman responded by growling friendlily.

Can he talk?

Yes, but only in his Yeti language, which I can fortunately comprehend. Please tell me if you want to ask him anything, and I'll translate.

The Yeti growled again.

He wants us to come inside so he can close the door.

There was a fireplace inside the cave, along with scant furniture. Once they settled, Pandora thought: *Peter, ask him about his state of mind. Is he sad or happy?*

Peter screeched, and the Yeti growled back.

Your screeches and growls all sound the same.

There are subtle differences, if you can notice. That's how our language works.

What did he say?

He said for the moment, he's happy. There's a cozy fire inside with a visit of a good friend: me.

So, what's his story?

Peter screeched, and the Yeti responded…

~O~

I was meant to live in the human world. I was born in a forest in the Rocky Mountains along the Pacific Northwest. We had a Sasquatch community with many members, with my mother, father, and three siblings.

At that time, we lived in a virgin forest, untouched by anyone but us and other animals. We lived in harmony with the elements, and peace reigned.

Soon, Man arrived at our home and ruined our way of living. Many trees were cut down for timber, and our land was slowly encroached, so we had to leave. Our kind scattered throughout the Earth. My family and I went to the Himalayan Mountain Range to make a home of our own.

My mother and father weren't used to the cold weather, but we three younglings soon adapted. Our pelts turned white. However, our parents couldn't adjust to the frigid atmosphere and soon died.

My brother and sister didn't want to stay in the Himalayas because of the sad memories and longed to return to the Rocky Mountains of their birth. They soon left, leaving me all alone.

Before long, I realized my kind was meant to be alone. Even as a family unit, we were still solitary creatures and always went hunting and foraging on our lonesome. Thus, I stayed within the Himalayan Range and on occasion, met some curious and surprised humans along the way.

Then, one day, I chanced on a human female and her Sherpa guide on a precarious trek to Mt. Everest. The Sherpas knew of my existence and greeted me congenially, but the female was, at first, taken aback. Once the Sherpa explained that I was well-disposed and had no intention of harming them, she assented and became friendly.

I was curious and followed them. I never understood why humans wanted to climb Mt. Everest since many people had died attempting to reach its peak. Their bodies are particularly ill-equipped to reach these heights. They don't even have fur all over their bodies, and their clothes scarcely protect them.

However, some of them have an iron will that allows them to do the impossible, similar to this woman I followed. No matter how cold and harsh the weather was, she still trudged on until she reached the top.

I marveled at this woman and her capability to do the inconceivable that other humans like her couldn't. It renewed my outlook on human beings, and some of them can be amazing and worth our time.

So, for the rest of my life, I ventured to be helpful and friendly towards humans who trekked the Himalayan Tundra. I sometimes saved them from snowstorm-related mishaps and brought them to safety. If they got lost, I showed them the right path. I soon became somewhat of a legend for a while, until it was my turn to figure in an accident and depart that life.

But I wasn't dead. Instead, I was transported to the Realm of Complete Happiness. I met all sorts of friendly creatures who treated me like family. I thought I would be happy to be among them, but regrettably, I didn't. I became sad, and I can't explain why. Maybe I just missed my old life back in the Himalayas.

So, I was cast off to this realm that truthfully, is relatively better. I get to be alone most of the time and be sometimes visited by some good friends like Peter.

~O~

Please ask him if he is happy here. If he says no, tell him if he wants to join us, Pandora thought.

After a few growls and screeches later, Peter replied: *He said yes, and he will come with us.*

But is he happy here?

The Yeti beamed but nodded his head.

He said only fools can be completely happy. Being sad sometimes isn't a bad thing, and in fact, it enabled him to feel empathy for others.

Wow. I didn't know Bigfoots can be so deep.

You can learn a lot of things from him.

Tell him to pack his stuff, and you will return for him tomorrow. For now, we have to go.

Where do you want to go?

Coming here gave me an idea. We have to find other creatures with fantastic abilities to recruit.

Chapter 41 Mayor Eddie, the Skillful Huntsman

Mayor Eddie wanted to return to his job as the head of the local government in Gintongbayan. He thought he had given all the help and advice he could contribute to the perpetually troubled Ponce de Leon clan. However, it made him rethink everything that had transpired.

Learning about all the supernatural and magical stuff happening in his town brought a well-deserved shock to his senses. He was, first and foremost, a realist and had never concerned himself with any news about it since he wasn't a believer like many of his constituents. Yet discovering the truth didn't change his steadfastness of being the town leader. Instead, it made him more fearful because it had an unknown and unpredictable element he never cared to learn about.

He was afraid of the implications and effects that the supernatural events brought on everyone he knew and loved. Would all this turn his town into a hellscape where mythological creatures reside and torment the citizens? It might happen and have scared the shit out of him.

Then it hit him. The only thing he could do with his capacity was to go straight to the source and cease any possible attacks happening to his beloved town. He would use his skill as an experienced hunter and stop it before it overwhelmed his beloved Gintongbayan.

~O~

His adept hunting ability came from his father, who used to hunt wild game in the mountains of Gintongbayan. He joined him on many hunting trips throughout his prepubescent and teenage years. He learned the intricacies of hunting with a rifle and became a marksman and expert tracker.

Many wild animals like wild boar, deer, and duck were present during his youth and were allowed to be hunted by the Philippine government. However, new laws were soon passed that made hunting with a rifle illegal, so he had no choice but to stop. He went on learning about other more useful things like governance and political science, which consequentially made him a dependable town mayor.

Nevertheless, his hunting proficiency was still present and never forgotten and became necessary, as he discovered later.

~O~

A plan was formulated in his head, and he wanted to talk to everyone present. His erstwhile secretary Esmeralda hadn't arrived yet from her crystal ball-locating task, Lola Sabrina was upstairs resting, and Henry and Angelica were nowhere to be found. Only Ruby Rose was there, looking like she was on the verge of sobbing.

He sat down and pondered about the plan and waited patiently for the others to arrive.

Hours passed, and Lola Sabrina, Angelica, and Henry showed up successively. Then lastly, Esmeralda arrived, with a crystal ball in her hands, which was the size of a basketball. The blue ghost also appeared out of nowhere, which slightly irked him.

He watched as Lola Sabrina murmured something incomprehensible to the crystal ball, and its murky coloration began to alter. It looked like fuzzy lines on a TV screen at first, slowly becoming clearer and brighter. A human figure suddenly appeared, which looked like Pandora. They looked for any indications it was her, and Lola pointed out the red hooded cloak she wore that she especially made for her.

Everyone rejoiced, and Ruby Rose cheered the loudest.

They saw Pandora was unharmed but doing something almost inconceivable: it looked like she was in deep conversation with two mythological creatures in a snowy valley. Lola Sabrina said that Pandora was in Batala, in a particular location she knew about.

Then, everyone began talking simultaneously, but only Mayor Eddie remained silent. He was still thinking about the plan and was willing to wait for everyone to talk themselves out. It was clear that they truly cared about Pandora and wanted to bring her back home safely.

Lola Sabrina said she was contacted through telepathy by someone she knew from her past. Pandora had to remain there for the time being to help the creatures in a particular predicament. Once it was resolved, she would be returned home.

Everyone became silent and looked uncertain. It was the opportune time for Mayor Eddie to tell his plan. He said: "Listen, everyone. I know you are all worried about Pandora and want her home. But after what Lola told us, she couldn't come here yet.

I'm proposing something we could do to make sure she will get home safely and also help our town become safer. Some of us, including myself, will go to this enchanted kingdom underground, help my goddaughter Pandora with her dilemma, and bring her home. Then, we will destroy any entrances and doorways linking both our worlds, so no more residents from Gintongbayan will ever be abducted or assaulted by the beasts in that realm. I have a responsibility as mayor in this town to keep the people safe, and I'm willing to do everything in my power to accomplish it."

Everyone nodded in agreement, but Lola Sabina didn't and became pensive instead. She said: "Destroying those portals won't stop them from coming. Remember, these are magical creatures, and some have the power to teleport themselves from one place to another. But please, do go on."

Mayor Eddie continued: "Who will join me? I know Esmeralda will come since she's motivated by money and will be adequately compensated. The ghost boy too because he has to. My other goddaughter Ruby Rose shouldn't come because she's still young and will remain here to care for Lola Sabrina. And I want Henry and Angelica to come as well. Does everyone agree?"

Everyone nodded except Lola Sabrina.

"Lola, is something wrong?" Mayor Eddie said inquisitively. He was worried that Lola Sabrina didn't seem to concur with his plan, and made him unsure. She was the person he needed to agree with him for the plan to reach fruition.

Instead of responding, Lola Sabrina stood up and exited the dining room.

"What's wrong? Is she okay?"

Everyone had blank looks on their faces. Mayor Eddie stood up and was about to follow Lola Sabrina outside but was stopped by Angelica. She shook her head and beckoned him to sit.

He did. He still had many questions to ask Lola Sabrina and resolved to wait for her return. She just needed time to take everything in.

Chapter 42 Going a-Travelling with the Gang

The time has arrived for the two brothers, Jacob and Wilhelm, to escape. Wilhelm had convinced the *Lakivot* to aid them in this precarious venture that, if discovered, might make them an early meal for their abductors before the festivities even started. It was now or never.

Feeding time was the best time to escape. While everyone was eating the mandatory slop, Jacob and Wilhelm climbed on the back of the giant civet, lay face down, and hid themselves in its thick fur. They held on tight as the Lakivot made its usual rounds for the last time during the day.

Once done, the giant civet went outside the enclosure and positioned himself in its usual spot at the back entrance. He waited for the other guard, the *Lobo*, to return to its place in front. When no one was looking, it quietly backed away towards the light side of Batala.

Soon, they were free and clear from any possible danger, and Jacob and Wilhelm sat upright. They were overjoyed and hugged each other. Wilhelm asked the Lakivot if it was all right, and it nodded.

They had agreed to take them to the pathway leading to the giant termite mound above ground, which was the doorway going to the human world. After that, the Lakivot would look for its remaining family of talking civets and try to rebuild their lives.

By pure coincidence, they came upon Pandora, Peter, and Bigfoot, traveling the same footpath in the opposite direction. They marveled at each other's appearances and stopped at the same crossway. Bigfoot was the most friendly and initiated conversation among them.

The talking civet was overjoyed by its newfound freedom. It eagerly replied to Bigfoot's questions. It said: "I'm so happy to meet all four of you. It's been a while since I'm able to talk to anyone freely without being reprimanded."

"That's great. But wait a minute. What do you mean 'all four or you?' There's only three of us: me, Peter and Pandora," said Bigfoot.

"I can smell her. There's a little fairy with you inside the saddlebag."

Peter was surprised about the revelation and grabbed the saddlebag behind him with his beak. Everyone heard a faint yelp from inside the bag as it was thrown onto the ground. Nixie peeked his head out and saw everyone's face looking at her inquiringly. She searched their faces, trying to gauge if they had a malicious bone in their bodies. They seemed to have a friendly disposition, which lowered her guard.

"What are you doing here, little fairy? Are you hiding?" Bigfoot said.

"Yes, and I'm sorry. I didn't want to bother anyone. I'm just a traveler hitching a ride."

"Why didn't you tell us? We would've let you ride along. What we don't appreciate is you sneaking around, listening to our conversations in secret."

This fairy is a spy, Peter thought.

How do you know? Maybe she's telling the truth, and perhaps only a hitchhiker, Pandora replied.

I don't believe her. She's hiding something.

"I should have told you, and I'm truly sorry. We *Diwatas* of the Lake are peaceful and non-confrontational creatures. We prefer not to be a nuisance to others, especially with beings bigger than us, so we tend to travel hidden from general view."

She looks harmless.

I don't trust her. If she's going to travel with us, I'm keeping tabs on her.

"Where do you come from, little sprite?"

"I reside in the Water of Life. Do you know about it?"

"We all do. Well, except the humans."

"What's the Water of Life?" Pandora asked.

"It's a magical lake where the Fountain of Life is located. Those who drink from it are granted enlightenment and eternal life."

"Lola Sabrina never told me about it."

"It's because it is kept a secret to humans. Only beings like us know about it and have drunk from it."

"Have any human tried consuming it? But what I really asking is: can I drink it?" Wilhelm said.

"To my knowledge, no. I don't know what effect it could give to a human being's body and it might not be safe for you. Us magical beings are made of sterner stuff, unlike you that are merely composed from blood and bone."

"As you can see, I may need it. Every day I spend in this place I age one year but my brother doesn't seem to age at all. Can any of you explain this to me?"

"No one knows why time passes differently for each person here in Batala. Bakunawa the Serpent-Goddess is one of the oldest beings here and might know the reason. We will ask her when she reappears from whence she traveled."

"Little Sprite, do you want to join us in our travels?"

"I will, if everyone is fine with it."

I'm not.

It's going to be alright, Peter. She's just a teensy thing. What harm can she do to us?

You're still young and too trustful. When you grow older, you will learn that some people have ulterior motives and lie. When she's around, promise me you will keep your guard up.

Alright, I promise.

"Can we join in your travels? I'm intrigued about this Water of Life and want to learn more about it," said Wilhelm.

"Sure. There's safety in numbers. This way, we can accomplish our goals quicker."

"What goals?"

"We are looking for beings with special abilities that are willing to join us in our fight against Axe-Grinder and his dark army."

"We will help you. The Lakivot and his family will want to join since they were also aggrieved by Axe-Grinder."

"Yes. I can get them later and bring them to us," the Lakivot said.

"By the way, where are we going?" Wilhelm asked.

"If we are going into war, we need the most powerful creature in the whole realm of Batala to come with us," said Bigfoot.

"Do you know of someone?"

"No not someone. Some*thing*. We will need a dragon."

"A dragon?!" Everyone uttered in amazement.

"Yes, a dragon. Similar to me, this creature used to reside in the Realm of Complete Happiness and like me, it was also exiled into this realm."

"What did it do?"

"It's not what he did but what he won't do. This dragon is a complete coward and doesn't want to get into any kind of conflict."

"Then it would be useless to come with us if it wouldn't fight."

"We just have to convince it to come with us. You've convinced me to join, we'll have to do the same to the dragon."

"Yes, a mighty dragon will really make a difference."

"Where can we find this dragon?"

Chapter 43 Sharing Joy and Sorrow

Lola Sabrina sometimes felt overwhelmed by the bombardment of ceaseless information that her faulty old brain couldn't process everything coming in. She had to find a quiet place in the house to relax and resettle her thoughts so all the vital data would be stashed away properly in the storage facility of her mind and brought up when necessary.

She went to Pandora's favorite secluded spot under the Juniper tree, which had been converted to an outdoor picnic shed, complete with a wooden table and chairs. She sat down and exhaled deeply.

She tried to connect telepathically to Jabber to inquire about Pandora's condition, but she couldn't seem to do it. She needed to clear her mind and loosen up for the entire exercise to work, so she made herself comfortable on the chair and closed her eyes.

She willed herself to relax and lowered her heart rate. After reaching the optimum state where her mind and body were one, she whispered: *Jabber, are you there?*

Still no response. She took a deep breath, then exhaled and reiterated the question.

Yes, I'm here.

Thank goodness. For a moment, I thought I'd lost my telepathic ability. Getting old is difficult sometimes. How's everything there? Is Pandora with you?

No, she isn't, but she's safe. She's with a tremendously capable creature who acts as her protector and means of transport. She's on their way to Bakunawa to be taught the same things you've learned when you were here before.

But will she be safe for the entire time there? She's still a teenager and, with her condition, quite sensitive to the elements.

Don't worry, Sabrina, I'll make sure nothing happens to her. She merely needs to be instructed on the vital teachings from the Book of Shadows, which will truly help our cause.

Alright. I trust you, Jabber.

I will keep in touch. DO NOT WORRY. Goodbye.

'Bye...

The connection suddenly dropped off on Jabber's end, which slightly miffed Lola Sabrina. She *did* trust him, but he was stubborn sometimes, which irked her so. She also didn't like being suddenly forced into a situation without asking her permission first. She knew about the dangers in Batala, and Pandora was in a risky position she shouldn't be in. It wasn't her fight, and she should never have been involved.

But she did owe him a favor in return for all the help he did throughout the years, and something like this was bound to happen. She inhaled and exhaled deeply again as if expelling the troubles currently plaguing her and, in a fleeting moment, worked. Her sorrow was temporarily extinguished.

She stood up and returned to the house, where everyone was waiting.

~O~

The dragon lived alone on a small flying plateau atop a grand waterfall. It was big enough to carry its mammoth frame and had sufficient space to walk around. The dragon liked living in it because the flat tableland afforded the necessary outlet to hide itself from everyone.

It was a fearful and timid creature, very much unlike its siblings, who were courageous and powerful. It was the runt of the litter and was used to being the last for everything that it never bothered to assert itself to its kinsfolk. It was relegated to being the family doormat and was soon cast away due to its perceived weaknesses.

The newly formed gang arrived in the mountainous region of Batala, where a sparkling river flowed from a cascading waterfall. They glanced up to where the dragon was supposed to be hiding. Bigfoot volunteered to talk to it and rode onto Peter to go where the magnificent but timid beast was situated.

The rest remained on the ground waiting, and to while away the time, they decided to go for a swim in the stream. For a moment, everyone was joyful as they playfully splashed each other and swam the lovely body of water.

Nixie, the only semi-aquatic member of the gang, expertly swam from one end to the next and also underwater, with ease. She was like a happy fish swimming in the ocean, her feet functioning as fins, propelling her to the deepest corners and back.

Pandora hasn't even tried swimming in any body of water in Gintongbayan because everyone in her family discouraged her from doing so due to her sensitive condition. Since no one would reprimand her, she went ahead, and clumsily dove in with a huge splash. Everyone screamed with laughter and clapped their hands as her head sprung from the surface, showing a wide smile.

The water felt good and was warm enough to lift everyone's spirits. They frolicked and larked about without a care in the world. Even Pandora, who had been like a little bird living in a gilded cage, experienced a newfound sense of freedom she hadn't felt before. For a brief while, they shared joy with themselves, and all the incoming troubles were momentarily forgotten.

Meanwhile, Bigfoot and Peter reach the top of the flying plateau and find the dragon sleeping. They landed in front of it, right underneath the nose.

Even though it was regarded as the runt of the litter, it still looked magnificent. It was still humongous, with thick dark scales all over its body, sharp claws and teeth, and smoke from its nostrils.

They contemplated waiting for her to wake up or arousing her from slumber. They decided on the latter since they were in a time crunch.

How does one wake a sleeping dragon? They speculated. Every scenario they conceived of doing didn't look good for them. They would either end up in a pile of burnt flesh, or perhaps an after-nap meal, or maybe being squeezed to death with its sharp claws.

They changed their minds and waited instead for the beast to wake up. They sincerely hoped the rumors were true and that it was merely a giant scaredy-cat.

Chapter 44 The Frog King

Axe-Grinder felt he was losing hold of his followers. His scouts had reported back to him that many of his enlisted creatures in various hotspots had left their posts and either joined the enemy or went back to their communities.

Why is this happening? He thought. He missed his loyal acolytes, the seven dwarves who had supplied him beneficial counsel in the past. They were gone, either passed away or banished from the realm. He had no one to bounce ideas with, so he had to rely on his wits, which he wasn't used to. He examined the recent events.

They had lost all the previous battles they fought against their lighter counterparts, and many on their side had perished. His men might be fed up with always losing, so the solution was obvious: win this time.

How can we win? He still had many of the most fearsome and terrible creatures by his side who could wreak havoc on many communities, but they were mindless and couldn't be trusted with strategic warfare. He needed smart and trustworthy followers who could rein in and control them to accomplish a win. A general in any army needed capable lieutenants to carry out the plans.

But alas, no one in his army had stepped up as replacements for the absent seven dwarves. He was like a frog king with useless flies as his loyal subjects, making him ineffectual, with nothing better to do but croak in despair.

He was engrossed in his thoughts on his dilemma when a scout arrived, bringing him the latest news: Pandora, the girl who had defeated them in the human world and sent them running, was spotted in the dragon abode by the waterfalls. The scout also mentioned they had successfully recruited creatures to join them and planned to enlist the dragon's help.

This piece of news dismayed him further. If they were able to make the dragon join them, then they were in serious trouble. He had to do something to get them out of the mess they were in and get a win for once.

Then, he had an idea. He would hit them where it would hurt: Pandora's family in the human world. They were left unprotected and ripe for the picking. He will be kidnapping the most vulnerable and weakest member of their household: her best friend Ruby Rose, and use her to get a win this time around.

~O~

Their conversation was fruitful, and everyone seemed to agree with Mayor Eddie's plan. Even Lola Sabrina concurred, even though she looked worn out. They were going to enter the realm of Batala through one of the underground rooms, which they discovered was a secret entryway to the enchanted kingdom. The golden skeleton key was in their possession, and they would use it to open it.

Mayor Eddie said he had to go back to his office to let them know he would be gone for an indefinite time and file for vacation leave. They will reconvene the next day to begin their rescue mission.

Esmeralda wanted to go home to prepare for the journey and bring the necessary supplies. She reiterated the pay she was going to receive from them upon the success of the mission, and Lola Sabrina reluctantly agreed.

Angelica and Henry went back upstairs to make sweet, sweet love again before anything drastic happened that might hinder them from doing it.

Lola Sabrina went back upstairs to her bedroom to rest. Ruby Rose was also exhausted and followed suit, and went to her room in the servant's quarters. Everyone needed a respite from everything that had transpired in the past few days to recharge their batteries.

~O~

The next day came. Everyone was well-rested and ready for the journey ahead.

Mayor Eddie was the first one to come in. He was dressed in full hunting gear, with head-to-foot polyester camo, high-topped insulated hiking boots, and a Fierce Mountain Reaper, the best and most accurate hunting rifle money could buy. He also brought a stainless-steel hip flask filled with whiskey that he described as "liquid courage."

Esmeralda arrived the next and was equally impressive. She wore an all-black ensemble tactical thief outfit that made her look like a character in a medieval fantasy epic. She had two smallswords sheathed on her back, a handgun holstered on her hip, and two bullet belts on top of each other.

Henry and Angelica came down from the bedroom, dressed simply in loose-fitting denim and sneakers. They each brought two large knapsacks filled with their food and sleeping gear. Henry also had a pistol tucked in his waist and two cartridges full of bullets in his pants pocket.

There was someone still missing, which was a vital member of the group: Andreas, the ghost. Upon mention of his name, he suddenly appeared out of thin air. Since ghosts never rested, he had always been in Casa de la Noche, roaming and haunting the hallways, unseen. It was up to him to make himself seen by others, and he was getting good at it.

Everyone was ready. Lola Sabrina and Ruby Rose led them toward the underground room that was also the passageway to the Realm of Batala. The pathway to it was intentionally labyrinthian to discourage possible intruders from finding it. But Lola Sabrina knew the way and brought them there in record time. Esmeralda was designated as the keyholder; she took out the skeleton key made of gold from her pocket and unlocked the door.

Mayor Eddie opened the door widely. It was pitch-black inside, so he took out a flashlight and shone the way. Before taking his first step, he took a swig of liquid courage to make himself braver.

There was a rugged pathway leading to an unforeseen destination. They said their goodbyes and closed the door behind them.

Andreas went ahead for reconnaissance purposes and let himself be unseen. He could travel speedily due to his ethereal entity and traversed great distances in seconds. He didn't find any potentially dangerous elements along the pathway, so he went back to the group and reported as such. They continued walking.

Chapter 45 The Pack of Ragamuffins

The dragon finally awoke.

Peter and Bigfoot had been waiting patiently for almost an hour and were amazed by the marvel of the flying plateau. They walked the entire space of the flat tableland and even looked under it and tried to determine how it truly worked. It was floating in the air with nothing attached above and underneath to hold it in place.

Bigfoot—who was naturally curious and had spent time in the human world—was familiar with their law of physics and wanted to find out how it could float on its own. The likely presumption he ascertained was that it was held in place by magnetism. The entire space cavernous of Batala may have large iron deposits that allowed the island-like humongous rock formations to float in the air.

They dug in the ground and found out it was indeed made of magnetite and iron ore, which were highly magnetic. They were in the middle of this unusual and fantastic discovery, and they didn't notice the dragon had awoken and was quickly getting antsy by their appearance.

Since both couldn't talk conventionally like the others and relied on their animalistic vocal emissions via growls and screeches, they tried to converse with it using this form of communication first. It didn't seem to understand them, so Peter tried the telepathic way, which worked.

The dragon's large and fearsome eyes changed its gaze towards Peter's, and telepathically replied: *What do you want?*

We come in peace. We are here in front of you as friends and citizens of Batala. If you are not yet aware, there are creatures from the darker side of this realm intent on harming the place your family resides.

I don't care about them anymore. Please leave.

I understand you were banished here by your dragon kin.

Yes.

I may already know the answer to this question, but I want to hear it directly from you: why did your family ostracize you?

Because I only want to be left alone. They wanted me to join in their raiding missions, and I always declined.

But how will you eat if you don't go with them?

I'm the only dragon that refuses to consume meat and can survive by eating plants for sustenance.

So, you're saying you're a vegetarian dragon?

Yes.

And not cowardly?

Does it make me a coward by refusing to eat meat?

No. It makes you noble since you don't want to cause harm to other creatures. Then how did the rumor spread that you're a cowardly dragon?

I don't know. Maybe it came from them since their definition of bravery is being able to hunt and eat meat.

Can you still hunt prey?

Yes, of course. I'm still a dragon, remember? But what I would never do is kill to eat.

How about killing to protect someone innocent?

It is a different matter. If you are protecting someone and have no other choice but to kill, then it is morally justified.

That's good to know. It makes our job easier.

What do you mean?

As I said earlier if you aren't aware yet…

~O~

Mayor Eddie was a natural leader, which was a useful trait in his job as the mayor of Gintongbayan. He had an easygoing demeanor and a way of talking to his constituents, and it never felt like he was bossing them around when he wanted something done. He used this ability in every situation, which always garnered positive results.

The current situation he found himself in was unlike anything he experienced before and was otherworldly, but he was confident he could still handle himself well. He looked at the other group members: they might ostensibly be like an inexperienced pack of ragamuffins, but everyone brought something to the table.

He looked at Esmeralda first, who was the most lethal among them. He wanted to find out if she had killed someone before but didn't know how to put it into words properly. Also, she wasn't trustworthy since she had lied to him before when she posed as his secretary. She was there only because she would be paid handsomely for it, so he made a mental note to keep her at arm's length and not let her out of his sight.

He glanced towards Henry and Angelica, the recently reunited couple. They could be trusted since he knew about them and their families for a long time. All three came from old stock and had ancestors who were the original settlers in Gintongbayan.

Both had the potential to be useful. Henry especially, since he spent many years in Batala as a captive. He would have some knowledge about the realm's geography and its inhabitants and could provide crucial information when necessary. Meanwhile, Angelica was fearless and would do anything to rescue her daughter and return her safely.

The only wildcard was the ghost since he couldn't predict his actions. One minute he was there, and the next, he was gone. He only hoped he was doing what he was supposed to be by being a scout and reporting to them if he found any danger.

Nonetheless, he was still confident of their odds. They traversed the rough pathway of Batala, with him leading the way to the unknown.

~O~

Nixie, the water sprite, was still inside Peter's saddlebag, watching everything that had transpired in the dragon's abode on top of the floating plateau. She couldn't understand what they were saying since all she heard from them were growls and shrieks. However, their expressions didn't show anger or any other negative emotions but with sincerity and friendliness. Their conversation seemed to be going well, and everyone looked to have agreed on something.

It was the first time she had seen a dragon up close. It looked magnificent with its large size and dark scales. It reminded her of the *Nanreben*, a fearsome sea serpent that guarded the Fountain of Life in her home lake. Both were akin in their terrible but beautiful attributes, which made her glad it would be a friend and not a foe.

However, it also dismayed her because she was a spy after all, and had to report this new crucial detail to Axe-Grinder by way of his roving scout. She was beginning to like her new friends and felt bad she was betraying them.

But for her, Axe-Grinder's soon-to-be reward of being able to fly was more important. She would do anything to take flight and leave everything and everyone in the dust once she had this ability.

Chapter 46 Kidnapping Sleeping Beauty

Ruby Rose felt weird all by her lonesome in her new room. Lola Sabrina had let her transfer to the former butler Pluto's old one. It was bigger than the others in the servant's quarters and had more furniture. She wasn't used to it since she had spent her formative years with her father in his room.

Lola Sabrina said it was only temporary and she would get another more suitable soon. She needed to be away from her father since he had been bewitched by a devil lady and needed time to return to his normal frame of mind. She was worried and wanted to do more for him but had reluctantly agreed because she trusted Lola's assessment of the matter.

She considered her new room carefully. It was filled with strange stuff representing the former owner's offbeat temperament. The furniture didn't match and was strangely positioned in the room. Some footwear was on top of the bed, an assortment of clothes on the shoe rack, a few pillows on the floor, and trash scattered everywhere. The only normal thing (but still odd, nonetheless) was an old spinning wheel and a small wooden stool at the corner of the room.

There was also a large antique wardrobe in the corner, which had strange markings on the front. She resolved to tidy up the room and then examine its contents later.

She had belatedly learned that Pluto was a supernatural creature masquerading as a human butler, so everything strange in the room was attributed to it. His father had discovered the charade and had gotten rid of him most strangely.

After cleaning up, rearranging the furniture correctly, and packing Pluto's things inside cardboard boxes, she sat down on the wooden stool. She felt strangely drawn to the spinning wheel, even though she didn't know how to use it. There was a ball of yarn already attached to the bobbin, so she unwound it from the spindle. She accidentally pricked her finger, and blood immediately spurted out.

She felt drowsy and lay down on the bed. She slept instantly.

~O~

The antique wardrobe was, in fact, a mini doorway to Batala. Pluto had discovered it a short while ago, as he was cleaning one of the underground storage rooms. He also found the spinning wheel. Both were dusty and covered in cobwebs, which he later cleaned.

He knew both items had magical properties. He recognized the markings on the wardrobe as an old dwarvish language often used by Axe-Grinder whenever he uttered magical incantations. He brought the pieces of furniture to his room and had planned to utilize both in some capacity but ended up not doing anything because he had already perished.

However, he had sent a message to Axe-Grinder about the existence of both articles of furniture before his passing. Axe-Grinder had been aware of their particular functions and whose magical attributes would manifest on their own volition.

He opened the wardrobe from the inside and saw Ruby Rose sleeping soundly. He saw droplets of blood on the bedsheet and glanced at the spindle on the spinning wheel. He smiled and was amazed by how unexpected his good fortune was. *Finally, great things are coming my way,* he thought.

He picked up Ruby Rose, carried her on his shoulders, and reentered the wardrobe.

~O~

Lola Sabrina awoke from her nap and felt something was wrong. She sat on her bed, took a deep breath, and cleared her thoughts. This process enabled her mind to be like a beacon that received signals from any of her family who might be in trouble and needed her help.

She felt a strong signal from Batala. It didn't come from Pandora or anyone from her family but someone else who she still cared about: Ruby Rose.

It couldn't be, she thought. She stood up and rushed towards her new room in the servant's quarters. She first went to Matteo's room and told him to follow her to his daughter's.

Lola Sabrina opened the door to Ruby Rose's room, and as expected, she wasn't there. Matteo followed inside and hastily looked everywhere for her: in the bathroom, under the bed, or inside the strange-looking wardrobe. She was nowhere to be found. He hurriedly went out to do the same thing in all the other rooms in Casa de la Noche.

Lola Sabrina stared at the antique wardrobe. She searched her thoughts. She couldn't remember ever seeing it in her entire life in the house. *Where did this thing come from?*

However, she remembered seeing the spinning wheel before when she was little. Her mother used to make yarn from wool with it, which had fascinated her. However, when newer automated methods to make yarn became available, it was stashed away in one of the underground rooms, never to be used again.

She correctly assumed that Pluto may have found both furniture pieces and brought them to his room for unknown reasons and perhaps held some clues to Ruby Rose's whereabouts.

She discovered the blood droplets on the bedsheet, which alarmed her. It implied that something or someone had caused Ruby Rose to bleed before her disappearance, which made the situation dire.

She sat on the bed, closed her eyes, and concentrated again to make her receptive to pick up trouble signals. She felt a faint signal wave from Ruby Rose, who was purposely incapacitated. She was being carried off by an *Amomongo,* a man-sized ape with a white-bearded *Dwende* wearing a gold tunic leading the way. They were close to arriving in the dark side of Batala, where a dark army was stationed and gearing up for war.

She opened her eyes and was horrified. She needed to let the gang know about what had happened so they could rescue her. She knew Ruby Rose would be used as a bargaining chip and thus make their tasks in Batala more difficult than it already was.

Chapter 47 Noone Can Beat the Queen Bee

Esmeralda unsheathed one of her smallswords and felt its blade for sharpness. It was sharp enough to slice through any human or supernatural being, which could happen shortly if the ghost detected any enemies approaching them. She was raring to go so she could return home and collect the reward.

She looked at the members of a newly formed gang of so-called rescuers. She reckoned that no one among them had experienced fighting or killing someone before, and she was right. To her, they were a bunch of rich and privileged snobs who never encountered any hardships in their entire lives.

She, on the other hand, had lived a hard life and clawed her way to the top. She had to fight and sometimes kill to get what she wanted. She learned not to be merely a worker bee in any colony but the queen and prevailed over all.

Mayor Eddie might think he is the leader of the group, but when push came to shove, he wouldn't know how to handle an attacker, she thought. *Once this happens, everyone will look to me to save them.*

She needn't have waited long. The ghost appeared and reported a small group of creatures approaching their direction who looked scary and dangerous. Mayor Eddie told everyone to prepare themselves.

Esmeralda checked her gun, cocked it, and put it back in its holster. She unsheathed both smallswords and clanged them together. Sparks flew.

She went to the front of the group to get the brunt of any incoming assault. She prepared herself using the dual-wielding combat stance.

She saw three dark creatures approaching them, which she didn't recognize. Henry yelled behind her: "*Aswang!*" He unholstered his gun and aimed.

The three Aswangs were huge weredogs with scraggy black fur, sharp teeth, and claws. They were also frothing at the mouth and trotting towards them. The first one quickened its pace and then lunged itself in Esmeralda's direction. She easily sliced through it like butter, and its dead carcass dropped on the ground. She then decapitated the head.

The others opened fire on the two remaining creatures. As they lay bleeding and covered in bullet holes, she also severed both heads. "You must always cut the heads off these creatures, to make sure they're really dead. Do not give them a chance to reconstitute themselves and wreak havoc again."

"Good idea. How did you know about it?" Said Mayor Eddie.

"It's common sense. We are dealing with supernatural beings who aren't human and don't follow our laws of nature. We have to be careful the next time if we want to beat them."

"What should we do?"

"We were lucky. We could handle three creatures with our current weapons. What if there are more than three the next time?"

"Then we have no choice but to fight."

"We can but we'd lose. But our chances would definitely increase if we add more to our number."

"You mean recruit more join our group?"

No. I mean, we have to find Pandora and the other creatures allying with her. It would decidedly even the odds."

"The ghost boy will have to find them and tell them where we are."

"Yes, and for the meantime, we have to hide ourselves and not be sitting ducks to these awful monsters."

"Yes, we should," everyone said in unison.

"Henry, since you have spent some time in this place, where should we hide?"

~O~

Peter and Bigfoot flew down from the floating plateau to their awaiting fellow travelers. They had happy looks on their faces. Peter whispered telepathically: *Pandora, we did it. The dragon has agreed to join us.*

Pandora beamed and said: "They did it! The dragon will help us in the fight against the dark creatures!"

"Hooray!" Everyone yelled.

"A mighty dragon can easily crush them with its size and terrible fire coming from its mouth."

"What will happen now?" Pandora said.

"We have to get back to Bakunawa. You have crucial lessons to learn from her."

"Okay."

They were now a large and formidable group that could rival any of Axe-Grinder's platoon of terrible monsters. The dragon was especially essential since it could easily crush hundreds with just one blow of its massive paw.

They walked together to Bakunawa's dwelling hut while Peter and Pandora flew ahead. Nixie was still inside the saddlebag being a nosy spy, without their knowledge.

~O~

Axe-Grinder went inside his dwelling house to check on Ruby Rose. She lay on an ornate golden bed cushioned with heaps of flower petals and was covered by a semitransparent red linen shroud. She was also guarded by the same *Amomongo* who had carried her before. He stayed for a few minutes, admiring his handiwork and envisioning a future where he and the army were finally victorious.

He went outside and considered his massive army who assembled among themselves by their fearsome breed. He was a general without lieutenants, but what he lacked in loyal minions, he had in superiority of numbers. He was going to defeat the enemy through the chaos of overwhelming force.

And if everything had failed, he still had an ace up his sleeve: the sleeping girl, which he would use as leverage.

Things were looking peachy for Axe-Grinder, and he was confident that he and his army were going to win this time around and rule over the Realm of Complete Happiness.

~O~

Andreas saw Pandora mid-flight, riding on a strange-looking winged beast he hadn't seen before. He was able to match their speed of flight and followed close behind. He would wait for them to land and let himself be seen.

They landed in due course, and Andreas made his bluish ethereal presence show. Pandora smiled once she saw him and whispered: *Andreas! You're the last person I expected to see in this place! How did you find us, and why are you here?*

I just followed the breadcrumbs. Lola Sabrina sent me here to find you. Your parents and Godfather Eddie are also here. All of us are here to help you go home.

I can't go home yet. I have to help these beings with their current problem.

We know, and we are here for that.

Where are the others?

They're hiding for the moment and waiting for my return.

Alright. Go back Andreas, and take them to this exact place where we landed. We are going to devise a plan of action against the dark creatures. Go quickly because time isn't on our side.

Chapter 48 The Rose in Dreamland

As Ruby Rose lay unconscious for an indefinite period, she dreamed.

She never envisioned herself as someone important and nothing more than the gardener's daughter and apprentice maid, but her dreams told her otherwise.

She was a royal princess in her dream, with many loyal subjects at her beck and call. Her father, the king, was stricken with a mental disorder that rendered him incapable of rule, so she was handed the keys to the kingdom and became the Queen Regent. She became the best ruler the kingdom had ever known, and peace and prosperity reigned. She was, for once in her life, not a supporting player or a damsel in distress but the heroine in the story, even though it was only in the realm of dreams.

However, it wasn't only one she had, but a continuous stream of interchanging dreams. With each one, she was the most important person in every dream scenario who could move mountains. She was always a mover and shaker, the big cheese, or the head honcho. In them, she was the person who solved problems or the one everybody depended on to fix conflicts and disputes.

In one dream, she was a hard-nosed private eye trying to solve a case of a missing heiress, Theodora Lioness. She was the renowned Sherlock Rose, who had singular detective skill by finding clues out of the most mundane objects. She was assisted by her loyal sidekick, the bungling but well-intentioned Doctor Whatchamacallit.

Sherlock Rose and the good doctor arrived at the heiress' ancestral home to look for clues and speak to her family. She found out that the heiress had a penchant for partaking in Angel Dust, which was a hallucinogenic drug. She had been buying it from a notorious drug dealer by the name of Alpha Golf, who was a chunky midget and had an affinity for wearing gold jewelry.

She discovered the bad guys' hideout in a massive underground bunker by the old docks. It had a dingy hole in the wall that was frequented by lowlifes and drug addicts. She infiltrated it by wearing a disguise as a pimp and Dr. Whatchamacallit as his prized prostitute. There, they found the missing heiress drugged out of her mind and close to death.

They easily rescued her and took her to the nearest hospital. The dream ended joyously after the heiress was reunited with her family.

In another dream, she was Katniss Everose, a poor but courageous girl living in District 12, the poorest and smallest district in the dystopian and tyrannical nation of Panem.

It was during the events when her sister Primadora was supposed to be chosen as the district's female tribute in the annual gladiatorial games called the Hunger Games. Instead, she volunteered to take her place. A male tribute was also selected, and both represented District 12.

She saved her sister from harm and defeated the tributes from the other districts, and both won the Hunger Games. She hugged her sister Primadora, and with her winnings, lived happily ever after with her family in relative peace and harmony.

Since her sleep was continuous and ceaseless, she continued dreaming in countless dream scenarios and always played the part of the savior. It filled her with confidence and bravery, attributes she sorely lacked in the waking world. Slowly but surely, she was imbued with a fearlessness and skill that rivaled any brave warrior in the realm.

~O~

Lola Sabrina was responsible for these dreams, which she had cast to Ruby Rose in a type of conjuration called a Courage Spell. It was the most she could in her capacity. She knew Ruby Rose would be woken up at some point in Batala, and she needed to be brave and not be scared of what was transpiring.

She concentrated again and made herself become a beacon to accept telepathic signals. The strongest one she detected came from Jabber the *Kapre*. She whispered to him: *Jabber, can you hear me?*

Yes, Sabrina, I can hear you. What do you want?

What's going on? Are you mad?

A little. I'm sorry for being rude. I'm just frustrated about something unrelated to our current problem. How can I help you?

It's about a girl Pandora's age who's been forcibly taken to Batala.

A kidnapping? Who took her?

It was the Dwende Axe-Grinder. He somehow gained entrance into our house and took her there. He put a sleeping spell on her that made her sleep endlessly.

What do you want me to do?

Please find the others and tell them. They already have a lot on their plates, and I wonder if this would be too much for them.

It would be. They are already fighting an uphill battle, and I don't know if they could still handle this.

Then what should I do?

Do not worry, and leave it to me. I'll keep you informed.

Thank you, Jabber. You know, I…

Jabber suddenly cut off his telepathic connection to her. It was the second time Jabber had done it to her, which made her wonder.

~O~

A small dark *Sigbin* arrived, which was one of the roving scouts Axe-Grinder employed. It had a brand-new report coming from one of his spies, a small *Diwata* named Nixie. It recounted a dragon being enlisted to join their enemy's side. He knew this would happen and wasn't surprised at all.

He went inside his dwelling hut to look at the sleeping Rose, yet again. He noticed her eyes rapidly moving in REM sleep, which he knew was due to dreaming. He wondered what she was dreaming about and considered bringing her out of her sleeping trance. He noticed her mouth forming into a wide smile that bothered him.

What is she smiling about? He thought. He wanted to wake her but knew the trance wouldn't allow him to. The only way for her to wake up was a kiss from someone who truly loved her. He scoffed at this idea and went back outside.

Chapter 49 The Elves of Greenwood

There was a consensus among the citizens of Batala that all *Dwendes* were evil, which had to do with their innate greed for gold. Nevertheless, a handful weren't and lived separately from Axe-Grinder and his minions. They were elves who resided just a stone's throw away outside the Golden Mountain's tunnel entrance. This small patch of forest was called Greenwood, which was hidden from general view.

These elves chose to live in this wooded grove to avoid any conflict their cousins were always participating in. They loathed any violence and preferred to live among themselves in peace and harmony with nature.

These woodland Dwendes didn't only behave differently but looked unlike their cave-dwelling counterparts, who were short and thick and whose appendages looked disproportional from their bodies. They have otherwise similar heights but have proportional extremities.

There was also another reason they lived away from Axe-Grinder and his ilk: they had intimate knowledge about the secret portal leading to the Realm of Complete Happiness. They knew its location and how to enter it if one or many were visiting. They didn't want anyone to know where it was, especially their more savage cousins.

However, Axe-Grinder did find out, and the creatures of the Realm of Complete Happiness blamed the elves of Greenwood. Thus, they became more reclusive than they already were and made themselves almost invisible to the naked eye. They became masters of camouflage and shunned everyone.

Yet Bakunawa, the Serpent Goddess, knew about their importance and had been thinking of ways to make them their allies. She had been trying to find them many times before but had failed. Her magic didn't seem to work on them. They were extremely proficient in hiding and exploited the natural surroundings to disguise themselves, even from her.

She decided to try for the last time to find them, and if she still failed, she'd return to the light side of Batala and fight the impending war without them. She was willing to attempt one more tactic.

She went to Greenwood and stood at the clearing, and passionately conveyed her case. She had prepared a speech and stated its finer points. She knew the elves were there and listening, even though she couldn't see them. Once it ended, she resolved to wait for them to appear or say anything.

But no one did.

It made her disappointed. But she was glad nonetheless that she at least tried and resolved to go home. She transformed herself into a giant white snake and slithered away from Greenwood.

Nevertheless, two elves by the name of Tinker and Blinker were listening intently and were greatly impressed by her passionate plea. The others didn't pay much attention and went about their elvish lives, while the two decided to follow Bakunawa a good distance away and in secret.

She didn't go to the usual entrance through the tunnel under the Golden Mountain but a different one via a giant termite mound. They waited a few minutes, and once the coast was clear, they followed suit.

Nevertheless, Bakunawa did know she was being followed and waited to arrive at her domicile to confront them. But what she didn't count on was that an assortment of humans and magical creatures were there waiting for her.

A pale girl wearing a red cloak she didn't initially recognize was the first one she saw. Upon closer inspection, she knew instantly who the girl was and the reason she was there. She transformed back into a less frightful and acceptable form of a woman and stood up. She said: "Welcome everyone, especially you, Pandora. You're here to finish your training."

"Finish? I haven't even started yet."

"Your grandmother had been preparing and teaching you before. You are already a powerful witch but what you lack is focus and control, which I will teach you."

"You mean those stories she told? Those were lessons?"

"Yes. You were already born with these gifts. She was merely teaching you self-confidence and bravery, exceedingly important traits to be a powerful witch. The Book of Shadows even has a prophecy about you.

"Me? What did it say?"

"It is written there about a pale-faced young woman clad in red will unite the fractured realm of Batala and bring peace. There's even a picture of you there."

"You really think it's me?"

"Yes, and the same prophecy mentions two elves who will play an integral part."

"Elves? You mean our enemies the *Dwendes?* I thought they were all evil."

"That's a common misconception. There are a few who are good and two of them have followed me here," Bakunawa said. She looked behind her and pointed at two medium-sized boulders.

The boulders behind her moved, then changed into two gray-colored elves dressed in leaves and vines. They looked imploringly at everyone who gawked at them in bewilderment.

"Do not be afraid, we mean you no harm. Please come forward. We want to meet both of you."

Tinker and Blinker held hands and hesitatingly advanced. They stopped a few paces from them.

"Hello. We are elves from Greenwood. We heard your speech and want to help," Tinker said.

"Welcome my friends! And thank you for coming."

"How can we help?"

"As you can see, we are an assortment of magical beings, along with a few humans. We have one goal in mind: defeat Axe-Grinder and his dark army once and for all, so they won't create problems to any of us ever again. They have been causing trouble above ground in the human world and here in Batala. They are also planning to attack another kingdom close to ours, which is the Realm of Complete Happiness. We must stop them at all costs."

"We?"

"Us from the light side of Batala oppose him and his rule. As you can see, we have enlisted many to help us in this fight. We have a young and powerful witch, a couple of skilled humans, different magical creatures with abilities, and we even have a dragon. Some will join later. Both of you has a crucial role to play in this, so we have to begin the lessons immediately."

"Lessons? Us?"

"Yes. I will teach the girl Pandora and both of you a few lessons from the Book of Shadows. Please come with me," Bakunwa said and entered her dwelling hut.

Pandora, Tinker, and Blinker quickly followed.

Chapter 50 Dumb and Wise Folks on Both Sides

The war was imminent.

Both sides had agreed to fight for the last time, and whoever lost would never create trouble again. Whoever was left alive from the losing side had to leave Batala definitively and look for another place to live, somewhere with no humans present. Whether their intentions were good or not, they have knowingly and unknowingly damaged the lives of many human beings, and their overall influence was detrimental in the long run.

Bakunawa, the Serpent Goddess, had a backup plan in case they lost, wherein the surviving beings from the light side of Batala would be living among the well-disposed creatures in the Realm of Complete Happiness. Despite anything to the contrary, she was confident they were still welcome there because they were all well-intentioned creatures and had fulfilled its primary requirement, which was providing a positive influence on humans.

Their dark-skinned kin were very much unlike them in every way.

Axe Grinder and his minions had been exploiting the humans and even used them for meat consumption.

He was aware his evil and corrupt acts left him and his ilk unwelcome anyplace they went. He planned to fight and fight until his last breath. The only other option was death.

And if they did win, their prize was gaining possession of the Realm of Complete Happiness. He imagined living in this place where its inhabitants were stripped of all negative emotions and granted the feeling of eternal bliss. He longed to feel this way and had grown to hate his constant lust for gold and domination.

Bakunawa was confident of their chances, and almost all probable outcomes she foresaw had them winning. Only one outcome had her losing, but nothing had happened yet that could likely cause it. A kidnapping of a human girl close to Pandora didn't occur yet, and she would start to worry when it did.

Bakunawa found out later about Ruby Rose's kidnapping, which instantly made her worry. It was one link in a chain of events that would make them lose the war, so she had to find a way to fix it.

~O~

Bakunawa had to leave Pandora and the elves and try to handle the situation with Ruby Rose. She had given a magic wand to Pandora to help her focus her magical ability and told her to practice with the elves supervising her. She then left.

She first went to Jabber the *Kapre*, who had informed her telepathically about Ruby Rose's kidnapping. She wanted to talk to him directly and not rely on telepathy since lying can be easily done. Actual face-to-face conversation was better in gauging truthfulness.

Jabber wasn't in his dwelling hut among his community of *Kapres*. His kin told her he had been traveling back and forth from Batala to the Realm of Complete Happiness. She was surprised he knew the entryway since this type of information was supposed to be a secret. It made her wonder.

Nonetheless, she was stuck. Should she wait for Jabber to come back or find another way to deal with the situation of the kidnapped girl?

She chose to do the latter since she didn't want to wait around doing anything. She could always get back to Jabber or even summon him. She had to look for another way to handle the dilemma of the abducted girl.

~O~

The rescue squad of Mayor Eddie, Esmeralda, Henry, Angelica, and Andreas soon arrived. The parents were happily reunited with their daughter, but there was no time for idle talk. They were updated with the plan and other pertinent details. They were introduced to the other creatures who were allies in the same fight.

Meanwhile, Pandora was having immediate success in practice. She could focus her light-blasting power on the tip of the magic wand and limit its flow of intensity. She could control and adjust it to stun but not scorch the target and soon became good at it.

The wand allowed her to regulate it and make it a useful tool or a powerful weapon. She could use it like a flashlight and illuminate any dark pathway or as an energy-blasting instrument of death that could incinerate any human or supernatural creature in seconds.

She realized she was quite adept in this type of power, and in their limited timeframe, she decided to concentrate on it to make it better. She soon found out she could make light do anything she wanted and even produce a hologram of anything. She tried to duplicate the body and size of the dragon using her power, which she could do successfully and astonishingly. The holographic dragon looked eerily similar to the real one, and its only downside was its intangibility.

The wand was useful in making her confident in her abilities. The elves were good helpers by being helpful and encouraging to her. They reminded her of troll dolls she used to play with when she was little, which were her favorite toys.

Tinker and Blinker were initially shy and reserved since they weren't used to conversing with other creatures, not their own. They soon found a close affinity with her and were glad she was on their side. In the short time they were together, they became steadfast allies, along with Peter Griffin, Bigfoot, and Nixie. All six of them became close-knit and grew to rely on one another.

They would have preferred to have the dragon as part of their clique, but it was too much of an unknown entity that they decided to keep it at arm's length. The dragon had unpredictable mood swings that made them afraid of being trampled.

By and by, Nixie the Water Sprite became guilty. She had grown to like her new friends and began to hate being a spy. She decided to bide her time and wait for something drastic to happen and tell them her real intentions, otherwise, she would remain in the status quo.

Everyone on the light side of Batala was momentarily joyful. There was a period of calm weather, but a storm was fast approaching, brought on by Axe-Grinder and his dark army.

Chapter 51 The Shroud of Mystery

When Bakunawa, the Serpent Goddess, was trying to find any information concerning the girl's kidnapping, she learned that the girl was put to sleep and covered by a curious red linen shroud. She remembered something about it mentioned in the Book of Shadows. She wasn't sure what it was, so she had to go home to look at the book for herself.

When she arrived home, she noticed everyone was busy preparing for the coming fight. They were practicing among themselves and exercising.

She was in two minds about telling Pandora about her kidnapped friend or not. Upon seeing Pandora with her family and new acquaintances momentarily happy, she decided to refrain from saying. This unfortunate piece of information would take her away from her gradual progress, and she needed to be focused on the task at hand.

She left them alone for combat rehearsals and went directly home to where the Book of Shadows was kept. She leafed through its thick pages, trying to locate the footnote about the red shroud.

She hit paydirt and found the annotation describing the red linen. It said:

Beware the scarlet shroud when draped over an unfortunate sleeper

It can turn the meekest lamb into the fiercest monster

Be certain to remove it before the seventh day of slumber

Or else the wolf will stay forever.

She realized that the red shroud had the power to change anyone draped under it into a werewolf, cursed to thirst for blood during the night of a full moon. She wondered how her mortal enemy Axe-Grinder got hold of this dangerous piece of apparel.

She read further about it in the Book of Shadows, which devoted one full page, along with a few illustrations. It also had a story about its origins:

~O~

The red linen cloth was originally part of a Maria Clara ensemble worn by an unnamed woman during the Philippine Revolution more than a hundred years ago. It was a long red scarf donned over the shoulders.

By day, the woman was a high-society matron who was part of the *Illustrados,* or the educated upper class. By night, she was a spy who worked in secret to undermine the enemy efforts of the Americans.

Her husband worked as a diplomat and was among the few in the government who advocated for the Americans to be the new colonial masters after the

Spaniards. This small group of affluent upper-crust Filipinos wanted to remain rich and in power against everything Andres Bonifacio and the revolutionary organization of the *Katipunan* stood for, which was independence from all foreign powers.

The woman spied on her husband and reported to the Katipunan. She soon discovered that her husband had another surprising and terrible secret: he had allied with supernatural creatures who lived underground and had been supplying him with large quantities of gold in exchange for subjugation.

The supernatural creatures discovered the woman's spying activities and had her attacked by a blood-sucking weredog, an *Aswang*. She was killed and ravaged to pieces. Her red scarf was the only one left, which the leader of the supernatural creatures took as a keepsake.

~O~

Bakunawa realized that the annotation was describing her mortal enemy Axe-Grinder as the "leader of the supernatural creatures" and the piece of clothing was cursed. She read further and found out how to neutralize the cursed apparel: by burning it with a magical fire.

This type of fire can only originate from a magical source, from either a magical person or object, which means magic can only be defeated by another form of magic. She only knew two sources of this kind of magical fire: one coming from their magical illuminating trees and one from Pandora and her light-blasting power.

After thinking about it, she decided that Pandora's ability had a better chance of burning the cursed shroud. She had to do it before the seventh day of the girl's endless sleep, meaning she had to move up the timetable and start the war early.

~O~

Axe-Grinder was getting antsy. He had a bad feeling he was supposed to do something important that he had forgotten. He knew it had something to do with the sleeping girl. *But what?* He thought and was angry at himself.

He returned inside and stared at the girl covered in a semitransparent red cloth. He could see she was still dreaming, her eyes rapidly moving in REM sleep. *What is she dreaming about?* He thought frustratingly.

He knew the sleeping effect from the spindle prick would only last one week in human time, but they were in Batala, whose time duration was different from theirs and highly irregular. He wanted her to be as compliant as possible, and being perpetually asleep accomplished that. Yet, something told him he had to wake her up or else something bad was going to happen. *Is this the thing I'm supposed to do?* He wondered and began scratching his head.

He hated being unsure of himself at this particular point in time since the war was close at hand. At this stage, he should have been confident and prepared, but alas, this *thing* was nagging at the back of his mind. *What should I do?*

As Axe-Grinder was figuratively banging his head on the wall out of frustration, someone diminutive in stature was approaching him. At first, he didn't recognize this tiny creature, but then he remembered: it was his spy, the water sprite. He stared at her for a moment and beamed. He had an idea. It was like a fluorescent bulb atop his head was suddenly switched on.

With this idea (which he thought was brilliant), he felt a huge weight lifted off his shoulders. He beckoned the minuscule *Diwata* towards him and said: "Come here little fairy. I assume you're here to report about your spying activities."

"Well, yes but I also have something else to tell you."

"Save it. I want you to do something for me for one last time, and once you're done, your obligation with us is over and you will get your reward."

"You mean you'll give me wings to fly?"

"Yes, little fairy. Soon you will fly."

"What do you want me to do?"

Chapter 52 The Donkey Among Battle Buddies

Andreas observed his comrades in arms participating in the war preparations, which included exercising, sharpening bladed weapons, and combat rehearsals. He wasn't sure how the other creatures would react after seeing his ghostly blue form, so he opted to stay invisible until further notice.

He didn't bother to pay attention to the human contingent and eagerly watched the amazing magical creatures readying themselves. Each was more fantastical than the next, and everyone had something to contribute to the war effort. While a few of the humans were formidable in their own right, they were no match for the awesomeness and might of the supernatural beings, who had extraordinary and incomparable abilities.

Looking at everyone made him feel like an out-of-place donkey in a corral full of magnificent steeds. He felt inadequate in the coming battle and questioned his effectiveness. Being dead and a ghost was already a difficult pill to swallow, but he did manage to overcome it and even found its usefulness. Yet there was still a nagging question in his mind: would all his efforts be enough to allow him to enter paradise?

He knew his ultimate destiny was connected to Pandora, and since she was an integral part of the incoming battle, then perhaps allowing himself to be seen and be useful was sufficient for the war effort.

Then, he had an idea. He went to his human friends and reactivated his blue spectral light.

~O~

Esmeralda kept busy by getting acquainted with her fellow warriors from the supernatural contingent and learning everything about them. Each showed a great capacity for courage and ferocity, whose traits she greatly admired.

She found a kinship with Bigfoot since it was the only creature who had spent time with humans before and was used to people like her. Bigfoot could not speak but still understood human language, so it often used hand gestures for communication.

And like everyone else, she was fascinated by the dragon and was mesmerized by its size and magnificence. She made certain she admired it from a distance since she had heard it was sometimes moody and unpredictable. Also, she wanted to make sure that the dragon saw her as an ally and not be mistaken for the enemy so as not to be accidentally incinerated or trampled on.

After learning everything she could about her magical brothers-in-arms, she returned to her squad of humans. Andreas, the ghost, had been waiting for her, which surprised and made her curious. Pandora was with him and spoke on his behalf.

"Esmeralda, my friend wants to ask you something."

"You mean your *ghost* friend? Don't you find it weird saying that?"

"Not really. He was my boyfriend when he was still alive, but now I don't know how to describe our relationship. I'm also indebted to him because I'm the reason he was killed in first place, so I'd appreciate it if we could extend any help if he calls for it."

"Fine. As long as your Lola pays me, I can do anything you want me to."

"My friend has a request to you."

"What is it?"

"Can he enter your body and become you for an hour?"

"What do you mean?"

"I'm talking about spirit possession. He will walk in your shoes for a short while. Are you okay with it?"

"Whoa. I'm not sure I'm fine with it. It sounds a bit invasive. Can I ask the reason why he wants to be me?"

"He said you are the most skilled fighter he had ever seen and he wants to find out how you do it, so he can use it in the coming battle."

"Well, as long as he won't poke around in my head for some personal stuff that's totally unrelated, then I guess I'm okay with it."

Did you hear that, Andreas? Only access memories of anything concerning her skill of fighting and self-defense, and nothing else. And don't take too long in there, or else, you might get lost. And she still needs her body to practice, Pandora whispered telepathically to Andreas.

Yes, just for a short while.

"How are we going to do it?"

"You'll not do anything. Just stand there and Andreas will do the rest."

Andreas floated towards Esmeralda and took over her entire physical and mental being. He was simultaneously like a shark and puppet master: devouring her prowess and fortitude, then controlling the strings to make her move. He felt her strength and bravery coursing through her veins, invigorating him.

Esmeralda, on the other hand, could only see what was going on but had no control over her senses. She was like a passenger trapped in a car, unable to drive or even get out.

She felt Andreas accessing the filing cabinet of her memories, going through them and looking for two specific folders: B for Bravery and F for Fighting. She allowed it to happen, which opened the floodgates to create a new kind of spectral but living entity.

The two disparate beings melded into one, who wasn't exactly Esmeralda or Andreas. This new person opened her mouth to speak but hesitated like she hadn't spoken for a long time.

Pandora said: "Andreas, are you in there?"

"Yes, I'm here. She's also here with me but I'm in control."

"Do you feel any different?"

"I feel her hands and they are strong, which makes me strong as well."

"Can you try to do what she does with the swords?"

Andreas (who controlled Esmeralda's body) unsheathed the smallswords on her back. They felt like extensions on her arm, and she knew instantly what to do with them. She expertly swished and swayed the swords to and fro like a proficient swordsman.

"It's strange. It's like I know how to wield these swords, even though it's my first time."

"It's her talent influencing and—like a disease—infecting you. Give in and use it."

However, Andreas could sense that Esmeralda was hiding something. She returned to the filing cabinet of her memories to access S for Secret Files but couldn't since there was a lock on the particular drawer.

Andreas brushed it aside and went back to practicing.

Chapter 53 The Three Children of Fortune

The three teenagers—Pandora, Ruby Rose, and Andreas—were still children at heart, and to them, adulthood was a million years away. Before hell had broken loose, they lived innocent and carefree lives and never entertained the notion of adult issues and hang-ups. The worst problems they encountered were mostly related to their social status in high school, like who was dating whom, who was the most popular, or who had the most friends and followers on social media.

But now, TikTok or Instagram be damned. Each of the three children of fortune had experienced misfortune of epic proportions. One even died, and the two were forced into situations where the result might be their demise.

And only one had the power to change all their destinies: Pandora. Their respective redemptions were up to her, which was right around the corner, approaching them like a slow-moving hurricane.

~O~

Bakunawa, the Serpent-Goddess, had children on her mind. She didn't want to adopt or bear them since she couldn't anyway.

A *Diwata* like her originated from the order of fallen angels who opposed God and didn't follow Lucifer to hell but remained on Earth in limbo. The enchanted kingdom of Batala was borne from the humans' understanding of its complicated history, and other creatures like her soon came into existence.

Her kind was immortal, and being godlike precluded her from bearing children. Yet she still cared for human beings and their offspring, which was an attribute she still kept in her heart from her time as one of God's messengers. Lucifer had successfully corrupted her, and not a day had gone by that she regretted consorting with him. The fall from God's grace was difficult to bear, but she understood later that it had to be done. They had betrayed their maker and committed an unforgivable sin. From then on, she promised to make amends and be a positive force in the physical and supernatural worlds.

Similarly, Axe-Grinder was a mutated offshoot of Lucifer's fallen angels but the kind who had chosen to remain corrupted. He still espoused Lucifer's teachings, which had garnered support from other like-minded creatures.

Even though the war brought on by Axe-Grinder and his dark minions was forthcoming, Bakunawa's thoughts were mainly occupied with the three kids under her wing. They were all young and innocent and were put into situations they were forced to. She felt a tinge of guilt, even though their respective troubles weren't her fault.

The ghost boy especially, since he had already been killed by one of Axe-Grinder's minions, and the only thing that could be done was to ensure his place in paradise, which was a difficult undertaking. The two girls were in danger and could be put to death if events soured.

Her thoughts concerning them were bleak. *What's going to happen to them?* She thought. Not doing anything seemed like the worst thing to do. She decided to tell Pandora and Andreas what had happened to Ruby Rose and see what they could all do to alleviate the situation.

She went outside her dwelling hut to find them.

~O~

Lola Sabrina had similar thoughts. She was worried more about the two girls since the boy's fate was out of her hands. Ruby Rose especially, because she had no knowledge of self-defense and would probably run away if there was any whiff of trouble.

And her father, Matteo, her wise and most loyal servant. Due to recent events, those adjectives wouldn't be an apt description for him. His normally trustworthy conduct was overpowered by Esmeralda's devilish machinations. Lola Sabrina had managed to excise him of her bad influence, but he was never the same again.

Nevertheless, Lola Sabrina still trusted him and would never terminate his tenure. She treated him as part of the family, and more so her daughter, who was like a sister to Pandora.

She went out of her room to look for Matteo. He was nowhere to be found in his usual hangout spots in the house if he wasn't working. He wasn't even in his room. She asked the other helpers where Matteo was, and no one seemed to know.

If she rested well and felt particularly clear-headed, she could utilize her telepathic ability as a GPS and locate the intended person within a five-kilometer radius. Currently, her mind felt tired and worn out, but she tried to nonetheless. Her ability pinpointed Matteo's location in the forest near Casa de la Noche, within the area Pandora went and got lost as a child.

She knew exactly where he was off to. She took a deep breath, exhaled, and telepathically whispered: *Matteo, can you hear me?*

No response from him.

First-time recipients of telepathy would usually take longer to respond since confusion and bafflement were their first reactions. Once they realized what was happening and a few minutes had passed, they would have the presence of mind to reply.

Lola Sabrina whispered for the second time and waited.

A few minutes passed, then he replied: *What's happening? Who is talking?*

Matteo, it's me, Lola Sabrina, and don't be afraid. We're merely talking with our minds.

Ma'am Sabrina?? Is that you??

Yes. Come back home. The giant white snake is busy and won't meet with you, and it's useless to go inside the termite mound because you can't. Only magical beings could.

How did you know where I was?

I'll explain everything when you arrive home.

Alright, Ma'am.

Lola Sabrina cut communication with Matteo and exhaled deeply. Her mind was about to reach the breaking point, and when this would happen, she would start blanking out. Some days, she would even forget she had this ability and yell in confusion if someone tried to contact her telepathically.

She needed rest and lots of it. She wanted to be in tip-top shape if the situation had gotten hairy. She went straight to her room, lay down, and slept instantly.

And she dreamed, albeit unintentionally, which was the last thing she needed. Even though she would never remember her dreams once she woke up, she would still be stressed out by them. This particular dream was no different.

It was the same dream she had before when Pandora was born, but now it was vivid and clearer. The pale figure raising her hand was Pandora, in the midst of the chaos and confusion of war. Pure light was coming from her hands, disintegrating everything and everyone in sight.

No one survived the onslaught of her own making but her.

Lola Sabrina suddenly woke up and sobbed.

Chapter 54 The Hut in the Forest

Matteo was dumbfounded by what had just transpired. He previously had an intimation that Madam Sabrina was a *Mangkukulam*—a witch, but he never saw any proof. He was aware of some people in Gintongbayan gifted with this type of supernatural power and even employed the services of one in the past, so he had seen supernaturalism up close. It was the first time he experienced her witchy ability, yet he was still blown away by it.

Ma'am Sabrina knew his reason for going to the forest: to find the giant white snake and ask for its help in getting his daughter back. He had brought a young goat as an offering to gain its favor and waited a couple of hours for it to slither into his immediate proximity, but nothing happened.

The buckling was bleating profusely. He had tied a piece of rope on its neck, and it was trying to get away from him. He was getting irritated and restless, and after Madam Sabrina telepathically contacted him, he immediately turned around and left, dragging the kid with him.

After a few minutes of experiencing willful disobedience from the hardheaded goat, his arms were beginning to get tired from all the pulling. The kid also sounded like a crying child, which freaked him out. He decided to stop to let the both of them rest.

From a distance, he saw a small hut in the forest. It looked ordinary and featureless, like any other hut made of nipa and bamboo that people living below the poverty line inhabited. He wanted to look closer and tied the rope attached to the goat in a protruding root on the ground.

Upon closer inspection, he saw someone moving inside. By happy chance, the figure appeared to be an old woman he had met previously: the cross-eyed witch, whom he had bought a magical potion before. He saw her inside cooking something in a large cauldron that expelled bright red smoke.

He tiptoed closer and like before, the witch already knew he was coming. She turned around and looked at him expectedly with her crossed eyes. She said: "We meet again, young man. I've been expecting you."

"Do you live here? I thought you lived in the Land of Broken Dreams."

"I still do. This is another place I own where I concoct powerful and dangerous potions that might cause harm to my neighbors in the squatter's colony. Please come in my humble abode."

Matteo went into the small hut and sat on a bamboo bench. He said: "What are you cooking in there?"

"Something especially potent, which will be useful to you," the old woman replied and stirred the cauldron with a large wooden spoon.

"You made potion for me? Sorry, I won't need it. I have some prior problem that won't need the kind of potions you make."

"Oh, but you do. You will need it to bring back your daughter."

"Do you know where my daughter is?"

"Yes."

"But how do you know this?"

"*Mangkukulams* like me have ways to get information about anyone, similarly to your employer."

You mean Ma'am Sabrina? Both of you are witches?"

"Yes. A long time ago, we were part of the same coven. There were thirteen of us, and now only two remain."

"Did you have a falling out?"

"No. We merely grew old and some of us died. We were all white witches who used our abilities to help people. Your employer's specialties were telepathy and divination, while mine was potions making."

"I didn't know about all this."

"Of course you don't. It's because our coven was secret. Not even our respective families knew about it, only us."

"Oh, okay."

"Whenever your employer uses her telepathic ability, it was like a radio signal that broadcasts her conversations to people like us, so I've heard and know everything. I've been trying to contact her but couldn't. It's like someone's blocking my messages to her."

"Why didn't you just go to Casa de la Noche and talk to her?"

"I shouldn't."

"Why? Everyone is welcome there, and more so an old friend of hers. She'd receive you with open arms."

"Do you see what I look like? I'm a scary cross-eyed old hag. People who notice me become afraid. I'd rather remain in the shadows where no one sees me."

"She's a good person and will accept you as a long-lost friend. Anyhow, you mentioned you made a potion to help me?"

"Yes. This one I'm making is quite powerful, and when I'm done, you should handle it with care."

"How much is it? The last potion you made for me was quite expensive. I don't have enough money to pay for this new one."

"Don't worry about it."

"Oh, I forgot. I have a young kid tied up outside. It's yours if you want it.

"A goat? Yes, I would like to have it. I'll make *kaldereta* or goat stew with it for my family in the Land of Broken Dreams. Thank you."

"No, it's you I should thank. You're making a magical potion to help my daughter, out of the goodness of your heart. By the way, what's in it and how will it help her?"

"I'll explain everything later. For now, I have to recite incantations and finish adding all the ingredients. And so please sit down and keep quiet."

"Alright. By the way, what's your name?"

"My name is Luna."

~O~

Axe-Grinder had just finished telling Nixie her part in the plan and sent her off. If she became successful, the tide of war would be turned in their favor.

He got information from one of his scouts that Bakunawa and the rest of his enemies would take a sip of the Water of Life before the battle began to reinvigorate and make themselves stronger. He had given Nixie a tiny flask filled with poison to dilute the water's reinvigorating properties and make them ill.

If Nixie would fulfill her task, they would be fighting a weaker enemy and surely win the battle. It would only take one blow to topple each one down. Axe-Grinder smiled, and for the first time in the longest time, he was confident of their chances of winning.

Chapter 55 Sweet Porridge

The *Lakivot, or* the giant talking civet, and Wilhelm had become best buddies, while Jacob was still freaked out about the general state of affairs and mostly kept his distance from everyone. They were constant companions and always in deep conversations.

Wilhelm nicknamed it "Sweet Porridge" for its affinity for the rice gruel it used to eat as a guard and its apparent sweet nature. He still thought of it as an "it" even though it was a male of its species. It looked like an adorable cat he used to own as a pet who just happened to be gigantic and could talk.

And it was a chatterbox. It likes to talk about everything and anything under the sun and would seldom become bothersome to others. Only Wilhelm was patient enough to listen and often indulged it in its numerous flights of fancy.

He found out they had many similarities. They liked exploring the immense cavernous space of Batala and marveling at its beautiful spaces and magnificent residents.

He often rode on its back while exploring the breathtaking surroundings to while away the time when combat rehearsals were done for the day. It was light-footed and fast, which made him hold on to its fur tightly so as not to fall over.

After one such rambling trip, they arrived at the boundary of their light side territory, thus facing the magical force field separating them and the dark side. Wilhem disembarked and approached it, marveling at its crystalline-like quality. He touched it, which felt strong and sturdy, like an immense wall made of diamond.

He could still see through it, but everything on the other side was distorted and undistinguishable. He asked Sweet Porridge: "Can we go through?"

"The force field has a mind of its own. It chooses the ones who can go through or not. To my knowledge, most winged creatures can enter and a few terrestrial beings like me can. If you cannot then there is a good reason and nothing can be done. You'll have to find another way in. Anyway, we shouldn't be here, it's too dangerous."

"Can you go through?"

"Well, yes," it said and demonstrated for him. It walked into the force field steadily, like going through a transparent curtain, and immediately returned to its side. "I shouldn't have done that. We have to leave right now or else something on their side sees us."

And something did. They noticed a figure moving from the distance approaching them. They couldn't see what it was due to the distortion. It was something similarly large, like Sweet Porridge, and walking on all fours. It stuck its face out of the force field and had features exactly like it, furry face and all.

Sweet Porridge recognized it instantly as its brother, who was likewise forced into subjugation by Axe-Grinder. The difference was it stayed as one of Axe-Grinder's acolytes while Sweet Porridge had left. There was no love lost among them. They growled and bared their teeth.

"Porridge, what's going on?"

"Get away from here! There's going to be trouble," it shouted. Its doppelganger lunged, and both were in an immediate and chaotic catfight. Wilhelm ran away and climbed on a rocky ledge for safety.

He also got a clear view of what was happening. While both Lakivots were fighting, numerous dark creatures were amassing on the other side. They tried to go through but couldn't. Some had horns and tried to force their way in by ramming their heads, but to no success. The force field was strong and seemingly impenetrable. It persisted and prevented them from entering.

Wilhelm looked on in horror as his newfound buddy fought a losing battle. Sweet Porridge was ravaged, bitten, and had become a bloody mess. Its sweet nature was its downfall since it lacked the ferocity to counteract the equal size and strength of its foe. The other Lakivot was about to deliver the final death blow, but its ear perked up. There was an approaching noise from afar.

Wilhelm belatedly heard a commotion coming from a distance on their side. It was his comrades in arms running to them. The dragon was the first to arrive and lurched towards the enemy, aiming for its head. It proceeded to bite it clean off, swallowing it whole. It threw the remaining carcass away to a belowground cavern.

He saw the dark creatures on the other side began to retreat. He came down from the ledge and rushed towards his bloody friend, who was barely alive. It was covered with bite marks all over its body and had a large gash on its neck.

Bakunawa came forward and watched the almost-dead Lakivot.

Wilhelm said: "Please help it, goddess. It is, I mean *he* is my friend."

"Death is different for us magical beings here in Batala. Your understanding of death may be the permanent end of life, but for us nothing is permanent. We continue living in another level of existence indefinitely. You see your friend as about to die, but in truth, he isn't."

"I don't understand."

"What I'm saying is you don't have to tell him 'goodbye' yet, but 'see you soon'."

"I still don't get it."

"Don't worry, I'll take care of him. It's dangerous here and all of you have to go back."

"Alright goddess," said Wilhelm and slowly returned to their encampment along with the other creatures, who had rushed to help them. He glanced back at his fallen friend and saw Bakunawa performing a magical ritual on him. A tear fell on his face, which he quickly dabbed with the back of his hand.

He saw his brother Jacob walking among the creatures, looking at him with fear and uncertainty in his eyes. He had lost a friend, but he still had a brother who appeared to be distressed.

He realized his brother needed him. He was younger in years but older in countenance and matureness. They have to stick together to be able to survive this ordeal.

He quickened his pace to walk beside him.

Chapter 56 Death's Messengers

Nixie, the Water Sprite, put the flask filled with poison in her tiny backpack, along with another one with the Water of Life in it. She never considered that the two flasks looked similar and might cause a mix-up later. She just closed her bag and wore it on her back.

She was happy that she would finally get her wish to be able to fly, and once it occurred, she would leave immediately. She didn't want to get involved in the incoming conflict between the two warring sides and wanted to be as far away as possible.

She needed to return to her home lake, where the Water of Life was located, to blend in the poison. She knew her new friends would hardly miss her since they were busy with combat rehearsals and practice.

She began the long trek home, which she didn't mind. Once she was gifted with flight, it would be easy to go from one place to another.

She knew of a pathway appropriate for her minuscule size where no one from either side would notice her, which she took.

She arrived at her home lake. Her *Diwata* community of water sprites was situated shoreside along their dwelling spaces in various ground holes since they were the only semiaquatic beings in the lake. The others, like the *Sirenas, Syokokoys,* and other merfolk, were full-time lake dwellers. She never worried about them since they were gentle creatures and never caused anyone harm.

She was more concerned about the *Bacobaco,* or the giant sea turtle who ruled over the lake and its dreaded protector: the *Nanreben,* who was a sea serpent that had shining eyes like torches, horns like a water buffalo, long tusks and teeth, and tough scales throughout its body. She had to find a way to get past them to get to the middle of the lake, where the Fountain of Life was situated.

She removed her travel garments and took out the poison-filled flask in her backpack. She regarded the entire breadth of the lake to specifically look for the two fearsome creatures she wanted to avoid. She only saw a couple of merfolk swimming in her direct line of sight, and no Bacobaco or Nanreben can be seen.

She held the neck of the flask in her teeth and cautiously went into the lake. She swam downwards to the ground level since she knew she was safest there. She walked on all fours and steadily crawled toward the middle.

The Fountain of Life was a natural water outflow in the middle of the underground lake. It had a small enclosure surrounding it, made of rocks that looked like a smaller lake within a bigger lake, with the fountain in the middle.

Nixie arrived at the rocky enclosure without anyone seeing her and climbed upward to reach the smaller lake. Once she reached the top edge, she uncorked the flask and poured its contents in. She swam away immediately towards her stuff left on the shore.

As she was about to arrive ashore, something was blocking her watery path: the *Bacobaco*. The giant sea turtle stopped her from swimming and said: "Little sprite, where are you off to?"

"Sir, I'm sorry. I was just taking my daily swim. I hope I'm not bothering anyone."

"These are dangerous times, little sprite. Have you heard about the forthcoming war? We are not part of it, since we are peace-loving creatures, but we should always keep ourselves from harm's way. You should never venture out anywhere alone and always have you kin with you."

"Yes sir, I will sir. By that way, where is the Nanreben? I haven't seen him recently."

"Alas, he was tempted by the dark forces of Axe-Grinder and joined them."

"But who will be our lake's protector?"

"In the absence of the sea serpent, *all* of us will be our lake's protectors. We must protect the most precious element in our lake: the Fountain of Life. Someone might come here to try to steal its invigorating properties or destroy it. We must all be cautious."

"Oh… Really? Thank you for the information, sir, I'll try to remember it."

"Always remember to beware death's messengers, little sprite. They might be hiding in every nook and cranny in our lake. Now go and spread the message to your Diwata community."

"Yes sir."

Nixie quickly swam towards the shore, dressed up hastily, and left.

~O~

Axe-Grinder got a new message from one of his scouts that the water sprite had fulfilled her end of the deal and successfully diluted the poison in the Water of Life. He was a man of his word, so he would grant her the gift of flight.

He went to his special room in his dwelling hut, where he created magical concoctions. He had a separate pantry that stored many ingredients for magical spells and potions. There were numerous flasks in various cupboards and shelves and a cauldron by the fireplace.

The last concoction he created was the poison for the lake, and there were still a few droplets left in the bottom of the cauldron. He poured its contents into another flask and stored it away.

A flying potion was not difficult to concoct, and he had all the ingredients available. He knew it by heart: two parts Mandrake root, one part Hellebore, one part Nightshade, three parts Henbane, and four parts

Wolfbane. He went to the pantry to gather all the ingredients, measuring each to the right quantity.

He mashed everything together in a mortar and pestle and poured it into the cauldron, where it would boil for thirteen minutes. He uttered the proper incantation to activate its magical properties.

In the thirteenth minute, he took the cauldron off the flames and poured the liquid mixture into an empty flask.

The flying potion was done. Once the sprite arrived, he would congratulate and present it to her.

However, he decided he wasn't done with her. He took out another flask on a shelf filled with crushed bark juices of the magical illuminating trees and poured one drop into the flying potion.

Chapter 57 The Bright Sun Brings It to Light

Since Batala was located underground, there was no sun. However, the magically illuminating trees functioned as the source of light and heat for the residents. They came into existence at the same time Batala originated, and everyone accepted it as part of the realm's supernaturalism, and no one ever questioned them.

Nevertheless, the magical trees had a self-defense mechanism that only the two oldest inhabitants—Bakunawa and Axe-Grinder—knew about. They never considered triggering it simply because it would cause the destruction of everything and everyone in Batala.

The trees gave off just enough energy to provide heat and light to the residents, and if someone posed a threat, like cutting either one of them down, they would give off too much radiation that could scorch everyone into ashes.

Axe-Grinder was thinking about this as he waited for Nixie to arrive in front of one such tree. Setting off the mechanism didn't enter his mind, but upcoming events had forced him to consider all options.

He already had backup plans using the sleeping girl and the water sprite. When worse came to worse and all plans and strategies had failed, he would reach a point of desperation, then trigger the mechanism and kill his enemies, which included sacrificing his minions. Then he alone would escape unscathed through a magical antique wardrobe going to the house of his former ally Marcus Ponce de Leon. He still had loyal followers masquerading as humans in the aboveground town of Gintongbayan. He would regroup and plan another assault on the enemy.

But he wouldn't let it go that far. Activating the self-defense mechanism of the magical illuminating trees was the final and desperate plan if all else had failed. He had to ensure they would win and get the ultimate prize in seizing the Realm of Complete Happiness.

He could see the little sprite jogging towards him from a distance. She looked excited about finally getting his gift of flight. He beckoned her towards him and then said: "Little sprite, did you fulfill your task?"

"Yes, sir, I did everything you told me to do. I poured the contents of the flask into the Water of Life. Will you let me fly now?'

"Yes. A promise is a promise. Here it is," he said and handed a tiny flask. "To activate the flying formula, you must go upside in the human world, face east, and wait for the first ray of the sun to hit your face, then drink it."

"Then what happens?"

"You will get what you want. You are free to go little sprite, we are done with our business."

"Thank you, Lord Axe-Grinder," Nixie said. She was overjoyed with her gift. Finally, she could fly like her cousins, the woodland fairies, and the birds in the sky.

She knew of both pathways going to the aboveground town of Gintongbayan and decided to take the safest route via the giant termite mound. The other passage through the tunnel under the Golden Mountain was utilized by many dark creatures, which she didn't want to encounter. She preferred to travel hidden and alone.

When she finally arrived in the forest of the human world, it was still dark out. In a few minutes, the sun would shine, and she would fly.

She hadn't seen the sun before. She had spent all her life in the underground lake with her *Diwata* community, along with the other aquatic beings. The only kind of lighting she had experienced was the magical illumination trees, which supplied heat and a source of light.

In her knowledge, the sun was an extremely blistering star located more than one hundred and fifty million kilometers from Earth. It was too far to cause any damage to anyone.

Nixie saw the early rays of the sun peeking from the eastward horizon and hitting her face. It felt warm and inviting, which gladdened her. She felt something sprout out of her back—the wings she had been wishing for all her life. It felt painful, but she endured it.

As the wings reached full growth, she tried flapping them up and down, up and down, up and down. Slowly at first, then quickly like a hummingbird. Then she rose from the ground.

She was finally flying!

Up, up, up, she flew towards the sun. The sun still felt warm and inviting, but then….

She couldn't stop. Her wings made her fly upwards without her control. The sun began to feel hotter and hotter, then became painful. She felt a burning sensation in her skin, which she could do nothing about.

Pain was her last thought as her skin started burning quickly, and her entire body was engulfed in flames. The wings were the last piece of her body to burn, and thus, she fell to the ground, turning into a small pile of ashes.

~O~

One of Axe-Grinder's scouts—a *Sigbin*—reported what had happened to the *Diwata*. It said: "She fell to her death, just like you said."

"Did she burn?"

"Yes, my lord. She burst into flames and fell to the ground floor in a heap of ashes."

"Good, as expected."

"My lord, can ask you a question?"

"Make it quick, you still have work to do."

"Yes sir. Why did the fairy had to die? She did what she was told do, I see no reason for her death."

"She wasn't one of us and couldn't be trusted. She already had friends on the light side and sooner or later, she would betray us and join them."

"But how did you know sir? She was just a little fairy that won't cause harm to anyone. She wouldn't matter in the grand scheme of things."

"Are you questioning my judgment?"

"No, my lord. I'm only trying to understand why she had to die."

"I already told you. Now begone! The war is upon us. You should go to you Sigbin kinsfolk and prepare yourselves."

Yes, my lord. And I'm sorry, my lord."

Chapter 58 The Peasant in Heaven

Henry thought he had made a big mistake.

He had participated in the mandatory practice and combat rehearsals, which were grueling and backbreaking. He felt tired, out of place, and ill-equipped, and started to regret coming back to Batala in the first place. He was just a simple country boy with peasant-like sensibilities who never intended to become involved in any conflict, much less a war.

He had spent uncountable years being kept for slaughter in one of the various people pens throughout the realm. While imprisoned, he had promised himself never to return if he had a chance to escape. Yet he broke his promise and returned to the one place he didn't want to go.

He did it because of his daughter Pandora, whom he planned to rescue. And because of fortuitous circumstances, all three of them, including Angelica, were now together as a family. They should get back home. It wasn't their war, and no way should have been part of it.

He was resting and thinking deeply about this quandary when Angelica approached him. She, too, had been practicing but was enjoying the entire experience. She said: "This whole place is amazing. And have you met our comrades? They look incredible. The Bigfoot is cool, and the dragon is scary, so keep your distance."

"Yes, I know. I've been with these type of creatures for many years."

"What's going on with you? You're snippy today."

"We shouldn't be here and have to go back home. This isn't our war in the first place."

"But our daughter is part of it and an integral cog in the machine. As her parents, we should support her no matter what."

"Yes, I know. But you realize that we are in a very dangerous environment and could be killed any second, and to a greater degree our daughter."

"I already know that. I'm not stupid. But have you seen our daughter practicing with her power? She has become quite adept with it and formidable. If anyone would even attempt to harm her, she would blast them to the next world. No one could touch her."

"Yes, I've seen our daughter with it and I'm proud of her. But…"

"No buts. We stay here until it's over. Don't be a coward."

"Wait a minute. I'm no coward, it's you who—"

"Mama, Papa. What's going on?" Pandora said, approaching from a distance. The Greenwood elves

Tinker and Blinker were following her like loyal puppies.

"Nothing, dear. Your father and I were just talking."

"I've spoken to Bakunawa, the Serpent-Goddess. She said the evil dwarf had taken Ruby Rose as a hostage. She's in some kind of sleeping spell. We have to do something."

"Oh my gosh. How did it happen? Does her father know about it?"

"Lola Sabrina and Matteo only found out later after she was kidnapped. Mama, what should we do?"

"We have to talk to your Lola; she would know what to do."

"How about Jabber, Lola's *Kapre* friend? He would know how to handle this kind of stuff."

"Good idea. Where can we find this Kapre? Up a tree, I suppose?"

"We'll ask around our new friends."

They found out later that Jabber was with his Kapre community in a faraway area in Batala. He had gone there to convince his kinsfolk to join the war. He was supposed to arrive shortly, with his kin with him.

Henry volunteered to go ahead and meet them halfway. He knew Jabber since he was the one who rescued him from captivity and would bring him back quickly. Peter Griffin also volunteered to help as a means of fast transport.

They were off.

Henry rode atop Peter's back and held on tightly. He had seen creatures similar to Peter before in many years of his captivity but never experienced riding on one. The griffin's body felt smooth like a warm carpet, and he could anchor his legs firmly onto the griffin's backside like on horseback and not fall midflight.

They soared high above Batala, where they could see everything from a distance. They spotted the Kapre community walking up ahead of the main pathway. They swooped down to find Jabber, among many tree giants who looked similar to each other. All of them were covered in fur and smoking tobacco, so it was hard to distinguish one from the other. Even the females were undistinguishable from the males.

Henry surmised that Jabber was probably at the head of the group, leading the way. He motioned Peter to stop at the front of the walking tree giants and got down.

The Kapres didn't seem to notice him. They were massive and lumbering creatures, and compared to him, he was just a small obstacle on the road that they could trample on. He scrambled to and fro, looking for the right Kapre since they looked alike. He started shouting Jabber's name many times, and finally, one of them looked in his direction.

Was it his former rescuer, Jabber? He still wasn't sure, so he went closer. The patchy fur, the long hair, and the beard appeared familiar. *He looks and moves like Jabber. Perhaps it's him,* he thought.

He remembered something. He yelled: "*Rumpelstiltskin!*" It was the word Jabber whispered to him before to mention to Lola Sabrina. This time, the Kapre stopped and crouched down. He said: "I remember you. You're the one I rescued from the human pen. You're Sabrina's son?"

"Son-in-law. Well, soon to be, anyway, if all goes well."

"What are you doing here?"

"I'm here to get you. We need your help. Please come with us quickly."

"You made a mistake in being here. I'm not coming with you."

"Why? You and your kin are on your way to us anyhow, you'll be merely arriving first."

"No, you don't understand. *We* are not joining you but with Lord-Axe Grinder."

"What do you mean?"

"I'm saying that me and my kinfolk are uniting with the dark side."

"What?! Why???"

"I don't need to explain to you," he said, then told another Kapre beside him: "Kill him."

The tree giant hurled himself and grabbed Henry by his massive hands. Peter was startled and flew atop the group, where no one could reach him.

The Kapre hugged Henry and began squeezing him. He couldn't breathe and was quickly suffocating. His bones began to break like brittle twigs.

In less than a minute, Henry was squeezed to death.

Peter Griffin looked on in horror, then flew away.

Chapter 59 The Aged Mother

Angelica noticed she had been getting older speedily in her short time spent in Batala. She had heard from the others about the unusual effects the place had on humans, with some growing old rapidly and some not at all. Henry was of the latter, whose growth had seemingly halted in his period spent in the realm.

While she was of the former and aging quickly by the day's passing; she also discovered wrinkles on her face and strands of white hair on her head. She also felt her bones hurting after completion of the combat rehearsals for the day.

She was approaching seniority at an accelerated pace and began reconsidering Henry's proposition to go home. She regretted calling him a coward and wanted to apologize once he returned.

However, she couldn't tell him sorry anymore because he was dead.

When the news came that Henry was killed by a *Kapre*, she didn't feel anything. She had been accustomed to her life without him, and his death didn't seem to affect her any longer. She was numb to it.

Pandora was disconcerted by the whole ordeal. She was bombarded with many feelings coming from all corners of the emotional spectrum that caused her to become discombobulated. She didn't know if she had the right to feel sad, angry, or vengeful since she only spent a short while with her father.

When confronted with the unfortunate news, both mother and daughter awkwardly hugged each other and didn't even shed a tear. They didn't feel horrified when their comrades told them that Henry's body would likely be slaughtered by the Kapre community, who were largely maneaters.

Nonetheless, the deadly confrontation changed their standing on the situation: they would find a way to rescue Ruby Rose. Once done, they'd depart Batala immediately and leave the war to be fought by the supernatural creatures without their help.

Pandora felt she was especially exploited by being brought to Batala as a ruse in the first place. Jabber the Kapre had forcefully taken her using deception, which she had believed. Now, she realized he had lied and betrayed her and even was the chief instigator of her father's demise.

Angelica told the humans about the plan, and they readily agreed. Even though Batala was a beautiful place filled with amazing creatures, it was still dangerous for ordinary people like them.

When everyone else was asleep, Angelica, Esmeralda, Pandora, Mayor Eddie, Jacob, Wilhelm, and Andreas snuck away from their encampment to rescue Ruby Rose.

~O~

By fortunate happenstance, Ruby Rose was, for the most part, left unguarded. She had been situated at Axe-Grinder's dwelling house, where she still continuously slept and dreamed various scenarios in which she was forever the heroine.

Her time was running out. She was approaching the seventh day of slumber, and if no one would rescue her soon, the cursed scarlet shroud covering her body would transform her into a werewolf. Pandora was told this crucial detail by Bakunawa, which made their rescue mission all the more determined.

A few dark creatures, who were appointed as her guards, were called off to go someplace else, and for the moment, no one was keeping watch. Andreas was doing reconnaissance and recognized this as the right time. He quickly went back to tell the others.

They had to find another way into the dark side. All of them tried going through the force field, but only Pandora and Andreas were able to, so all of them had to go the longer and farther way in, which was through the tunnel under the Golden Mountain.

They moved quickly and ran in half-pace due to the time element. They wanted to reach Ruby Rose in time before she became a monster or else be eaten by it. They dreaded it and were tired of mainly being subjected to the monsters' foodstuff.

They finally arrived at the innermost cave entrance to the dark side of Batala. They hid behind a large boulder and sent Andreas to scout the area and find where Ruby Rose was confined.

They could barely see anyone from their vantage point, and no one seemed to be moving. It was also dead quiet, and not a supernature creature was stirring, not even a were-mouse. Andreas arrived momentarily and telepathically told them Ruby Rose's exact location. Not a soul was present in the whole expanse of the dark side.

Which was curious. They had to be there to amass as a legion of horrifying soldiers to take part in the war. If no one was there, there had to be a valid reason why.

Esmeralda smelled a trap, and she voiced this concern to the others. Someone might have told them they were coming and were waiting in the shadows, ready to strike.

Esmeralda wanted to test her theory by volunteering to rescue Ruby Rose all by her lonesome. The others were amazed by her courage and true grit but were secretly glad they wouldn't need to go anymore.

She was an expert in sneaking around due to her vast experience as a world-class thief. She was adept at being unruffled and stealthy to make as little impact as possible in any place she would infiltrate.

She asked about the location of Ruby Rose's confinement space, which was inside Axe-Grinder's dwelling hut. It was situated the farthermost in the entire domain of the dark side, where no other domiciles were built. It was deliberately solitary, which was Axe-Grinder's preference.

She was ninja-like as she crept soundlessly and furtively from one hut to another, and indeed, no one was there. Each hut she passed didn't have a single creature within its vicinity, which creeped her out. She soldiered on despite the hair on her neck standing up. She felt it wouldn't be this simple, and she would face an unforeseen obstacle.

And she was right. As she was approaching Axe-Grinder's hut, a curious thing was standing outside the doorway. It was something she never thought she would encounter in an underground enchanted realm: a gray alien.

Or perhaps not.

To her, it did look like the prototypical extraterrestrial being from another planet as described in popular culture: a large head, long arms and legs, gray skin, and a nonexistent sex organ. It reminded her of an octopus, with its appendages resembling tentacles. She surmised it was probably a supernatural creature she wasn't familiar with.

This tall, man-like creature stared at her blankly with its large black eyes. It wasn't moving and seemingly didn't notice her, so she sidestepped to get past it. Yet it saw her and tried to grab her with its tentacle-like arms. She had expected it to happen, so she unsheathed her smallswords and slashed at both limbs. They fell to the ground and slithered away like snakes.

Esmeralda saw its appendages slowly growing new ones. She retreated, hoping that it would follow her. She wanted to lead the creature away from the doorway so she could enter it, but it didn't work. She looked for other entryways, but it was the only one, and the only way through was to defeat it.

She slashed away like cutting tall but impenetrable grass that grew right back after each cut. A few minutes of this, and she recognized the futility of her actions, so she stopped and retreated far back.

She noticed a red fog accumulating from a distance. It looked eerie because it was moving quickly on its own volition towards them. It skipped her and went straight for the gray alien.

It formed into a small tornado. It began enveloping and slowly disintegrating the gray alien from within. Soon, it turned to dust.

The red fog began changing into something familiar— and to her surprise—to a man who looked like her jilted lover, Matteo.

And indeed, it was Matteo, who had drunk a magic potion to transform him into a red mist. The once ardent lovers were again face to face in another circumstance, more strange than before.

Both were speechless.

Chapter 60 The Poor Man and the Rich Man are the Same in Death

Matteo had patiently waited for Luna to finish concocting the magical potion. He wanted to ask her how the potion would work, but she was still busy muttering incomprehensible incantations and mixing the reddish mush in the cauldron.

His imagination had been running wild. What was the potion supposed to do? Will it enable him to fly or become as strong as the Hulk? Or maybe make him teleport from one place to another in a blink of an eye?

He needn't have to wait long.

The witch was about to finish reciting the incantations that activated the supernatural properties of the ingredients, each coalescing with the other, rendering magic to happen. This point in the conjuration process was the most dangerous, and one mispronounced incant or incorrect ingredient measurement would make the potion explode.

Nevertheless, Luna was an expert potion maker and completed the concoction, with nothing drastic occurring. The reddish mush had transformed into a bright red liquid, which she poured into a transparent flask.

She handed the magic potion to Matteo and said: "Now listen carefully and I'm going to tell you specific instructions in taking it. If you won't follow it to the letter, then it will kill you."

"I'll do anything, for the sake of my daughter."

"Alright. Tonight is the full moon, where witches like me are the most powerful, and the potions are the most potent. At exactly three in the morning, the witching hour, go outside and face west to the setting moon. Uncork the flask, and before drinking its contents, say: '*Ego creo quad ego loquar.*'

"Then what happens?"

If you follow the instructions precisely, then you won't die."

"But what will it do to me?"

Then suddenly, in the hut in the forest, Luna, the mysterious cross-eyed *Mangkukulam*, and everything related to her had disappeared. Matteo stood alone in the forest and noticed the young goat was nowhere in sight. She had magicked it with her.

He looked at the flask in his hand and went home.

He set his alarm clock at 3 a.m. and tried to sleep early but couldn't. He was still tossing and turning close to midnight and thus decided to forego sleeping altogether and wait for the witching hour to arrive.

At exactly three in the morning, he went outside and brought the flask with him. He faced the full moon, uncorked the vial, and downed the bright red contents.

Once done, he felt he had forgotten something from the instructions. Then it dawned on him: he forgot to utter the Latin chant before drinking the magic potion.

Shit, he thought aloud. *Am I going to die?*

Then, something peculiar was starting to happen. The consistency of his fleshy body was beginning to change. At first, it became like glass, then sand, and lastly, similar to a cloud that was colored deep red. His transformation into the red mist was complete.

He was able to alter the substance of his body through will and be a free-flowing fog, then return to his solid human state. He discovered he could destroy anything by turning himself into a tornado and surrounding it.

He quickly became acclimated to his new power. He ran towards the giant termite mound, turned himself into a red mist, and easily seeped through it. In his foggy form, he quickly flew through the Batala tunnelway, desperately looking for his daughter.

~O~

Mayor Eddie had been dutifully complying with what everyone told him to do. He had been learning much about combat from the supernatural contingent of warriors and was taught to heighten his natural aptitude for sharpshooting. He could utilize his Fierce

Mountain Reaper with deadly accurate force from quite a distance, more than he was used to.

His bullets were also magicked to inflict terrible damage to anyone or anything they hit, even deadlier to the supernatural element. Their previously impenetrable skin could now be blown away to smithereens by his rifle bullets.

Even with his lethal weapon and sniping prowess, he was relieved he could finally go home. After all, he was still the mayor of Gintongbayan and needed to go back to fulfill his mayoral obligations.

And it looked like they were surely going home since his goddaughter was about to be rescued, and his other goddaughter Pandora was safe and sound. Yet in his short time spent in Batala, he felt danger was always afoot, and death was forever lurking around the corner.

And he realized he shouldn't feel relieved, yet since the task wasn't done. He hadn't seen Ruby Rose with his own two eyes free from any danger.

He couldn't see Esmeralda from his vantage point behind a large boulder. He inferred that she should've been with them by now if no one hindered her rescue efforts. If it took this long, she may likely be in trouble.

A few minutes turned to an hour, yet either Esmeralda or Ruby Rose had arrived. After Esmeralda, he was the most proficient fighter among them, so he volunteered to find out what happened.

When he arrived at the hut in question, no one was there, but he heard a commotion coming from inside. It sounded like growling and yelling noises. He rushed to the door and kicked it open.

His eyes fell on Esmeralda first. She was all bloody, with slashes on her arms and torso. She was holding both smallswords in combat stance up ahead of a large and snarling wolf. He also saw Matteo, which surprised him. There was also something weird happening to his body, which looked hazy for one moment, then solid the next.

He realized the wolf was his goddaughter, and they were too late to rescue her. The curse had attained finality and turned Ruby Rose into a damned creature of the night.

He aimed the werewolf with his Fierce Mountain Reaper and cocked it. As he was about to fire, Matteo transformed into a killer fog and enveloped him in a tornado-like fashion.

The two disparate individuals coming from different sides of the fence became one in blurry chaos, turning round and round and round.

Both disintegrated into nothingness.

Chapter 61 Rumpelstiltskin's Return

Axe-Grinder had realized—because he was the general in his army of dark fighters—he needed a second-in-command or a lieutenant general, someone who would make sure his orders were followed precisely. Since most of his trusted inner circle of the seven dwarves had perished, he needed the one surviving member beside him to carry such orders: Rumpelstiltskin.

He amassed his remaining fighting force to rescue him in the darkest corner of Batala, where the worst of the worst supernatural creatures were imprisoned. It was a realm within a realm: another pocket universe similar to the Realm of Complete Happiness. It was a domain called the Realm of Utter Hopelessness, a prison dimension where the most troublesome and vilest creatures were cast off from all of Earth's mythologies.

When Rumpelstiltskin and Pandora were sucked into a black hole, he was purposefully sent to this dimension by a race of mysterious beings who monitored every interdimensional passageway in all the realms and levels of existence. Little was known about them, and even Bakunawa, the Serpent Goddess, and Axe-Grinder, two of the oldest supernatural creatures in Batala, knew less. Those who had seen them described them as having grey skin, long arms and legs, and large heads. They were known as the "Gatekeepers."

The Gatekeepers had cast away Rumpelstiltskin to the Realm of Utter Hopelessness due to his inherent ability to cause a rip in the spacetime continuum, which would engender a cosmic cataclysm or the end of all things. It would happen if someone would call out his name with him close by, thus prompting the tear.

Axe-Grinder had recently discovered this ability from a new follower named Jabber from the clan of *Kapres* and wanted to use it as a weapon for the upcoming war. Hence, he decided to take his strongest warriors to the realm and free the imprisoned Dwende.

The entire domain was a prison institution shaped like an octagon. It was a series of interconnecting buildings with small cells housing each terrible creature. He had sent scouts to scope the whole facility, and they reported to tell him of one way in: from above.

The scouts had discovered that the protective covering atop the whole prison was made of the same material as the force field that separated the light and dark sides of Batala, which, curiously only the winged creatures and a few terrestrial creatures could go through.

He sent out his various winged warriors, the *Wakwaks* (vampiric birds), *Minokawas* (gigantic dragon-like birds), and the *Manananggals* (winged vampires that can separate their torsos from their bodies) to find the imprisoned *Dwende* with a powerful name.

Their search directed them to the middle of the facility within the octagon, where the most dangerous creatures were jailed. There were no guards since the cells were bewitched, which hindered escape. Rumpelstiltskin's jail cell was magicked with a powerful spell that neither winged beast could overcome. One Minokawa went back to Axe-Grinder to bring him up to date.

Axe-Grinder rode atop its back to fly towards Rumpelstiltskin's cell. When he arrived, he noticed it was enchanted with a powerful protection spell that had encroaching vines as strong as titanium covering it. The Minokawa's powerful claws couldn't even scratch it.

Axe-Grinder knew how to neutralize the spell and break Rumpelstiltskin free. He brought his wooden staff wherever he went, not only to help him walk but also to focus his sorcery and make it more potent. He pointed its bottom to the crisscrossing vines and uttered the chant, which was a reversal spell: "*Quarum sacra fero ne auderet contradicere.*"

The vines then lost their magical potency and became like any other vascular plant that can easily be ripped with both hands. The dark dwarf Rumpelstiltskin seized them and tore them away.

He was free.

Axe-Grinder approached his last and most loyal follower and hugged him. There was no need for conversation with like-minded *Dwendes* like them. They had spent eons together in a united front. For them, talk was cheap. Their actions did the talking for them.

Rumpelstiltskin rode on the same Minokawa behind his lord Axe-Grinder and flew away from the Realm of Utter Hopelessness with a renewed hope for the inevitable.

~O~

When Pandora and the remaining humans, along with Andreas, went to Axe-Grinder's hut, only Esmeralda was left unconscious and lying in a pool of blood. Mayor Eddie and importantly, Ruby Rose were nowhere to be seen. Jacob and Wilhelm carried Esmeralda outside and away from the encampment of the dark side. They made a makeshift stretcher for her conveyance.

Angelica determined that Esmeralda's wounds were too severe for any mortal man to remedy. They all decided to bring her back to the light side where someone with a healing power could fix her up, particularly Bakunawa, the Serpent Goddess.

They tried to go the shorter route through the force field, which allowed them all to pass.

They arrived with Esmeralda in tow. Bakunawa and the supernatural contingent met them and shared their sorrow, especially with Pandora and Angelica, who had undergone so much.

Bakunawa approached the still-unconscious Esmeralda and performed a healing spell on her. The deep gashes on her arms and torso and the various scratches and bruises all over her body slowly healed. In a few minutes, she was as good as new.

Esmeralda opened her eyes, and the first person she saw was Pandora. Tears fell down her face and mouthed the words: "I'm sorry," to her.

Pandora approached her and said: "It's alright. It's not your fault and you did your best."

"No. I've done so much bad things to your family and yet you've accepted me as your friend. Now, you've even saved my life even though you have every right to leave me there."

"Don't worry about it. It was really a group effort and we didn't want to leave you there to die."

"Thank you, all of you."

"By the way, what *did* happen there?" Angelica asked.

"First there was an alien, then Matteo arrived as a red fog and ate it up. When we entered the room, there was a wolf, and then—"

"Slow down, *slow down* please! You're not making any sense. Maybe you should rest first, and we can talk later."

"But something else happened..." Esmeralda said and immediately nodded off.

"I put her to sleep for her own good. All of you should rest as well. We will reconvene tomorrow and discuss further plans."

"Yes Goddess," everyone said in unison.

Chapter 62 The Crumbs on the Table

Lola Sabrina couldn't telepathically contact anyone in Batala, as though someone was intentionally blocking her from going through. From all her knowledge about witchcraft, there shouldn't be a reason why she couldn't talk to Jabber, Pandora, Andreas, or even Matteo since they were the most receptive to telepathic communication.

If someone was blocking her on purpose, this "someone" had powers equal to hers or even more. This person, or maybe a supernatural being, had specific training in necromancy to undermine her white magic or perhaps knowledgeable in specific excerpts in the Book of Shadows.

The clearest memory she had in her time spent in Batala was reading particular chapters in the sorcery book related to her two most potent endowments: divination and telepathy. She remembered one excerpt in particular: *entities who can create a powerful barricade against telepathic signals have an extensive understanding of black magic.*

She speculated by using a process of elimination, that there was only one who fulfilled those prerequisites; someone powerful enough and filled with malicious intent was their nemesis, the dark *Dwende*Axe-Grinder.

By doing it, he had everything to gain and nothing to lose. He knew of her power and influence and wanted to subvert whatever assistance she provided.

She was all alone, left helpless and nothing to do. It was like she couldn't eat a full meal and only left with crumbs on the table. She was still hungry for information and getting desperate with each passing second.

What am I to do? She thought loudly.

You have to stay calm, or you will lose your mind again.

Someone was telepathically whispering back to Lola Sabrina, which meant the invisible barricade blocking the signals was starting to crack. Someone with powerful white magic was able to break through.

She was incredulous.

Who is this? She replied.

It's me, Luna, your former coven-mate. I've been trying to contact you, but something or someone has been blocking my messages.

Luna! I'm happy and surprised to hear from you! How long has it been?

It's been years. How is your family? Oh, sorry, bad question.

Not good, Luna, not good at all. Right now, they're in a dangerous place where I'm too old to go and give any help. I can't even contact them.

I know everything, Sabrina. I've been listening to your telepathic conversations. You use it like yelling through a megaphone for everyone like me to listen. You might consider dialing back the volume, so to speak so others won't hear you.

Oh my gosh. I'm sorry. I'm losing it.

It's what happens to all of us as we grow old. For you, some of your mental facilities are slowly disintegrating...

And you?

For me, it's my looks that are decaying. If you see me now, I surely look like what a witch is supposed to appear: a cross-eyed old crone.

You're too hard on yourself.

But my mind is still as sharp as a tack. I could still make complicated magic potions from memory. I've recently made one such concoction for your gardener, and I think he made a mistake in taking it.

Matteo? You know him?

Yes. I've given him a potion to enable him to teleport from one place, or another so he can rescue his daughter. However, something must have gone wrong since he should be there now.

Knowing him, he is sometimes foolhardy and often rushes to judgment. Did you give him proper instructions?

Yes, I told him exactly how to take it and the consequence of not following instructions.

It means they're in more trouble than they already were. Oh, Luna, what should we do?

For you, nothing. You're too old and fragile to make any impact. For me, I could still do something that affects change positively.

What will you do?

Do what your gardener was supposed to: take his potion properly and rescue your family.

Oh, thank you, Luna. Thank you! How can I repay you?

No need. We're only the two surviving members of our coven, and we should help each other when one of us is in trouble.

Yes. All these years, I should've reached out to you. I'm sorry…

Don't worry about it. Your family is rich, mine is poor, and we don't mix. I completely understand.

Yes, and it shouldn't be. You could have come here and knocked on my door for a visit. Catch up on old times.

No thanks. I try to avoid things like that due to my scary looks. Children are known to run away when they see me.

It can't be that bad.

It is that bad. In any case, I really should go. I have to make the same potion again, and take it this time, then look for your family.

I owe you a debt of gratitude, Luna, and once everything is over, please come and visit. We have a lot to talk about.

We'll see each other soon…

Her telepathic imprint was gone.

Sabrina breathed a sigh of relief. It was like a dark cloud in her mind had parted to let the sunshine in. She felt glad that the former member of her coven had contacted her out of nowhere and offered help. Yet she was also guilty that she hadn't given her any financial aid since she was poor and lived in a squatter's area in Gintongbayan.

She knew of the reputation of his family in town as misers who rarely went out of their way to help the less unfortunate segment of society. She promised to change that, be a more helpful and productive citizen, and encourage her family to do the same.

I hope I'll remember when it's over, and my family is safe and sound.

Yet at the back of her mind, she knew her faltering old brain wouldn't allow her to, much less retain it. But she was still hopeful, and her kind of hope had wings that enabled her to fly.

Chapter 63 The Golden Goose

For Pandora, everything was going from bad to worse. She had been trying to contact her Lola Sabrina via telepathy, but for some unknown reason, she couldn't. It was like someone had created an invisible wall that restricted any telepathic communication to go through.

She and the remaining humans had been having the worst luck, and everything they did or attempted to do had seemingly crashed and burned. She needed advice from her Lola to get themselves out of the jam.

She thought of their present state of things: Mayor Eddie and Matteo had mysteriously evaporated or were probably dead, along with her father, who was likely made into Kapre grub. Her best friend Ruby Rose had become a werewolf and was likewise missing. Her Lola Sabrina would know what to do.

They were back in Bakunawa, the Serpent-Goddess' camp, which was the last place she wanted to be, and this sentiment was shared by her mother Angelica, and the remaining humans. They didn't want to participate in the upcoming war and wished to go home instead.

Bakunawa needed her because she was their golden goose who could invariably turn the tide of war. Her powerful light-blasting ability was the key to defeating Axe-Grinder and his dark army of terrible creatures. Without her, Bakunawa and her alabaster troops would be surely defeated.

Since getting away was fruitless, Pandora decided she might as well join in the war preparations and told Angelica and the remaining humans to do the same. They had to make the best out of a bad situation. She'd try to find a way to contact her Lola again later.

The only thing that put a smile on her face was the two Greenwood elves, Tinker and Blinker. They looked like troll dolls she used to play with when she was little. She often was transfixed by their actions, which sometimes verged on the silly. They were like goofy and weird-looking puppies that followed her wherever she went. They were a delightful respite from the presumed troubles in the coming future, which they couldn't escape.

Even though she didn't want to think about it, the time for war was getting closer, and she couldn't do anything about it. She felt tension in the air that was icy cold and sharp like a knife's edge. Everyone was nervous, irritable, and unable to relax. Small quarrels sometimes occurred among the supernatural contingent for no reason other than pure restlessness. They had too much nervous energy and had to remove through combat practice and rehearsals.

She considered the numerous armaments on display for them to choose and wear, like battleaxes, swords, bows, arrows, and armor. They were all properly sharpened and polished, and ready for use.

She had chosen a lightweight suit of steel armor that particularly fit her lithe frame. It was composed of steel plates linked by internal leathers and loosely closed rivets to enable her maximum freedom of movement. She tried it out to test its comfort and viability, and after donning it for the first time, it felt a little heavy, but she became used to it quickly.

She had seen Esmeralda's smallswords and wanted something similar to them. She selected a *Naginata* or a type of polearm with a long wooden shaft with a curved blade attached at the end. It was a useful weapon for close-quarter combat in case her light-blasting power failed her in the heat of battle.

She practiced her new weapon with Tinker and Blinker, who helped her immensely. They took turns standing on each other's shoulders and roleplayed the part of a tall enemy carrying a weapon. They playfought for the whole day until Pandora became used to the Naginata.

She saw the other humans were doing the same.

Her mother, Angelica was making good use of her time by befriending the supernatural creatures who were on friendly terms with them, especially with Bigfoot, who always had a nice smile on his furry face. He could understand her but could only respond in growls and grunts.

She knew her fighting skills were inferior, but she was adept at making friends and used it to her advantage.

She planned to make as many friends as possible who would hopefully fight in her stead when the time for hand-to-hand fighting came.

Meanwhile, Esmerald's wounds had healed nicely, thanks to Bakunawa. She resumed practicing with renewed vigor and became surprisingly accommodating to the others who didn't have her fighting prowess. She was particularly helpful to the two brothers, Wilhelm and Jacob, and taught them the proper usage of bows and arrows, which were their preferred weapons.

Pandora looked for Andreas, but he was nowhere to be found. She was aware of his newfound ability to enter anybody and possess it. He could be anywhere, taking possession of anyone like a vampiric sponge sucking essential information out of its victims. She telepathically inquired him of his whereabouts, but no response. *Either he's avoiding me, or the invisible wall doesn't only block telepathic communication to and from Lola Sabrina but to everyone inclined to it,* she conjectured.

She thought about her Lola Sabrina and how worried she might be. She tried to think of another way to communicate with her other than telepathy, but she couldn't think of any. *If there was only a way to send word,* she thought.

Then suddenly, she slapped her forehead and had an idea. She laughed at herself for being so stupid and not thinking about it earlier. The elves! She could send the funny-looking elves Tinker and Blinker to her Lola.

They had a knack for camouflage and could leave Batala and go to Casa de la Noche almost unseen.

And they would readily agree to it with no questions asked. She stopped practicing and ran towards her mother, Angelica to tell her about her plan, with the two elves following close.

She found her with Bigfoot and Peter Griffin, sitting on a couple of loose boulders, resting and talking with them. She yelled from afar: "Mama, I found a way to talk to Lola!"

"Huh? What are you shouting about? Come here and say it again!"

When Pandora arrived, she said: "Mama, how are you talking to them? Both can't talk and you aren't telepathic."

"They can understand me but can't talk back. They just shake their heads, nod or growl to respond. What do you want to talk to me about, dear?"

"Mama, I discovered a way to send a message to Lola: these two elves! We can write it on a piece of paper that they can take to her, and also bring back her reply to us. They can do it in a day's time."

Tinker and Blinker fervently nodded, still with silly grins on their faces.

"See? They always agree. I love these little critters!"

"Alright. What are we going to write about?"

"Everything. About Henry, Matteo, her traitorous *Kapre* friend Jabber, everything. I hope she'll know what to do."

"I hope so…"

Chapter 64 The Devil's Sooty Brother

Rumpelstiltskin has returned to the fold. He was the final jigsaw piece in his lord Axe-Grinder's dark puzzle of terrible warriors to set the war plans in motion. Another crucial piece was the Kapre contingent, led by a new believer in the cause called Jabber.

Axe-Grinder had dubbed Rumpelstiltskin as the "devil's sooty brother," behind his back. It wasn't an insult but a term of endearment. It was a known fact they were all Satan's offspring, and it was high praise to be mentioned in the same breath as him.

Axe-Grinder had been greatly surprised when Jabber offered his help since he was widely recognized as an ally to Bakunawa and the magical humans. He promptly accepted him and never doubted his conviction since he knew how difficult it was to decide to betray someone.

He planned to bring the two like-minded individuals together, work with each other, and bring forth assured victory. Rumpelstiltskin was already present and accounted for, and he was waiting for Jabber and his *Kapre* community to arrive.

From a distance, he saw them approaching. They were like a troop of gigantic orangutans who were more ape-like than men, with huge hairy arms swaying from side to side and mammoth legs rambling along the pathway. Each was smoking a comically large rolled tobacco, with black smoke accumulating at their headspace. They rambled towards him and stopped.

Jabber took two steps forward. If he didn't, no one would distinguish him from the others due to similar appearances. He raised his right hand semi-upwardly and yelled: "All hail Lord Axe-Grinder!" The rest of the Kapres followed suit.

"Jabber and the clan of Kapres. Welcome! The war draws near but before it happens, let us all be merry! Prepare a feast for our new brothers! Go to the people pens and slaughter a couple of humans!" He told some of his minions.

"My Lord, we also brought human meat. This particularly had escaped from one of your pens, and we caught them for you."

"Wonderful! Hand it over to them," Axe-Grinder said. The Kapres followed the dark minions to the feasting area. "Jabber, come here. I want to introduce you to someone. However, we cannot say his name yet because it holds power. We will say it when the right time comes during battle. In the meantime, you can call him 'Sooty'."

Rumpelstiltskin smiled and offered his hand to shake. Jabber's massive mitt grabbed his tiny hand and shook it.

"Come! Let us talk about battle schemes and strategies."

"Yes, my Lord," both said in unison.

~O~

Ruby Rose's consciousness was trapped in a hellscape inside the body of a terrible beast.

Lola Sabrina had tried to neutralize her werewolf curse with an enchantment of continuous life-affirming and encouraging dreams filled with heroism and bravery, but it was sorely lacking. She still transformed into a mindless creature of the night, with her conscious mind held hostage.

She had hoped she was still dreaming, but alas, everything felt real. The last thing she remembered was being inside her new room in the servant's quarters and accidentally pricking her finger with a spindle from an antique spinning wheel. When she woke up, she was in a humongous cave that she could only suspect was Batala.

It was like riding her car with someone else taking the wheel. She could still see, hear, and feel everything, but without her in control. She felt helpless and couldn't do anything as her beast body had ravaged Esmeralda almost to death. Then, it escaped the dwelling hut and was momentarily lost in the deep caverns of Batala, taking her along as an unwilling participant and hostage.

She saw a pack of similar were-creatures going to an undisclosed location, and her beast body followed. The place they were going to become darker and murkier, and she could hear a commotion ahead.

The were-pack was going towards other similarly dark creatures, who were feasting and merrymaking. She was filled with horror, as she saw the type of meat roasted on spits: humans. The terrible creatures were munching at them with gusto, with oil dripping down their mouths. If she could vomit, she would.

She could hear the creatures' huge mouths and sharp teeth crunching at the bones like they were eating fried pork rinds. She could feel her beast's body getting hungry, its mouth drooling. Her mind was sickened, but her body had a powerful desire to devour meat.

To her utmost horror, it looked like her beast body was going to indulge in the feasting, and if it would happen, she wondered if she could handle it or might go insane. But thankfully, it didn't and went away from the banqueting and went to three disparate creatures in deep conversation. He recognized two of the dwarves, but the other one she didn't, but from the looks of it, was a *Kapre*.

She knew that her beast's body was drawn to its lord and master, Axe-Grinder, the older of the two dwarves. It was programmed to follow him wherever he went like a loyal pet. The other one she recognized as the dwarf who was sucked into the same black hole as Pandora. If the two were there, then trouble was surely afoot.

Her beast body went to Axe-Grinder's side to be petted and was rewarded with a scratch behind the ear. They were all talking in Dwarvish language that she couldn't comprehend. After a few minutes of listening, something strange began to happen: she was slowly able to understand them.

The previously alien speech started to make sense to her and soon became understandable. She could only surmise that her mind was slowly melding into her beast body, and before long, her consciousness as Ruby Rose would vanish, and only the mindless werebeast would remain.

She was stricken with fear and helplessness. She was trapped, and no one was going to help her. Then, she heard a name mentioned by the Kapre that offered a glimmer of hope: Pandora. He said he knew of a way to get to her when she would be alone. He would only need a handful of loyal warriors to go with him.

Axe-Grinder motioned her beast body to go with the Kapre, along with the other dwarf.

The three of them left while the feasting and merriment continued. Nevertheless, her hope was renewed. He looked forward to seeing her best friend Pandora, who would hopefully recognize it was her and find a way to change her back into her true human self.

Chapter 65 The Grave Mound of the Starman

Lola Sabrina visited the grave of her late husband Galileo, at the local cemetery. It was his death anniversary. She brought a bouquet of white Lillies and packed a small lunch in her bag since she planned to spend the whole day there.

The weather was downcast, which mirrored her current emotion. She always felt this way during the anniversary of Leo's death that in truth, may be alive since he was bitten by a were-animal when her daughter Angelica was still a baby. He might still be roaming around in the mortal world or the nether regions of Batala as a cursed creature of the night.

Nonetheless, deep in her heart, she was aware the man she knew and loved was long dead. It was already too late, and nothing could be done about it. If a werewolf bit someone, it wouldn't take long for the mindless animal to take over the human consciousness.

She always forgot what her husband looked like, so she kept a small picture of him in a golden locket worn on a necklace and often glanced at his bespectacled and balding appearance. He might look homely to everyone else, but he was handsome in her eyes. He was the only man who loved a woman like her who had lots of emotional baggage.

He was buried in the family mausoleum along with other members of the Ponce de Leon clan, who, like Leo, were mostly men who died young. She placed the bouquet atop his grave mound and said a short prayer.

"Deep peace to the running waves to you. Deep peace to the flowing air to you. Deep peace to the quiet earth to you. Deep peace to the shining stars to you. Deep peace of the infinite peace to you."

She chose a pagan prayer that was more of a chant, rather than a Christian one. She considered herself a lapsed Catholic who only went to church whenever she remembered it. She had been deeply religious after Leo's death up to the time she took Pandora to church when she was still a toddler, and the incident happened. She was shaken to her core by it and thus completely abandoned her devotion to Catholicism.

Once done, she sat on one of the marble benches, unwrapped her homemade egg sandwich, and took teensy nibbles. She wasn't hungry but forced herself to eat because she hadn't consumed a full meal since the day before.

She opened the locket holding Leo's picture that was already faded with age and looked at it intently. She waited for memories of him to pop up in her head.

The memory that always came to her was the first time they met when he asked to know his future by reading his palm. More than anything, he wanted to learn if he was going to marry and if he did, who would be his future wife.

He had arrived in Casa de la Noche, rang the doorbell, and was brought to the drawing room by the majordomo, where she had set up an area to admit customers. She sat behind a table and motioned him to sit in a spare chair in front of her.

He said: "Good morning, madam. I've heard from people around town that you can tell my future. I'm curious: how do you do it?"

"There are many ways, but the easiest and quickest would be reading your palm," she replied.

"Which hand, right or left?"

"Well, it is important to analyze both hands. The non-dominant hand will reveal your character and personality, and the dominant one will show how these traits are manifested in practice. Together, they will show how you're using your potential in this lifetime. Should we start?"

"Yes, please. But first, what's your name?"

"Sabrina. And you are—?"

"Galileo Montalban, and I prefer you call me Leo."

"Galileo? It's a good name, quite unique. Don't you like it?"

"I hate it. I've been bullied my whole life because of it. Leo will suffice, if you don't mind."

"Alright. Were you named after someone from your family?"

"No. It's the name of an Italian man who discovered the stars."

I don't think that's right."

"What do you mean?"

"Your namesake didn't discover the stars. I think he became famous for another thing but still related to stars and stargazing. The ones who discovered them were more likely cavemen before history was recorded."

"Maybe you're right. I never paid attention to it when it was explained to me by my parents."

"They were well-meaning parents who gave you a good name. I don't understand why you were still bullied."

"When I was little, kids used to call me 'Gay Leo.' I'm not."

"Not what?"

"Not gay."

"Really?"

"Why? Do I look gay?"

"Not particularly."

"What do you mean?"

"Nothing. I'm just making conversation."

"I know what you're doing. You're making me all riled up to get me to admit personal details, which you will use for my reading."

"I've done no such thing. I'm merely doing small talk and it's you who's getting easily upset."

"I'm sorry. All those bad memories of getting bullied came roaring back, making me mad."

"Don't worry about it. Please give be both your hands."

"Sure," said Leo and handed them over, palms up.

"Alright. Let's see…" She said. She was silent for a minute and observed all the features of his hands. "You have well-manicured hands, soft and never calloused, which meant you grew up in the privileged class and never did any manual work in your life."

"You're right, but any idiot would know that."

"It's merely a superficial observation. We haven't done the actual reading yet. But what do you really want to know?"

"I want to know if I am going to marry and if I did, then who."

"Your hands will give us clues to answer your questions. For your information, they are portals that provide invaluable insight. They have lines, creases, mounts and plains that tells the story of your future."

"Where does it tell me who am I going to marry?"

"Don't you want to know other information about your future?"

"No, just the stuff about marriage."

"Alright. For that, we will look at your heart line, which is the highest horizontal line on your palm. Hmm…"

"Your heart and life lines are curious."

"Why?"

"Both are short and broken."

"What does it mean?"

Suddenly, she saw a vision of Leo's future, which inexplicably and surprisingly, she was a part of. She saw both of them in church, standing before a priest at the altar and about to be married. After the priest told him to kiss the bride, his face suddenly transformed into a wolf, close to biting her.

She snapped out of the daze caused by the vision and stared at the confused look on Leo's face.

"Are you alright? For a moment, it looked like you were about to puke. What happened?"

"Telling one's future is sometimes confusing. I'm sorry I appeared out of sorts."

"What did you see? Do I get married?"

"Yes."

With who?"

"Well, *me.*"

"You?"

"Uh-huh."

"Are you making fun of me? Is it because of how I look?"

"No. What do you look like?"

"A rich sucker who always doesn't know he's being scammed."

"I'm telling the truth. Why would I lie to you? My family is already rich and I'm only doing this to help people. If you're not satisfied with my reading then you should leave."

"Wait a goddamn minute. I just want to tell you—," Leo stopped abruptly because, for the first time, he ran out of things to say. However, he was intrigued by Sabrina's prediction and suddenly saw her in a brand-new light. There was something about her that fascinated him.

And it was the beginning of their short but sweet love affair.

She remembered everything as if it was yesterday. She knew it was only a momentary clarity of thought and would soon return to ceaseless forgetfulness. Yet, she was still thankful that she remembered him, her Starman, who taught her to discover the real stars in her life.

The memory of how they first met reinvigorated her, and she decided to forego her whole day vigil of his grave mound. She wanted to go home immediately because she suddenly thought of how to help her distressed kin in Batala.

Chapter 66 The Old Beggar Woman Who Wasn't

When Lola Sabrina arrived at Casa de la Noche, she noticed an old beggar woman she hadn't seen before, wearing unkempt clothes, standing aimlessly in front of the main gate. She paid the driver of the rented tricycle she rode, disembarked, and walked towards the stranger.

"Who are you and what do you want?" She said congenially.

The old woman faced her stoically, her wrinkled face looking unreal and wooden. Then, her whole body suddenly separated in two right at the waist, and two small faces peeked out from both bodily structures. It was the Greenwood elves Tinker and Blinker in disguise. One had been standing on top of the shoulders of the other to form a realistic representation of an old beggar woman.

Upon closer inspection, Lola Sabrina noticed that the elves used plant materials to create the perfect disguise: her clothes and hair were made of vines, leaves, and ferns, and her face, arms, and legs of intricately carved wood. She sensed that the elves had worn this disguise before and were proficient at it.

She was taken aback and wary since her experiences with supernatural creatures in the past weren't always good. However, she saw one of them holding a letter with her name written in big black letters. She opened the gate quickly and ushered them in.

She had been alone in the house since she left for the cemetery earlier in the morning. It was Sunday, and all the household helpers were out on their day off. She was relieved they were alone, and no one would ask questions or disturb them.

She grasped the letter eagerly and tore it open.

She recognized that it was written in Angelica's cursive, with five short paragraphs filling in the short bond paper. She slowly read its contents. Some she knew already, but many she wasn't aware of. The most devastating parts were Jabber's apparent betrayal and Ruby Rose becoming a werewolf.

The part about Ruby Rose, while it was appalling to read, had reinforced the idea she had earlier. There was something supernatural in her room responsible for her kidnapping and werewolf transformation that she had to find, something she could use and perhaps exploit.

She went to her room in the servant's quarters, with Tinker and Blinker following close behind, like little puppies who found a new master. She brought along the household keys and chose the appropriate one for Ruby Rose's room, which had been the quarters of the previous butler named Pluto. She opened the door and went in.

Pluto had been a strange nut recently discovered as a shapeshifting *Pugot* masquerading as their human butler, who was now gone. It looked like he had amassed peculiar furniture and accessories as the chief steward. He kept all of them in his room for unknown reasons. The oddest thing in the room that Lola Sabrina gazed at straightaway was the spinning wheel.

She wondered where he had gotten it since she didn't recognize it as one of theirs. She guessed Pluto may have found it in one of the underground rooms and brought it to his. She came closer and discovered droplets of blood from the spindle going to the bed. She unhooked the spindle with crusted dried blood and put it in her pocket.

They glanced at the elves staring raptly at a different piece of furniture: an antique wardrobe. This, she recognized as theirs that her grandfather Marcus used to display in his room. They were looking particularly at the markings in front.

She asked them if they knew what it meant and quickly realized she hadn't heard them speak before and if they were able to. Thankfully, they did. Blinker then replied: "It's in our language. 'This is a doorway that will take you to where you want to go.' It says."

"How do you think did these strange pieces of furniture get here?"

"In the past, before the conflict between our kind began, some were in friendly terms with a few of the humans in town, including your grandfather. We gifted them with magical items that could help them with their day-to-day living. However, most of them became greedy and didn't use them properly, so these articles of furniture became corrupted. We told them to destroy those, but some like your grandfather didn't seem to listen."

"I could only guess what happened. Instead, my Lolo Marcus hid them in one of the secret rooms and our former butler found them and brought them here and thus, causing a lot of mischief."

"We should destroy them."

"Not yet. We will use them to help my family who are apparently trapped and in danger in Batala. Once all of them are out of harm's way, then we will destroy these items."

"How will we use them?"

"We will need the help of my old friend Luna. I only hope she is still here and had not gone to Batala yet."

"Why would she go there?"

"She reached out to me earlier and offered to help us. She is also witch like me and a master alchemist. We can use this magical wardrobe to go to where she is."

Blinker opened the wardrobe and entered, with Tinker and Lola Sabrina following close behind.

~O~

Luna was about to finish the magical potion she had concocted when a door suddenly appeared out of nowhere and opened. To her surprise, it was Sabrina, along with two elves in tow.

"So, this is where you live. Is this the Land of Broken Dreams?" Said Lola Sabrina.

"Yes. How did you get here? I never imagined you having this ability to teleport."

"I don't. We discovered this magical wardrobe in our home that can take us to where we want to go. However, it's been debased, so we don't know how long it will hold. We'll have to do this quicky."

"Speaking of teleportation, I'm about to finish my potion that could enable me to teleport from one place to another. It will allow me to go to Batala and rescue your family."

"Oh, thank goodness! I have something I need to give you," Lola Sabrina said and handed her the spindle. "It has the blood of my granddaughter's best friend who has been turned into a werewolf and is roaming around in Batala. You could use it to pinpoint where she is and maybe cure her?"

"I think I have those…" Luna said. She opened a shelf on the top cupboard. "It is where I store my most dangerous potions that I only open in dire situations."

"What potions will help her?"

"Here they are. A wolfsbane potion. A small sip from this will cure the girl. And a locator potion will enable me to find her. Give me the spindle." She said and took it. She opened the vial containing the locator potion and dunked the pin with the dried blood. The colorless liquid suddenly turned black and recorked it. "It's done. Once I'm finished with the teleportation potion, then I'll leave for Batala."

The magical doorway was beginning to break apart. "We've better go back. I don't know how I can thank you, Luna. You're really putting your life in danger for helping my family."

"Don't worry about it, Sabrina. I consider you like a sister and I would do anything for my family. I'll see you soon."

Sabrina and the elves reentered the magic portal to return home to Casa de la Noche.

Chapter 67 Six Soldiers of Fortune

From all the war preparations and training the white army did for a few days, six had shown promise and were particularly skillful and brave: Esmeralda, Pandora, Bigfoot, Peter Griffin, Andreas, and Wilhelm. Bakunawa, the Serpent Goddess, recognized this, thus elevating their roles and making them platoon leaders.

They did all that they could do with their platoons. They got to know the soldiers under them, identified the skill sets that made them effective fighters, and formed plans and strategies in the short time allotted. However, only two things remained unclear—where the battle would take place and when it would begin.

Bakunawa summoned the six soldiers of fortune in her dwelling hut. They had hoped this would be for final preparations and all lingering questions would be answered.

Once inside and seated, Bakunawa stood up and said: "We are approaching the endgame, and any time soon, the battle will start. Prepare your soldiers for this eventuality and may fortune favor you."

They had expected a long and inspiring speech from her, but they got what they needed and didn't say anything in return. They stood up about to leave, but Bakunawa said: "Pandora, please stay. I want to talk to you."

The other five glanced at her, and she nodded back, reassuring them. One by one, they ambled outside, leaving the two of them inside.

"Pandora, we haven't really talked. I know there are many things on your mind and now is the time say all of them," Bakunawa said, with kindness in her eyes.

"Goddess, can I speak honestly?"

"Yes, you may."

"My family shouldn't be here and I'm including all humans in this equation. Except for me and Andreas, they don't have supernatural abilities to fight back. Their courage and natural fighting talent could defend themselves momentarily but if faced with a powerful creature like a *Kapre* or *Aswang*, they surely would be defeated and killed."

"What do you propose?"

Can we go home?"

"I'm sorry, but no. We need you, Pandora. Once the fight is over, then you can leave."

"Alright. I will do what you ask of me as long as you keep my mother and the other humans out of this."

"Very well. What about Esmeralda and Wilhelm?"

"I'll ask them."

"Anything else?"

"My friend Ruby Rose, who has been turned into a werewolf. What can we do to help her?"

"Do not worry. I will personally look for her and bring her back. Your only concern is your role in the war that can happen anytime soon."

"This is my first time to take part in a battle or any large-scale conflict, so I don't know what to expect."

"You just follow my lead. You only worry about the soldiers in your platoon and if they are doing what you are telling them to do. Anything else?"

"Nothing else, goddess."

"Please tell the others to prepare their soldiers. Make sure they have enough weapons and armor and we will leave in a few hours."

"Where will we go?"

"Do not worry about it, Pandora. I will be in the lead and all you have to do is follow me."

"Yes, goddess," said Pandora and went out.

The other five were waiting for her. Esmeralda said: "What did she tell you?"

"She asked me to tell her any concerns or issues I may have, and I told her. She said that, except for me, all the other humans don't have to fight, even you Wilhelm and Esmeralda. You have the choice to stay behind."

"No. You need me. I've grown close to the giants and hybrids in this army, like the *Lakivots, Tikbalangs,*

Gisurabs, Patakodas, and the like. They only listen to me and do what I tell them," Wilhelm said.

"Me too. My platoon are good hand-to-hand combatants, and they need me to guide them," Esmeralda said.

"Okay, we all stay. My mother and other humans can stay behind. What's on your mind, Peter?"

I've developed a rapport with the dragon, and it can watch over us from above and demolish anything in our way.

Good. How about Bigfoot? Can you ask him if he has anything to add?"

Peter screeched, and Bigfoot growled back in Yeti-speak.

He said his platoon will be ready to fight.

Andreas? Where are you? Are you alright?

I'm here, and I'm fine, Pandora. It's almost done, and I can finally cross over.

"Yes, it will be over soon. Thank you, all of you. We will wait for the goddess to come out and then we will go."

"Where are we going? To a battlefield, I presume where we will fight?"

"I don't know. She told me to just be ready and we will all leave soon."

~O~

The Gatekeepers were keenly observing everything closely. They were watching what was transpiring from afar through their interdimensional image transmitter. Among all the worlds, dimensions, realms, and levels of existence in the cosmos, they had been particularly monitoring the goings-on in Batala due to its impending war that could alter the fabric of the universe.

Their policy had always been to observe and only intervene in circumstances of great consequence. When a situation has potentially disastrous implications, some would go in and make adjustments to prevent it from happening. Thus, adhering to the overall narrative the Masters had mandated for everything in the universe to conform to.

One such situation came into existence. However, one human got the upper hand and prevented an adjustment from occurring. They needed to find some other event in this particular space-time continuum and attempt it again. Another was dispatched to Batala to make the required adjustment, but this time in disguise. They didn't want to make the same mistake again because too much was at stake.

The necessary adjustment would be directed to a young girl with a powerful supernatural ability, who was on her way to battle. To them, she was an anomaly. Her existence was an offensive act to the narrative, and anything she did or would do had universe-altering consequences.

The Masters described her as an Aeonian Being, someone who should have existed outside the narrative, but due to a flub in the cosmos, she was born in the human world. She should have been a god similar to them.

The Gatekeepers had to be cautious in dealing with her...

Chapter 68 The Thief and his Master

Between Jabber and Rumpelstiltskin, it was clear to Ruby Rose who was the master—Jabber the *Kapre*. Even her beast body, which she had no control over, recognized him as the alpha and followed behind his giant footsteps.

Rumpelstiltskin had a thief's gait and walked furtively like he was about to commit a felony. Of which, in essence, they were going to.

Jabber planned to kidnap Pandora before the war began. He said he knew of a secret way leading to her, and each of them had a role to play in the abduction. Ruby Rose, in her werewolf form, would give distraction and force all interlopers and stragglers away from her, while Jabber and Rumpelstiltskin would do the actual kidnapping. Once done, all four of them would escape through a portal activated by mentioning Rumpelstiltskin's name.

They were walking in a slim pathway towards an unknown destination. Jabber was leading the way, followed by her and lastly Rumpelstiltskin. Ruby Rose looked ahead and was confused since they were approaching a dead-end.

Jabber was curiously in a hurry and walked hastily, which perplexed her further. *Where are we going?* She thought. *Maybe there's a secret doorway we're not able to see yet.*

As they arrived at the dead-end, Ruby Rose saw a crevasse on the cave wall. It was a normal-looking fissure that could not fit any individual like them. Jabber reached out with both hands, embedding his massive fingers in the dented cracks, and wedged it open, like forcibly opening an elevator door. She surmised that even a creature as mighty as a *Kapre* could never open a cave wall using only the strength of his fingers.

Yet miraculously and impossibly, he did, which didn't demonstrate his brawniness but appeared magical. With little knowledge Ruby Rose had about Philippine mythological creatures like Jabber, she wasn't aware that *Kapres* knew magic, but he did, by the looks of it.

Jabber was seemingly opening a portal that led to another area in Batala, and to follow the plan, to a place where Pandora was supposedly alone. She looked through the portal with her beast body's eyes and indeed saw her best friend Pandora standing by herself.

But how would she recognize her in her werewolf body? She thought. Then she remembered. Pandora knew how to pick up telepathic whispers. She was like a powerful receiver that could register signals of telepathy.

Since Ruby Rose had no control of her beast body, Pandora might not hear or even recognize her. It would be like listening to whispers in the darkness, which probably would provoke fear and confusion.

She had to shout, and with all the force of her captive mind, she yelled: *PANDORA, WATCH OUT! EVIL CREATURES ARE HERE TO HARM YOU!!*

And Pandora heard. She glanced over quickly at the source of the telepathic shout and saw the three, all fearsome creatures, intending to hurt her. From all the training she had—and she was a quick study—she smoothly reached for the wand tucked underneath her belt like a seasoned gunslinger to focus her light-blasting ability. The wand ignited at its tip like a welding torch and fired at them with short and disabling blasts, which weren't deadly. Yet.

The three were caught off guard and fell, discombobulated but unhurt. It was enough time for Ruby Rose to let herself be known to Pandora: *It's me, Ruby Rose! Please help me!*

Ruby? Where are you?

I'm right over here! It's me inside the werewolf, and I'm trapped! I can't control it!

Help is on its way! I've sent a message to Lola Sabrina, and knowing her, it will arrive here soon!

What kind of help? Something that would lift this curse?

I don't know. Just hang on!

The three of them had shaken off their confusion and reengaged their planned abduction. Some soldiers of the white army were stationed close by and noticed the commotion. They were running towards them at full speed. It was going to be a fight.

By good fortune, help arrived in the form of Luna, who suddenly appeared out of nowhere in the middle of the two hostile groups. She was wearing a fanny pack holding numerous vials filled with magical potions. She picked one and threw it to the ground a short distance away.

Black smoke burst out and enveloped everyone, providing cover to escape. Before the smoke spread, the werewolf suddenly lunged at Luna with its mouth open, baring sharp teeth. As it was about to reach her, she quickly took another vial, uncorked it open, and threw the contents at it. The creature yelped and suddenly fell to the ground, unconscious.

It was the cure for the werewolf curse. As the thick smoke billowed everywhere, Luna dragged the sleeping wolf to safe ground. The cure was taking effect, and its black fur, sharp teeth, claws, and every feature belonging to the terrible creature slowly vanished. Then, Ruby Rose's familiar and pretty face started to appear.

As the smoke dissipated, they heard a loud voice shout: "Rumpelstiltskin!" And as it finally cleared, the thief and his master had disappeared.

Pandora approached the sleeping Ruby Rose, naked from head to foot. The spell was finally broken. She awoke, and the first face she saw was Pandora. She broke into tears and hugged her. She said: "I'm so sorry Pandora, for everything."

"It's not your fault. You were held against your will by these evil creatures and turned into a terrible beast. Thanks to her, you're saved." To Luna, she asked: "By the way, who are you?"

"I'm your Lola's friend. My name is Luna."

"I'm Pandora, and this is Ruby Rose."

"I know about the both of you from your Lola."

"You came at the right time, and saved my friend. Nonetheless, big trouble is still coming and I don't know how we can get away from it."

"We are going to. I'm here to bring all of you home."

"I can't. I made a promise to the goddess to stay here and help her. The others you can take home."

"The goddess?"

"Bakunawa, the Serpent Goddess. She's the leader of the white army, which are in conflict with the dark army. Didn't Lola Sabrina tell you about this?"

"She didn't, but I'm privy to the goings-on in Batala."

"A war between them is forthcoming, and I have to be a part of it. Can you take my friend and my mom back home?"

"Of course, and I'll be back for you. Are there other humans you want me to bring home?"

"I'll find out. There are also many humans imprisoned here in people pens for slaughter. Do you know about that?"

"No. What do you propose we should do?"

"Free them, of course."

"One problem at a time. Once all of you are safe, they we can consider saving those people. When will I come back for you?"

"Soon, but only after."

"After *what?*"

"The war."

"When it will happen?"

"Soon, very soon…"

Chapter 69 The Sole Man Without Purpose

Among the two brothers, Wilhelm became useful and proved himself valuable to the white army. Yet Jacob, who was only slightly older than Wilhelm, had a younger brother's sullen temperament, thus representing himself as inept and left without purpose.

He felt like a useless supporting character in a story who ought to be killed. And if abiding by what had happened to other talentless and cowardly humans like him, he would either be murdered by one of many dangerous creatures inhabiting Batala or held captive again to be used for slaughter.

He would rather die than be jailed once more in one of those human pens where he and his brother had been put away for many years. The most excruciating feeling was waiting for his turn to be butchered for meat. He didn't want to feel that way ever again.

Now, the so-called war was fast approaching, which he was forced to join. He should have been like his brother Wilhelm, who had fostered many friendships with scores of supernatural creatures, becoming soldiers in his platoon.

He was looking for an opportunity or any reason to relinquish himself in the army. When he heard Pandora was rounding up humans who wanted to return to the mortal world, he immediately made himself known. He was then told to wait under the magical illuminating tree for someone to teleport them to safety.

He was so happy that he forgot to tell his brother what had transpired and immediately went to the meeting place under the tree. He forgot to ask which one since there was more than one magical illuminating tree in Batala. He decided to go to the nearest in his proximity since it was most likely there.

When he arrived, he was surprised that there was only one present. There should have been more humans like him who were raring to go home and sick and tired of the Realm of Batala and all it entailed.

He resolved to wait, even though he acknowledged he may have no home in the mortal world to return to and everyone he knew from his old life was probably dead. Yet, anywhere was much better than remaining in Batala.

He didn't have to wait too long, and someone appeared out of thin air. She expected a human and didn't want to see another supernatural creature, but he did, to his dismay.

It was Lord Axe-Grinder, along with his two goons, the traitorous *Kapre* Jabber and the sooty-colored *Dwende* Rumpelstiltskin. Both were yelling repeatedly Rumpelstiltskin's name. Then, scores of dark and terrible creatures appeared consecutively, some heavily clad in armor and bladed weapons, and most only garbed by their frightfulness.

Jacob was confused at first, then hit him like a ton of bricks: Axe-Grinder was taking the war to them, and by the looks of it, they were scarcely prepared.

He sprinted towards the white army stationed just a short distance away. He ran and ran like his life depended on it, which was. His immediate task was to arrive there before the enemy got to him and warn them. For a brief moment, he was proud of himself for being brave and doing the right thing. For an instant, he was blessed with a glorious purpose.

But alas, a high-flying *Aswang* swooped down and snatched him like he was just weak prey. It took him up above to the cave ceiling and bit his neck, then sucking his blood dry.

His lifeless body was dropped to the ground with a mighty thud.

~O~

Nevertheless, Peter Griffin had seen the Aswang take a bite out of Jacob and promptly informed Bakunawa and the other platoon leaders immediately what had happened. Wilhelm was shocked by the news but had to swallow the hurt to ready his troops.

The war, which everyone had been preparing and training for, was finally at hand. Bakunawa rushed to the forefront and yelled: "Today, we fight to end all future battles. This is for us and our friends the humans! Attack!"

The war was gloriously fought on both sides. All supernatural creatures dark and light, who at one point were brothers living in peace and not separated by the color of their skin and a magical force field, fought valorously. Even the handful of humans allying with the light side were courageous in their campaign of alliance and peace.

Pandora was magnificent in battle. She utilized her wand to direct her energy-based power in creating different blasting ranges. As a result, no enemy could come close to her and if one did, be obliterated immediately. Her platoon was energized by her courage and followed her example.

Equally impressive was Esmeralda, who used her smallswords with deadly accuracy. She directed her troop of blade-wielding creatures to slice and dice any enemy approaching them. Various body parts littered the cave floor, which made the fighting tricky but still manageable.

Andreas employed his various ghostly powers to the fullest extent. He made himself many and possessed one dark creature after another to force them to kill themselves and their ilk.

Wilhelm was wrathful by his brother's death but used it effectively. He rode atop a Lakivot who looked like his dead friend Sweet Porridge and directed his soldiers of giants and hybrids to smash any dark creature approaching their way.

Peter Griffin and his flying platoon ruled the air. The dragon was his most deadly warrior, who wiped out any enemy that flew their way.

Bigfoot and his platoon utilized brawn and brute strength to overwhelm the enemy forces.

Bakunawa, the Serpent Goddess, oversaw everything and even fought when necessary. She knew victory was within their grasp but still directed her army to continue fighting.

There was a clear dividing line between both sides due to their contrasting appearances. If viewed by an outside observer, it was apparent at the onset who the superior fighting force was: Bakunawa and the light army. They were organized and fought with a goal in mind.

The majority of the dark creatures were mindless beasts who fought indiscriminately. Even though they were bigger and more ferocious, they lacked organization and thus were readily overcome by the much smaller but more proficient enemy.

Before long, it looked like victory for the light side was imminent. The bloody and dead bodies of the dark army littered the ground floor. Yet Lord Axe-Grinder had a final and desperate backup plan unless everything else failed, and it was about to. He was going to inflict damage to the magical illuminating tree, thus triggering its self-defense mechanism, which would give off deadly radiation and poison everyone.

He looked at the remaining survivors of his dark army. Most were dead and strewn about on the cave floor, and some retreated to the dark side of Batala. Jabber the *Kapre* was nowhere in sight, but Rumpelstiltskin was still alive but injured.

Both of them went back to the area where they first appeared close to the magical tree. Axe-Grinder lifted his staff and magicked it to become a sharp axe. He proceeded to chip at the sturdy tree trunk, breaking bits and pieces of the bark away.

It was enough to trigger it. The damaged portions began to give off a thin gas that didn't look harmful at all but was nevertheless deadly. Axe-Grinder yelled Rumpelstiltskin's name, thus opening a magical portal to which they escaped.

Chapter 70 The Star Money Owed

The Gatekeeps saw through their interdimensional image transmitter everything that had happened in Batala and especially with their inside man who had screwed up again miserably. The war they were trying hard to bring into desirable coordination had gone in the opposite direction, and they knew the Masters would not be happy. They would have to pay them back the star money owed to appease them.

They waited for their man inside to come and explain himself. If his explanation won't be accepted, then they would have no problem in offering his head on a plate to the Masters.

However, he didn't arrive at the stipulated time. They went back to look for him at the interdimensional image transmitter, but he was nowhere to be found.

Where is he? They asked each other, but they could only guess. They surmised he may have changed skins to avoid detection. If that was the case, they had to go and look for him themselves and also stay clear from any of the inhabitants of the realm since one of their own was accidentally killed by someone they perceived as a lesser lifeform.

~O~

Jabber the *Kapre* had intimated what would happen, and he got away just in time before it became messy. He had been wrong in assuming that they would easily win the war and that their strength and mindless ferocity would be enough to overwhelm the enemy. Nevertheless, they were soundly defeated by a weaker but more organized fighting force.

By the looks of it, every one of his supposed clan had perished, along with many creatures of the dark army. Yet he didn't care since he wasn't a Kapre or any creature native to Batala, but only masquerading as one. He wasn't even someone from the mortal world. He was a higher lifeform from another dimension who had a job to do but had failed spectacularly. He was a Gatekeeper, and his kind will be coming for him very soon.

Their mission was supposed to be simple: hinder the growth of an Aeonian Being born in the world of humans and never let her develop to full potential. However, every attempt they made only pushed her further into the maturation of her abilities that rivaled them and the Masters.

He had to change skins and leave Batala immediately. He was planning to go above ground to the mortal world, lay low, and become a human. His kind would never think of finding him there.

~O~

Three Gatekeepers arrived in Batala using their invisible interdimensional craft in the immediate aftermath of the war. No one alive was in their immediate proximity, which afforded them enough time to fix a few mistakes they made. The first thing they needed to do was to stop the spread of radiation caused by the damaged magical illuminating tree.

They used their abilities to envelope the area surrounding the tree that the radiation had spread with a force field, thus ceasing its dispersal. Once safety was assured, they changed to their invisible skins.

It was too late to make adjustments, so they would only observe the goings-on in Batala and perhaps find some clues to the whereabouts of their errant Gatekeeper kin.

~O~

Bakunawa, the Serpent Goddess, surveyed the bloody battlefield that had been unfortunately situated too close to home. Dead bodies littered the ground floor; some from the light army but most from their dreaded enemy. All his platoon leaders were alive, except for Andreas, who was already dead in the first place but a formidable ghost.

She assembled them to speak to them. She said: "All of you have fought gloriously and bravely, and did what you were trained to do. You have brought pride to your kinsfolk, and blessings will be showered to all.

To Pandora, our youngest and strongest fighter, I bestow you the gift of hindsight. It will aid in your inborn abilities of telepathy and light manipulation to make you understand how you can use them for the benefit of everyone."

"Thank you, goddess."

"To Bigfoot. You are an altruist and truly show unselfish concern for others, even at your own expense. I, for one, am unaware by the wishes of someone like you. What is your ultimate wish?"

Bigfoot growled in Yeti-speak, while Peter Griffin telepathically translated to Bakunawa what Bigfoot said: *I want to return to the home of my parents and sasquatch community, to the Rocky Mountains along the Pacific Northwest in Canada.*

But wasn't it destroyed by man? They might not be there anymore.

I'm aware of that. But can I return to an earlier time when we were all together, and our home was unaffected?

Yes, I can send you to that particular period. However, your time there would just be brief. Humans would still arrive and cut down the trees in your forest and leave all of you without a home.

Yes, I know, and I still want to. It was the happiest time in my life, and I want to feel that way again, even for a moment.

Alright. You will get what you wish. She continued in normal speech: "To Esmeralda, the cunning. You have shown a surprising capacity for goodness, despite your past life as a criminal and thief. I grant you all the gold you can carry, and you will use it to change your life for

the better. If I find out you didn't, then there's going to
be repercussions."

"Oh, my god. Thank you, goddess. You don't need to
worry about me. I'll use it to make good with my life
from now on."

"To Wilhelm, who had lost his brother in the war, for
which I am truly sorry. I give you the gift of eternal
youth, where you can live a long and happy life
unaffected by the severity of age."

"Goddess, thank you."

"To Peter Griffin, who had provided essential aid at
the right times. I grant you the ability to speak all
languages, so can converse to any individual or creature
in all realms and worlds in the universe, thus gaining
the ultimate gift of knowledge."

Peter screeched in gratitude.

"And lastly, to Andreas. I know what you wish for,
which is to finally cross over to the afterworld.
However, I have the capability of giving you something
better: the gift of life. Do you want to be alive again?"

Yes, goddess.

But your new life will not be the old one anymore. You
will be born again in a different body, and all your
memories will be lost. Do you still want to?"

*In that case, then no. I want to keep all my memories, especially
the ones about Pandora. It's my time to proceed to the realm of
souls.*

"Alright," Bakunawa said and glanced upwards. A raven swooped down and perched atop her right shoulder. "You know what to do."

The raven cawed and alighted on his shoulder. They looked at each other and agreed to their previous arrangement: that it would finally take him to paradise. Andreas glanced at Pandora for the last time and left, walking towards the horizon of shining light that suddenly appeared ahead.

Goodbye, Andreas, may you have eternal peace, said Pandora.

Chapter 71 The Owl Sees All

A long time ago, at the dawn of the creation of the cosmos, there was a Parliament of Owls who perched at the end of the universe, watching over every world, realm, domain, plane of existence, and dimension. They called themselves the Masters, led by their leader, the Grandmaster Owl.

At that time, there were only a few domains they monitored, but as eons passed, many sprang up and soon were too much to keep tabs on by themselves. Thus, they looked for other creatures in the universe to take their place, but for a fee paid them in star money, which was the universal currency.

Soon, many hyperintelligent and higher lifeforms took on the challenge and became Gatekeepers, but temporarily only. One way or another, they did something that displeased the Masters, and once they fell out of grace, they would have to relinquish their posts and return to their home world.

Then, the cycle begins anew.

The current crop of Gatekeepers came from an advanced planet of super-intelligent creatures with uncanny abilities who had yet to pay their allotted star money. This didn't sit well with the Grandmaster Owl, who had been looking for any reason to eliminate them.

Then, their consecutive screwups began to affect the well-oiled machinery of the cosmos, and its proverbial nuts and bolts were loosening and coming apart. This was what the Masters were waiting for, and it was the right time to replace them.

The Grandmaster Owl took flight from the end of the universe to find the Gatekeepers, get the star money owed, and finally terminate their tenure.

~O~

Axe-Grinder and Rumpelstiltskin were hopping mad. They were back at the dark side of Batala, which was empty of its inhabitants. Even the human pens didn't have guards.

They were the only two remaining survivors of the dark army that they knew of. Some had retreated and escaped the battle, which didn't sit well with them, especially with Axe-Grinder. He was particularly angry with Jabber, whom he thought was a good addition to his army but proved ineffective. Once he found him, it would be hell to pay.

Axe-Grinder decided to go to the human world above ground, in the town of Gintongbayan, where he still had a slew of cohorts masquerading as humans. He would regroup them and reassess his options, then find a new plan moving forward.

He wasn't down for the count yet. There was still a chance to rise and overcome the enemy. Then, he had an idea of a new target to direct their wrath: the witch Sabrina, the granddaughter of the traitorous Don

Marcus. She had always been a thorn in his side, and by killing her, he could still have a victory that he had yearned for a long time.

He glanced at Rumpelstiltskin, who was equally vengeful like him. He smiled and seemed to know what he was thinking about. They gathered their necessary belongings, and Rumpelstiltskin murmured his name. A portal then opened, and both went through.

~O~

Lola Sabrina exhaled a deep sigh of relief. Everyone important in her life was finally back in Casa de la Noche: Angelica, Pandora, and Ruby Rose. Nevertheless, some casualties also saddened her: Henry, Mayor Eddie, Matteo, and Andreas.

The family curse had struck again. All the men close to her had perished, leaving themselves, the women, alive to deal with all the problems in the world. Although, for the most part, the general state of things had worked themselves out for the better.

Even her coven-mate Luna came at the right time to help her and was instrumental in engendering a positive outcome to the problem. However, there was still one thing left to do that was altogether a difficult undertaking: bring back every abducted human confined in the numerous people pens in the dark side of Batala.

Luna and Lola Sabrina couldn't do it themselves with a task as humongous as this, which needed an equally large form of magic. They were merely two old women subjected to many limitations due to age. Even with Pandora helping them wasn't enough. They needed someone who knew the area and was powerful enough to move mountains, which Bakunawa, the Serpent Goddess, could provide.

Yet Lola Sabrina wasn't sure she would help, since they parted ways not on the best of terms, but she had to try nonetheless. She went to her room to be alone and to concentrate. She reached out to her through telepathic channels and said: *Goddess Bakunawa, are you there? It's me, your old student Sabrina.*

No answer came, so she reiterated her inquiry again and again. Her telepathic whispers should be able to go through since the one responsible for previously blocking them was out of commission.

She had become patient and not agitated like before, so she had no problem doing it repeatedly.

Then she hit paydirt, and someone whispered back: *I'm here. What can I do for you?*

Goddess, is that you?

Goddess? Sure.

We have to do something about the humans still held in those pens in Batala.

Humans? In Batala?

Yes. They are being imprisoned for slaughter by the creatures on the dark side. We need your help to free all of them and return them to the mortal world. We can't do it alone.

Is Pandora with you?

Yes, of course.

Alright. We also need her for this to work. All of us with supernatural abilities need to help each other to bring everyone there. We also need a large, open and deserted area to transport all of them, someplace without anyone bothering us. Do you know of an area like that?

Yes, I think I know of a good place empty of people, in a squatter's colony, called the Land of Broken Dreams. I'll have to speak with my friend Luna first. I'll talk to you later.

Their extrasensory communication was over.

Lola Sabrina suddenly had a headache after the conversation ended. She tried not to let it affect her and went downstairs to talk to Luna.

As Luna was briefed on the situation, she suddenly blurted out: "You got it all wrong, Sabrina. The squatter's village doesn't have a large open area. On the contrary, there's no space available. We're too many people jampacked in an area too small to accommodate us."

"I'm not done yet. Of course, I'm aware about it. I've lived in Gintongbayan my entire life. The one who responded to me earlier wasn't the goddess, but someone else impersonating her. I'm setting up a trap for this impostor, with your help."

"But what about the people imprisoned in Batala?"

"We'll deal with them later. We have to take care of this first."

Chapter 72 One Eye, Two Eyes, and Three Eyes

The three Gatekeepers, still invisible to the naked eye, had followed the breadcrumbs accidentally left by their errant kin masquerading as Jabber, which led them to the town of Gintongbayan. At the same time, they likewise left clues, albeit also unintentionally, that the Grandmaster Owl picked up.

Each Gatekeeper was known by how many eyes they had, which was an inconsequence of their biological makeup. Everyone in their race had the same visual acuity despite the number of their eyes. Therefore, One Eye's oculus has the same faculty of vision as Three Eyes' oculi.

They were ill-prepared for the world of humans. They didn't bother to research them since they looked down on them and previously assumed they were merely a primitive and unintelligent species. Yet they were sorely proved wrong many times before.

As a result, the human skins they brought as disguise weren't lifelike at all and looked exceedingly fake. Nevertheless, they weren't aware of this fallacy and continued putting them on.

They strolled along the bustling main street in Barangay Poblacion wearing their brand-new skins to acquaint themselves with the human world. They didn't notice the townsfolk staring at them in shock and disbelief because of the absurdity of their appearance. They looked clownish and hideous simultaneously in their completely unconvincing disguises.

They stopped outside *La Cocina Secreto* and inhaled the odor inside, and instantly became hungry. The aroma smelled like their favorite food on their planet called *globula,* a green slime-like substance packed with necessary nutrients their cephalopod bodies need. They went inside and occupied a spare table.

They were familiar with the dinner customs of humans from what they had seen through monitor screens and asked for the food they smelled earlier. The waiter said they were cooking *paella*, the restaurant's specialty, and took orders for three servings.

When the food arrived, they stared at their plates filled with saffron rice, shellfish, and chicken that didn't look like globula. Nevertheless, it still appeared to be enticing. They quickly devoured it in a few seconds, which horrified the waiter.

They stood up to leave but were halted by the waiter for payment of the food. One Eye scrounged in his pocket and took out a wallet, an integral part of the disguise. Inside was a photo I.D. with his human face and a wad of cash that he gave the waiter to pay the bill.

With their hunger sated, they went outside and continued strolling along the sidewalk, with nothing yet in mind but aimless wandering. One way or another, something would undoubtedly pop up in their pocket navigational system to provide information about the location of their missing Gatekeeper kinfolk.

Then it happened. They heard a ding that pointed to a place far away from the town proper, to an area with too many people crammed into ten hectares of governmental land: a squatter's colony called the Land of Broken Dreams.

~O~

The errant Gatekeeper, who had been impersonating Jabber, was wearing the human skin of a *taong-grasa*, or a homeless man. It was an impressive disguise, complete with long, unkempt hair, dirty and tattered clothes, and grime all over his body. It hid its many imperfections by how grubby it looked.

He had planned to hide in plain sight as a pathetic beggar. He was relatively free to roam the streets of Gintongbayan, with no one giving him a second glance because of his loathsome appearance, hence, making his disguise perfect. He was able to do all sorts of crazy things that a normal citizen couldn't do due to his looks and the general outlook of people like him in town. The citizens would either avoid or promptly forgive him for his shenanigans.

Consequently, he could scope the entire town unobserved and unseen by anyone. He even saw his three Gatekeeper kin from the outside making a fool out of themselves inside a restaurant. He also found out where Lola Sabrina and Pandora lived.

He also discovered a place far away from the town proper where homeless and poor people like him lived temporarily, in a squatter's area called the Land of Broken Dreams.

With all this information and idle time roaming around, he began to formulate a plan of his own, a plan that would enable him to be the hero for once and not be merely a supporting character in someone else's story.

~O~

The Grandmaster Owl flew faster than the speed of light towards Earth, all in good time. His anatomical arrangement and abilities made him impenetrable to the rigors of space, traveling through millions of galaxies, star systems, and dimensions in the blink of an eye.

He was the first Aeonian Being born at the same time the universe was created. He was yet a formless matter floating in space without the ability to reason. As eons passed, he slowly became sentient and transformed into the avian variety of his preference and could mold similar Aeonian Beings like him. Soon, the Parliament of Owls was formed to be the guardians and watchers of the cosmos. They called themselves the Masters.

Yet, on rare occasions, Aeonian Beings were born outside the Grandmaster Owl's knowledge and supervision. Whenever this occurred, he had to look for ways to hinder their growth, and if things didn't turn out as planned, termination was the final solution.

He entered the Earth's atmosphere like a fiery comet and landed in the forest at the back of Casa de la Noche, just a stone's throw away from the makeshift hut owned by two dwarf brothers, who were recent prison escapees.

They heard a crash ahead and rushed towards the smokey crater. The Grandmaster Owl was encased in a protective outer layer, which slowly dissolved after he landed. He flapped his wings to dust off all the refuse matter accumulated from space travel. He flew towards the awaiting midget spectators.

He recognized them as formidable little people, which he could exploit to find the Gatekeepers. He imbued them with special but temporary abilities and transformed them into tall and muscle-bound freaks. They were his puppets that he could control from above.

He had picked up a strong signal to their whereabouts, which he gave his muscular minions to locate.

Chapter 73 Odds and Ends

The teleportation potion that Luna concocted and drank hadn't worn off yet, so she could teleport herself, Lola Sabrina, and Pandora, to her home in the Land of Broken Dreams. She tried to go back to bring the Greenwood Elves but she couldn't anymore. It had completely worn off at that point, but she had instructed them to follow immediately by themselves if she couldn't come to get them.

On an ordinary day, the squatter's colony was disorderly and dirty, filled to the brim with the most impoverished people of Gintongbayan. There were no garbage receptacles or means for waste disposal, so trash, waste excrement, and other refuse matter were scattered everywhere. The settlers lived in decrepit and makeshift houses that could easily be destroyed by strong wind or even a push by a strong man.

Most of the settlers lacked the normal mental facilities to function in general society and thus had been relegated by the powers that be, to reside there. Some of the more conventional thinking inhabitants like Luna were assigned leadership positions as *purok* or zone leaders to rein in the loonies and at least have a semblance of organization to the whole colony.

However, the one thing lacking was empty spaces, which was what Lola Sabrina had preferred for the plan to work. Yet when they rethought the plan, it became apparent the so-called disadvantages of the colony were advantageous to their overall strategy, which included dealing with the impostor posing as Bakunawa, the Serpent Goddess.

The chaotic nature of the squatter's colony was a practicable place to usher in supernatural elements since most potential witnesses were already too crazy to be considered or even believed. Any individual intending to cause harm would be overwhelmed by the chaos that can likewise become an obstacle to their designs.

All they had to do was wait and let any malicious individuals come and deal with them one at a time. Thus, also allowing the helter-skelter quality of the Land of Broken Dreams to be their helper.

~O~

Everyone was drawing close to the Land of Broken Dreams. Lola Sabrina and Pandora were already in Luna's house, with the prearranged plan in place to take effect.

They didn't know who the impostor claimed to be Bakunawa, the Serpent Goddess, but had devised a plan to deal with this mysterious faker. They already had an intimation of who it might be and the only thing they were sure of was this goddess pretender was supernatural. Hence, they prepared something similar to counteract any potential transgression.

They also knew others would come and had devised numerous measures and countermeasures against them.

And someone did approach their house, but it wasn't who they expected: it was Henry, who they thought had perished at the hands of the Kapre clan. They were surprised at first, and Pandora was even moderately glad. However, they immediately knew it was a ruse.

This individual masquerading as Henry approached them and said: "Pandora, Lola Sabrina, I'm alive! I escaped the tree giants who had taken me and immediately came to find you."

"Oh, is that right? Peter saw you being squeezed to death by one of them. If what you say is true, then you've escaped death the second time, which is incredible," said Pandora.

"Well yes, I did and thank you. I'm your father after all, and our family is known for being amazing."

"No, you don't understand. Anyway, why didn't you just go back home and wait instead of coming here? And how did you about this place?"

"I'm here to offer my help. You can't face them alone."

"*Them?* Do you even know who 'them' is?"

"Of course. The Gatekeepers, who have traveled millions of miles from a faraway world to find you."

Lola Sabrina, Pandora, and Luna were astonished by what they heard and tried to hide their befuddlement.

Then Lola Sabrina said in an offhand manner so as not to sound too curious: "Gatekeepers, huh?"

"Yes, Gatekeepers…" and the individual posing as Henry then disclosed everything about them: their origins, particular tasks, their association with the Masters, and ultimate purpose that unfortunately included Pandora.

Lola Sabrina, Luna, and Pandora were blown away and momentarily forgot about the plan. Pandora said: "How did you know about this, uh… Dad?"

"I just know. Trust me, the Gatekeepers and the Masters are coming for you Pandora, and you need my help." Then, the impostor posing as Henry suddenly disrobed, including the human skin. Then, out came a lanky creature they hadn't seen before with four black eyes, grey skin, and tentacle-like appendages. It said: "My name is Four Eyes."

"Are you one of them?"

"I was. But now I'm an outcast due to some mistakes I made. They're also coming for me, so it would be to both of our bests interests to join forces."

"How do I know you're telling the truth? You've lied to us before, impersonated Jabber and many others, and even killed my father."

"Everything I previously did were orders from them. I had no choice but obey."

"How can we trust you?"

"You have to. All your combined powers alone couldn't stop them. The Masters are interdimensional Aeonian Beings who are virtually omnipotent. The Gatekeepers have amazing powers as well, as you can see."

"What can we do?"

"You have to tell me everything about the plan you've made. This way, I could include the things I could help you with and maybe make better."

"Okay. Here is what we had wanted to do…"

~O~

The Grandmaster Owl hovered over the Land of Broken Dreams to determine the breadth of the area and its inhabitants. His first impression of it was the same as everyone who had seen it for the first time: chaotic, overpopulated, and messy. Someone careless might get lost and overwhelmed by all the confusion.

He glanced at the two muscular freaks below, who were his temporary minions and under his control. They were approaching the main entrance of the squatter's colony, about to be let in by the appointed guards. However, they were made merely to be mindless morons who couldn't properly respond to any questions, so a fight began to ensue, which only lasted a few seconds. The guards were quickly and soundlessly dispatched.

He directed them in the general direction of the Gatekeepers in the middle portion of the squatter's colony. It was clear to him where they were, but due to the disorderly nature of the area, it would be similar to finding a needle in a haystack.

Nevertheless, the mindless brutes moved on like impregnable boulders rolling down a hill, demolishing everything in their path. Any person or object in their way was mowed down.

They approached their general location which was occupied by houses packed together like canned sardines, with just tiny spaces in between as passageways. The Grandmaster Owl commanded them to stop since the proceeding venture needed finesse rather than brute force. He swooped down towards them and transformed into a homely-looking and balding man who could pass off as a colony resident. He told them to wait and then went along.

~O~

The three Gatekeepers had entered the Land of Broken Dreams without incident. Their off-putting appearance was not unusual and right at home among the unbalanced segment of the squatter's colony. Their pocket navigational system directed them to a particular house in the middle area.

Due to the colony's disorderly and overpopulated quality, they couldn't pinpoint exactly where their errant Gatekeeper kin was. He could have masqueraded as anyone and be anywhere within the vicinity, and they would have to take extra special care in finding him. Besides, their pocket navigational system only had a ninety percent accuracy, so ten percent of the time, it missed the mark.

And to compensate, they needed to split up. This way, they could cover more ground and find him quicker. One Eye went to the left, Two Eyes to the right, and Three Eyes straight on.

One Eye went to the eateries, where various food stalls, canteens, and *carinderias* were located. *Pagpag* was the primary food served, which was leftover restaurant food scavenged from garbage sites and cooked into various dishes.

One Eye was the most voracious of the three and couldn't help himself. He went to a particular carinderia and partook in one of the servings sold by a proprietor, which was refried chicken and rice from Jollibee. Everything looked delicious to him. He then ordered other dishes that he ate with gusto.

Two Eyes went into the location of the local gymnasium, where a basketball game was ongoing. He was transfixed by it and wondered what was in the ball that everyone was trying to take hold of. It had to be something precious that they were fighting over.

One player saw him and yelled at him to join. He nodded and ran towards them.

Meanwhile, Three Eyes approached the right location where Four Eyes was situated. He was in one of the biggest homes in the colony, owned by one of the zone leaders, and also a local *mangkukulam*.

He stopped a few blocks before it and hid behind a thick utility pole. He had a good vantage point to see everyone come and go and planned to wait indefinitely. One way or another, he would likely catch Four Eyes in the act.

~O~

Luna knew every resident in the squatter's colony and was immediately aware if outsiders entered the premises. She had an overall understanding of its unique environment, a type of situational awareness that made her a dependable zone leader.

Even though her physical features were deteriorating with age, with no depth perception due to her crossed eyes, her mind was still as sharp as a steel trap. She also had a natural intuition that can be construed as a second sight, so she immediately felt something supernatural close by with malicious intentions. She told everyone her suspicions and to be ready.

She was also worried they overthought it and that there would be no room for improvisation if something unexpected happened. If someone they haven't prepared for did appear, then they would be in trouble.

As if fate would have it, someone did come forward: their old foes Axe-Grinder and Rumpelstiltskin. They weren't wearing any disguises, which took her by surprise. Nevertheless, they had planned for this contingency and were prepared for them.

Rumpelstiltskin yelled his name, and a humongous portal appeared out of thin air. Dozens of humans started piling out that looked like ordinary *Gintongbayan* citizens, some she even recognized. At first, Luna thought they were the people supposed to be rescued from Batala, and their old foes may have turned over a new leaf and were helping them. However, she immediately knew it was not the case since they began transforming into terrible and dark creatures like *aswangs, manananggals, pugots,* and the like.

Due to the cramped spaces in the squatter's colony, they became stuck in the narrow passageway between households going to Luna's house and couldn't move. The more they tried, the more stuck they became.

Luna, Lola Sabrina, and Pandora had expected this to happen.

Pandora took out her wand, directed it to the middle of the cluster of monsters, and discharged an all-encompassing energy blast that surrounded them.

They were disintegrated in seconds.

Amid the ashes of the fallen monsters, their two dark foes were still alive, looking like they were caught with their pants down, with fear in their eyes. Pandora aimed again and blasted them away to another world. Hopefully, somewhere, Luna thought, they couldn't escape and be trapped for all eternity.

~O~

Three Eyes saw everything that had transpired and recognized the three females from the monitor screens in their interdimensional image transmitter, especially the one they targeted and failed to adjust. He reckoned it wasn't too late to create modifications involving her but quickly disregarded it since it wasn't his decision.

Yet the one he was looking for was nowhere to be found. Four Eyes had to be there since the pocket navigational system pointed directly toward them. He glanced left and right and wondered where the other two were and what took them so long.

He recognized it as an opportune time to make a move since they were busy dealing with the failed attack and had let their guard down. He quickly changed to his invisible skin and approached them quietly.

As he came closer, he saw Four Eyes inside the house, unskinned and with his real cephalopodan features. He was sitting on a chair, looking at everything happening as if anticipating it.

He walked slowly and softly to them, trying his best not to be noticed. Yet despite his efforts, the cross-eyed witch looked in his direction as if she had detected his presence.

He stopped and remained still. The witch wasn't doing anything but still facing him. He didn't know what to do next. Should he retreat or move onward? He was stuck and couldn't move.

He saw the witch whisper something to the girl, who then took out her wand and pointed it in his direction. The last image he saw was a bright light coming towards him and blasting him to pieces.

~O~

"You got another one," said Luna.

"How did you know where it was, since it's invisible?"

"I just know. Each of us witches have a measure of extrasensory perception but some like me, have enhanced it to be usable."

"Do I also have it?"

"Yes, but you have to hone it through meditation and practice. You're still young, you have time to do it when you grow older. I will help you."

"Are there more coming?" Said Lola Sabrina.

"We have to ask our new friend Squidward here."

Four Eyes stood up and was gladdened by the occurrence. What he had hoped to happen *was* happening, and all he had to do was sit and wait. His new friends would eliminate anyone approaching them with harmful intent.

Nonetheless, he knew there were at least two of his kin still coming and possibly more from the Masters. He had furnished them with his pocket navigational system so they would have additional knowledge of anyone approaching.

"How does it work?" Asked Pandora.

"It's functions like the GPS in your smartphone and uses your satellites to find people you want to find. However, it doesn't work for humans like you and only detect alien biosignatures."

"*Alien?*"

"I mean us. In your world, *we* are the aliens, but if you come to our planet, then you're the aliens."

"Do you also have magic in your world?"

"It's space magic. It is a form of magic that draws power from the cosmos. I'm able to access it, and even *you* can."

"*Me?*" said Pandora incredulously.

Four Eyes was silent. He was of two minds whether or not to confide her real ancestry. He had nothing better to do and nothing else to lose, so he decided to proceed.

"Yes, you can. You are different from the other humans. You are an Aeonian Being like the Masters. You should have been borne like them but due to a cosmic mistake, was caused to be born here on Earth. Your biology is still human but your essence, the intrinsic nature of your spirit, originated from them."

"From the Masters? Can you tell me more about them?"

"They are basically *gods*: all-powerful and almighty. They are as old as the universe itself. They are celestial bodies that have become sentient after billions of years. They are the supreme authority and protectors of the universe, responsible of its state of existence."

"And all of them are coming here?"

"Perhaps not all but I'm sure some will come, and only you have the power to defeat them."

"Me? I couldn't. If what you say is true then they are essentially supreme beings and no one, not even me can beat them."

"You have their powers—"

"But I don't know how to use them. I can hardly even control my energy blasting ability."

"She's still young. In time, when she grows up, she will know how use all of her powers," said Lola Sabrina.

"It's time that we don't have. We can only make do with the abilities she currently has."

"You mean my light blasting power?"

"No, the other one. Your telepathy."

"But it's a useless power for this occasion. How can transferring thoughts from one mind to another be used to defeat the undefeatable?"

"I can help you, dear. Don't worry. You can do it," said Lola Sabrina.

"But how, Lola?"

"Here is what you need to do…"

~O~

The Grandmaster Owl wore a better and more life-like human disguise. He had searched the minds of the humans involved, and the person he purposely chose to mimic was the most likely to cause them unsettlement.

He knew he was approaching the house where a troublesome Gatekeeper and another Aeonian Being were located. He commanded his minions situated not far from him to move towards his direction, in which he was about to invade the premises.

Yet someone was blocking his way, who looked like an old beggar woman with a wooden face but discovered she wasn't. He saw through the disguise of two little people standing on top of each other, who had utilized plant materials as clothing to complete their masquerade.

He thought nothing of this oddity and quickly bypassed them. Yet they were on a mission to thwart him and tried to grab at his shoulder.

He was surprised by their grit and even admired them for it. He had an otherworldly fortitude honed by eons spent at the universe's end with his ilk, the Parliament of Owls. Galaxies and star systems couldn't budge him, let alone two lowly creatures from a primitive world. They were like bugs trying to move an entire planet.

He looked at the Greenwood Elves with pity in his eyes, which suddenly glowed like two bright stars. Then, an intense monochromatic beam of light issued forth from his pupils, hitting and subsequently disintegrating them into nothingness.

He saw his two muscular minions approaching him. He turned around, and all three walked towards the house in question.

~O~

Lola Sabrina, Luna, Pandora, and Four Eyes stood beside each other outside the house, waiting for the inevitable. Four Eyes was the most scared since he was already aware of the abilities the Masters possess and how powerful they can be.

Lola Sabrina glanced at Pandora and noticed how calm and confident she looked. She had seemingly grown to maturity since the attack in the gymnasium that changed all their lives forever. She was extremely proud of her.

In such a short time, she had become a formidable witch in her own right and had altogether grasped the intricacies of witchcraft that rivaled even her and Luna. She was confident that the instructions she had given to her earlier would work and even make it better.

It was high noon, and Lola Sabrina sensed a showdown was coming.

From a distance, she saw three people approaching, snaking their way through the narrow passageway towards them. The first one looked exceedingly familiar, and once she could see him just a few paces away, she was appalled by the sight: it was her husband Leo, whom she thought was long dead.

However, she realized instantly it was a trick since he still looked the same when he went missing many years ago. He didn't seem to age a day. Even though she knew it was a deception, she was nonetheless bothered and couldn't seem to shake it off.

The impostor posing as Leo said: "It's me Sabrina, your Starman. I've come back to you."

"This again? Why do people we know had died would then come back to life to bother us?" Luna said.

"Maybe they're zombies," said Pandora.

"Zombies?" said Leo, who was the Grandmaster Owl.

"Yes. Even your bodyguards look like the living dead."

"Sabrina, it's me. You know it to be true."

"No, you're not. My Leo is long dead. And how dare you use his image in trying to fool us? My granddaughter over here has already pulverized some of your kind and she will do it again."

Four Eyes shook his and whispered: "Watch out. He's not a Gatekeeper but a Master. Do be careful."

Lola Sabrina nodded and said: "We know who you really are. Can you take off your mask?"

The Grandmaster Owl suddenly transformed into his real anatomical form of a Great Horned Owl, whose most distinguishable feature was tufts of feathers on his head to mimic horns. He was man-sized compared to his smaller North American counterpart.

"He's a bird. Am I really seeing this right? I have problems with my eyes, you know," Luna said.

"We're looking at the same thing and you're correct, he is a bird and particularly a giant *owl.*"

"Oh my. He's not just *a* Master, but *the* Master. He's the Grandmaster Owl in the flesh," Four Eyes said.

"What's the difference?"

"He's the leader and more powerful."

"Here I am, unmasked with my real face. Gatekeeper, where are your kinfolk? I've tracked all of you to this place."

"I'm not with them anymore, Master. They've cast me off, so I'm on my own."

"That's not entirely true. You're an opportunist and infiltrated any group you've encountered, in the guise of helping but in reality, are more concerned for your own interests. You've betrayed everyone, even your own kin. You're doing it right now."

"You're wrong Master. I've only done what I'm being told to do. The fault lies with my clan who had made terrible decisions."

"Yes, everyone is at fault, and I blame myself. Too many mistakes have been done already. It's time for you and your Cephalopodan kinfolk to cease your term as Gatekeepers."

As if on cue, his two muscular minions dragged both One Eye and Two Eyes in their midst, bound and gagged.

"What will happen to us?"

"You have yet to pay the star money you owe me. And once you do, like all the others before you that have ended their tenures, then you can all go back to your home planet."

"You won't kill us?"

"I have no reason to. But for your friends there…"

"We're not friends. By the way, how did you know the face you chose was significant to us?" Said Lola Sabrina.

"Because I am all-knowing and all-seeing. That face was your husband's, is it not?"

"Yes, and he's been missing for many years."

"He's dead."

"Yes, I know, and seeing you using his face was really strange."

"What will you do to us?"

"Your granddaughter is special. Did you know that?"

"I've always known about it and I've also been told recently of her apparent 'otherworldliness.' Is it true?"

"Yes. She is like us. The Gatekeepers had failed to impede the growth of her abilities and it seems she had become powerful in her own right. *Too* powerful, which can become problematic in the future. Hence, I'm giving her two choices: terminating her life right now or coming with me to the end of the universe and be a Master."

Lola Sabrina was appalled but didn't show it. She said: "Can she stay here instead? She won't have to use her powers and be a normal teenager. I'll be with her and make sure of it."

The Grandmaster Owl shook his head. "It's too much of a risk. Using her powers has universe-altering consequences. And you're old, you can't remain with her forever."

She threw a glance at Pandora and whispered: *Now, Pandora. NOW!*

She took her wand out to focus her power and pointed it directly at them. Instead of a bright light from the tip, invisible sound waves began to emit toward Grandmaster Owl, his brawny minions, and the remaining Gatekeepers. Lola Sabrina had taught her to use her telepathic ability to its full capacity, unleashing soundless supersonic screams that the recipients could only hear.

The minions were the first ones affected. They covered their ears, trying to dampen the intensity, but to no avail. Their heads slowly began to bulge, with blood spouting from their orifices. After a few seconds of continuous protrusion, their domes suddenly burst like smashed watermelons, and the lifeless bodies fell to the ground.

The Gatekeepers were made of sturdier biomass, so the intense noise wasn't as caustic to their cephalopodan makeup. Their bodies were used to extreme pressure from their planet's atmosphere, and it wasn't the first time they experienced these ultrasonic noises. Yet they were still affected, inducing them to excrete black ink from their pores and knocking them unconscious.

The Grandmaster Owl wasn't accustomed to any aggressive force used against him. He was usually the instigator of many of the universe's calamities and seldom experienced backlashes, so it was his utmost surprise that someone dared to cause injury to him.

And it proved to be injurious. It was a type of earth-shattering noise akin to the sound of the Big Bang that birthed the universe and consequently himself. It tore at his insides, which were made of dark matter. A crevice began to form in his nether region, getting bigger and bigger, and becoming a black hole.

The black hole had an extremely high gravitational field and slowly pulled everything in. Lola Sabrina, Luna, and Pandora could hold themselves steadfastly and hinder their entry, but not for long.

Pandora remembered the time she was drawn into a similar opening along with Rumpelstiltskin sent both of them to Batala, and didn't want it to happen again. She was scared and didn't know what to do. She fearfully glanced at Lola Sabrina and was surprised at how peaceful she appeared. She whispered: *Lola, what are we going to do?*

This portal will disappear when one of us goes in, and it has to be me.

What?! Lola, no!

Don't worry, dear. Tell your Mama I love both of you and don't take my death too hard. It's simply a part of life. Luna is like a sister and will be in your life in any way she can. I see Leo, my Starman, across the doorway, waiting for me. It's time for us to be together again. Goodbye.

Lola Sabrina walked into the black hole that immediately closed behind her, leaving only Pandora and Luna, staring at open space.

Epilogue

Luna and Pandora went back to Batala, by way of the long route through the giant termite mound. They went to Bakunawa, the Serpent Goddess, to ask for help to rescue the humans still imprisoned in the encampments.

Bakunawa had previously destroyed the force field separating the dark and light regions, so they went directly with nothing or no one impeding them. They saw the human pens were left unguarded. They easily unlocked them and set everyone free.

Along with their aid, Bakunawa was able to reestablish peace throughout the realm. Some dark creatures who didn't join the war returned to the fold afterward and were welcomed with open arms. She also decided to give all the gold to the humans since it was the main root cause of the conflict in the first place, and they had no use for it.

The Gintongbayan townspeople elected a new mayor after the demise of Mayor Eddie and honored his memory with a statue built in his likeness in the middle of the town square. Everyone became wealthy, and the separation between rich and poor ceased to exist. The Land of Broken Dreams was torn down, and its residents were transferred to government resettlement homes, where they were given the help they deserved.

The citizens never knew how close they came to total devastation and of the people involved who stopped it.

Peace and prosperity prevailed over the town, with the supernatural creatures watching over them in secret.

With Luna's help, Pandora created a coven with twelve other witches. They espoused white magic and promised never to use it for evil purposes, only for good.

Angelica and Pandora were momentarily sad about Lola Sabrina's passing but soon accepted it like a warm and comforting embrace. They decided to remove the sign and do away with the name of *Casa de la Noche* for their home since it provoked fear among the townsfolk. They opted for a nameless residence and used it as a base of operations for a charitable foundation in Lola Sabrina's name.

Pandora vowed never to use her godlike powers to the full extent since she knew it would attract beings from the stars. Yet she also acknowledged it wasn't the last time she saw them. They would come back for her in the future, and by that time, she would be ready.

Sometimes, during nighttime, she'd look up at the millions of stars in the heavens and wondered if her Lola Sabrina was one of them. She would then whisper in the darkness of the night sky: *Lola, are you there?* She waited and hoped that one day, she would reply.

THE END

About the Author

Lemuel Lomeda

Lemuel has been working as a municipal clerk for two years and part-time as a freelance online content writer. He previously wrote feature articles in his local paper. He wrote his first novel during the pandemic and liked the experience so much that he went ahead and wrote the second one.

He is an avid reader and loves reading novels by Stephen King, Dean Koontz, George R.R. Martin, and Lee Child. He lives with his two kids Marcus and Danica, and is separated from his wife.